I0822464

LAST OF DAYLIGHT

VAST COLLECTIVE BOOK I

Nicole Hayes

Second Edition

Library of Congress Control Number: 2022921381

ISBN 979-8-9868220-2-0 (Hardcover Edition)
ISBN 979-8-9894105-4-5 (Softcover Edition)
ISBN 979-8-9868220-1-3 (Ebook Edition)

Printed in the USA

1st Edition Printed in 2020

nicolehayesauthor@gmail.com

THE VAST COLLECTIVE SERIES

Last of Daylight
By the Pale Moonlight
Asylum in Firelight
Nox's Verse
Glass Chains
Pyrite Prison
Restraining Silver
Featured Verse
Thirst
Levee
Flood
Featured Verse
Cascading Light

To my younger self who had just as many dreams about daggers and blood as she did about fairies and butterflies.

SECOND EDITION NOTE

I wrote the first draft of *Last of Daylight* when I was sixteen and revisited it during the beginning of the COVID pandemic in 2019. It was beyond far removed from where the series ends, and it didn't work anymore. I found it made me wince to read the gore, violence, and the age gaps which contrasted terribly with the wholesome content, pervading the series by the end of the second book, *By the Pale Moonlight*. So I rewrote the story to better suit the overall themes and narratives.

If you've read the first edition, hopefully you can see how this entry is more cohesive with the entire series. These additions come after years of honing the lore and learning the characters. Not to mention the enormous growth that comes with writing thirteen books.

If you've never read the first edition, and this is your first time reading The Vast Collective Series, welcome to a journey I hope you'll enjoy as much as I did.

To continue reading the series, visit www.nicolehayeswriter.com/ or Amazon.

TRIGGER WARNINGS

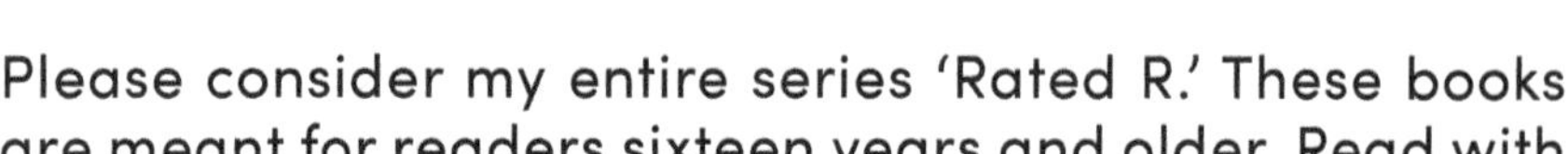

Please consider my entire series 'Rated R.' These books are meant for readers sixteen years and older. Read with the following triggers in mind:

- Graphic Violence
- Graphic Language
- Psychological Warfare
- Romantic scenes between barely adults and older characters
- Bondage/Domination Sadomasochism
- Diverse Relationships

CONTENTS

ACKNOWLEDGMENTS

I wouldn't be here without my magnanimous husband. My relentless torture on your patience backed me through drafts of each book, but you took the brunt of it with LOD. Sharing in my pride and love for these projects really gets me through them. Thank you for helping me find my confidence. Batman, you rock!

Jasmine Clark, you are an inspiration. Thanks for awarding me the best of Tameka, one of the most-loved characters. I appreciate your rousing writer pep talks during COVID. Your openness in conversations on diversity in a fictional apocalypse encouraged me to write kick-ass characters who happen to be minorities. You're a gem in a world of ash.

Firefly, my Croatian bestie and critique partner, thank you. I don't know if the book would be published if I didn't meet you on the eve of quarantine. Your feedback ultimately brought my characters to life and helped transform this book from the musings of a sixteen-year-old girl into a mature discussion on so many topics. I can't wait for the world to read Project Pomegranate.

ONE

FATE AND GIFTS—CHOSEN ONE? TRY CHOSEN FIVE

{SEPTEMBER 2002}

"THEY'RE REAL, YOU KNOW?"

From behind, a man's voice startled Rayne Callahan into dropping the book she'd been sorting. Bram Stoker's *Dracula* fell into a pile of its neatly stacked brethren and spilled onto the hardwood floor, stirring the scent of leather and ink. It had taken her twenty minutes to arrange the book display among the cozy stacks of the modest bookstore. Now it was a beautiful mess of the recently reprinted classic.

Rayne often helped out at her mother's bookstore after school for some allowance cash. It was near closing time, and the place was empty. Hence Rayne's teenage impersonation of a skittish kitten. Not only frightening herself, but likely terrorizing a customer in the process.

"I'm sorry, sir," Rayne called as she knelt to clean up her mess, tucking thick strands of her long dark hair behind her ears. Her sunburned cheeks flared as she regained her composure. "Welcome to Callahan's Books and Novelties. How may I help you?" When thick boots stepped into her line of sight, Rayne put on her best customer service smile and looked up for eye contact.

She froze.

The man wasn't human. He couldn't be. It wasn't only that he was handsome, but he was different looking. He was tall with long black hair pulled back to expose a face with gentle angles and a pleasant smile. But his eyes and his complexion...

They were inhuman.

When the customer knelt in his black cargo pants and tee shirt to help with the books, Rayne could see the details more clearly. His eyes were black and his skin was pale—

No.

That wasn't quite right.

The longer Rayne stared at him the more she made out a deep blue ring around his black irises. And his complexion wasn't pale Caucasian. It was light gray.

The faintest recognition stirred in Rayne. A glimpse, a ghost—

A grin.

The customer grinned, and the expression's kind warmth resonated in Rayne. It matched his voice as he said, "Here, let me help. I didn't mean to startle you."

That's right. His initial words had startled Rayne. It took shaking herself to stop staring at him and ask, "Can you please repeat what you said?"

While returning copies of *Dracula* to the display, the man gestured at the book. "They exist in a way. Vampires, I mean. They're aliens."

Rayne couldn't help herself. Between the grin on his face and the direction of the conversation, she giggled. "Seriously?"

Still smiling, he gave a shrug. "Yeah. They come from a planet in this galaxy. Their homeworld is one without stars in its night sky, and ash covers its plains."

His words sparked a twinge of pain between Rayne's temples. The man looked older than her fourteen years by a decade or so, but there was nothing menacing about him.

As he helped her reassemble the display, he kept sincere eyes on Rayne as if he'd noticed the oncoming headache.

He asked, "Not feeling well?"

Ignoring the pain, Rayne waved him off with an incredulous smile. "I'm fine except someone just told me vampires are real and come from outer space. So how did they get here for us to write fiction about them?"

He placed the last book and chuckled. "Oh, that's a long story. Are you sure you want to hear it?"

As Rayne opened her mouth to answer, Michelle Callahan's voice rang through the stacks. "Closing time, Rayne. I'm locking up."

The man put a finger to his lips and winked.

Taking the hint, Rayne called, "Okay, mom." To him, she whispered, "I'll take you to the back door," and waved for him to follow. "So, tell me more about Cinder."

The pain needled behind her eyes sharp enough to take her breath away as they reached the door.

His voice sobered behind her. "I didn't tell you the name of the planet, Rayne."

Yes, he did.

Surely, he did.

Then how could...

"Rayne? Did you finish the display, honey?" Her mom was coming closer through the stacks.

While a fine tremor overtook every muscle in her body, Rayne slowly turned and faced the stranger. There was a sadness in his eyes, and a frown had replaced his smile.

Concerned and old... impossibly old.

That's how he looked to Rayne.

She asked, "What's happening to me?"

He ducked his eyes before saying, "I can't tell you now. There isn't enough time."

Rayne opened the door to the backstreet, and he kept a respectful distance between them as he stepped through. Again, non-threatening nor imposing.

Between the genuine kindness in his expression and the sense of familiarity between them, Rayne trusted him.

She said, "Meet me at the Arkansas Skatium on Bowman on Friday. Have you heard of the place?"

"Yes. I'll meet you there in three days, but you'll have to wait until after dark."

Despite the flush of her Labor Day weekend sunburn, Rayne felt the blood drain from her face, accompanied by wooziness.

After dark.

Vampires.

Cinder.

The mysterious stranger clasped Rayne's shoulder gently to steady her. He said, "If it makes you feel safe, you can bring Tameka and Sagan."

Her two best friends. How did he know their names—

"Rayne, are you in the back already?"

She called over her shoulder, "Yes, momma." To the stranger, she asked, "What do I call you when I tell my friends about this?"

The man grinned again, and it softened Rayne's headache. With a nod, he said, "Just call me your guardian."

"There you are."

Rayne whirled around to find her mother right behind her. She tried to force a smile while thinking of excuses to explain the strange man on their backstreet when Michelle asked, "Ready to head home?"

Confused by her mother's casual tone and lack of curiosity, Rayne glanced behind her to find the threshold empty.

The mysterious stranger had disappeared without a sound, his last words lingering on Rayne's mind.

"Just call me your guardian."

It was finally Friday. The day Tameka Phillips would meet Rayne's mysterious guardian. Three nights ago, Rayne had called up her besties and told them everything. During the part of the story where the stranger knew the girls by name, Tameka had gotten chills.

Who could he be? And could he be trusted?

Tameka appreciated they were meeting him in a crowded venue, albeit not the best lit one, but at least the girls would meet him together.

Cinder.

Alien vampires.

Despite the twinges of pain, Tameka couldn't get it off her mind the entire bus ride to school. At fifteen years old, she was the oldest of their freshman crew, but between the three girls, Tameka would admit Rayne was their leader. If only because she'd dragged them in and out of the most impossible situations since they were twelve.

When they drove off course at the go-cart track into the woods. Or filled up water guns with Pepto Bismol to prank stingy adults during trick or treating. And that one time with the tiger at the zoo.

Tameka and Sagan would never let Rayne have a frappuccino again.

Now here they were. Meeting with some handsome mystery man much older than themselves.

Guardian.

The word felt ladened with significance.

"Hey, if you frown any harder, you'll get wrinkles. And then how will you get a date for homecoming?"

The voice from behind Tameka wasn't exactly a welcome one. With a lot of sass and a hint of frustration, Tameka said, "Kyle, it's not really any of your business who I date since we broke up a month ago." She turned and faced her ex-boyfriend.

They were filing out of the buses and into J. A. Fair's cafeteria. More of a bunker than a center for education, there were no windows in the vast space built to accommodate the nine hundred plus student body. Someone without taste or imagination had coated the cinder block walls in beige and stickered the floor with ugly white linoleum tiles. Six long tables, with attached stools, furnished the room. It smelled of canned vegetables and frozen patties.

Which still smelled better than Kyle Roberts' attitude.

He tossed his bag in their corner of the standing-room only space and leaned against a wall. Sulking. "Well, since *you* broke up with *me* a few weeks before my first high school dance, I guess I'm a little bitter."

Kyle was cute. His jawline could cut glass. Those forest green eyes really popped against the last remnants of his summer tan. And even though Kyle didn't take good care of it, the curly brown mess of his hair always fell in his a face in a way that made Tameka want to brush it back.

But the boy had one major flaw of which Tameka respected herself too much to overlook.

Rayne rushed into the cafeteria, "Hey, guys!"

And Kyle perked right up at the first sight of their best friend's big blue eyes. "Hey, Rayne. Are you going to the skating rink tonight?"

Yup. Kyle was obsessed with Rayne.

Tameka sighed and dropped her bag, saying, "We're *all* going."

Sagan Sterling came around the corner, and they all stopped to stare at her. She beamed and fluffed her hair. Yesterday, she'd been a brunette. Now, she was sporting a blond bob. It suited her violet eyes and tiny nose.

"Love the hair." Tameka meant the compliment as she pulled Sagan in for a side hug. While doing so, Tameka couldn't help but notice the slight blush on Rayne's cheeks as she admired the newly blond girl.

Kyle gestured up and down, assessing Sagan before saying, "See now *this* is how you get a date to homecoming. Take notes, Tameka."

Rayne and Sagan snickered while Tameka opened her mouth to chew him out—

The morning bell rang.

Perfect timing.

Tameka took a deep breath and exhaled all her irritation.

She was *not* about to let Kyle ruin this day for her. There was something momentous about the stranger—this *guardian.*

Cinder.

With a wince at her headache, Tameka headed out to get this boring day over with before the excitement of tonight. As they filed through the hub of the school with the cafeteria, gym, and administrative offices, Tameka considered the risks of listening to the mysterious stranger's story. All along the walk, she maneuvered through the crowded North Hall lined with old-fashioned wooden lockers and segmented by riot gates—metal grates which security rolled up to the ceiling every morning. They were a necessary precaution to isolate fights in the halls.

Bleak.

That's the word Tameka would use to describe J. A. Fair High School.

At the junctions of intersecting corridors, security guards and staff discouraged students from lingering at their lockers. Mrs. Mendax was the loudest among them. "Expeditiously! Move expeditiously!" Tameka supposed their principal's volume made up for her tiny stature. At five foot, five inches in heels, Rebecca Mendax demonstrated little command over her adolescent charges.

With Sagan buffering between Tameka and Kyle, he mused, "It sounds like Mrs. Mendax ate a thesaurus for breakfast this morning."

Beside Tameka, Rayne snickered which made the teen boy light up. Tameka rolled her eyes and changed the subject. "So, about tonight, Kyle. It'll be a girl's night."

He frowned at her and pressed, "Meaning . . .?"

Sagan took Tameka's hint and went with it. "Meaning we'll be talking about boys and clothes. And maybe you won't want to hang around for it."

Kyle scoffed. "Oh, you mean you three are planning on getting into trouble, and I'm not invited. Is that how it is, Rayne?"

Ah . . . Puppy dog eyes.

Even Tameka was weak to them.

But Rayne didn't buckle under pressure. Instead, she compromised. "We'll hang with you until around eight, and then we'll dump you off on Andrew for the rest of the night."

After dark.

Tameka glimpsed the same realization on Sagan's face. They shared a nod before Tameka dug in the spurs. "Who knows? Maybe you and Andrew can make it into a date?"

Andrew Holt was their fifth bestie. He went to Hall High across town, but they all met together at the skating rink on Friday nights. The mysterious guardian hadn't invited either boy, so while it sucked to leave them out of it—maybe not so much Kyle—it was probably for the best.

"Fuck off," Kyle grumbled and parted ways into a history classroom.

A puzzled frown crossed Rayne's face as she pondered aloud, "I didn't think he had history on 'A' days."

Tameka sighed. "He doesn't."

Sagan snickered into her hand.

The girl trio walked the rest of the way to their lockers at the end of the hall. They were silent, no doubt lost in the same thoughts.

Anticipation.

Nerves.

And something familiar about Cinder.

Tameka tried to imagine a sky without stars, and the thought left her melancholy. How could people dream without them? Or fall in love?

With her head in the clouds and nursing a slight headache, Tameka wandered into English, waving 'later' to Rayne and Sagan. Did alien vampires have emotions? Were they barbaric people or were they civilized?

Well, in order to travel to other planets, surely they were more advanced than humans. As a thought occurred to Tameka, she blinked at her completed homework from the night before. What if the aliens weren't friendly, and this *guardian* was here to warn them?

As agony lanced through Tameka's temples, she pushed the notion aside.

For now.

Last period.

Sagan couldn't imagine this day going by any slower, especially her advanced placement Chemistry class. At least her lab partner was awesome.

Lynn Renee's deep brown eyes matched her braids and flawless complexion. Said umber eyes were sharp as she carefully measured a solution into a beaker. Satisfied, she said, "There. Now we set it on the Bunsen burner—Hey, are you with me, girl?"

Sagan shook herself, saying, "Yeah. Sorry. We want to heat it to three hundred degrees Celsius." Even though Sagan had watched every step and documented their results, she couldn't keep her mind from Rayne's mysterious visitor. And despite the progressing migraine, Sagan continued to formulate questions about the planet called, 'Cinder.'

Beside Lynn and Sagan's lab table, another student warned his partner, "Hey, Justin. I think that's too hot."

Sagan looked over to see John inching away from the Bunsen burner of which Justin had cranked all the way open. The liquid in their beaker was foaming. She warned, "I wouldn't do that if I were you."

Justin's mouth lilted into something he thought passed for a sexy smirk, but it came across as condescending. The sleaze behind it filled his voice as he said, "Don't worry, gorgeous. I know what I'm doing. Here *and* in the bedroom." He blew her a kiss.

Sagan recoiled, and her stomach soured at his unwanted advance. She was only fifteen for fuck's sake. It didn't matter that Justin was conventionally attractive. His quarterback entitlement had always unnerved Sagan.

Unimpressed, Lynn leaned across the table, saying,

"Yeah, well. Are you planning to blow prematurely there, too?"

The beaker shattered, and glass went everywhere.

John yipped and ducked under their table.

Justin scowled. Under his breath he mumbled, "Whatever." Loud enough for the teacher to hear, he said, "Hey, we need another beaker. Genius John, here, disintegrated ours."

"Asshole." John, cute in a geeky best friend kind of way, folded his arms and sulked on his stool. He grumbled, "This better not affect my first nine weeks report card."

Sagan looked back to her beaker and gave a little cheer. "Woo! From clear to blue. We did it, Lynn!"

They high-fived, and when Sagan turned around to stick her tongue out at Justin, she froze.

For the split second before their eyes met, the strangest look was on his face.

Desire—

No.

Ownership.

The intensity of it chilled Sagan to the bone, and she looked away to hide her anxiety. Maybe she could use a guardian.

Mrs. Callahan picked up the girls from school for a three-day sleepover at Rayne's house. There, they ate pizza and prepared for the big night.

"Thanks for always remembering pineapple, Mrs. Callahan." Sagan gave Rayne's mom a thumbs up.

Michelle shuddered. "I'm glad you're enjoying it, dear."

Tameka owned the pepperoni and jalapeño with a knife and fork.

The Callahans were awesome enough to let Tameka and Sagan stay over regularly since they were kids. Between Michelle running a bookstore and Ray working graveyard at the hospital, they kept busy. With Rayne starting high school and her little brother, Jack, not far behind, they did their best, and Sagan loved them for it.

Rayne got her pale complexion and height from her mother.

As Ray rushed down the stairs and snitched a slice of cheese pizza, Sagan considered his contributions to Rayne's genetics. Bright blue eyes and thick black hair.

To his wife, Ray said, "Sorry, honey. No time to chat. I'm late." Then he kissed Rayne on top of her head.

"Dad!"

"I'll never apologize for it, sweetie. No matter how much it embarrasses you in front of your friends." Ray patted his scrubs before snapping his fingers and snatching the car keys from a side table. "Where's your brother?"

Jack emerged from the washroom. "Hiding from the girls." At eleven years old, Rayne's baby brother was growing up into a handsome little man. His hazel eyes scrunched as their dad ruffled his soft brown hair.

At the honk of the carpool, Ray kissed his wife and waved to the busy household. "I'm off. Have fun, kids."

The rest of the late afternoon was equally chaotic. In a whirlwind of tops, skirts, makeup, and hair spray, the girls tried their best to dress older than their ages but not so much as to upset Mrs. Callahan. It was a delicate balance. One Jack kept trying to interrupt despite his earlier complaint.

This was par for the weekend course.

Sagan loved braiding Rayne's hair, and judging by the goosebumps on the other girl's skin, she was enjoying it, too. It was hard not to crush on the prettiest girl in school, and Sagan had caught Rayne's admiration earlier in the day after the blond hair reveal. They'd almost kissed once during a sleepover, and Sagan would never forget how her heart had pounded from the excitement.

One day.

Tameka finished getting ready first. With her tawny brown complexion, darker brown freckles, and crystal green eyes, Tameka hardly warranted any makeup. Just eyeliner and mascara on her red lashes. She'd tied back her froth of red coils gifted to Tameka by her mother. Both women were simply stunning, and they shared a grace Sagan saw in Tameka well beyond her years.

Pragmatic.

That's how Sagan would describe Tameka.

An hour later, Mrs. Callahan dropped them off at the skating rink for four hours of parent-free fun.

Well, sorta.

It was mostly walking around with Kyle trailing behind them. He and Tameka argued while Sagan and Rayne brushed fingertips, sending Sagan's heart racing—

A glimpse of someone distracted Sagan.

Weird.

That was the second time she'd noticed an older man with blond hair watching them. What was his problem? It couldn't be the mysterious *guardian*. Rayne had described him as tall, gray, and handsome with black hair and eyes.

From behind, Kyle interrupted Sagan's thoughts with a groan. "Oh, great. Here comes Andrew."

Andrew rollerbladed up to the wall with a thud. "Hey, ladies." Flatly, he added, "Kyle."

Sagan and Rayne separated, flanking Andrew. "Hey."

Tameka climbed to her tiptoes and peered through the black-lit space toward the door.

Kyle snapped. "Okay. Who are you three looking for?"

Feigning ignorance, Tameka said, "I don't know what you mean."

"All night, you girls have been looking at the front door. Andrew's here now. So why are you still looking?" There was a tad bit of jealousy in Kyle's voice.

Andrew quirked a brow at Sagan, who looked over at Rayne.

With a defeated sigh, Rayne admitted, "We're meeting someone tonight."

Andrew made a delighted sound and asked, "Anyone as hot as you three?"

Tameka clicked her tongue. "It's a guy."

"Would you like me to repeat the question?" Andrew bounced his brows at Tameka's widening eyes.

Sagan snickered into her hand.

Despite everyone else's playfulness, Kyle looked hurt as he asked Rayne, "You're meeting a guy here tonight? What happened to the shit earlier about 'girl's night?'"

Rayne ran a hand through her hair. "You're right. It'd be much safer if you and Andrew were with us when we meet him."

Andrew leaned into Sagan and muttered, "Who are we meeting exactly?"

Rayne winced as Kyle reiterated, "Yeah, who?"

In frustration, Tameka threw her hands up in the air and gestured at Rayne. "Some mysterious guy came to the Callahan's bookstore to tell Rayne about alien vampires."

Andrew gaped.

Kyle frowned.

Bouncing with excitement, Sagan added, "The man said the planet was called—"

"Cinder."

Sagan pouted because Kyle ruined the big reveal, and she winced because the word spiked pain in her temples. But it posed an excellent question.

How did Kyle know?

Kyle did *not* like this.

As soon as the word, 'Cinder,' came out of his mouth, pain burst between his eyes. Tameka was rubbing her temples. Rayne was shaking her head. Sagan sat down and clutched her hair. Andrew's knee buckled until he held onto the wall to keep his skate from rolling out from under him.

The pain receded, and Kyle managed to say, "Okay. How the hell did I know that?"

Andrew—long brown hair, teal eyes, and bronzed from a summer on his grandfather's farm—took the initiative to suggest, "Maybe we should get some air and talk about it outside."

Rayne seconded the idea. "Let's get some water first. Tameka, what do you think?"

"I think there's something weird happening, and I think it's because of your guardian. But Andrew's right. Let's get outside."

As they headed for the doors, Kyle frowned. "Guardian?"

Rayne held up a finger to stave him off for now.

Meanwhile, Kyle noticed Sagan looking over her shoulder. He asked, "What's wrong?"

She whirled on him, concern marring her pretty face. "Nothing. I thought I saw someone, but I'm sure it's nothing."

Kyle pulled her in for a side hug as they walked into the back parking lot. He assured, "I think we're all spooked tonight."

In the cool September night air, Rayne told Andrew and Kyle her story about the strange customer at her mom's bookstore. Then she looked away with a blush.

Did Kyle mention already how much he didn't like this?

He couldn't keep it out of his voice as he admonished, "You mean you trust this guy 'cause he said he was your *guardian*—Whatever that means?"

"Step off, Kyle." Tameka got between them.

Around her, Rayne's face fell, and Kyle felt like an asshole. "Look, I'm sorry. It's just... Doesn't this sound a little crazy?"

Andrew nudged him, saying, "No crazier than when I first heard you and Tameka were dating."

Sagan snorted on a giggle, and Kyle wanted to bite Andrew's head off, until he noticed how the joke perked Rayne back up.

Kyle was about to ask more questions when Sagan stiffened, staring wide-eyed behind him.

Looking in the same direction, Tameka muttered, "What the hell?!"

Andrew straightened as well.

Kyle and Rayne noticed at the same time and turned to face…

A blond man.

Not the gray-skinned, dark-haired guy Rayne had described from her shop. Just a plain, almost indiscernible in a crowd dude.

Kyle swept his hair irritatingly from his face and tried his best not to growl when he asked, "You got a problem, mister? This is kind of a private party."

Sagan gripped Kyle's shoulder. "That guy's been following us all night."

Behind Kyle, Andrew asked, "Are you kidding?"

After Sagan shook her head in answer, Rayne stepped to the front of their group. "What do you want?"

Kyle admired her bravery, but if push came to shove, he'd get Rayne back inside the crowded skating rink.

When the blond man took a step forward, the teenagers took a step back. All the while, the guy said, "He'll come for you. Salvation girl. The Progeny." On top of his words not making any damned sense, the wild look in his eyes raised the hair on the back of Kyle's neck.

With her entire body stiff from tension, Tameka said, "I think we should go inside now."

The man advanced again, cutting them off from the back door. On and on, he droned with his psycho nonsense mostly directed at Rayne. "The most beautiful salvation. Even now, the Night King brings his armies for you."

Sagan cried, "Leave her alone!"

Tameka pulled Rayne to her side. "Fuck off, man, or we'll scream for security."

Kyle glanced at Andrew, who took the hint. They flanked the girls, ready to force their way back inside—

A blur—A streak of black and gray soared by Kyle. One second, the crazy guy was upright and spouting shit about armies, and the next, his ass was on the pavement.

Another man stood over him. Tall. Gray. With black hair.

Rayne's 'guardian.'

Making for quite an imposing sight, the guardian dude loomed over the sputtering zealot. His voice was icy, deadly serious, as he warned, "Come near them again, and you'll suffer the consequences."

Beside Kyle, the three girls exchanged wide-eyed glances. Andrew even gaped. While it impressed Kyle the supposed 'guardian' could move faster than Kyle could blink, he still wasn't convinced this situation was trustworthy.

The crazy stalker spat blood, but climbed to his worthless feet and shuffled back inside without another word or even a backward glance.

If Tameka's hand wasn't on Rayne's arm, Kyle was sure their leader would've taken a step toward her 'guardian' as she breathed, "Thank you."

The lightning-fast stranger turned with his hands up in a non-threatening gesture. Kyle narrowed his eyes. Sure, this guy was unarmed, but he'd just leveled a creep in the span of a heartbeat. How could they trust him?

Andrew, Tameka, Sagan, and Rayne seemed poised on the brink as their friend squad waited for the man to speak. When he did, it nearly floored Kyle.

"I got you."

Seriously?! Was that some kind of lame catch phrase?

A brilliant smile blossomed on Rayne's face, and the bubble burst. She asked, "Can you tell us about Cinder now?"

Andrew tacked on, "And why does the mere mention of it make my head ache?"

Sagan didn't mind intruding. "Are you an alien?"

"Is that why you can move so fast?" Tameka added next.

Kyle waited until the others finished with their deluge, which seemed to amuse the 'guardian,' given how wide he was grinning at their intense curiosity. Once they'd had their turn, Kyle asked the most important question.

"Can you teach us how to fight like that?" If Kyle could learn to defend himself like that, he could pass it on to his two little sisters.

The grin faded from the older man's face as he said, "Yes. We'll begin training tomorrow."

Rayne finally took that step forward. "Training for what?"

Kyle detected a hint of sorrow in the man's voice while he dropped a bomb into the conversation. "For Cinder's second invasion of Earth."

Second.

Invasion.

Sagan gasped, cupping a hand over her mouth. Tameka chafed the other girl's arm. Andrew shook his head and blinked, bewildered. Despite the shock, Kyle knew what would happen next.

Rayne declared on their behalf, "We're in. Now, what do we call you other than 'guardian?'" Her cheeky smile at the end made the man grin again.

"I'm Xelan. I'm an alien known as an Icarus. And I'm here to help you save the world."

Rayne beamed.

Nope.

Kyle did *not* like this.

While Andrew appreciated Rayne's trademark enthusiasm and reckless sense of adventure, there were still so many red flags about this night.

This Xelan guy clearly wasn't human, but what made his aliens any better than the ones who planned to invade? And what exactly would this training include?

They were high school students for fuck's sake.

Andrew tried to keep the skepticism out of his voice as he asked, "You're saying *we're* going to save the world?" He gestured at the five of them.

Xelan lowered his hands. "With the right training, yes, I think you can stop the invasion at the onset."

Kyle did not keep the skepticism out of his voice. "And we're just supposed to trust you?"

Andrew wanted to sigh at how Rayne's face fell. She was impulsive, so it was up to the rest of them to ask questions which would keep them all safe. Still, this had to dampen her whole 'world savior' mood.

When Xelan frowned at Kyle's terseness, Tameka took the lead. "If there's a way we can help, of course we will. But... You have to understand why we're hesitant to trust you."

Sagan said, "I'm not."

The friend group turned to face her with matching expressions of disbelief. Except Rayne. She was glowing at her best friend.

At the center of attention, Sagan explained, "The way I see it we come out on top either way. Say the invasion isn't real... At least this way, we get super fit and fast and capable of defending ourselves against weirdos like that one guy. And if the invasion actually happens, we could be heroes."

Rayne cried in delight and threw her arms around Sagan.

Andrew considered her argument.

Fit.

Awesome.

Heroes.

He turned back to Xelan and said with a shrug, "All right. Count me in."

Stronger than she looked, Rayne roped Andrew into the hug between the girls. When Tameka sighed, saying, "Same," Rayne latched onto her, too.

They all looked over at Kyle, sulking with his arms folded. But Andrew knew all about Kyle's home life. There was no way he would turn down the opportunity to learn how to kick ass.

"I'm in."

Five-way hug commenced.

Rayne beamed at them, and among the huddle, she promised, "We won't regret this."

Tameka glanced over at Xelan, who was waiting for them to finish. She sounded more than curious as she said, "I want to learn more about Xelan."

Andrew clocked the narrow-eyed glance Kyle shot his ex-girlfriend at the slight dreaminess in her voice. Yup. Teenage hormones were a go.

Sagan said, "No matter what happens, we'll be together. Everything will work out as it always does."

This was true. Things always worked out in the end. Even with the tiger.

Andrew smiled when they gave a final squeeze and broke apart. As he faced Xelan, he said, "All right. We still have some questions, but first, where are we meeting for this 'training?' Do we need a gym membership or something?"

Xelan grinned. "No. I have something else in mind."

The next night, Andrew stood blinking at the physical education abomination built near Rayne's backyard. In the woods bordering her neighborhood, obstacles ladened a cross-country race track, and rocks formed the circle of a sparring ring. Glow wands and lanterns provided some visibility. Under the dappled moonlight through the oak trees, it smelled of the oncoming autumn splendor and ice from the massive open cooler off to the side. Xelan had filled it to the brim with water and sports drinks.

The alien—Icarus, whatever—Xelan held his arms wide to encompass the outdoor facility. "I've uhm... been preparing for a while now."

To Andrew, there was something so familiar and inviting about the man's earnest dedication and focus. Even the haphazard lack of exposition seemed familiar.

And Rayne ate it up. "Where do we start?"

It made Tameka and Sagan smile. Kyle couldn't suppress a smirk.

With his hand on his hips, Xelan peered out at his creation as if considering Rayne's question. When he clapped his hands together, the five teenagers startled. He said, "For each lap around the course—minus the vaulting walls, you're not ready for those, yet—I'll answer one of your questions."

Tameka shrugged. "No problem. It can't be more than—"

"It's a full kilometer." There was an amused sparkle to Xelan's eyes as Tameka's widened.

Sagan raised her hand, and when Xelan called on her, she said, "I have weak ankles."

Xelan assured, "Don't worry. I'll run it with you to prevent any missteps. I won't ask something of you I wouldn't do myself."

That was enough for Andrew. "All right, you heard him, people. Let's get going. I have questions which need answering." Not trying to impress anyone, he started down the course. It snaked through the underbrush and crossed over creeks. Ditches formed gaps for them to leap.

It wasn't the hottest night in September, but as the humidity thickened among the leaves, Andrew felt it in his lungs. Sweat dripped down his back, prompting him to strip off his shirt and tuck it into the back pocket of his cargo shorts. He felt bad for the girls, who trooped along in step with their shirts on. None of the five teenagers looked eager to push themselves for a faster pace, and each of them huffed air into their lungs with great effort.

Not Xelan.

He kept lock step with their strides, but the man wasn't breaking a sweat with his perfect runner's form. Andrew mimicked it without being told, but as he tried to mirror the older man's breathing, Andrew struggled. This was more activity than he'd see in a month.

And that was without the walls.

Along the course they passed obstacles of varying height and scalability. Some had pegs for grip, but the tallest one was sheer at over three meters.

Incredulous, Andrew gestured at it with his thumb. "You seriously think we'll climb that one day?"

Xelan only answered with a grin.

By the time the finish line came into view, Andrew's calves and quads were screaming at him. His lungs begged him to collapse and crawl the rest of the way there, but he held steady. Nothing would rob him of answers.

With hands planted on his hips, Andrew completed the kilometer run gasping for air. The girls and Kyle fared the same. Shit, after a month of this, they'd better get fit enough to save the world.

Xelan was an optimist. It was in the enthusiastic thumbs up he gave them as he said, "Good job, today, team. We'll do it again tomorrow."

Kyle groaned. "Seriously?"

Rayne jumped with excitement. "Really?!"

Xelan nodded. "You'll spend your weekend nights here, and I think I'll train with each of you individually one night every week on your home turf."

After gathering her breath first, Tameka asked, "I gotta know. Why only at night?"

"Oh." Xelan looked sheepish. "I burn under the radiation of your sun."

"Cool."

Bewildered, Andrew and the girls glanced at Kyle, who shrugged. "What?"

Xelan assured, "No. It's a good point. You should know your enemy's weaknesses."

Andrew frowned at his phrasing, and Rayne asked the question on his mind. "Enemy? But you're our guardian, right?"

Sagan plopped down on a boulder, asking, "Are the Icari our enemy?"

While Andrew perched beside her, Xelan finally gave some explanations.

"Yes. And no. Cinder is ruled by a King, who suppresses our race's capacity to evolve in intelligence and physical ability. The Icari obey him because they are capable of nothing more."

Tameka muttered, "That sounds awful."

Rayne asked, "And that's who we're supposed to fight. This 'Night King?'"

Xelan slumped gracefully onto a patch of grass. He sounded tired, old beyond the years on his face. "Nox. His name is Nox. And yes. It's my hope that if you defeat him at the start of the invasion, we can prevent further casualties of those only following orders because they must."

Something about the way Xelan kept repeating the onset or start of the invasion bothered Andrew. He asked, "What makes you so sure we can stop it before it begins?"

Kyle added, "And why was the crazy bastard from last night saying this King guy was bringing his armies to us? Why *us*?"

Xelan said, "I think it will make more sense if I explain why they're invading. Cinder is dying under the explosion of a red giant kept at bay by a shield around the planet. Eight thousand years ago, the Icari invaded the Earth to escape Cinder's inevitable demise."

Rayne asked, "Why Earth?"

"Because human blood harbors a similar nutrient to our primary source of sustenance. We came by it from a plant on our homeworld, but since Li—our sun—exploded, we can't grow the Vittle crop as once before, despite our best efforts to revitalize it."

Andrew noticed Tameka kept sneaking glances at Xelan which had nothing to do with a mysterious back story and everything to do with teenage hormones. She pressed, "But what happened with the first invasion?"

A streak of moonlight fell across Xelan's face, and Andrew could see the sorrow from here. "Your ancestors, hybrids of our two races, fought Nox back to Cinder and sealed him from returning. Sealed me here away from my people and my home."

While a quiet settled over the clearing, Rayne left Tameka and Kyle's side to sit on the grass with Xelan. It broke whatever melancholy had gripped him, and he smiled kindly at her.

Andrew wondered about Xelan's life—Separated from his people, at war with his homeworld, and yet still he could smile like that at Rayne.

The warm expression faltered as the Icarus went back to answering their questions. "So, that's how I know the invasion will start with you, because Nox is fixated on his revenge. You've had spies following you since birth. Before, even."

Andrew balked. Kyle scowled. Tameka, Sagan, and Rayne exchanged worried glances.

Xelan continued, "In all transparency, we've had our own people watching over you. It's no accident your family lines have remained close after all these millennia."

This was too much. Andrew's head was about to explode. "Look, about all that... You helped us out with that creep last night, so we have enough trust in you to join you for this jaunt in the woods. I'm speaking for myself when I say I'll continue this training to get more kick ass, but as far as the rest, I can barely keep my head above water with school. I don't know how I'm supposed to stop an invasion. Besides, you said Cinder was sealed, right?"

Grim. That's how Xelan looked as he said, "Every day we get more intelligence reports about Nox's efforts to breach the conduit which connects our worlds. Estimates say anywhere from six months to several years—"

"Six months?!" Rayne cried.

Tameka muttered, "How are we supposed to get in fighting shape in such a short amount of time?"

Sagan added, "That's a pretty broad window."

Kyle humphed. "Twenty bucks says it never happens." Obviously, he wasn't convinced by Xelan's story.

But Andrew was.

"It looks like I'll be seeing you every night on the weekends, and how do Thursdays sound for our one-on-one sessions?"

Because regardless of if the five teenagers accepted their fates, after meeting Xelan, their lives could never be the same.

TWO

IN THE DARK WHERE MY ENEMY WAITS PATIENTLY

THE BEAUTIFUL GIRL WITH BRILLIANT BLUE EYES. The sweetest smile... She would save Cinder.

Yes.

Yes.

It was worth the Justice's ire to have laid eyes on salvation. Eyes the blond man now lowered to the ground as he bowed on hands and knees to the procession. Enforcers weren't permitted to view their gods. Overhearing the Night King's heavy boots was blessing enough. A reward for the blond man's loyal defense of this compound and the precious secret within.

How many had he killed to protect the Icari?

Dozens. Surely. And all their faces flashed through his eyes—The couple necking in the woods, homeless people seeking a place to sleep for the night, and the occasional curious trespasser. Spies made up the bulk of his victims.

The blond man killed for the Icari without knowing what they looked like. The eternal Night King and his Silver General. Like the blue-eyed girl, they must be beautiful to look upon...

He glanced up—for a second, for a heartbeat—and turned his eyes down.

Beyond human.

The Enforcer knew Heaven existed for angels were among them. Could he make it to their feet and kiss them before the Justice caught him? Would she revoke his claim to eternal life if he dared break rank?

Could he contain himself either way?

The blond Enforcer bolted onto his feet and ran through the crowd of kowtowed cultists.

"Stop!"

It didn't take long for someone to notice, but the Enforcer was only four meters from touching divinity—

Powerful arms swept him up and held him back. "No! No, please! Master!" Tears sprung to his eyes and blurred his vision as he reached for the angels. "Please..."

But the Night King turned his back and walked away with his blood female. More Icari worked about the courtyard, carrying gigantic crates between them onto train cars.

The Silver General's eyes stared through the Enforcer as other members of the Cult of Night wrestled him to the ground. Staring into such purity was mesmerizing until the Justice stepped between them.

From her short height, she looked down her nose at the blond Enforcer to say, "You are out of line."

"How could I deny such beauty?"

Behind her, in the most angelic tenor, the Silver General called, "Bring him."

The Enforcer's voice broke as fresh tears poured. "Thank you. Thank you."

The Justice's smile was twisted. "Oh, I wouldn't go that far." She nodded, and the cultists tied his hands and ankles together.

This was fine. He would bask in the presence of sheer glory. Even as they dragged him roughly to the Justice's office, the Enforcer counted his fortunes for this opportunity—

And there it was.

The Silver General assessed the Enforcer with careful intelligence behind a gorgeous countenance of eternal youth and wisdom.

The Enforcer wept on his knees and muttered his thanks to the cosmos repeatedly.

It didn't even offend him the way the General pointed at him and asked, "Is *this* what you call security, Justice?"

The short woman said, "We foster unquestioning loyalty, but for some, it can become overwhelming in its concentrated dedication."

"Angels... And blue-eyed salvation."

The Silver General pinched the bridge of his nose and sighed, which prompted the Justice to shift her weight in a nervous gesture. When the god hiked up his slacks to crouch to the Enforcer's height, a distant chorus sang.

Blessed.

"Did you go near the blue-eyed Progeny girl?"

The Justice scoffed. "None of my congregation would dare—"

"Such beauty and pure love. She will save Cinder," the Enforcer repeated his truth.

The icy look the Silver General shot the short woman made her tremble. It frosted the elegance of his cadence as he said, "Resolve this. We can't have your people undermining our efforts after millennia of preparation. Let me put it to you frankly—The invasion carries on according to plan or no 'eternal life' for you."

Between one blink and the next, the General gripped the Enforcer's throat and squeezed like an iron vice. All the while, he kept his eyes on the short woman.

Enraptured, the Justice bowed. Her voice came out on a breath as she said, "Yes, Master."

Inky blackness engulfed the blond man's vision as he gasped for air.

Please, look at me.

Please, grace me with divinity one final time.

When the Silver General turned and faced the Enforcer, clarity brought him peace.

The Enforcer would meet the same afterlife as those he'd murdered, with no hope of finding true Eternity. And that was okay. It was worth this short time among angels, worth the years of his life listening to Cinder's Verse, and worth the momentary pain of the General snapping his neck.

The angels would win this day.

Amen.

A welcome guest paid Xelan a visit at his installation. IONA-01 was bustling with activity, both to prepare for the invasion and to maintain their front as a private airline outside of Little Rock's East End, among other locations.

"Lucas, my old friend. Why am I not surprised to see you?"

As another Icarus left behind after Nox's banishment, Lucas worked with other Icari to field relations between Earth and other galactic entities and monitor the Progeny—Xelan's name for all those descended from Rayne, Sagan, Tameka, Kyle, and Andrew's ancestral lines. But The Brethren were also Xelan's overseers.

In a bespoke three-piece suit, Lucas excelled at the part of the diplomat. Framed in the doorway of Xelan's office, Lucas answered, "Well, seeing as I'm keeping your activity with the Progeny a secret from The Brethren, I thought I'd check in and see how first contact went."

Xelan came around his desk, leaned his butt against it, and folded his arms. "It went well. I think they're taking everything in stride."

Lucas stepped further into the room and closed the door behind him, saying, "Of course, I agree with you. It's in their best interest to prepare. I simply wished we could've left them oblivious to live their lives as The Brethren had decreed."

This bothered Xelan. How could The Brethren expect those five teenagers to stand a chance against Nox and his invasion force without an ounce of training or support? At least Lucas saw reason. Even so, Xelan admitted, "I understand to an extent. If I thought they could survive without this burden, I never would've contacted them. Unfortunately, I see no other course of action."

"Have they inquired as to the source of your speed and vitality?"

Lucas touched on something Xelan would rather avoid. "No, but I will tell them, eventually. They'll need to understand nacres and how the nanites within nacre bearers lend unbelievable advantages to the opposition."

The shorter Icarus ran a hand through his sandy-brown hair. Lucas' golden eyes—true, molten gold—flashed as he raised a brow. "And if they ask for nacres of their own?"

Xelan sighed. This was a difficult subject. Ultimately, the Progeny should remain unaffected by Icarean relations, but there was no fine line between sitting duck and super soldier. Xelan said, "I'd like to leave them whole for as long as I can, but if the worst comes to pass, then we'll see if Enki will grant them nacres."

Lucas gave a solemn nod. "Very well. I won't speak of it again. I suppose they don't know who you are—to them or to the Icari?"

Xelan shook his head and unfolded his arms to lean back against the desk. "No, and I don't plan on telling them. I need them to trust me, and how could they if they knew my part in this? Fully, I mean."

"Lying by omission—Xelan, I know you. My friend, martyring yourself may cost you their trust later." Lucas made an excellent point, but...

"One thing at a time," Xelan said, biting his thumbnail. "Right now, I'm grateful they listened to me and agreed to training. For the sake of Earth and Cinder, I'll build them into a fighting force capable of facing Nox."

Lucas stepped into Xelan's line of sight, demanding his focus as he asked, "And Rayne? Does she know her part?"

Xelan shuddered and looked away from Lucas' earnest concern. Xelan said, "Not yet. She's so young, and I don't want to overburden her."

Lucas smiled congenially and placed a hand on Xelan's shoulder. "As if telling her the fate of the world rests on their teenage shoulders isn't burden enough?"

This time Xelan met Lucas' eyes as he said, "Exactly. So the rest can wait until I've earned more of Rayne's trust."

With a nod, Lucas conceded. "Fair enough. Keep me updated on their progress, and I'll lend you whatever support I can garner from The Brethren. But Elden help me if they ever find out I instigated your contacting the Progeny before the invasion."

Elden help them both.

That night, Xelan put the Progeny through their paces on the training course. Tameka and Sagan were still staying the night at Rayne's, so that was convenient. Kyle had told his mother and sisters he was off to see a movie with Andrew, who was the only one with a car.

This might take more delicate maneuvering than Xelan had first assumed.

"Perhaps every night on the weekends isn't feasible," Xelan declared to the five teenagers, who'd collapsed with varying degrees of over-exertion. "I'll just come to you after dark on your designated week nights until you're older." He didn't want to cause any trouble in their households.

The Progeny barely mustered a thumbs up in response from where they'd splayed out on the grass, panting. It made Xelan smile. Maybe another two months of this, and they'd tackle the course with ease. They could even progress to the vaulting obstacles.

Yes, the first six months would take the most out of them, but they'd get there. Now, onto the genetic memories.

Xelan cleared his throat before asking, "Have any of you had any unusual dreams or thoughts?"

Rayne perked up. "What do you mean?"

"Well, I was wondering if you'd experienced any memories which weren't your own?"

Tameka got to her feet and dusted herself off. "Do you mean like flashbacks or something?"

Xelan nodded.

Kyle always sounded suspicious when he addressed Xelan. "Why? Should we be seeing shit?"

Andrew said, "I did last night. I dreamt of a desert, but that was all."

Sagan nudged him. "How do you know it was a flashback?"

"Because I could smell the sand and feel the sun—It was unlike anything I'd ever experienced."

Xelan wasn't sure if this was a good thing, but he'd try for as much transparency as their mission could afford. He said, "The desert in Egypt is where Cinder's conduit opens into Earth. It's where the First Wave of Progeny sent Nox back during what we call 'the Vacating.'"

Rayne's bright blue eyes shone with curiosity. "Who were the Progeny? Can you tell us more about our ancestors?"

Xelan nearly winced. How much of the truth could he tell without overwhelming them? There was one simple place to start. Xelan pointed at Rayne and said, "Celindria." Then he pointed at Tameka, saying, "Merit. Devis was Kyle's ancestor. Andrius was Andrew's—obviously a family name. And you, Sagan. Your ancestor was called 'The Afflicted One.' T.A.O. for short."

Sagan frowned. "Why?"

That was a story for another time, so Xelan offered a shorter answer. "It's the name she gave herself. The Progeny weren't born. They were genetically engineered to combine the best of our two species. Strength, speed, enhanced senses, but without the Icarean hunger and aversion to Sol's radiation. The Progeny came into this world as fully grown adults."

"Cool." Sagan glanced at the others as they looked at her and gave a cavalier shrug. "Either we can let everything Xelan says overwhelm us, or we can accept that we descended from totally badass hybrids. I'm choosing the latter, and I'm taking Tuesday nights."

Tameka helped Sagan to her feet, saying, "When you're right, you're right. I'll take Wednesdays."

Andrew stood, and Kyle followed. The latter ran a hand through his knotty curled hair with a sigh. "Mondays already suck. May as well go all out."

Rayne remained seated and beamed up at Xelan. "I'll take them all."

His eyes widened. "What?"

"Every night after you finish with each of them, you come and train me."

Sagan nudged Rayne. "I know you're famous for insomnia, but what about school?"

The other girl refused to budge, shaking her head solemnly. Then Rayne impressed Xelan by saying, "Nothing is more important than preventing the invasion. Besides, it's not like I'll lose any sleep because of it." She turned those bright blue eyes on him. "Please, Xelan. I want to help."

Aside from fierce determination, Rayne was nothing like her ancestor. And for the first time in several thousand years, Xelan realized it was a benefit and not a hindrance. She could really make the difference between victorious success and utter defeat.

Xelan grinned. "Every night. I got you."

Nox, King of Cinder, reviewed his General's estimates in silence. As much silence as one could come by in such a place. Outside the walls of his quarters, the Cult of Night celebrated another load of fresh recruits. None of which were of any interest or concern to Nox. He let the humans carry on as if they weren't harboring a hundred thousand Icari, fresh from Cinder.

Although, Nox would admit, without these humans none of this would be possible. They saw to the surveillance of the Progeny after the Vacating. They also built these compounds to house the Icarean troops for the invasion. And without them, Nox would never have acquired the blood from Celindria's descendant to breach the conduit, however limited the window.

Still, work needed doing and how could they get any done when they found every excuse for a celebration—

"Your majesty, would you like me to shut them down?"

Ah . . . General Korac had detected Nox's growing agitation and, like the best soldier, he aimed to rectify it. Either that or Korac was equally bothered by the constant ruckus.

Nox shook his head. "No. Let them stay the course as if we don't exist. Better to keep them in high spirits while we rely on them for a discrete source of food. Speaking of, how do we fare if we ration the warrior caste?"

The fireplace cast an orange glow on Korac's exotic features—white hair, white eyes, and white skin. He was shorter than Nox, though most Icari were, but only by a few inches. Dressed in pressed slacks and a silk black button-down with the sleeves rolled back, Korac had assimilated a mite too quickly—almost eagerly—to modern Earth fashion. With a keen sharpness in his quiet observations, Korac had always proven useful in diplomacy and combat. Although, he was quieter and much less carefree in recent millennia.

The Vacating had sobered them all.

Korac said, "As the report states, I've disseminated our troops in CoN compounds across the world at key strategic locations for the full invasion. With the high number of human volunteers, we shouldn't need to ration even the warriors for several years, if it should take so long. They're prepared to mount the assault on your say."

The report also stated CoN—short for Cult of Night—leadership only agreed to such terms under the condition Nox would grant them nacres after the invasion began. 'Eternal life' as they preached it. But Nox wasn't remiss to note only the leadership would receive the nacres. Not the underlings.

Humans.

Nox stood and went to the front of his desk, leaning back against it. He bit his thumbnail as he considered the question Korac no doubt wished to ask.

When?

Raking a hand through the length of his hair, Nox asked, "What of Celindria's descendant?"

Korac smirked with a knowing glint in his eyes. "I had wondered when you would get to that. Coincidentally, the traitor has already broken his exile and engaged the Progeny. As we predicted, he started with Rayne."

Well, wasn't that interesting? Nox pressed, "Who was your source?"

With a sweep of his white hair over one shoulder, Korac leaned against the fireplace, folded his arms, and crossed his ankles. "A rogue CoN Enforcer. He went off mission and actually confronted the Progeny—Yes. Yes, I know. They are forbidden to do so. He blamed it on the girl—Celindria's descendant. He said she was too beautiful to stay away from. I dealt with his punishment, and the Justice assured me it wouldn't happen again."

No doubt to keep her claim on a nacre. The Justices—compound leaders—disgusted Nox the most, but they'd proven vital to his operations in the past. Still, there was always something... off about them.

On the subject of Rayne...

Too beautiful to stay away from. Nox humphed at the thought. She was only fourteen. Although the reincarnation of someone like Celindria would certainly possess dangerous gifts, he doubted she could bewitch a grown man into stalking her.

Back to the question of 'when.'

Nox said, "The girl needs a nacre before we can proceed. Surely, the traitor will see to it. If not, we'll see that he does. Until then, I want firsthand knowledge of their interactions. If he intends to train them against us, we should counter it with subterfuge. Are you up to the task?"

The General straightened and gave a solemn nod.

The best soldier.

Nox nodded his approval. "Good. See if Colita wants to play a role." No doubt the Icarean female would appreciate some use of her talents.

"Very good, sire."

Quick to fulfill his current mission, Korac made to leave until Nox called, "Leave Celindria to me."

It was slight, but Nox noticed Korac stiffen before he faced his King once more. "You wish to encounter her before she's ready?"

Korac rarely questioned Nox, so he'd allow it. He said, "I will. Tonight."

With a bow of his head, Korac conceded. "As your majesty wishes."

Nox's General left without another indication of his thoughts. The pale Icarus kept his opinions behind a mask of composure, but his eyes gave away what only Nox could see after a lifetime together. Korac was restless and angry.

They all were.

Millennia they'd spent starving, half their species dying off on the brink of extinction. All under the glaring blaze of Li, their pitiless and hungry star.

Had it driven Nox mad?

Perhaps.

Or perhaps now he finally understood a creature like Celindria. Heartless and steeped in ambition—Yes, sacrifice everything for the righteous cause.

No love.

No mercy.

Only cold genocide would do.

Celindria had delivered upon the Icari unspeakable suffering with the Vacating. Now Nox would exact vengeance from her reincarnation.

And then some.

Nox would not stop until he'd devastated her race and claimed her planet for those more deserving. For eight millennia, the Icari endured the Wrong Side of Eternity. Celindria's descendant would bleed for as many years to rectify the First Progeny's crime. There would be no haven for her—No end to the agony.

Salvation in blue eyes.

Truth be told, it was all Nox could see.

Korac sighed outside of Colita's quarters.

It was hard to imagine that dour brood passed for a good mood these days with Nox. But then again, it was hard to imagine anything but Rayne's tears bringing the King of Cinder any relief or joy. And they would wring them from her until Celindria's descendant cried blood.

Fuck, Korac wasn't in much better spirits.

Why?

Why was Nox asking him to do this? Not that reconnaissance was beneath the General. In fact, the personal touch was one of his fortes. But...

Dream invasion?

It was unheard of—borderline uncivilized. To enter someone's sleeping consciousness intruded on their deepest fears and darkest desires—It just wasn't done.

And it seemed like an extremely fucking bad idea for Nox to intrude on Rayne's mind. After everything Celindria had put Nox through, it could only bring more anguish and further sour Nox's mood. It was rare to see him in any other state, and only occasionally did Korac see a glint in his King's black eyes—When torturing Celindria's descendant was in his thoughts.

Obsession.

There was no remedy for this. Once they commenced with the invasion, they would have their revenge.

Simple.

Colita answered after forcing Korac to knock a second time. She languished in a silk robe, clinging to her skin. Her blond tresses were still wet from the bath, where two of the male Icari from her harem awaited further in the room for Colita's return. Cinnamon mingled with other scents rushed into the hallway. Her lids were lowered headily around sky-blue eyes, extending an invitation to Korac.

One he would always turn down.

"Colita, Nox wants you performing subterfuge for the Progeny. Are you still in possession of the capsule we gave you for the task?" Korac enjoyed that his professional manner in the presence of Colita's nearly naked body agitated the viper.

Her eyes flashed as she said, "Of course. I wouldn't dare toss it after how much Razor charged us for it. Does Nox even know how you came by those credits?"

Ah... So Colita thought she could elongate her fangs at Korac? A little blackmail because he'd spurned her advances?

Korac wouldn't give her the satisfaction of a response. "Begin the reconnaissance, tonight." He let his eyes wander down her body, taking in the silk surrounding her slender curves, before Korac met Colita's eyes again. They shone with wanton need. Korac smirked. "And remember your place as consort to the King. Find your dignity and try to maintain it for more than five seconds at a time."

Korac walked away, leaving Colita scowling in the doorway. The ugly twisting of her pretty features better matched her insides. He felt the daggers of her eyes in his back all the way to his quarters down the hall.

This compound was tighter living than Nox's Castle on Cinder, but the humans in the Cult of Night tried their best to appease their gods. As General and Nox's second-in-command, Korac warranted a decent-sized apartment, with a massive bed, fireplace, and an en suite. As did Colita as Nox's blood consort and third-in-command.

Korac went to the sitting area and sat in an armchair before the fire. He stared into it, imagining this setting was as good a place as any to introduce himself to the Progeny. But which one would he meet first?

Oh, hell. Korac knew without asking. He'd wondered over the years how T.A.O.'s descendants had fared. Did any of them inherit her affliction? Or her gift?

It was time to find out.

Korac straightened his slacks, swiped any wrinkles from his button down, and checked his manicure. He muttered to himself, "Shit." Yesterday, when he'd disposed of the fanatic Enforcer, he'd dented his black nail polish.

While Nox refused to assimilate to human clothing, preferring to remain shirtless in leather pants, Korac indulged himself in shiny shoes and tailored garments. And there was something to be said that Nox had given his General the freedom to do so.

A thought to consider for another time.

Korac noted the time was three in the morning before swallowing the subconscious capsule. Sleep claimed him within moments.

Sagan Sterling appeared, facing the fireplace with her back to Korac. She was the shortest of the Progeny women at five feet, three inches, and she looked especially small in her pajama pants and sleep shirt. He watched a moment as she peered around, taking in the space. While Sagan acclimated, Korac propped an elbow on the chair and rested his face against his hand, observing.

Young. Fifteen years old. Born a brunette, Sagan had bleached her hair a few nights ago with a fresh cut. Her stance was one of someone with no experience in combat—as was her physique. Sagan Sterling was simply a teenage human girl—

With wild, violet eyes.

When she'd turned and faced Korac, it was a shade he'd recognized instantly. A forgotten pain twisted in his heart.

An innocent being, Sagan raised her hand in a stiff wave. "Hello." To herself, she muttered, "Wow. Weird dream." There was wonder in her voice, and a soft friendliness in her smile.

This required a change in tactics.

Korac stood, and Sagan took him in, fearlessly. Despite him towering over her by a foot, her smile never left her lips. He said, "I'm here from The Brethren. Xelan sent me to train you in an arena where you can't be harmed."

Sagan's smile blossomed into a brilliant grin. "Awesome. I'm Sagan." She held out her hand.

When Korac took it, Sagan's warmth enveloped him. He actually returned a smile of his own. "I'm Korac."

"That's a pretty name. Are you Icarean?"

Korac fought to keep his eyes from narrowing as he wondered what version of the truth Xelan had told the Progeny. He said, "Yes. I was left behind after the Vacating. While we work, you can catch me up on what you already know." As he spoke, Korac pushed the chairs aside to clear the space. "Have you sparred with anyone, yet?"

Sagan helped with the last chair, saying, "Oh, no. We can barely run the course without dying, but I'm eager to try out some moves since you're here to teach me." Yes. The enthusiasm glittered in her violet eyes, further warming her ever-present smile.

Was this underhanded tactic beneath Korac?

As soon as he questioned it, he recalled the sensation of being pulled inside-out by the conduit as Celindria and the Progeny sealed them behind it on Cinder.

"Let's begin with your stance, and you can tell me all about your training so far."

Sagan dodged the first blow, but dropped her defenses and took the second one to the gut. Air whooshed out of her lungs as Sagan choked on her breath.

"Again."

Korac gave orders like a General who was accustomed to compliance. He'd whooped Sagan's ass for the last two hours, and she'd loved every second of it. With his help, she would surely become a better fighter.

Again, Sagan stood and centered herself, raised her fists in a pose which defended her face and core. This time when Korac came at her with the first blow, she swept aside so the second strike kissed the air beside her.

There was no time to celebrate as Korac used his greater reach to grapple Sagan against him. Even though this was a dream, his warmth seeped through her pajamas along her back. As his arms enveloped her, she felt trapped, suffocated.

Panicked, Sagan abandoned her short-term training and struggled in his grip.

Korac released her immediately, taking a step back and giving her some space.

Deep breath in. Pause. Ease it out.

As Sagan recovered, Korac assessed her with sharp eyes. They were so strange. From a distance, they were simply white, but Sagan had gotten close enough to see the dark flecks of gray surrounding his pupil.

Korac also smelled like a cold winter night in a orchard of evergreens. The silk of his shirt felt as soft as it looked. His long fingers held a wealth of strength controlled in gentler touches—

Okay.

Sagan was crushing.

Hard.

The Icarus was gorgeous, and there was a smooth cadence to Korac's voice which hypnotized Sagan every time he spoke. She couldn't wait to share this dream with Tameka and Rayne—

"Your fight-or-flight instincts require reprogramming. You try to flutter away like a butterfly when you should ground yourself and flip me off of you like a tiger."

Korac kept his distance and left his hands loose at his sides, non-threatening, but Sagan knew how fast he could strike.

And how painfully.

It was strange experiencing sensation in a dream.

Sagan stretched her sore limbs before settling back into her stance, ready to fight again.

Korac's keen eyes flickered with some unknown response before he shook his head. "No more, tonight. You'll need rest to build your strength."

Yeah. Sagan was *not* Rayne, and she had a quiz in the morning. Still... She could stand to spend a few more minutes getting to know this Icarus. "I can't wait to tell Xelan. Will you be training the others, as well?"

Again, Korac shook his head solemnly and shame replaced the intelligence in his eyes. He confessed, "I'm not supposed to be here. Not with any of you." He swallowed before taking a step toward her. "Sagan, I lied to you."

That took her aback, and she frowned.

Remorse thickened Korac's voice as he said, "Xelan didn't send me. I'm here against orders not to interfere with your training, but you're so vital, I couldn't stay away." He took another step, beseeching. His eyes begged Sagan to believe the sad sincerity. "I fear without extra combat skills, you'll never reach your full potential, and I couldn't allow that."

Sagan let Korac closer, hearing him out. "Why would someone order you not to interfere?"

The same something—respect or regard—flickered in his eyes again before Korac said, "The Brethren. They want you to live normal lives. Even Xelan could face major consequences for contacting you. As would I. So please. Don't endanger his plan to train you further by mentioning me, and we'll keep our sessions a secret."

Sagan stood before an Icarus in the throes of regret. What he said made sense. This 'Brethren' had kept the Progeny's birthright a secret from them all their lives. From their parents—hell—from the world. If they'd known this invasion was coming, why were they keeping it hush-hush?

With Korac's help, Sagan could advance faster, and she could better stand a chance at protecting her friends and the Earth. She'd have to limit how much of her progress she would let Xelan see, lest he notice, but Sagan could manage that.

Boy.

Tackling an advanced placement curriculum sure seemed hard enough before Sagan learned the fate of the world depended on them. Now, she was looking at training sessions with two badass Icari while trying to maintain a social life. Maybe even dating.

Maybe even dating Rayne.

Korac waited patiently like a gorgeous statue while Sagan considered their situation. He wasn't pressuring her, and this didn't feel like conniving manipulation. He simply asked a favor of her.

Sagan smiled. She could deliver. "Sure. How often would you like to train together?"

Lord, when the Icarus smiled, it lit Sagan up inside. Korac said, "Every night, if you can."

Every night with him.

"Yeah. I think I can manage that."

The glaring red numbers of Rayne's alarm clock told her it was five in the morning. Was she finally tired enough to sleep? After all the excitement of this weekend...

Sagan sighed prettily in her sleep before rolling onto her side away from Rayne. For the thirtieth time, Tameka kicked Rayne, where she was snug in between her best friends. It was almost as if Rayne's parents had bought the queen-sized bed for this exact reason.

All night, Rayne replayed the events of the past week, and all night, she thought of Cinder. Of the Icari. Xelan seemed like a wonderful person, but what of Xelan's people? Did they deserve exile? He'd said they had no choice but to follow their King's orders regarding the invasion. So, didn't they need saving, too? And how could Rayne help?

Even in sleep, she couldn't escape the recap. She dreamt of conversations with Xelan.

"Wait a minute, Icarus was that Greek story. The wing-ed being who flew too close to the sun? That's what you call yourselves?"

"Where do you think the story came from? Many of your stories and much of your language came from us." Xelan gazed up at the stars. "Your civilizations were in their infancy when we invaded. You were just learning the meaning of history. Like children, it was easy for you to believe we were gods. So much so the Pharaohs who came long after continued the farce."

"What about spreading your vampiric nature with your bite?" Rayne bared her canines, and her nose crinkled as she made a hissing face.

Xelan chuckled, and it warmed Rayne's heart. "No. None of that. It's not a virus that can spread through our saliva, and I've seen firsthand what drinking Icarean blood does to humans. It's not pretty. We can reproduce with your kind, but the offspring rarely survive. Altogether, we're not terribly compatible without nacres."

As a young girl from Little Rock, Arkansas, Rayne couldn't imagine aliens had invaded human civilizations of 8,000BCE without the world maintaining some recorded knowledge of it. But there was something about the pain in Rayne's temples whenever Xelan came around. It told her she understood. She knew.

Deep in Rayne's bones, she *knew*.

The dream shifted, and clouds swirled above. Xelan faded away seconds before lightning struck and ignited Rayne's blood. The pain flared into white, searing agony. With her palms pressed to the side of her head, Rayne watched the sky shift as she fell to her knees. She screamed as her world split apart like a filmstrip, leaving a vast emptiness behind.

Sights, sounds, and even smells—not all of them good—assaulted Rayne's senses. A shadow of a man stood in front of an electrified portal. She couldn't make out any of his features, but she sensed a wave of hatred and malice that tested her resilience.

Rayne's fist closed and broke a familiar, glass object in her hand. Warm liquid spilled down her fingertips. A high-pitched, keening sound pierced through her ears, and a roar of wind shuddered around her. The portal swallowed the shadow with little resistance.

The pressure increased. It drew thousands upon thousands of Icari into the conduit like air vacating a depressurized plane. At first, terror overwhelmed Rayne. The portal might take her too, but it didn't draw her in at all. She stood there, unharmed, until all the Icari were sealed behind the conduit.

Once done, the torn fabric of space shimmered into nothing. Beyond it, stood a mirror. The mirror reflected Rayne as a mysterious woman with dark skin and brilliant blue eyes. She and the woman were the same.

"You've kept me waiting, Celindria."

To face the voice, Rayne turned her back on the mirror and found herself in a different space altogether. A high stone ceiling replaced the storm clouds, and loose red soil replaced the desert sand between her bare toes. A pyre blazed in the center of the cavernous chamber.

The flames were black. No heat; no smoke.

Through the licking peaks of the fire, Rayne made out a figure sitting on a stone throne. Devoid of ornament, the plain rock structure was enormous. It could easily sit three of her. The figure, however, had no trouble filling it out.

Along with the change of scenery, Rayne's clothes were different. Rather than the white billowy gown of the woman in the mirror, Rayne wore loose black pants, laced rather than zipped. They swept the soil as she moved around the pyre. The top clung to Rayne, a wrapped black material revealing her arms and midriff. At least the neckline was a modest scoop. Rayne's hair was tied back from her face with some of it braided close to her scalp.

The figure remained seated as she tiptoed closer. Built like a mountain, his biceps were as broad as her waist.

Should Rayne engage this dream or wait for it to pass? It felt different from the genetic memory. Like she was awake.

"You are very much asleep, safe in your bed." A deep rich baritone came from the shadow, hiding his face. He tilted his head as he said, "I expected you earlier. Are you having trouble sleeping?"

Rayne stopped a few steps away—Well, a few for her. It was probably one gigantic stride for him. Prepared to run at a moment's notice, she shored up enough courage to ask, "Are you real? Do you want something from me?"

Without seeing his face, Rayne could feel his smile. It felt cold. He said, "Yes, I am, and yes, I do."

The man stood and towered a foot over her, cast in the shadow of his monolithic build. Rayne was the tallest of her three besties at five foot, six inches. The stranger was even taller than Xelan, but with a different aura entirely. The air around the figure blurred until she couldn't make out any distinctive features aside from his stature.

Rayne didn't take a step back. Not from the tiger, and not from this figure. She asked, "Who are you?" Despite her resolve, Rayne's wavering voice betrayed her mounting anxiety.

"There is no hiding who I am."

A chill down Rayne's spine raised the hair on her arms and sent her heart racing. When she swallowed her fear, it made an audible sound. "Nox." His name came out breathy. Clenching her fists, Rayne wet her lips and tried to regain some ground. "Where's your crown? Should I curtsy?"

Better.

Despite the filter over Nox's face, Rayne detected a smirk as he said, "Crowns on your world denote power. On my world, my power is known and requires no ornamentation. You'll soon learn what I mean."

A shiver overtook Rayne, and she hugged herself. It probably didn't look very badass, but she couldn't deny the impulse.

Nox enjoyed her discomfort. It was in the ease of which he faced her, and the satisfaction in his tone. "I aim to do more than discomfort you, Celindria." He took a step toward Rayne, putting himself right in her space.

She set her jaw and looked up—way up—to meet Nox's eyes. Whatever filtered his face kept Rayne from discerning individual features separate from his entire face. For instance, his eyes glittered like pools of black ink. His cheeks, brows, and jawline were cut from severe angles. But his lips might soften the harshness, full as they were, if Rayne could marry the complete picture together.

Her nightmare was handsome.

And despite how much Nox frightened Rayne, she glared at him while saying, "Xelan will teach me how to take you down."

"Always so formidable, Celindria."

It bothered Rayne that Nox kept referring to her by her ancestor's name. She opened her mouth to say so when light exploded in her eyes as an iron fist backhanded her across the chamber.

When Xelan said the Icari were wing-ed, Rayne was excited to maybe one day fly. As it turned out, flying wasn't all that much fun. Mostly because of the landing.

The loose red soil grated Rayne's skin from her sensitive nerves as she skidded before a wall put a stop to her momentum. Her body begged Rayne to stay down, while every instinct screamed for her to get up before—

Nox's considerable fist closed around Rayne's throat and pinned her against the wall. On her knees, she scratched at his hands, but it only made him squeeze tighter, until black coffee grounds peppered her vision.

Seething with anger and hatred, Nox spat, "Has he told you that your ancestor condemned our people to starve under our glaring sun?"

Rayne could only manage a squeak as she tried to answer. Her eyes felt enormous, and they watered, staring into the unforgiving iciness in Nox's onyx glare. Before the darkness claimed Rayne, Nox loosened his grip enough for her to cough out, "Yes." She gulped a painful inhale of life-giving air. "He did. And I feel for your people. I want to help."

The separate features of Nox's face loosened from their tightened snarl into cold calculation as he considered Rayne's words. When he let her go completely, Rayne collapsed and coughed into the dirt, until her chest and ribs concaved into themselves.

Nox stared into the black flames, and they danced in the reflection of his eyes. After a long moment, he said, "Perhaps, there is a way you can help."

Despite the raw agony of her throat, hope flushed through Rayne. She croaked, "Anything," and meant it.

"Every night we will meet, and we will fight. There are worse horrors than myself ahead of you, Celindria. You must know what you're up against if you're to survive what awaits you. Tell your guardian of this, and ask him for a nacre—It is all that will save you, now."

A nacre.

Xelan spoke of nacres in a way that made Rayne believe the Icari were born with them. But… "I don't understand. How will us fighting and me receiving a nacre help the Icari?"

Nox met her eyes then, and eight thousand years of solitude weighed down on Rayne. "You are Cinder's salvation. You simply aren't strong enough yet. But I can make you strong and teach you Icarean fighting styles. Yes, you have your guardian, but I will be far less delicate with you. You will fight better for it."

Cinder's salvation?

Rayne would tell Xelan about this encounter and get some answers. But in the meantime…

"Yes. I'll train with you."

Nox gave a single chuckle, and despite the rich effect of his baritone, the sound came out bitter and ugly. "Not training. Fighting. Every night, I will kill you until you're strong enough—fast enough—to hold your own. Can you endure this, Celindria—"

"My name is *Rayne*." The four words escaped on a reflex through gritted teeth. She was tired of Nox calling her by the other woman's name. "And in case you missed it, I'm a teenager from Little Rock, Arkansas. Not some ghost from Egypt. I write stories and sing in choir. I'm always surrounded by people who love me, and I feel nothing personal toward you or your people. I want to help, and if you think killing me every night will make me strong enough to save the Icari from you—Then bring it."

On the last, Rayne stood and assumed the basic fighting stance Xelan had shown them earlier in the night. She knew it was weak. Her core wasn't stable, and her throat was still aching from being strangled. But she was not about to let this Icarus push her around without putting up some kind of fight.

"There's the warrior's spirit. You'll need it."

Nox punched Rayne fast and hard.

She heard a crack and startled awake, heart pounding and breathing heavy. Sagan awakened enough to pull Rayne's arms around her. The blond was always the little spoon, but tonight, as Rayne laid awake and watched the sunrise, she could've used the comfort of being held.

THREE

RESISTANCE ISN'T BUILT IN A DAY

A KALEIDOSCOPE OF SHAPES AND COLORS EXPLODED IN KYLE'S VISION. He gripped onto something tight, hanging on in the howling confusion of colors, tastes, smells, and sensations. When Kyle could see again, he was standing in the desert under a night sky. Heat from a forge blazed nearby. A woman with beautiful skin the deep color of a purple calla lily and bright blue eyes held something out to him. He could barely make out the shape of the object.

It was a glass heart pierced by a golden dagger, and blue liquid shimmered inside.

As the woman spoke, Kyle smelled jasmines on the night air. "Devis, your brilliance will save the Progeny from Nox's devious designs. You will be Earth's savior."

Devis was Kyle.

The hand with which Kyle reached out to receive the object was the same deep shade as the woman's. The billowing white sleeve of her dress lingered on his skin as they held the device between them.

It was a warmth Kyle ached to know more.

He regained consciousness, crouched over a toilet near the school's cafeteria. The act of ejecting his breakfast rocked his already pounding head. Genetic memories sucked.

The desert. A forge. Some weird trinket. And a beautiful woman.

A beautiful woman with the same eyes as Rayne. That's where the similarities stopped. Celindria was shorter and curvier than her descendant, with long hair in locs and braids. While Kyle found Rayne's ancestor extremely attractive, her eyes lacked the same warmth as Rayne. Too much cold intelligence pressed from behind the cobalt blue irises.

"Yo, Roberts. Are you okay in there?"

Kyle recognized Pablo Suarez's voice and nearly cursed. This was embarrassing. With a groan, he stood and said, "Yeah. Yeah. I'm fine." He opened the door to find concern in his Nicaraguan classmate's warm brown eyes.

Pablo volunteered, "Mi madre always gives me ginger soda and salted crackers for a stomach bug. Maybe you should see if the cafeteria has anything."

Kyle muttered, "Nothing can help me now."

"What?"

The genuine kindness emanating from Pablo's worried frown took away some of Kyle's gruff. "I said thanks, man. I'll go check now."

It was a lie, but at least it seemed to put his classmate at ease. Pablo smiled and said, "Anytime."

The smell of discount lunch meat and cheap vegetable medleys nearly sent Kyle back to the toilet. He'd have to start bringing his own lunches, anyway, since Xelan put them on a strict protein macro diet. Grilled chicken and steamed broccoli.

Hooray.

Outside the cafeteria, where the teachers parked out back, students gathered for some fresh air at a cluster of picnic tables. Tameka, Sagan, and Rayne were huddled around a table, and Kyle knew as he approached they were talking about this past weekend.

About Xelan.

Being Monday, and being Kyle's night to train solo with the ancient alien, the last thing Kyle wanted to talk about was Xelan. He ran a hand through his hair, tearing through the knots in frustration.

"You look a little stressed."

Oh, thank goodness. A welcome distraction and possibly a new date for homecoming. Kyle turned and faced Nikki with a grin. "Hey, beautiful. Your solo is coming along nicely."

Nikki gave him an incredulous look, which really brought out the freckles on her translucent skin. "You were skipping in the auditorium again?" Despite her admonishing tone, a blush crept onto her cheeks.

Kyle feigned shame, saying, "Yeah. You caught me spying on your rehearsal. I guess you'd better punish me for it." He winked.

Nikki's blush deepened as she giggled and swatted him. "You'd like that, wouldn't you?"

"Hah! More than you know."

Her eyes were an icier blue than Rayne's, but sparkled all the same as she stepped closer to murmur, "But I know why you were really there." They both looked over at the girl in question still huddling with Tameka and Sagan. "Don't worry. I'll keep your secret if you take me to homecoming."

Kyle tucked a strand of Nikki's dishwater blond hair behind her ear and whispered into it, "Deal."

"Hey, you two."

The short girl gazed up at Rayne with a secret smile. "Hey."

Kyle asked, "You three planning to bring your alien boyfriend to homecoming?"

Rayne's eyes tripled in size, and she glanced over her shoulder where Tameka and Sagan were still conspiring to fill Kyle's weekends with training. When Rayne turned back, her frown affected him. "Kyle, we aren't supposed to tell people."

Nikki blinked. "Uhm... Alien boyfriend?"

"I know. I know." Kyle held up a hand to placate Rayne. "If we tell anyone, they'll lock us up in the loony bin. But at least now you have an excuse for your *guardian* to include Nikki here in the apocalypse training. Unless you *want* her to die in an alien invasion?"

The color drained from Rayne as she stared at Kyle, mortified. He felt kinda bad but…

Nikki's trust in Rayne was open in her eyes as she waited patiently for the brunette to fill her in or freeze her out.

To Kyle, Rayne said, "I'd planned to ask Xelan after his session with you." She met the other girl's earnest expression and smiled. "Nikki, we need to talk."

Good.

Before the two girls walked off together for that bizarre conversation, Kyle made a point to say, "I'll call you later, Nikki, and we can talk about homecoming."

When a smile blossomed on her face, Rayne's reaction wasn't what Kyle had expected. How could he get over her if she insisted on smiling like that?

Kyle blocked Xelan's kick with both arms crossed at his front. Still, the blow rattled his bones, until he cried, "Son of a bitch!" As his voice rang through the trees of his backyard, he worried his mother would hear.

Xelan likewise scanned the perimeter for intruders or maybe more spies while he waited for Kyle to recover.

"Show me that kick again," Kyle demanded, eager to learn everything he could from their *guardian.*

The Icarus grinned with a warmth Kyle realized was signature to his personality as Xelan said, "A tornado crescent kick is a little advanced. Let's try a good old-fashioned roundhouse, first." He demonstrated the kick, slowing the movements. It should look ridiculous in cargo pants and a t-shirt, but apparently, the Icarus didn't own any other clothes.

Dressed in workout shorts and a tank, Kyle mimicked the move. Slow at first, and then he tried faster. He knew without asking that it would get easier and feel more natural with practice and strength. More training. But at one day a week, it would take forever.

Kyle asked, "What can I do on my own to speed up this process?"

Xelan nodded approvingly. "Hit the gym. Train upper and lower body, and don't forget cardio at least four days a week. Thirty minutes of it at minimum. As you get older and gain more freedom from your parents, we'll work on the training course."

Freedom.

Did Xelan know about Kyle's home life? The young man wasn't about to volunteer it, and the second Xelan hit the road, Kyle was teaching his sisters everything he'd learned tonight. They'd taken the news of the invasion pretty well, and the siblings had prepared a strategy for when the day finally came. His sisters wouldn't tell their mother, not for fear of eviction or worse, hospitalization.

Kyle shuddered.

"Are you cold?" Xelan asked while packing his stuff.

With a frown, Kyle shook himself back to reality. "No. Are you heading out?"

Xelan swung his duffle over his shoulder like it weighed nothing, despite all the gear Kyle knew it held. Xelan asked, "Do you want more than two hours?"

Wow. Two hours.

Kyle shook his head. "Naw. I don't want you keeping Rayne up too late. I can't believe she volunteered all her nights for this."

"She's a surprise, that one." Xelan's fondness suffused his voice.

It grated on Kyle. "Well, you would know, spying on her and shit."

Xelan didn't look upset by Kyle's accusation. Instead, his features softened with sadness. Almost enough to make the younger man regret the ugly remark. Xelan said, "I've looked after all of you from a safe distance until the situation called for intrusion. Every night, I pray to Elden the reports of Nox's progress are wrong, and none of this is necessary. But I couldn't live with myself if the invasion went down with you five unprepared."

Kyle sighed. "Look, I don't mean to come off as ungrateful, and I'm sorry for accusing you of being a weirdo. But you are kind of a weirdo. It's taking some adjustment on my part to trust that you're really on our side." Especially with Rayne, but he left that part out.

Xelan patted Kyle's shoulder. "Don't worry. I'm no more a weirdo than you. See you next week."

"Say 'hi' to Rayne for me."

Walking away, Xelan's grin was in his voice. "If you're lucky, I just might."

Asshole.

"Kyle says 'hi.' I think he likes you."

When Rayne blushed and ducked her eyes, Xelan wondered if he should've kept his assumption to himself. He opened his mouth to say so, when she held up her hands.

"It's okay. I just don't see him like that, you know?"

Yup. Xelan had stepped into a beehive of teenage hormones by accident. He dropped his duffel and busied himself with pulling out supplies as he said, "Sure. It's not really any of my business, anyway." Gloves. Defense pads. Jump rope. That should do for the night. He peered up at the window facing the backyard. "Should we be worried your parents might see?"

Rayne shook her head. "That's my room." She let out a sigh and wrung her hands. "Uhm, Xelan, I need to talk to you about a few things."

Moonlight cast across the green lawn onto the gray brick of Rayne's house. When she stepped into it, her skin glowed with the reflection. It was eerie with the concern in her sparkling eyes, so like her ancestor's.

Xelan tossed her the gloves with a smile, saying, "You can tell me anything, Rayne."

She fumbled one, trying to catch it, and a bashful smile overtook some of the anxiety. "Well, first, I kinda told a friend about you and the whole invasion thing." She winced with her confession.

Honestly, when telling a bunch of teenagers the world could end any day now, one must expect a few slip-ups. "Go on."

Rayne had expected him to reprimand her. He could tell by the way her body let out a sigh of relief. She said, "I was hoping you could train her, too."

If it were up to Xelan, he would train the entire human race for the invasion, but The Brethren had forbidden him from training the Progeny. So why not? "Sure. Arrange everything, and I'll turn up."

Rayne's beaming smile was contagious, and it felt heartwarming to have this kind of rapport with someone—

She threw her arms around Xelan's waist and pressed her cheek to his chest. "Thank you."

How long had it been since his last hug?

Unsure how to proceed, Xelan cautiously squeezed back, but not too hard. He was afraid of hurting her.

Rayne stepped back, ducking her eyes again. She sounded embarrassed as she said, "Sorry. That wasn't really 'badass warrior' of me."

"Oh, warriors *do* hug." At her hopeful glance, Xelan added, "They often give the best ones. Are you ready for practice? Show me your form. Good."

With growing confidence, Rayne took her stance and held up her fists. She confessed, "I hope you don't mind, but I ran the course this morning before school."

Xelan's immediate response was a flush of pride, but concern quickly replaced it. "That's pretty early. Did the girls run with you?"

Rayne looked caught, and she dropped her arms with a sigh. "No. I went out before they were awake. I couldn't sleep after..." After a shiver, she hugged herself and looked away. Xelan thought he'd need to push, but after a moment, she said, "I dreamt of a black pyre, a throne, and a man—an Icarus—built like a mountain."

Nox.

How could he invade Rayne's dreams? Was he here? Xelan nearly cursed he was so angry. The Brethren swore to him they'd monitor conduit activity. He'd ask Lucas tomorrow. Even if Nox was still on Cinder, Xelan would need to investigate a means of dream manipulation. But for now, the lost look in Rayne's eyes told Xelan his silence had unnerved her.

He knelt on one knee in front of her so she'd meet his eyes. "Did Nox hurt you?"

When Rayne nodded, Xelan's heart broke. She was so young, and now she was burdened beyond her years. Rayne swallowed loud enough for Xelan to hear before she said, "He told me he would kill me every night to make me strong, and he said to ask you for a nacre."

Every.

Night.

If not for trying to reassure Rayne, Xelan would let his disgust for the King of Cinder show on his face.

Monster.

"It's okay, Rayne. I'll teach you how to defend yourself against him, and you won't need a nacre. It's complicated, but I can't just give you one, and I don't know if I would if I could."

She tilted her head to the side, holding back her question.

Xelan put a hand on her shoulder and said, "A nacre will permanently alter your body and change you forever. It's such an irrevocable conversion of your physical being that it isn't up to me, anyway. There are channels and permissions. We can't simply introduce nacres to the human race. Please understand... I intend to make you more than a match for Nox without one, but I'm also prepared to advocate on your behalf should it come to that. Do you understand?"

"I'm not afraid of Nox, and I was happy to have the chance to tell him to his face."

Xelan's mouth almost fell open. Brave and determined, Rayne looked the part of a warrior with her chin high and her eyes sharp. He grinned at her. "All right. Then let's teach you some moves to surprise him tonight—Oh, I'm always a phone call away if you ever need me. Tell me any details you want. Write them down afterward, and maybe we can use them to build strategies."

Rayne smiled. "Thanks. I'll do that." She stepped back and resumed her stance.

The similarities and differences between her and Celindria still surprised Xelan. He returned the expression and held up two pads. "Punch as hard as you can."

When Rayne complied, he didn't feel it. Xelan ordered, "Again, and put some muscle behind it."

The second time was better. "Good. Now jab with your left arm."

She went to do it, and Xelan smacked her in the head with his pad. "You let your guard down."

Rayne's hair clung to the static of the vinyl material as she glared at him.

He ruffled her head a little extra until it made a wild, kinetic mess. "There. Much better."

Xelan actually felt Rayne's next punch.

"There's my badass warrior."

Wednesday nights with Xelan.

Tameka sat cross-legged in her backyard, waiting for him to show up. In the meantime, she checked a small compact mirror. Black eyeliner emphasized the bright green of her eyes, made all the more exotic for her black freckles and tawny brown skin. She'd tied back her red coils and dressed in workout gear, completely confident in the sports bra without a shirt.

A duffel bag flew over Tameka's privacy fence and landed on the plush grass. Her heart raced as Xelan followed with the easy bound of a graceful cat. Only then, did Tameka wonder if her parents could see them. She spared a glance over her shoulder to ensure the enormous boughs of her family's oak tree sheltered their training space.

Yup.

All alone.

With Xelan.

"Hey." Tameka tried for casual, but the greeting came out breathy. How could she help herself? He made cargo pants and a t-shirt look good, filled out by his muscular thighs and broad shoulders.

Xelan gave her a radiant smile, oblivious to her attraction. "Hey. All set?"

She clapped her hands in their fingerless gloves. "Yup." Aware of how much he was about to kick her ass, Tameka assumed their first basic stance.

"Here. Bring your feet closer together. And..." Xelan adjusted her fists so her arms better blocked her face. "There."

The contact left Tameka breathless. He smelled cozy, like the Callahan's bookstore. His hands were hot, unusually so. In fact, he radiated warmth in every sense of the word. Again, she breathed, "Thanks."

Xelan gripped a vinyl pad in each hand, saying, "So like with Kyle, Rayne, and Sagan, you punch this as hard as you can."

Tameka gave it her all.

"Good." When Xelan grinned, it melted her. "Have you done this before?"

Feeling a little proud of herself, Tameka preened. "I've taken some self-defense classes."

He dropped the pads and faced her. "All right, then. Show me what you've got."

Tameka feigned a punch before kicking Xelan's knee.

Before the kick landed, he jumped back and caught her foot.

Quick to react, she spun and kicked him with the other leg.

Xelan leaned out of the way and dropped her foot.

Never one to forget a skill, Tameka kip-upped back to her feet.

With wide eyes, Xelan looked impressed. He nodded with approval and said, "Awesome."

While his praise meant the world to Tameka, she was too busy leaning over and breathing hard to celebrate. She held up a finger. "Give me a second."

With his hands on his hips, Xelan looked up and admired the stars, while Tameka caught her breath. He chuckled unexpectedly, and when she quirked a brow, he said, "I should've known you would put up the best fight."

Tameka straightened and dared to step closer, gazing at the stars with him. "Why is that?"

"Did your parents tell you anything unusual about the day you were born?"

That widened Tameka's eyes, but she knew what he was speaking to. "About the lights going out in the hospital?"

Xelan faced her with regard and awe in his eyes. "You were the first Progeny born in this generation, and the entire grid went down. Not only the hospital complex, but the surrounding area."

Tameka felt the need for activity, so she grabbed the pads and handed them to Xelan. While he got in position, she said, "You're talking as if you know from firsthand experience."

"Well, I was there."

Tameka blinked.

Xelan's eyes softened with sorrow as he said, "We look after the Progeny. I cared for your mother as I care for you, but I couldn't be in your lives. Not for thousands of years now."

After she landed a right hook, he nodded for her to go again. While they trained, she asked, "Why not?"

Again, the sorrow haunted Xelan. "Persecution. I would visit, leaving them alive and thriving. But within the next decade, when I returned, I would find their homes had burned to the ground. Or worse. Being born different is dangerous, so The Brethren stopped informing the Progeny of their birthright. Even now."

Tameka wet her lips before asking, "Xelan, can I tell my mother?"

He looked away and bit his thumbnail, respecting her question with thorough contemplation. After a long moment, he said, "Only if you trust her completely to believe you. Otherwise, you risk endangering your freedom to train, at best. Or at worst, she may call the cops on me and send you to a mental health facility."

Well, wasn't that discouraging? But Tameka wanted to protect her family from the invasion. How could she do that without telling them?

"I think I know where you're headed with this. The Brethren have assured me of measures to protect the Progeny—all the Progeny—when the day comes. Me training you is simply another precaution."

Tameka nodded. "Yeah. That makes me feel better. Is there anything else I should do?"

Xelan blew the air out of his cheeks as he considered her question. He said, "You can stash weapons at places you frequent, so when the Icari invade, you're prepared." Gently, he gripped Tameka's shoulder. "But the best thing you can do now is train."

Stronger and faster didn't happen overnight.

Tameka gazed up at Xelan and admired the midnight ring around his otherwise black eyes.

Wait.

Tears.

Why was she seeing tears—

Light exploded in Tameka's eyes, and she went numb—

Not numb.

Sucking agony throbbed in her chest while blood poured from a gaping hole in her sternum.

{6,000BCE}

"You were right!" Xelan cried from the entryway. Under normal circumstances, that phrase delighted Merit to hear. Unfortunately, this time he followed it with a grunt as he fell to one knee.

She dropped the Icarean book and hurried to his side with a cry. "My love!"

Xelan slumped face first to the earthen floor.

Merit pushed him over onto his back and hissed. "Who did this?!"

There was a hole in his chest. It gaped and gushed rich, blue blood. More astonishing than the wound itself, was that it would not heal. Merit hissed. "What happened?"

"Colita. She revealed our plans to Nox." Xelan winced as she peeled cerulean-soaked cloth from skin. Through pained gasps, he said, "Korac ambushed me and took me to Nox's chambers. He told me to stand aside and let him deal with the vermin, himself. Then he repeated everything back to me that I'd confided in Colita over the last two years."

Merit asked, "Do they know of the Pretiosum Cruor?" Her tone was urgent and firm.

Xelan looked down the length of his body to her hands on the wound as he said, "No. I never told her of it. Please give me more credit than that."

Merit pulled her wrap off her red hair and packed his wound. "Why does this not heal?" She tried to conceal a sniffle with her words.

Xelan must have heard the panic in her voice and reached for her dark hand with his pale, bloody one. "Merit. Love, look at me."

Slowly, she brought her eyes to meet his. Xelan said, "It will not heal any longer."

Merit cried, "No, no, why not?" Her voice shook, and tears filled her eyes.

With a wince, Xelan cupped her cheek. "Nox took my nacre."

Merit shook her head, still cradled in his hand. She asked, "What will we do? Tell me, what can I do?"

"Leave me. Warn Celindria and the others. None of you are safe—"

Another cry tore from Merit's lips. "I will not leave you!" She took his hand from her face and laced their fingers together. His pale. Hers dark. Yin and yang.

The salt of her tears burned her face, and the gravity of her decision weighed heavily on her heart. "Wait here, Xelan. I will fetch you some water."

Xelan muttered between choking coughs. "Must. Tell. Celindria."

Merit turned the corner into his laboratory. She found a razor-sharp instrument on his worktable. Jabbing a cork stopper into her mouth, she shoved the instrument under her breastbone. The immediate pain brought her to her knees, and she furiously bit into the stopper to stifle a wail. Yet even as she worked, she could feel the regenerative properties of the nacre healing the fresh wound around the scalpel. Quick. She had to work quick.

After several tries and much screaming around the bit, Merit returned to Xelan. He was laying where she'd left him. Still. So very still. "My love?"

No answer nor flinch.

Not a single reaction.

Merit said, "Xelan, I brought the water." She set her emerald eyes on the face she loved for forty years and crashed to her knees beside him. "No! You cannot leave me!"

Xelan's eyes were fixed to the ceiling, unblinking and unseeing. Blood streamed from his gaping mouth.

Merit gritted her teeth, vowing, "I will not allow you to die!" Ripping his shirt, she considered the wound.

Just below the brain stem in Xelan's chest, Merit found a chamber similar to the one near her heart. She pulled the delicate pearl computer from the folds of her wrap and worked her way into his chest cavity. Sweat beaded on her brow and dripped from her lip. The salt mingled with her tears. Her vision swam with little black dots, and it became more difficult to breathe. All that aside, she smiled when she felt the chamber swallow the nacre.

"Yes! Save him!" Merit croaked. She rocked on her knees as she watched. Until finally she swayed all the way over, laying along the length of him. She forced her lungs to drink air in and expel it out. Heavy eyelids refused to stay open. A hitch caught her breath, and she felt it echo in her pulse as it slowed. She was dying.

But Merit only wanted to live long enough to see him move his eyes. In a voice light as air, she commanded, "Breathe."

Xelan's chest heaved hard enough to bow his spine. His great swallow of air punched into his lungs. The wound stitched closed as if the two halves no longer wanted to be apart.

She knew how they felt.

Merit rasped, "Xelan, listen. I cannot be with you much longer, for I fear your desperation."

Slowly, he turned his head, with his mouth gaping for air. Xelan's fresh tears told Merit he was listening.

"I will not risk you for the revolution needs you far greater than it need I." She coughed and copper blood filled her mouth. "Thank you for finally seeing me. All I ask is that you not waste time with the next love. See them and know them. Be with them. Know that I am . . . always . . . with you."

Horror and grief filled Xelan's eyes. Unable to take the sight any longer, Merit thrust the instrument the rest of the way into her heart.

As she considered whether she believed in an afterlife, Merit decided she wanted her last words to make a mark. To leave the most lasting impression and summarize her personality in one last breath.

"Take . . . The bitch's . . . Head."

{SEPTEMBER 2002}

Air.

Tameka tried to breathe, but she couldn't take in any air—

A punch to her sternum brought Tameka back to her actual body, laying on the grass in her backyard. Xelan stopped pumping compressions onto her chest and wiped an unsteady hand down his face. Into it, he said, "Tameka. Tameka, I'm so sorry."

Questions flooded her mind, but first...

She reached up and cupped Xelan's jaw. Not only did he let Tameka do it, but he leaned his face into it with a little hiccuping sob. So warm. Xelan's soul felt like a well of kindness from which Tameka would never completely draw to the bottom.

He swallowed and said, "I tried to revive Merit, your ancestor, but I couldn't. Nox ripped my nacre from my chest, but I escaped before it killed me. I escaped to warn Merit, but she... She thought herself worth less than me and gave me her nacre before I could stop her. Then, she..."

Tameka had felt the knife to her heart. The resolve to keep Xelan from reversing the nacre swap. But above all of it, she'd felt Merit's love and devotion for him. Tameka said, "She would never have forgiven you if you'd died while she could save you. Don't tarnish her sacrifice with guilt."

Xelan turned his closed eyes up to the sky and swallowed hard enough for Tameka to see the movement, as if he could physically swallow his grief. When he met her eyes again, he'd found some peace. Gently, he took her hand from his jaw and placed it with the other on her abdomen.

"Thank you. What about you? Are you all right?"

Tameka had to give the question some serious thought. Her ancestor and Xelan had been an item, which had ended tragically. Feeling all of Merit's emotions actually made Tameka feel better about her crush on Xelan. Like he'd earned her trust across multiple lifetimes.

"Yeah. I think I am. Will you help me up?"

Xelan lifted Tameka easily to her feet, and for a second, she stared up at him a breath apart. Awkwardly, he stepped back and cleared his throat before asking, "Uhm. Are you sure you're okay?"

Tameka flexed her fists, feeling in command of her own body. She resumed her stance and squared off with Xelan. "Let's get back to this."

He was still frowning with concern as he said, "We can call it a night, if you need—"

"No. No, because now I have a personal vendetta to take up with the King of Cinder and his blood whore. Teach me how to kick their asses so I can repay them for Merit's death."

A little grimly and a whole lot determined, Xelan said, "Gladly."

Andrew had braided his hair for training in a style he'd hoped Xelan would recognize from his ancestor's genetic memories. Over the course of the last week, Andrew had experienced three memories, and all of them were pretty chill. He was proud to say his ancestor was probably a cool guy with a talent for convincing people to take his suggestions seriously. The Progeny known as Andrius had also amassed an enormous family before...

Well, that's what bothered Andrew. There was one memory where he was talking to the woman they'd all accepted was Rayne's ancestor, Celindria. But the two ancient Progeny were on opposing sides of the discussion and then nothing. That was Andrius' latest memory so far.

The mystery of how Andrius' life ended left Andrew needing to know more. Hence, the hairdo. He was hoping to segue Xelan into some answers.

Unlike his friends, Andrew lived in an apartment, so no backyard for training. Xelan agreed to meet him at Boyle Park, within walking distance of the complex. He stood in a field of freshly cut grass, and the smell merged with the scent of wet earth from Rock Creek's nearby banks. The drying leaves of surrounding oak trees heralded the coming of autumn, as fireflies danced their last waltz of the summer.

A Jaguar X-Type pulled up to the gravel lot, and it surprised Andrew to see Xelan step out of it, duffel bag in hand. The Icarus waved like a dork. "Hey."

Andrew frowned and said, "I thought you could fly or something."

The other man chuckled as he made his way over, asking, "What part of 'low profile' are you and the other Progeny having trouble understanding? I'm not looking to be on some government scientist's slab for dissection."

"Oh." That made sense. When Xelan dropped the bag, Andrew dug through it and grabbed the jump rope. "Kinky…"

But Xelan wasn't paying attention to Andrew's hilarious joke. He was peering at the younger man's hair.

Oh, good.

Andrew said, "Yeah. I've had a few other memories of Andrius. Can you tell me anything about him? And what's a 'Pretiosum Cruor?'"

Xelan hid a wince, but not before Andrew glimpsed it. He said, "I'll answer after you give me three solid minutes of jumping rope."

Pfft. Like that was hard or something?

After three minutes, Andrew was spitting between gasps for air. This road to fitness would kill any chance of him becoming a smoker. "Okay," he managed between deep inhales. After a ragged exhale, he croaked, "Tell me."

Xelan didn't smirk or taunt him. He seemed completely aware of the tolls this sort of training would take on the human body. They obviously weren't the first humans he'd gotten into shape. He said, "I was hoping to tell everyone about it as a group, but I suppose we'll have to cover this one at a time. The Pretiosum Cruor is a device Kyle's ancestor—Devis—created to seal the conduit to Cinder. Did you see what it looked like?"

Fully recovered, Andrew retrieved the jump rope, ready to go again. "It was a glass heart thingy with a gold dagger through it, but there was nothing inside."

At Xelan's nod, Andrew resumed jumping rope for another three minutes. The Icarus said, "When filled with blood, it genetically locked the conduit to the donor." While Xelan spoke, he paced around Andrew as if he couldn't keep still while telling the story.

Breathing heavy already, Andrew strained to ask, "Celindria?"

"She took it upon herself, yes. So the conduit can't open without her blood."

Wait.

Andrew frowned. Between skips, he asked, "But she's dead, right? So, why are you worried about Nox invading?"

Xelan stopped pacing, stood in front of Andrew, and stared. Hard. There was entirely too much gravity to his solemn expression, and he seemed unwilling to speak the answer aloud.

How else could Nox come by Celindria's blood—

Oh.

Andrew stopped jumping prematurely and stared at Xelan with his mouth falling open.

Rayne.

"Does she know?"

Xelan sighed and ran a hand through his hair, exasperated. "Like I said, I wanted to tell you altogether, but first I'd hoped to ease you into it. So, no. I haven't told her, but I'd plan to when she's older and more grounded in this invasion business."

Andrew pulled on the back of his neck with both hands and blew the air from his cheeks. "Shit. I don't think I want to know this."

"Well, you do. So you can tell her or wait until I think she's ready."

Nox would target Rayne, specifically. She was in danger, and Andrew knew it. His voice came out soft as he said, "Please, don't leave this up to me. I want to help her."

Xelan nodded as if something had occurred to him. "You can, and I think I know how. Can you commit to extra work—" He held up a warning finger before Andrew blurted out his answer. Xelan added, "In secret. The others can't know."

If it meant helping them... "Yeah. I can."

Without another word, Xelan took out his cell phone and made a call. There was no greeting or conversation exchanged. He simply gave their location in the park to whomever had answered.

Andrew's brows went up, bewildered, and Xelan didn't offer any further details. Instead, he said, "Get a few more minutes of cardio in while we wait."

Ten minutes later, a Mercedes S-Class pulled up beside the Jaguar. When the man stepped out, Andrew knew he wasn't human. He wasn't as tall as Xelan, but there was a certain confidence in how the Icari carried themselves.

Majestic.

That was the word.

The Icarus with sandy-brown hair crossed the lawn, accumulating grass stains on his fancy business suit. With molten-gold eyes, he took one look at Andrew and said, "You're Andrius' descendant. It's a pleasure to meet you. I'm Lucas." He held out his hand.

Andrew's hands went sweaty, nervous to meet another human-appearing alien. Still, he shook Lucas' hand. "Hi. My name's Andrew."

"I know." After the other man shone him a magnificent smile, they both turned and looked expectantly at Xelan.

"Lucas, you told me The Brethren were looking into a human member. How about a Progeny?" Xelan grinned as if this were a spectacular idea.

But as Andrew realized what he was saying, the young man frowned.

The Brethren.

Lucas looked cautiously optimistic. "It's a sound idea, but how will I explain meeting a Progeny after The Brethren warned *you* to stay away from this generation of descendants?"

Mischief sparkled in Xelan's eyes as he said, "Well… *I* was. *You* weren't. This must be your idea for it to work."

The incredulity in Lucas' answering smile spoke volumes of the friendship between the two Icari. They were clearly accustomed to each other's antics. After shaking his head, Lucas asked, "Andrew, how do you feel about this? It's a bigger commitment than I'm sure this mad scientist has made clear."

There was no question. No doubt. Andrew said, "I want to help with the invasion. To help keep Rayne safe from Nox. Our families... Everyone."

Something flashed in Lucas' golden eyes for an instant before it vanished.

Was that respect? Appreciation?

Whatever it was, Andrew hoped to see more of it. "I'm ready to do whatever it takes."

Lucas and Xelan exchanged an approving glance before Lucas said, "Very well. Tomorrow, I'll introduce you to The Brethren. You'll need to act as if it's the first time you're meeting Xelan, and you can't breathe a word to the rest. Otherwise, we'll risk exposing Xelan's secret training plan."

"Yeah. I'll tell my mom I got a part-time job at the Callahan's bookstore."

Xelan patted Andrew on the back. "Perfect. Then you can fill me in on all the duplicitous schemes Lucas here refuses to tell me."

Lucas leaned over and whispered into Andrew's ear, "Play along as if I'm telling you a juicy secret."

Andrew almost gaped, but for real. The spicy scent of the shorter Icarus was so intoxicating, he'd almost held onto Lucas to draw in more.

Xelan brought Andrew back to the here and now when he sulked. "Don't keep me hanging. What did he say to you?"

Lucas chuckled, a warm rich sound.

With a shake of his head, Andrew recovered himself enough to play along. "That's for me to know and for you to lose your mind over not knowing."

Lucas winked, and Andrew swallowed.

Were all the Icari this hot?

Andrew was so in over his head.

"I'm keeping your secret, as promised, but I want something in exchange."

Sagan was feeling bold. Hence, her demands on an Icarean warrior in her dreams.

Korac had pulled his hair back in a high ponytail tonight, exposing more of his delicate bone structure and making it slightly easier to read his expressions. Right now, he was smirking. And oh, boy. Sagan's heart couldn't take it.

"Be careful of what you ask. You may get more than you bargained for."

Yeah...

Yeah.

That was *not* a deterrent. Sagan shook herself before she could drool on her pajamas. A little nervous to pry, she wet her lips and asked, "Can you tell me what it's like on your homeworld?" More than anything, she'd wanted to ask Xelan about Cinder, but talking about his planet always seemed to make him mournful.

Korac's eyebrows raised at her question. He was wearing a white button up tonight with a waistcoat left undone to sway with his movements. Because he'd rolled his sleeves up again and his pinstripe slacks sported some dirt and wrinkles, it looked like the end of a long day of hard work.

Yet here Korac was, training Sagan in his free time. Gratitude left her warm enough to smile nonstop. It seemed catching as he smiled or smirked more tonight than in the last week.

"I'll tell you, but I want fifty push-ups while I do it."

Eager to comply, Sagan hopped down and began counting. She was pretty proud of her progress so far, as push-ups came easier with every night.

Korac paced around, hands clasped behind his back as he obliged her. "Our sun burns around us and never stops. At first glance, it's maddening. How could we not perish under such fire? But Elden protects us from certain death."

There was that name again.

Elden.

Sagan's arms shook halfway through her count, but she kept pushing.

And Korac kept talking. "The world is scorched. Forests of charred trees can't replenish their foliage without clean water. Even the oceans churn ashen black foam onto cliffs of volcanic rock. But near the conduit to Earth, the air is cleaner. It smells of sediment and rain. It rains less on Cinder than in Earth's driest desert."

Against the rug, Sagan murmured, "It sounds beautiful." She hit the fifty count and curled on the floor to gaze up at him. "Awesome and tragic."

Korac sat in front of the fire with her, one knee up and his wrist resting on it. His expression was unreadable as they sat together. When he'd said nothing, Sagan feared she'd offended him. Then Korac startled her when he suddenly reached for the desk nearby. Out of a drawer, he retrieved a sketchbook and a pencil.

As Korac sketched, Sagan leaned closer to peer at the page. And he let her. Within a few seconds, she made out a cliff face under a harsh sky, streaked with glaring light. Their red giant of a sun. A blocky castle or fortress dwarfed a ruined temple set across a thoroughfare from it. Beyond those structures was a shimmering portal.

Finished, Korac set the sketchbook on their laps between them and pointed. "This is Li Mountain. It's the highest peak on the planet. There, you see, that's Nox's Castle."

"What's this?" Sagan pointed at the shimmering energy.

He said, "It's the conduit to Earth."

Nox's Castle sat at the entrance to their planet. Was the King of Cinder so dedicated to taking Earth that he'd build his castle near the entrance? It gave Sagan a chill, and she shivered.

Korac reached for the blazer on the back of his desk chair and slipped it around her bare shoulders. Sagan ought to sleep in workout clothes rather than skimpy tops, but dressing this way for bed had gotten her in his jacket. His crisp winter scent emanated from it, surrounding her.

"Can I keep it?"

Korac looked confused at first.

Sagan giggled. "Not the jacket. The sketch. It's amazing."

He smirked again, saying, "Finally. Someone who appreciates my artistic talents. You can't take it with you, but I'll make sure you get it."

A little thrill went through Sagan.

Korac stood and held out his hand to her. "On your feet. We still have drills to run."

Sagan took it, and he lifted her easily. For a heartbeat, they stood close, staring into each other's eyes. Her pulse fluttered, and, almost as if he'd sensed it, Korac took a step back.

Like a General, he ordered, "Back to work, soldier."

Sagan almost pouted.

Three hours later, her alarm clock woke her before Sagan could land the cartwheel kick she'd tried to execute all week. And the bad luck kept coming as she ripped her favorite jeans at the knee. There was only one remedy for this. Sagan took some scissors and cut the jeans into shorts. Using a lighter, she burned the fringe off and...

Sagan glanced around the kitchen to make sure her parents were gone for the day. Then she pressed the scorching hot lighter to her skin, letting the metal sear her arm. She sucked air in through her clenched teeth, as endorphins flooded her synapses with all kinds of 'should not be doing this.'

Whatever.

There were worse things for a teenager to get into, and at least this gave Sagan some relief from the near miss in her dreams.

The dose of serotonin and dopamine got Sagan through the bus ride to school before arriving in the cafeteria where the others waited for the bell to ring. Kyle was snuggled up with Nikki, the two likely discussing their date tonight at homecoming. Sagan liked that Tameka wasn't the least bit bothered, and despite her obvious crush on Xelan, she'd gotten a date for the dance tonight, too. When Rayne's eyes met Sagan's across the cafeteria, more endorphins flooded through her.

The two girls were attending together in secret.

A date with Rayne.

Talk about thrills.

Although, Sagan couldn't ignore the cloud over Rayne's head this last week. She'd seemed more tired than usual, and Sagan was pretty sure the other girl skipped an essay in history. Which was totally unlike her.

When Sagan joined Tameka and Rayne's conversation, the latter brushed Sagan's fingers and put her at ease. Everything was fine because they were together. Aside from that, the morning looked uneventful as they made their way down North Hall to their lockers. It was a journey accompanied by the soundtrack of Mrs. Mendax's constant encouragement to move faster. Their short principal wasn't standing correctly in those heels, and Sagan bet her feet hurt by the end of every day. Poor lady.

Sagan opened her locker prepared to hide a ten-centimeter pocket knife within the wooden cubby, per Xelan's recommendation, but she paused.

Nestled inside with her textbooks and binders was a sketchbook.

No fucking way.

Suddenly breathless, Sagan opened it in the shelter of her locker enough to glimpse the sketch from her dream. Other sketches beckoned her curiosity, but this wasn't the place. She quickly hugged it and her morning textbooks close to her heart. Tameka and Rayne rummaged through their own lockers down the hall from her, unaware of Sagan's secret.

Should she feel guilty or ashamed? She felt bad for keeping her dreams from Rayne, but…

Some part of Sagan enjoyed the secrecy and wanted Korac all to herself. Their dreams were professional training and innocent fun. Harmless, really.

Really.

That evening, Sagan and Rayne held hands under a table while Tameka and Kyle danced with their dates on the gym floor. The homecoming committee had transformed the space into a magical wonderland of leafless trees, glowing white with fairy lights. They'd strung them from the rafters and basketball goals. Glittery flakes of silver and navy blue—the school colors—snowed down from above.

Even while Sagan caressed the back of Rayne's hand with her thumb, the scenery made her think of Korac. She felt bad for hiding the sketchbook and keeping a secret from Xelan and Rayne.

The aforementioned hotty wore workout pants and a tank to the dance, saying, "I couldn't see the point in buying a dress to only wear it once, and we never know when the invasion will happen. So..." Rayne shrugged by way of explanation.

Meanwhile, Sagan felt overdressed and a little superfluous in her backless black dress. She'd even curled her short hair, hoping Rayne would notice—

The blue-eyed girl reached over and tugged on a curl. "Have I told you how much I love the blond bob?" Rayne beamed.

It warmed Sagan to her toes, infecting her with a huge grin. "Thanks. Did you braid your own hair like that?"

For all that Rayne didn't dress up, her long black hair was tied in an intricate knot of braids. She snickered while saying, "No way. Mom insisted I look somewhat nice for the dance." Then she looked conspiratorially left and right before leaning to whisper in Sagan's ear. "Do you wanna get out of here?"

Sagan's heart skipped a beat. She swallowed before nodding emphatically. More than anything, she wanted to be alone with Rayne.

Her best friend, hopefully girlfriend, nodded toward the nearest exit. There were no chaperons guarding it, and the girls slipped out, heading for the football field.

"C'mon."

Rayne's mischievous smile beckoned as she pulled Sagan under the stands. Among the metal framework, the girls found a pillar outside of the streaks of moonlight. Here, there were no parents. No mysterious Icari. Just Rayne's ethereal glow and dazzling eyes.

Butterflies fluttered in Sagan's stomach, and her lips went dry. What if she wasn't a good kisser?

Rayne said, "You're shaking," as she pulled Sagan to her.

"I'm nervous."

Her best friend whispered, "Close your eyes."

Sagan did and took a steadying breath. This close, Rayne smelled sweet like a flower Sagan couldn't quite place. The softness of Rayne's lips surprised Sagan. Their kiss was warm and exploring. Sagan could spend hours doing this—

A rustling broke them apart. The girls fell into fighting stances automatically, scanning the perimeter.

Wow. They were only one week into badass training, and already they could take on the world together. Sagan smirked and found a similar expression on Rayne's face.

"What are you two doing out here?"

Oh, shit. Mrs. Mendax.

Sagan's face burned as she ducked her eyes and stared at the ground. Good and caught.

At least Rayne seemed prepared. "Sagan lost her cell phone during the game. We found it."

Thinking quickly, Sagan held up her Nokia, saying, "See?"

The principal looked unconvinced, but also too exhausted to press it. "Get back inside, girls. You should be more careful."

Sagan almost sighed in relief. When Mrs. Mendax turned her back on them, Sagan shot Rayne a thumbs up, but the girl looked transfixed by Sagan. She quickly pecked a kiss on Sagan's cheek and ran ahead, snickering to herself.

It made Sagan grin until...

From behind the pillar, Justin emerged with an awful smirk on his face. Self-satisfied and toxic, that's how he looked as he blew a silent kiss at Sagan. She felt the blood drain from her body. That scumbag quarterback was the last person who should know the girls' secret.

Justin knew it, too. His eyes were hungry with the knowledge, devouring Sagan in whatever sick fantasies he was devising.

Now more than ever, she needed Korac's training to protect herself and to protect Rayne.

FOUR

BLIND ENMITY WON'T ALTER REALITY

{MARCH 2004}

EVERY NIGHT FOR THE LAST TWO YEARS, NOX KILLED RAYNE IN HER DREAMS. And every night, she returned with her feet planted sturdily in the dirt and her fists up in an increasingly effective stance. Only now, a storm was casting clouds of inner conflict in her brilliant blue eyes, electrifying them with purpose. Lightning in her veins.

Exactly according to plan.

Celindria's descendant sat across a long dining table from Nox, separated by a feast of Icarean dishes. He enjoyed keeping the young woman on her toes. Some nights she and Nox simply talked while dancing around the fire in combat. Tonight's lesson was one in etiquette and galactic protocol.

With a feign of ignorance, Nox asked, "How is choir?" All the while, knowing she'd dropped out to focus on training for the invasion, according to Korac's reports.

The reincarnation of the First Progeny ducked her eyes before saying, "I wouldn't know. I couldn't find time to fit choir in my schedule this school year." She never lied to Nox, which only deepened his mistrust.

What tactics was Celindria playing at inside the young woman's mind? Was this not a ruse to entrap Nox? Surely, she was biding her time to unleash all manner of pandemonium and suffering on him.

She looked exhausted with dark circles under her dulled eyes. When would she sleep? School during the day. Work at the bookstore after school. Training late in the evenings. And dying in her restless dreams.

All according to plan.

Once Celindria's descendant had accepted this was not a night for fighting, she gingerly grabbed a bore kabob and nibbled on it. After swallowing, she asked, "So, if there's etiquette for dining as a 'galactic leader,' does that mean you meet peacefully with other worlds? How many other worlds are there? And what are they like?"

Yes. Rayne was a curious creature. While they'd engaged in combat, she often asked Nox about Cinder and the Icari. It was a shared trait between her and The Afflicted One's descendant, Sagan. Korac reported some of their inquisitive conversations; although, Nox could tell the General had regularly withheld details. Perhaps concealing his progress in the wager.

The First Progeny's reincarnation waited expectantly for Nox's response, her expression one of earnest curiosity. Sometimes, he indulged her, but this time he said, "You should ask your guardian why he's left gaps in your education. You know, if he'd given you a nacre already, you wouldn't be so tired."

"If you'd let me have one night of sleep, I could get some rest."

Rayne's quick response brought a smirk to Nox's lips. "Quite." After some consideration, he said, "No. We don't meet peacefully with other worlds." Not anymore.

This seemed to disappoint the young woman, judging by her downcast expression. After taking a deep breath, she changed the subject. "How is my etiquette?"

Nox leaned forward, planted his elbows on the tabletop, and steepled his fingers. "It's customary when presented with such a feast to enjoy it with expressed enthusiasm. No one likes when an exquisite meal goes to waste."

Still frowning, Celindria's descendant examined the table covered in food with a forlorn expression before shaking her head. "I'm not hungry."

Excellent.

A silence stretched between them in which Nox observed Rayne's subdued behavior until she abruptly asked, "Nox, don't you want peace between Cinder and the other worlds? For trade and cultural exchange?"

Nox narrowed his eyes as a familiar sensation occurred to him. It was happening more lately. Every night in which she faced him with determination in her bright blue eyes, he'd felt it.

Respect. Regard. Even affinity.

It was a remarkable privilege to see a mind such as Rayne's take shape.

Nox flattened his arms on the table and said, "Cinder's reputation precedes us, and we are not welcome in peace. Before your guardian and your ancestor betrayed us, I was working to mend relations. Since the Vacating, I've had to resort to despicable acts to foster this invasion. Nothing will stop it. Not even you, Rayne."

Ah...

He'd used her name, and she'd perked up despite the context.

Strange.

With renewed hope, Rayne reached for her chalice and drank from it.

Victory.

Nox asked, "Is this enough for you?"

The young woman peered over the rim of the chalice. When she recognized Nox's triumphant signature, Celindria's descendant set the drink down, trembling. She'd figured it out. "You poisoned me?" Her offense in the accusation disappointed Nox.

"Never take bread or drink from an enemy." Nox leaned back in his chair and folded his arms, admitting, "If you'd possessed a nacre, the poison wouldn't affect you. True, it's a dishonorable and pitiful end for a warrior of your caliber, but you're not a child anymore, Celindria. You're a killer in training."

There.

Anytime Nox referred to the young woman by her ancestor's name, the storm raged behind her eyes. It flared with her electric temper. Exhilarated by her reaction, he said, "Count to two hundred and forty, and you'll wake safely in your bed—Once the poison liquefies your organs, of course."

The First Progeny descendant's eyes widened, and Nox could see the counting begin. Now, how would she spend these precious seconds?

A fine tremor overtook her. She gripped the table, glared at Nox, and said, "Humor me?"

This could prove interesting. "Yes?"

"I don't want any guilt for putting you down when you invade, so tell me. Will you be leaving behind any children?"

Nox narrowed his eyes, agitated by the direction of their conversation. "No."

"Good." Celindria's descendant spat blood and smeared it with the back of her hand.

So formidable, but how dare she mention family? Nox stood and walked toward her. "No children. No parents. I had a brother once, but your guardian took him from me."

Despite the agony racking her body, Rayne's heartache glistened in her eyes, and Nox believed it was genuine. She said, "I have a little brother, so I understand how you must feel. If anyone ever hurt him, I wouldn't stop until I found justice."

Justice.

Not revenge.

This young woman believed she was a being of restitution, to make right that which was wrong. It was something Nox understood.

As he approached Rayne, she fell to one knee, choking on blood. Nox knelt with her. Centimeters from his face, she groaned, "One hundred and eighty-two seconds in."

It was a slow death not fit for a warrior—Nox would not repeat this exercise, assured she'd learned her lesson. In an act he'd scrutinize later, he reached out and clasped her hand. To his astonishment, Rayne adjusted her smaller hand in his for a more comfortable fit and squeezed the lifeline. She choked, and he held her upright.

Staring into his eyes, the brave woman said, "Tomorrow, I'll beat you."

Nox smirked. "I look forward to it."

When she vanished from the dream like all the other nights, he couldn't help but notice a significant change. The absence of Rayne's warmth had left Nox cold. Touching her came with a price. One he couldn't afford to overlook, yet one he'd dare not abstain.

"Until tomorrow, Rayne."

Korac pinned Sagan to the rug. Her pupils dilated, and her thighs parted beneath his weight. Her scent, fresh and sweet, perfumed the air. Watermelon…

No.

Korac stood and backed away. Here, in Sagan's dreams, he glimpsed thoughts on the surface of her subconscious. Desires she'd dare not say aloud, but which haunted Korac throughout his days.

Make him laugh.

Kiss him.

Let him be your first.

It was a torrent of hormones and emotions which impeded on Korac's mission. Despite himself, he may yet win the wager against Nox.

Sagan spun her legs until she was on her feet, facing him again. She'd learned that move within the first month of their nights together, but she'd honed the muscles and reflexes to pull it off fluidly in the years since. Sagan was strong and agile, formidable. But also funny and full of hope. A little goofy, even.

Korac enjoyed their nights together, except...

Tell him how you feel.

How were they supposed to get any work done when every touch exhilarated her? And fuck Korac if he dared claim any detachment. The young woman was gorgeous, fun, and flexible. But above all...

"Step back and give me a butterfly kick."

Sagan obeyed Korac's commands like an obedient submissive, which only further aroused him. In her skimpier and skimpier pajamas, he tried not to admire her toned legs flexing through the movements of the kick. The way her bare abs bunched. And with the little flip in the middle, her breasts bounced—

Korac needed a fan to put out the flames between them or risk the fire consuming the sparring couple completely.

Breathless from the exertion, Sagan looked to him for approval, her violet eyes sparkling with confidence.

Elden help him. Korac loved the way she looked at him.

Sagan gave two thumbs up, asking, "Was that good?" She was so dorky. It should've killed his libido, but it only made it worse.

The Silver General, famous for inflicting pain with elegant splendor, was utterly infatuated with a girl from Earth. Korac smirked, saying, "You're doing well." He squared off against her.

Sagan raised her fists in a self-assured stance. "Am I doing well enough to kick Nox's ass?" she asked and threw the first punch.

Korac blocked and evaded the left jab. When she fell back into a flip and almost uppercut him with a kick, his chest swelled with pride. Sagan was coming along nicely.

Now for some subterfuge. "You know, nothing about this war is straightforward? No opponent is ever truly your enemy."

Sagan landed with a split and caught Korac's stomping foot. She pushed with all her might, throwing him off balance. He fell to the floor. There, Sagan grappled her thighs around his neck in a headlock, squeezing.

While Korac considered the irony of this position, she said, "I don't see the Icari as my enemy, but Nox has his sights set on Rayne. She's scared of her ancestor's significance, and I think it's taking a toll."

Intriguing.

Korac slipped his hands between Sagan's mostly bare thighs and spread them open despite her best efforts to hold the lock. Her freckled nose scrunched cutely with the effort. Once free, Korac locked his legs around Sagan while gripping her toned bicep and pulling her arm back at a painful angle. "What sort of toll?"

Sagan would not give up, even prone and gasping in agony. Centimeter by centimeter, she rolled onto her side. This put more pressure on her shoulder joint, but it also loosened her legs from Korac's grip.

Resourceful.

He could break Sagan's arm like a twig, but nurturing her confidence was vital to his mission. Instead, Korac let her rise to her knees, noting her ass looked nice in those tiny silk shorts—

A headbutt was always an interesting choice.

After pulling that little stunt, Sagan cried out, "Ow!"

Korac laughed as she fell back, rubbing her head. She mumbled another, "Ouch."

He couldn't help but smirk at the aforementioned goofiness he found so endearing. Korac said, "Let that be a lesson to you. Only reserve a headbutt as an absolute last resort. Are you all right?"

Sagan pouted, and it was adorable. "I'm fine. But about Rayne... She's not eating, and that's not good because she works out constantly on the training course. Her thighs are thicker than my head. I'm worried about her mood swings lately, too. She was always so vibrant, and now she's monochrome. Literally. She only dresses in black and white these days." Concern for her friend looked beautiful on Sagan. She glanced away as if confiding something momentous. "I think it's getting to her. She only talks about the invasion—tactics and scenarios. The rest of us are doing extracurricular stuff or..." She met Korac's eyes before saying, "Dating."

Nox's strategy was proving fruitful. Rayne was degenerating. This news would please Korac's King, but the ruse was starting to chafe. Two years of undercover work grated on Korac's nerves.

Diverting the subject from her crush on him, Korac said, "You told me once you wanted to date Rayne."

Sagan sighed. "Yeah, but her head is miles away on Cinder. I think, for her, the invasion has already begun."

If they only knew...

Korac stood and held out his hand. "That's too bad. Anyone would be lucky to have you."

The cute way she blushed would occur to Korac throughout the day. There was no getting around it. This wager was won, surely.

When Sagan stood, they were close again. Her subconscious betrayed her interest in Korac more so than her scent.

It was becoming more difficult to say goodbye at the end of the night. He gave a bow of his head. "Tomorrow, Sagan."

She smiled sweetly. "Good night, Korac."

The dream ended, and he awakened in his chair beside the unlit fireplace. Korac left his quarters to knock on Nox's door.

"Enter, General." Nox always knew when it was Korac knocking.

What the General found on the other side of the door unnerved him. The King of Cinder was searching a windowsill. It was still dark out, so no risk of sun exposure, but the impulse was an unhealthy strain of paranoia Korac had hoped to avoid.

"Sire?"

Nox muttered to himself, "There's nothing there." He faced Korac, saying, "Tighten security on the Progeny. I want you to monitor them. I sense..." He didn't finish the sentence because he didn't need to.

Korac nodded. "Yes, your majesty." He changed the subject. "I'm here to report on your progress with Celindria's descendant."

Graceful even with his mountainous build, Nox draped himself over a chair, one leg hanging over the armrest languid as a cat. An enormous cat. He peered at his signet ring on his middle finger, saying, "Go on." The ring's emblem of the Pretiosum Cruor reflected the firelight—a sign of things to come.

"She's restless and exerting herself without desire to replenish the energy. Sagan also reported depreciation in mood and other symptoms of a depressive episode. In her words, you're 'getting to' the girl."

Nox tilted his head as if conceding a point. "Dying every night would have such an effect. We would know, wouldn't we, General?"

Korac wondered if Nox had forgotten the wager or was blowing it off for an unknown reason. Or was this his approach? Wear Celindria's descendant down and conquer her? Korac almost shuddered. That wasn't for him, but it was exactly what Celindria deserved.

Nox was still staring at his ring as he said, "There's a strength in the young woman's vulnerability."

Was that admiration in the King's tone?

Korac ignored his initial response to raise both brows, and instead, treaded carefully. "I suppose there would be, your majesty. According to Sagan's accounts, there's much in common between Celindria's descendant and Cinder's greatest traitor."

That didn't go over very well.

With a brooding frown, Nox bound to his feet and crossed his expansive quarters in two strides. At his desk, he rapped his considerable knuckles on an open dossier.

"We'll need to leave before too long for the pre-invasion tour of the continental compounds. See that the fortress in Egypt is prepared for Phase II. And..." He glanced down at his ring. "Send in Colita. I'm in need of her services."

The blood whoring viper always appreciated being 'needed.'

"Yes, sire."

Korac made to leave when Nox called, "Begin the surveillance tonight. I don't care which Progeny you start with."

"Do you not wish to go yourself, your majesty?"

Nox's eyes flashed on the verge of Atramentous as he said, "It's not time."

Yes. This close to the invasion, they were all on the verge of losing control.

"Of course, your majesty."

Korac left to fetch Colita, excited for his evening plans. Sagan had taken up running track, and tonight was her first meet. How fortuitous.

"You'll kick ass tonight. Don't be so nervous, Sagan."

Sagan sighed. It was easy for Rayne to say. She made running that training course her life, where Sagan only trained at the pace of a normal human being.

As if to assure Sagan, Rayne captured her chin and kissed her, soft and quick. They were under the bleachers again—this time Sagan had checked to make sure they were alone. But...

In the dusk hour, the coming night felt alive with possibility. Almost every night felt that way lately. Sagan blamed a certain gorgeous man of her dreams for the constant nocturnal anticipation—

"Hey." Rayne kissed Sagan again. "Stay with me." Tonight, Rayne was in all black—a skater dress and tights with chunky-heeled combat boots.

Guilt and shame suffused Sagan. She was still keeping Korac a secret, even from her girlfriend. Worse, Sagan was confiding her concerns for Rayne to the secret soldier. She tried for a reassuring smile. "I got this."

"Damn straight." Rayne hooked her arm through Sagan's and pulled her out of the stands. "C'mon. I can't wait to cheer you on."

Parents, teachers, and students filled the bleachers, prepared to cheer on J. A. Fair's track team. This was Sagan's second meet, but in her first one, she set a new school record thanks to Xelan's training and possibly because of a genetic advantage. One day, Sagan would like for their guardian to come to a meet, but it felt silly asking someone who'd already dedicated so much time to them to take even more time for her school stuff.

With that in mind, Sagan glanced over at her team. Their coach was looking through the crowd, most likely searching for her. She hugged Rayne, saying, "Thanks for coming."

"I wouldn't miss this. Did you not invite Tameka?"

Sagan laughed. "It's Wednesday, remember? I wouldn't dare ask her to give up her Xelan night for me."

Rayne giggled. "It's so obvious, isn't it? Do you think he knows?"

That was a good question. Sagan shrugged. "If he does, he's playing it cool. As if he were capable of anything less."

"He *is* pretty cool. Okay. Look for me in the front. Break a leg, girl."

Another hug. "Thanks, babe. I'm so glad you're staying with us tonight."

The almost carnal mischief sparkling in Rayne's eyes took Sagan's breath away. "Me, too." The vixen promptly turned around and walked off.

Okay. Now Sagan had butterflies for a different reason. She made her way through the staging area and found her coach. "Hey, sorry. I was—"

Their principal, Mrs. Mendax, stepped in and patted Sagan's shoulder while she said, "You're up first. We want a strong start. You're our record-breaking star, so don't blow it."

The coach gave a helpless shrug.

Yikes.

Hurdles were nothing compared to the vaulting walls on the training course. Sagan had this. While she stripped out of her windbreaker pants, she practiced meditative breathing techniques, another courtesy of Xelan. The short running shorts beneath bared her legs to the cool March night air, and goosebumps formed down the striations of her toned quads.

Whistling brought Sagan around with a grin for Rayne—

It wasn't Rayne whistling at her.

Justin, allowed in the staging area because of his school athlete prestige, was devouring Sagan with his eyes. His 'cat that ate the canary' grin unsettled her. After hanging out with Icari like Xelan and Korac, the adolescent boy's tenor lacked appeal—all immature and smarmy. "Looking good, Sterling."

Sagan ignored him, tied her hair back, and stretched, preparing for another record-breaking one hundred meters and ten hurdles.

The toxic chuckle from Justin's direction turned Sagan's stomach before he said, "Act all high and mighty while you can. See you after the race."

A chill shot down her spine as he walked away toward the stands with too much self-assurance. He was up to something. Probably pissed because she'd emphatically turned down his advances over the last two years.

Only one thing would get Sagan back in the right headspace. She went to her duffel, plopped down cross-legged, and took out Korac's sketchbook. While her team warmed up, Sagan sketched them, adding to the compendium of landscapes and portraits.

All of Korac's work was beautiful and inspiring, but one particular portrait had caught Sagan's attention that first night.

A woman with a mohawk in the coolest battle gear Sagan had ever seen. Another, shorter woman, was snuggled beside her, also in badass clothes. Both were warriors judging by their physiques, and the loving glow Korac had captured made Sagan smile as she imagined her and Rayne in a similar picture.

Sagan wondered if she might recognize the two women in a genetic memory, but she'd yet to experience one. Out of their friend group, she was the only one without genetic memories. And when she'd asked Xelan, he'd said not to force it. Which only frustrated her further.

"Sagan, you're up."

Right.

She slipped her sketchbook back in her bag and went to the starting line. It wasn't hard to spot Rayne in the crowd with her parents. The other girl was waving wildly, contrary to Sagan's complaints to Korac the night before. It was enough to light Sagan up inside as she got in position.

Deep inhale through the nose.

Easy exhale through the mouth.

Calm. Focus. Relive Xelan's training and...

The gun went off and so did Sagan. The blond girl sprinted for her life and jumped one hurdle... Two... With all ten hurdles cleared, she crossed the finish line to roaring cheers.

Sagan had once asked Xelan how he could run so far and so fast without losing his breath, as she was now gulping air in great heaves. He'd said his nacre kept him from exerting himself. When she'd asked for one, Xelan told her they'd talk about it later.

Later never came.

So here Sagan was, dying for air with her hamstrings screaming at her. But if the thumbs up from her coach was any indication, Sagan had earned the breathlessness. Another record set.

Kick ass.

Pizza celebration tonight. Screw grilled chicken and steamed broccoli.

Boy, Sagan wished Korac had seen the sprint.

"Well, done, young lady." Mrs. Mendax was surprisingly stealthy for a woman stilt-walking in those uncomfortable looking heels.

Almost startled, Sagan managed a polite smile as the principal walked back to the stands. Sagan stayed in the staging area to cheer her team on until the meet ended. It was a night well won. As she went to collect her things by the athletics building, a nauseating voice alerted Sagan to her precarious isolation.

"Wear a dress Friday night. I'll pick you up in my truck."

Justin.

Sagan was in the middle of climbing into her sweatshirt and windbreaker pants. He'd focused his disgusting sneer on the last of her exposed legs before Sagan quickly pulled her pants the rest of the way on. "What part of 'hell no' don't you understand, Justin?! Even if I wanted to go on a date with you—which I don't—I spend every Friday at the skating rink with—"

"With Rayne?"

Sagan tensed. She didn't like the way Justin said it. Smug didn't cover it.

The bastard got in her face, bad breath and all, only centimeters away.

With that stupid grin, Justin said, "I know your secret."

Sagan glared, but inside she balked as she asked, "Which secret specifically? I'm a teenage girl, it's hard to keep track of them all."

"Rayne."

Justin may as well have slapped Sagan the way she recoiled and cupped a hand over her mouth.

"That's right." He was enjoying this. "I saw you two making out—"

Panicked flared as Sagan cried, "Shh! Shh. Are you crazy?! My parents are around." She glanced toward the stands to make sure they were alone, ready to kick his ass but also kinda ready to cry. "Why would you threaten me with this? Do you have any idea what might happen to us?"

Permanent grounding would keep them from training with Xelan. A conversion camp might ruin their lives.

Satisfied, Justin said, "Because you're the track and field star, and I'm the football star. You shouldn't be hanging out with those goth freaks. You should be doing my homework, waxing my truck in a bikini, and practicing with me on that bare-foot and pregnant trophy wife future of yours."

That was enough.

"No." Sagan raised her chin, prepared to stand up for everything. "I love her. Tell my parents. See if I care. They love me, and they love her. I know they'll accept it. Even if they didn't, not you or anyone else will tell me who I can and can't love."

Justin stepped closer so that he loomed over Sagan. He put his face in hers and jeered, "Sure, you can say that about your own parents, but are you willing to put Rayne through that with hers? Can you guarantee they'll be as accepting? After all, maybe they saw themselves with a dozen grandchildren in their future, and you'll be robbing them of that."

No...

Was Justin right?

Amid this, Sagan's instincts beckoned for disassociation—distraction—desperately asking for a way out of this.

Sagan turned her back on him so she could stare under the bleachers. In the worst moment of her entire life, Sagan saw something she must've imagined.

Korac.

He was leaning against a support column in jeans and a black t-shirt. A ball-cap hid his hair which was tied back from his face, but she'd recognize those cheekbones anywhere.

A hallucination.

Sagan was seeing Korac to help her through this hard decision. Justin was the universe's way of punishing her for falling in love with Korac and keeping him a secret. For lying to her parents about the invasion, and for feeling happiest in her best friend's arms. A *girl's* arms.

Resolute, Sagan turned, faced her worst nightmare, and asked, "What time should I be ready on Friday?"

"Six. Don't bother wearing panties, and if you say 'no,' I'll publicize your lesbo affair to the entire town. Starting with the Callahan's bookstore."

Hell.

All these secrets had brought Sagan to Hell, and Justin was the devil.

Rayne heard Sagan's muffled answer to her question, but couldn't believe she'd heard right. "I'm sorry. Can you repeat that?"

The girls were laying in Sagan's bed together, Rayne spooning her girlfriend as always, but something was wrong. Sagan was stiff and refused to face Rayne.

"I'm going out with Justin Friday night."

If the Earth opened up and swallowed Rayne right then, she might feel better for it. As it was, she wanted to vomit while simultaneously needing fresh air for the heartache. "Why? What about us?"

Sagan curled into a tighter ball, not answering.

Rayne wouldn't accept that. She hopped out of the bed and put herself in Sagan's field of vision, begging. "Talk to me. Please. Don't shut me out. What's happening to us?"

The other girl's violet eyes swam in tears as Sagan asked, "Don't you think it's time you grew up and dated a boy?"

Rayne recoiled as if Sagan had slapped her. "What?!"

"Keep your voice down. You'll wake my parents."

Had something sucked all the air out of the room? Because Rayne couldn't breathe. Her heart sludged, bleeding with every beat. This couldn't be happening.

Sagan reached out and cupped Rayne's cheek. Her hand was soft and soothing and so very confusing. Sagan said, "I can't stop loving you, and I've tried. You'll always be the most important person in my life, but please let me try to be normal."

Normal?

Normal?!

They were hybrids of a vampiric alien species and humans destined to save both worlds from an evil, sadistic King.

Normal?!

Rayne swallowed her tears and tried to keep her voice steady as she asked, "Can I use your cellphone?"

Sagan frowned, obviously not expecting that response. "Of course, but why?"

"I'm calling Xelan. I need to punch something."

Rayne's spinning aerial kick landed, and Xelan staggered back.

Three.

She didn't give him time to recover.

One punch.

Two.

A kick to his ribs.

Three.

Four.

Xelan blocked and evaded, but at least Rayne could tell he was putting some effort into it.

Five.

Six.

She actually made him grunt. All the while, she put all her aching heart into every swing.

On the other side of the Sterlings' garden shed, Rayne could grunt and shout all she wanted. With a war cry, she ran up onto the shed wall and almost swung her legs around Xelan's neck for the takedown.

Almost.

Rayne plowed into him instead, straddled his ribs, and swung at him.

Seven.

Eight—

Xelan gripped her wrists like a vice. "Stop."

No.

No, if Rayne stopped, she'd recall the tears in Sagan's eyes as she begged Rayne for normalcy. Something which Rayne didn't want or care to want. They weren't normal. Both girls found men and women attractive, and both girls were training for an apocalypse. Rayne had only one thing going for her.

She could be 'not normal' with her best friend. Together. But now...

Rayne burst into tears sitting on Xelan's diaphragm. How could Sagan just quit them? And for Justin?!

While Rayne hiccuped in sobs, Xelan gently rolled her off him and curled her against him in a much needed hug. He even kissed her hair, which made her cry more.

The best hugs.

They sat in the middle of Sagan's backyard with Xelan rocking Rayne before he asked, "Do you want to talk about it?"

No.

Yes.

Rayne mostly wanted to punch about it.

"Would a nacre help with a broken heart?"

Rayne meant her tenacity halfheartedly, and Xelan took it that way with a warm chuckle. "I'm afraid not. At least it never has for me."

That was a curious thing. She separated them enough to peer at him. "You've had your heart broken?"

Xelan nodded solemnly. "Many times, and I'm here to tell you that unfortunately this will not be your last heartache. It's a part of life, and I intend to see you have a long one."

Rayne sniffled and wiped her eyes. "Sorry. Sagan's shutting me out, and it hurts." Rayne realized how immature she sounded, shored herself, and stood. "But don't worry. I've still got my head in the game." With a squaring of her shoulders, she reached out a hand to Xelan.

For a few heartbeats, he stared up at Rayne before taking her hand. Once Xelan towered over her again, he said, "It's okay to experience your life, Rayne."

She looked away. There were other things on her mind than Sagan—

No.

Don't think about it. About *him*.

Unbidden, Rayne considered the heat of Nox's hand. How hers was so much smaller than his. In all the times Nox had killed Rayne, he'd never comforted her or showed any signs of caring.

Until last night.

After which, Rayne spent this morning writing about it in her private notebook. Sure, she'd shared the battle aspects of the dream with Xelan from another notebook. But...

Not their conversations. Or how Nox's smirk made Rayne's pulse flutter with something...

Something wrong.

Feeling for Nox was wrong.

Rayne was wrong.

Despite her mature act, a hot tear rolled down her cheek. "What's happening to me?"

Xelan wrapped Rayne in his arms, and she pressed her cheek against his chest, absorbing his wholesome comfort. Much needed. His voice sounded deeper this way as he assured, "You're growing up, and it's difficult for anyone. I can't imagine what it's like for someone with all this extra pressure."

"I hate it."

God, Xelan's gentle laughter was the kindness Rayne needed right now. He separated them and promised, "It will get better."

She looked around the shed toward Sagan's house, resigned to her fate. "Yeah, but how do I face it until then?"

He spoke against her hair. "You're mostly human. You need to do human things and spend time with your friends outside of training. Go back to the skating rink on Friday nights. Have movie nights with the others."

It sounded like a worthy endeavor. Rayne asked, "But what about training?"

"We'll still train, of course, but maybe we'll skip Fridays or Saturdays. You need something normal." Xelan smiled, and it lit Rayne up inside. "Go on a date, you juvenile delinquent."

Even though it was too close to what Sagan had said earlier, Rayne knew where Xelan was coming from.

He chuckled affectionately. "Don't let all this apocalypse business confuse you, Rayne. It's not your life until it is, and until then, enjoy what you have."

Honestly feeling better, Rayne beamed at her guardian. She shoved him playfully. "All right."

Xelan made a show of rubbing his arm where she'd nudged him and then snatched up her wrist. He examined her biceps. "I feel sorry for anyone who tries to take you out. Look at these bad boys! Kicking my ass and throwing me around this yard. More's the pity."

"Thanks, Xelan."

While Rayne was ready to fight Nox in her dreams, she wasn't really ready to see Sagan curled in a ball in her bed. Her best friend's back was to her, but Rayne could hear Sagan sniffling and saw her wiping her eyes.

Why was this so hard?

Disheartened, Rayne went to the living room and curled up on the sofa. The Sterlings wouldn't ask why they'd slept separately, and Rayne was too exhausted to worry about it.

Her dream brought Rayne to the same stony chamber with red soil and a black blazing pyre. After three years of coming here, she realized this was Nox's bedroom on Cinder. The table they ate at last night took up one third of the room. A desk and a set of armchairs took up another third. The bed, throne, and pyre comprised the final third.

Nox always began the dream on his throne.

Rayne checked out her change of clothes. Gone were the dancer's pants. Now, she wore tactical pants with a multitude of pockets. Nox switched the wrapped top for a sports bra, displaying her abs, shoulder caps, and biceps. Rayne didn't take offense. She knew Nox wasn't interested in her that way—

But what about him holding her hand?

Rayne hugged herself, asking, "Why the change of wardrobe?"

Nox stood from the throne and took a menacing step toward her. "I thought you would appreciate an ensemble closer to your own clothing. It will improve your training. Check the pockets."

Three knives of varying size.

One lighter.

And a length of chain, roughly thirty centimeters of it.

Rayne assessed the balance on the twelve-centimeter knife. "I find it funny that you'll arm me, but I still can't have shoes." For emphasis, she wiggled her toes in the dirt.

Nox chuckled, and she enjoyed the rich sound. "I may deign to explain myself eventually, but not today."

Tired.

Rayne's bones felt heavy in her skin, weighing her down like someone had replaced her marrow with lead. She wet her lips, thought about what she wanted to say, and then decided it was worth a try. "Nox?"

Maybe it was the pleading in her voice, but the humor died from his eyes as he stopped his approach. When he asked, "What's wrong?" Rayne wondered if the concern was genuine.

She hugged herself tighter, almost taking a step back, retreating to protect her broken heart. "Please. Just this one night, can you let me sleep? Please." Her voice shook with the last, on the verge of tears.

Nox resumed his approach, coming around the fire. Purpose glittered in his eyes, and Rayne felt tears spill over her lashes. She did *not* want this fight tonight.

"Please. Nox, I can't—"

Nox moved so fast, Rayne almost didn't see it. Before she could "yip," he'd scooped her up in his arms. Rayne felt tiny, and Nox's arms felt like sturdy tree branches around her. Warm ones.

Rayne still couldn't make out the entirety of Nox's face, and what she could see was unreadable. Almost as abruptly as he'd lifted her, Nox set Rayne down on... a blanket?

A fuzzy rug or blanket had manifested before the fire. After he lowered her onto it, Nox sat beside her, watching the flames dance with that unreadable expression.

Was this...

Was Nox letting Rayne sleep?

She feared more underhanded tactics, but as the seconds turned into minutes, her body relaxed one muscle at a time.

When Nox's voice broke the silence, it almost startled Rayne. "I won't let you go—ever—but you can rest tonight."

His words affected her in a way that she'd rather not scrutinize. Instead, Rayne curled onto her side, facing Nox. She could see the light dance in his eyes as he stared at the peculiar black fire. Nox's gaze was intense, as if he'd found the answers to all his questions in the flames.

Rayne felt like an intruder, so she rolled away and tried not to think about Sagan. Or these complicated stirrings in her chest.

And other places.

Everything was so hard and confusing—

Warmth suffused Rayne, and she tensed. Nox laid down along her back and threw an arm around her, tucking Rayne closer to his front. Against her hair, he whispered, rumbling in his deep baritone, "Sleep, Rayne."

Not only did Nox call her by her name, but he was giving her exactly what she needed. Held in Nox's arms, Rayne found a second layer of sleep and dreamt of saving the worlds with love.

FIVE

CONFUSION AND DISAPPOINTMENT

MATURITY AND RESPONSIBILITY

FROM THE SAFETY OF A HANGAR IN IONA-01, XELAN WATCHED THE SUN RISE. He appreciated the view through a nacre glass panel. The installation of which was Razor's suggestion, and every morning Xelan wanted to thank him for it.

"When are you expecting Andrew?" Lucas asked from the doorway to Xelan's office.

Xelan kept his back to his old friend and considered his question. "You know, he's skipping school and risking truancy for this, right?"

Lucas' loafers whispered along the slate floor as he stepped further into the room and closed the door. He sounded sincere as he said, "I know. He's a valiant knight defending his friends and family from a tyrannical King. But *The Brethren* need convincing of that, not me."

It was impossible for Xelan to keep the cynical incredulity out of his voice. "They've needed convincing for two years?" He turned and faced Lucas.

The shorter, better-dressed Icarus answered with an apologetic shrug.

While they waited for Andrew to arrive, Xelan considered his conversation with Rayne from the night before. She was excelling at her lessons, but perhaps too well. He worried about how she was managing her day-to-day life. Although Xelan impressed upon the Progeny the importance of their birthright, he'd never intended for them to give up on the outside world entirely.

Was that the case with Rayne?

And how could Xelan reverse it?

A Volkswagen Jetta pulled down the drive to the airfield. Fortunately, Andrew's mother had let him borrow the car for today's prowess review, likely under the impression the young man was driving it to school.

"He's here." Ever the terrible host, Xelan patted Lucas on the back as he returned to the waiting Brethren members in his lobby. Caedes and Frullop, a frowning pair of Icari, looked particularly agitated with the lack of hospitality.

Xelan's crew operated the installation, and he'd given them strict orders to carry on as usual despite their guests. A member of the crew let Andrew in through the front doors. The young man waved awkwardly, and Xelan could see the tension in his shoulders. Neither of them were happy about this.

"Welcome, Andrius." Frullop took it upon himself to initiate greetings in Xelan's territory.

Caedes glanced at Xelan. It was a dare to challenge them.

Politics.

Xelan rolled his eyes and waved for Andrew to follow him. With only a polite nod in Frullop's direction, Andrew let Xelan lead him into the indoor gym facilities.

"We'll conduct the test here."

Caedes stepped up. "Correction. *Lucas* will conduct the test here."

Xelan almost laughed out loud, and he tried not to acknowledge the burn on Andrew's cheeks. If The Brethren thought they were breeding discontent by pitting the young man against Lucas, they were blind *and* dumb.

Frullop's smug sneer only confirmed it.

Xelan fought not to grin. "If you wish. Andrew, please demonstrate what Lucas and I have taught you." After Lucas had introduced the young Progeny to The Brethren, they'd given Xelan special permission to train Andrew and only Andrew as a pilot to train Tameka, Rayne, Kyle, and Sagan in an official capacity. Xelan fortunately kept his unofficial efforts under wraps.

"Right." Andrew went to a mat and assumed a grounded stance. It would've looked perfect if he wasn't still blushing as Lucas faced him. The young man said, "Don't go easy on me."

Lucas smiled and slipped out of his suit jacket. "I wouldn't dream of it."

Xelan clapped a hand over his mouth to keep from snickering when Lucas started unbuttoning his shirt and Andrew's mouth dropped open a little. Xelan glanced over at Frullop and Caedes to see if they'd caught on, but they had not. The former was still sneering, and the latter frowned gruffly.

Perfect.

Lucas finished stripping down to his slacks and muttered something about not dressing for the occasion before he squared off with Andrew, who looked ready to faint. Without a nacre to regulate his blood flow, Andrew had flushed brighter than a tomato under his golden complexion. He shook himself out of it and focused the way Xelan had taught him.

Foreplay was over.

Caedes shouted, "Go."

Andrew punched Lucas, who deftly evaded. One blow. Two.

Lucas caught Andrew's next right hook and turned so he pinned Andrew's arm behind his back.

Thinking quickly, the younger man bent and flipped Lucas over him.

The capable Icarus landed on his feet, but not for long. Andrew swept the loafers out from under Lucas. Once he hit the floor, Andrew mimed stabbing him in the chest.

Caedes called, "Point."

Andrew helped Lucas to his feet, awkwardly muttering, "Sorry."

The Icarus laughed richly. "You don't apologize for taking an opponent down."

Xelan felt bad for how Andrew's face deepened to a purple shade as he said, "No. I mean, I stole your wallet."

The entire collection of Icari looked at the wallet Andrew held in his hand. He opened it and said, "Nice driver's license photo."

Lucas' golden eyes sparkled with humor and respect as Andrew returned his wallet. The Icarus mused, "Aren't you just full of surprises?"

"Yes. He's a trained thief."

After Frullop's ugly proclamation, Xelan took Andrew by the shoulders. The accusation had drained some of his color, and Xelan wouldn't stand for that kind of ugliness in his installation. "You did great. I'm proud of you. Few Icari could pull off that stunt against a trained warrior."

Andrew ducked his eyes, still uncertain, but he smiled despite it. "Thanks, Xelan."

Caedes' gravelly voice announced, "We've seen enough. The Progeny may state his case."

Xelan patted Andrew's shoulder and said, "You got this."

The young man stepped up to the members of The Brethren, represented here by Caedes, Frullop, and Lucas. Andrew said, "My friends still don't know about all of this, and I'm glad they don't."

Caedes narrowed his eyes.

Frullop smirked.

And Lucas raised a brow, intrigued.

Xelan trusted Andrew to speak for the Progeny as he continued, "They shouldn't know that the people responsible for tying our lines together kept the impending invasion a secret because of their own cowardice. You fear the King of Cinder's wrath if he returns to Earth and finds an army of Progeny trained at your hands. I'm getting that he's a force of nature, insane with vengeance, consumed with the need to make our ancestors pay for the Vacating. Obviously, you think if you don't train us or give us nacres, then maybe he'll go easy, not only on the Progeny descendants, but on Earth and The Brethren as well. I think you're wrong."

As Andrew spoke, Caedes' expression transformed from one of criticism into one of regard.

Frullop's smirk twisted into a scowl.

Xelan could tell Lucas was hiding a smile, one of pride, because Xelan was doing the same thing.

They let Andrew finish. "I think if Nox is so consumed with hatred, then he'll kill anyone not conscripted in his army and burn the world to the ground. All of us. Give us a chance to stop him, or at the very least, to put up some substantial resistance. Without training us—without nacres—Nox will take Rayne and unlock the conduit to Cinder. And then what will you do? Involving us is your best option."

"Thank you, Andrius." Frullop sounded so insincere. "We will deliberate your argument and provide an answer within a day or so."

Caedes agreed with a silent nod.

Lucas got dressed as he assured, "You did well. I'll deliver our decision, personally. Until then..." He bowed his head and left with the other two members.

As soon as they left the room, all of Andrew's confidence dissipated. "Xelan, how do you think it went?"

Xelan watched Frullop, Caedes, and Lucas climb into a tinted limo within the hangar before his crew let them out into the sun. Free of their scrutiny, Xelan let out a heavy sigh. He said, "Honestly? I don't know, but the second Lucas gives us word, I'll tell you."

Andrew deflated.

Xelan wouldn't have it. He said, "None of that. You delivered an excellent demonstration for the Progeny's sake, but let's just say I'm glad I broke the rules and trained the five of you, anyway—What are you doing?"

Caught, Andrew tried to hide something behind his back, but his smile was unabashed. "Sorry. I couldn't resist." He held out another wallet. "Frullop looks terrible in his driver's license photo. Also, it expired in the sixties."

Xelan laughed.

They were so dead.

Rayne wrote about kissing Nox in her notebook during English. She wrote about running her fingers through his hair in Algebra. In Spanish, Rayne wrote about pulling him down on top of her and—

Muy caliente.

She'd spent the entire day in a haze of hormones and curiosity. This was normal, surely. But... So very wrong.

It was better than facing reality.

Sagan sat with Justin and the other academic, athletic overachieving crowd at lunch. Rayne had never seen Sagan wear sweats outside of practice, but there she was, covered head to toe in silver and navy. No skin showing. No vibrant makeup—Hell, no makeup at all. Even her hair was flat and lifeless. Sagan looked scooped out, and that's about how Rayne felt, separated from her all day.

From way over here, Rayne heard Stacia, the oldest girl at Sagan's table, ask with ill-disguised disgust, "Why did you bring your own lunch? That's so weird."

Cecily, the youngest girl, copied their leader. "Yeah. Like... who eats steamed vegetables?"

Blond-haired and dark blue-eyed Lucy, twisted the curly ends of her hair around a finger, saying, "It looks pretty healthy to me."

Justin shot Lucy a glare until she withered and shrank. Then he grabbed Sagan by the arm to lift her. "C'mon. Let's get you in the lunch line. You need to put on some weight."

To Rayne's revulsion, to her heartache, Sagan complied without even the slightest protest.

"What's *her* problem?" Tameka sat down beside Rayne and took out her lunch—grilled fish and steamed vegetables—same as Rayne. Only unlike Rayne, Tameka was actually eating her food.

The smell of it turned Rayne's stomach.

Across from them, Kyle asked, "Are you all right?"

Beside him, Nikki finished a bite of her baked chicken with a dry swallow to add, "Did something happen?"

Raw and overexposed, Rayne looked away from the concern in her friends' eyes. "I don't want to talk about it."

The kind, wonderful people surrounding Rayne dropped the subject and started discussing weapons.

Kyle proudly admitted, "I'm all right with a quarterstaff, but I prefer projectiles."

Tameka preened, "Xelan said I was a natural with a rope dart. He'll let me upgrade to a chain one, soon. What about you, Nikki?"

The dishwater blond girl ducked her eyes shyly. "Well, I'm still learning blades, but we're moving onto swords this week."

When they glanced at Rayne for her input, there was no pressure or any forced expectations. They would simply let her fill in the silence if she was ready, and Rayne knew it. But her head... Her heart...

"I need some air."

Rayne didn't wait for them to acknowledge her statement or offer to come with. She burst outside the cafeteria and into the back lot, gulping the fresh March breeze. A weight on her chest made it hard to breathe, and her stomach somersaulted over the breakfast Rayne's mother had forced her to eat.

Because now Rayne knew an important truth. An ugly one at that.

Rayne could only be herself with Nox.

Tears brimmed her lashes, threatening her mascara as Rayne came to accept this harsh new reality. Nox understood what she was completely, and he would never tell Rayne she was wrong for feeling this way. True, he would simply punch her and carry on per usual, but there was something to be said for feeling comfortable with 'usual.'

"Rayne."

Oh, this would hurt.

Trembling with this latest emotional crisis, Rayne turned and faced Sagan. Rayne swallowed, but still couldn't find the words to speak.

Sagan took a step toward Rayne, but stopped as if she'd thought better of it. It was so strange for the girl putting them through this bullshit to look equally destroyed by it. Her voice even shook with it. "I'm sorry, Rayne."

Rayne almost laughed. It seemed like the correct response to how insane her life had become. "I still don't understand 'why?' Why choose 'normal' over me?"

Sagan winced. "It's not like that—"

"We don't hang out with the freaks."

Stacia.

Sagan whirled to find the older girl behind her, arms crossed in disdain. Cecily mimicked her stern stance a second later, as if she'd just remembered her role as a copycat. Lucy stared at the scene as if considering her place in it, curious and undecided.

Rayne expected Sagan to defend her, to tell them she wasn't a freak.

Instead, Sagan said, "Sorry. I just wanted to get something back from Rayne."

Lucy murmured, "Justin won't like it," which prompted Stacia to agree.

"Don't waste anymore time. Get what you came here to get, and we'll walk you back inside."

"Make sure it's the last time," Cecily added for good minion measure.

Rayne couldn't help herself. She gaped at this bizarre scenario. Especially as Sagan crossed the schoolyard and threw her arms around Rayne.

As the trio of Justin groupies gasped and scowled, Sagan whispered into Rayne's ear, "Please, forgive me." When she pulled away, the color had drained from her face, and icy resignation clouded her violet eyes.

Whatever was happening here had cost Sagan, dearly.

Before Rayne could respond or hug back or drag Sagan off with her, her best friend turned and marched back inside like she was headed for the gallows. Stacia and Cecily sneered at Rayne before following Sagan, but Lucy stayed and measured her.

What was Lucy seeing?

Rayne had no idea. The girl eventually went back inside, leaving Rayne alone in the most off-kilter day of her life.

She actually looked forward to seeing Nox tonight.

Tameka didn't wait for Rayne to come back into the cafeteria. When Sagan walked inside, escorted like a prisoner, Tameka went to her closest friend. She found Rayne outside, sitting on a picnic table near tears.

As Tameka sat down beside her, she smoothed a hand over Rayne's back. "Hey. You don't have to tell me anything, but I'm here for you."

"I love you, Tameka."

That came out of nowhere and took her aback. Before Tameka could ask, Rayne answered her question. "Maybe I didn't tell her enough. Maybe I pushed her away and didn't know it. So I'm telling you before you leave me, too. I love you."

Tameka tsked and pulled Rayne against her. "Girl, that ain't happening. We'll see the end of the world together, you hear me?"

Rayne squeezed a mite too hard, and something cracked. "Shit, I'm sorry!"

It hurt to laugh, but Tameka did it anyway. "I'm sure my rib will eventually heal. You've got to be the strongest of us now."

"I'll be more careful." Rayne promised it as if she feared Tameka would stop being her friend otherwise. Whatever was happening had done a number on the brunette girl.

Tameka stood and held out her hand. "Come on. We've got a quiz in history, and I know you haven't studied. You can copy my cheat sheet."

Rayne took her hand and stood. "Thanks. I mean it. Thank you."

Tameka pulled Rayne close against her side and chafed her arm. "To quote a certain Icarus, 'I got you.'"

That made Rayne smile. They walked together back into the cafeteria—

Oops.

Tameka accidentally bumped into a fellow redhead. "Hey, Matt. Sorry."

Matt Anderson, pale and freckled with short auburn hair, smiled, but it didn't reach his almost black eyes. He said, "No worries, ladies. Are you two coming to the game Saturday?"

Baseball. Not really Tameka's thing, but...

"Sure. Why not? I think this one could do with getting out of the house." She playfully nudged Rayne.

Subdued, but living, the brunette said, "Yeah. Of course, Matt. We'll see you there."

There was something about his smile that reminded Tameka of a shark. A handsome one, no doubt. The boy kept in peak physical condition, but it was like Rayne, who at least had the excuse of an apocalypse to drive her.

What drove Matt Anderson?

"Hey!" Kyle ran out of the cafeteria, distracting Tameka. He indicated with his thumb at the cafeteria doors. "You two are missing one kick ass fight."

Nikki followed, breathless. "They're shutting the gates."

Oh, it must be a big one.

Tameka dragged Rayne by the hand into the cafeteria, and yup. The security guards were rolling down the riot gates. No one in or out while the three guys in the center went at it. One of which, Tameka was ashamed to say, she'd dated. And how about that? He fought as clumsily as he fucked—

"Rayne, what're you doing?!"

Before Tameka even finished the question, Rayne jumped onto a cafeteria table, ran down the length of it, and leaped onto two of the boys. She pinned one and said something into his ear which stopped his struggling.

The second one swung at Rayne. She let his fist go by her before grabbing his arm and wrenching it behind him. Again, she whispered something in his ear, and he stopped.

Rayne faced the third boy and waved for him to come at her. There was something crazed in her expression, and Tameka worried she'd make a habit of picking fights.

Chock full of testosterone, the teen boy unwisely charged at her.

With ease, Rayne caught him and suplexed him over her head and onto the table. It clattered with the force of his landing, and he gaped like a fish, unable to take in air. Deftly, Rayne thwacked his chest, and he took such a deep breath that his spine bowed with it.

Wild.

That's how Rayne looked.

Tameka ran into the center of the cafeteria and grabbed her by the arm. Rayne let Tameka pull her into the crowd—

"Ms. Callahan."

Shit. Too late.

Mrs. Mendax emerged from the sea of students trapped inside the cafeteria. For all her five-foot, three-inch stature, their principal looked intimidating when she folded her arms and glared. "I expected better out of you, young lady."

A voice in the crowd shouted, "She started it." And others agreed.

Tameka glanced toward the voice and almost snarled.

Justin.

Locked in his grip, Sagan looked devastated and completely powerless.

What the fuck was going on?

Kyle called, "It's Rayne's first offense. You won't suspend her for this, will you, Mrs. Mendax?"

Behind Tameka, Nikki took Rayne's hand and squeezed. But the girl in question stared at the principal with the same wild look in her cobalt eyes. She was breathing hard from the exertion or... excitement? Tameka wasn't sure what was happening in her closest friend's head, and Tameka realized she'd need to talk to Xelan about it.

After a considering moment, Mrs. Mendax tugged on the lapels of her blazer, straightening it. "Rayne, you'll spend the rest of the week in detention." She grabbed the one boy on the table by the arm and dragged him off of it. "You, too. Don't disrespect my school again."

Tameka sighed with relief. Detention was manageable. Suspension was too harsh for Rayne's first offense. Not to mention, Tameka believed it was good for Rayne to get out of the house, even if it was just for school. Tameka glanced Rayne over. "Are you all right?"

"I'm fine." That was a damned lie. Rayne's pupils were dilated, and Tameka could see her pulse pounding in her carotid.

Kyle asked, "Do you want me to get detention so you'll have company?"

Nikki snickered at the suggestion. "We could all get it and join you in protest."

That was enough to snap Rayne out of it and make her smile. "Thanks, guys. I'm fine."

Bullshit.

Tameka hugged Rayne, assuring, "Whatever is happening to you, I'm here."

Rayne's response only furthered Tameka's concern. "Please don't tell Xelan."

As security arrived to collect Rayne, Tameka frowned.

How could she *not* tell Xelan?

"Stay down!" Xelan ordered for the third time. He walked away from Tameka and headed for the playground equipment. Their bags were by the rope tree.

Tameka's backyard opened onto an elementary school in the Meadowcliff subdivision. A great location for training. And making out. Though, Xelan was always too focused for the latter. Much to her disappointment.

And Tameka wanted none of Xelan's orders tonight. Her biceps bunched when she threw herself into a kip up and charged at him. Tameka's lungs burned, her head ached, and her bruises screamed. Why was she doing this again? Oh, yeah. Cause there was no chance she was ever staying down.

Tameka never made a sound, but she came at Xelan from upwind. Big mistake. As soon as she came in range, he spun into a tornado crescent kick, and sent her crashing back into the dirt. She groaned and coughed out the little particles of earth.

"You are so damned stubborn! You're by far the most tenacious Progeny I've ever met." Xelan stepped over her and reached out a hand. "Why can't you just stay down?!"

Above him, the stars winked and played in their games. It would be a shame to waste such a night.

Tameka gripped his hand and twisted a foot around his ankle. She pulled, and he came tumbling down on top of her. Elbows and knees jabbed in uncomfortable parts of her body until Xelan spread out above Tameka in a plank. Not well thought out, she'd admit, but it got him down on the ground with her.

Tameka took Xelan's face in both her hands. "Look at the stars with me?"

There.

An innocent request.

"Of all the things for you to do, and of all the things for you to say right now..." Xelan broke into a grin.

Tameka smiled in return.

"Fine. Ten minutes, then I'm heading to our fearless leader's house." Xelan rolled over beside Tameka. Not an improvement, but at least she had him for a little while.

Tameka shrugged as she said, "It's not like she sleeps, anyway." She was *not* about to ruin this moment with news of today's events.

Xelan grumped in agreement while he gazed into the night. He said, "There are better views. The city's too bright.

One day I'll show you a true night sky." He turned to her with a gorgeous, genuine smile.

Tameka's breath left her.

Future plans.

With Xelan.

His smile twisted just a little. "Breathe," he said.

Deep inhale. Tameka let it out on a sigh.

Xelan looked too pleased with himself.

A thought occurred to Tameka. "Why do you stare up at the stars so often?"

"The sun swallowed Cinder before I was born." Xelan expanded his hands to cover the entire sky, saying, "There are no stars. Only the fire." He stared into the black with his hands resting on his stomach. After a quiet second, he asked without even a glance at her, "Tameka?"

"Yes."

"What else have you noticed about me?" Xelan kept his eyes on the cosmos.

Tameka sputtered. "Well, uhm... You see..."

When Xelan turned to her, Tameka swallowed hard. A heaviness had settled into his eyes. So sad. A little lost. She reached out to him and touched his face.

Xelan let her.

Tameka traced the angle of his cheekbone and the strong line of his jaw. When her fingers brushed his lips, Xelan took her hand, saying, "Tameka, we can't."

"Why not?" Her voice sounded petulant even to her.

"Because you're too young. I was there when you were born."

Tameka drew her hand back and stifled a groan. The same old tale of how her birth signaled the oncoming invasion. It was history to her. "I'm eighteen." Tameka tried to ignore the urge to cross her arms and sulk. She turned away from him and looked back at the sky.

Xelan shook his head. "I'm ancient. I won't take advantage of you. You have an entire life to build. So many wonders to experience. It would be selfish of me to stand in the way of that even if I am extremely attracted to you."

Well, that got Tameka's attention, but when she opened her mouth to say something, anything... nothing came out.

Xelan dared poke her nose. "Besides, I'll still be devastatingly hot when you're old enough."

Laughter bubbled out of Tameka and then... the dreaded snort.

Xelan's smile broadened until all his teeth gleamed. "That's my girl. Now..." He made to stand up. "Let's tuck you in."

"Wait. I need to tell you something else." Yes, Tameka was about to use Rayne's bad day as an excuse to keep Xelan on the ground with her. "Rayne's going through something, and it's leaking into school."

Xelan frowned. "I know something's wrong between the other girls. I tried to talk to Sagan, but I won't force her to tell me what's wrong."

Tameka nodded, knowing the feeling exactly since she spent all afternoon trying to pry it gently from Rayne. "Can you talk to Rayne about it, tonight? She's got detention for the rest of the week."

Xelan's brows shot up. "Is it that bad?"

"I'm afraid so."

It wasn't his famous grin, but it was reassuring all the same. "I got you."

At the use of Xelan's catch phrase, Tameka snorted again.

"But, Xelan, I was only trying to break up the fight."

"I believe you, but learning to fight comes with a certain amount of responsibility."

Korac was careful to remain downwind of the training grounds as he stalked Rayne and the traitor through their paces. All the Progeny showed tremendous growth in their physical abilities in the years since the traitor first approached them. But not all of it was on him, though.

Celindria's descendant demonstrated killer instincts, a wildness to her offensives, reminiscent of a certain Icarean King. Korac could see Nox's influence in how the girl held nothing back, even with her guardian, and the General appreciated her growing defiance in the face of 'responsibility.'

Rayne dropped the dumbbells she was using for deadlifts to place her hands on her hips. "Don't you think I know that? All I do is try to live up to this enormous expectation, so forgive me if I needed to blow off some steam." She turned her back on her guardian and stared out into the woods in Korac's direction.

He slipped behind a tree as the traitor approached his ward. "You work the hardest, and you've made such significant progress. I'm so proud of you, Rayne. I only worry about how you're handling the stress of it all."

"Which stress, Xelan?" Celindria's descendant turned and faced her guardian once more, and from here, Korac could smell the salt of her tears. "Failing my classes because I don't see the point in homework? My girlfriend breaking up with me for some jerk? Or how the invading King kills me every night in my sleep or worse..."

The traitor went stone still, and the girl shied away from him as if she'd said more than she'd meant to.

"Rayne, what is 'worse?' What is he doing now?"

Celindria's descendant waved a hand in dismissal. "Nothing. Forget I said anything."

But her guardian wouldn't have it. He gently took the girl by the biceps and made her look at him. "You can tell me anything. I'm only worried about how you're doing."

Rayne sighed before saying, "Nox held me."

What?!

In an annoying turn of events, the traitor and Korac shared the same recoil to her confession.

No.

Korac abandoned his post, running through the woods faster than human eyes could detect. Once through the treeline and into an adjacent neighborhood, he hopped into the Porsche 911 he'd parked nearby.

This was not good, but it explained why Nox had asked for three brunette girls with blue eyes the night before. Obviously, Korac had realized the connection, but not the purpose. Feeding on the Cult of Night was essential to the invasion strategy. And so what if the King wanted Pleasers who'd resembled Rayne? Korac had thought nothing of it.

Until Rayne said Nox held her in a dream.

The Enforcer at the gate let Korac drive the convertible into the compound, and he abandoned it to their minions as he rushed to the royal quarters.

The Justice intercepted Korac, much to his irritation. The short woman asked, "Have you seen Melinda?"

There wasn't time for this. Korac remained composed despite his boiling frustration. "Who is Melinda, and why should I care?"

The Justice tugged on the lapels of her blazer, straightening it with some haughty authority. "Melinda is one of the Pleasers you collected last night. She didn't turn up for her rotation this afternoon."

Shit.

Fuck.

Korac said, "Prep your infirmary. I'll have her with you in a moment." He didn't wait for the Justice's response or any further questions as he rushed the rest of the way to Nox's quarters. Outside the door, Korac considered what he might find inside and if he even wanted to see it.

After a deep breath to steel himself, Korac knocked.

"Enter, General."

Inside, Nox stood before the fire, leaning an arm against the mantle. A crimson smear stained his lips as he stared hungrily into the flames. The aroma from the burning wood perfumed the air, but there was another odor beneath it. A darker scent.

A pitiful whimpering drew Korac deeper into the room. He found the first girl twisted on the floor on this side of the bed. Her blue eyes were swollen shut. The puffy, purple lids looked in Korac's direction as if she could hear him, and she whimpered again. Still in the bra and panties he'd brought them in, she made no attempt to move.

While Nox kept his eyes on the blaze, Korac knelt and checked the girl's pulse.

Thready.

She was dehydrated and pale—drained. That's when Korac noticed all the bloody divots torn out of her body at random, huge chunks taken out by teeth.

Nox's teeth.

Her limbs looked wrong, and she'd rested them at a strange angle—

Oh.

Nox had dislocated every one of her joints right down to her fingers and toes.

Without a nacre, this damage would take months to heal. All because Nox had held Rayne in a dream.

Korac said nothing—would *not* say anything to his King. At least the girl was alive. It was imperative to keep relations between the Icari and the Cult of Night civil as long as the invasion relied on their services.

As gently as possible, Korac scooped the girl in his arms. He was halfway out of the room, when he heard another whimper.

With his back to Nox, Korac shut his eyes.

Three girls.

Three trips.

Nox said nothing as Korac carried the first one out. The General brought her to the infirmary.

As he laid the girl on the first gurney, the Justice clicked her tongue and admonished, "How can you shame us this way, Melinda?"

Melinda groaned, but didn't form a sentence.

Korac glared at the back of the Justice's head as she continued. "Obviously, you angered the Master after he found you fit to bed. What did you refuse him? I bet you won't do it again."

Disgusted, the General went to retrieve the next girl, unwilling to correct the Justice on this issue. Unwilling to speak about it at all.

As Korac lifted the last girl in his arms in the same condition as the other two, Nox finally said something.

"I know you understand."

The girl weighed nothing in Korac's arms, her body clammy with so little blood. Should Korac say something? But what could he say? There were so many things hinging on this. If Nox could hold Rayne the night before, which he clearly had, then he was on his way to winning the wager.

Even though Sagan spent the last night awake and not in a dream with Korac, there was no time to waste. Or he risked a similar fate for Sagan.

Korac responded the only way he knew how. "Of course, your majesty."

As he deposited the last girl in the infirmary, Korac distracted himself from the impending storm. Instead, he thought of Sagan's bravery two nights ago when she'd faced that teenage piece of shit who'd blackmailed her into a relationship.

Punk.

Tonight, Korac would treat Sagan.

But first...

He knocked on Colita's quarters. Again, she didn't answer until the second knock. "Good evening, Korac."

Why was she always mostly naked?

Contempt clipped Korac's usually careful cadence. "Colita, you have yet to do your part with the Progeny descendants. What are you waiting for, exactly?"

Her wicked smile must tempt some men, but certainly not Korac. She purred, "Their age."

Korac raised a brow in question.

Scorned by his rejections and refusal to play her games, Colita sighed and flattened her tone. "I was waiting for *men* and not *boys*. Now they're old enough. I'll get to work tonight."

Korac shook his head, incredulous. "You're *opening* with the seduction angle? You're not even trying for a creative ploy?"

Colita smirked, raking a hand down her slender curves, as she assured, "Tried and true."

"Good night, Colita." Korac walked away without giving her assignment another thought.

She slammed the door in his wake.

In his own quarters, Korac desired an escape. He thought of violet eyes and fierce courage. A woman who smelled of fresh fruit and summer nights.

Sagan deserved to know the truth, but it wasn't the right time. She deserved an escape as well, and Korac aimed to give her one.

He fell gracefully into an armchair and popped a subconscious manipulation capsule.

The young woman appeared in the dream wearing more clothes than Korac had yet seen on her. Long pajama bottoms and a long-sleeved top hid most of Sagan's skin from view. When she turned and faced him, Korac tried not to react.

A black eye.

The light blue swelling and redness in her corneas reminded Korac of the girls from earlier in the night. Not as striking, but no less enraging.

Justin was breathing on borrowed time.

Sagan ducked her eyes, hiding in shame. "Sorry about last night, Korac. I didn't feel well."

He cupped her chin and positioned her face gently to better examine the bruising. Korac said, "I suppose you'll tell me you fell. Or ran into a doorknob?"

Sagan surprised Korac by staring him down. "No. I won't lie. Not to you."

Forgetting his composure just this once, Korac put his hand on his hips and stared down at his tapping foot. He was thinking... About everything.

And he decided.

This space was not about anyone but them.

Korac cupped Sagan's nape and kissed her. It was impulsive and probably a bad idea given her condition, but—

Sagan kissed back, moaning into his lips. She parted hers, and Korac took the invitation. They tasted each other, and he enjoyed her sweetness.

Even when they broke apart, they stared at one another with the same smile on their lips. Sexy, happy, and a little silly.

Korac held up a finger. "One second."

Sagan peered at him with naked curiosity but waited patiently as Korac went around his bed and held up his surprise.

Matching axes.

He tossed one to Sagan, and she caught it with a gleeful cry. "It's beautiful."

Polished to a fine shine, Korac admired the emblem of the Pretiosum Cruor on the axe heads. Double-bladed, they made for quite the pair of death-dealing weapons.

Sagan practiced her stance with her axe. With him pressed along her back, Korac corrected her arms for the best feel. Against her ear, he asked, "How's that?"

A little breathless in his arms, Sagan said, "It feels right."

Sure, preparing the Icarean tour of the Cult of Night compounds was a better use of his time, but that could wait.

Sagan was the only thing on Korac's mind tonight.

It was Andrew's turn with Xelan tonight. The young man groaned as he exited Hall High School and crossed the student parking lot to his car.

Every Thursday he trained with Xelan. And every Friday, Saturday, and sometimes even Sunday, his muscles ached from the workout. The DOMs sucked, and now that the Progeny were getting older and more independent, they were discussing training on Saturday nights at the training ground as well.

Fuck. That.

Although Andrew barely got around on the weekends, they still belonged to him. He protected his free time because if he didn't, Rayne and Xelan planned all kinds of exercises for their unit to do.

Between that and Andrew's responsibilities to The Brethren, he was tapped out.

With a sigh, Andrew plopped into the car and cranked up the radio. Insane Clown Posse made everything better. He sped on the drive to the park in his mom's Volkswagen Jetta. It was nothing fancy. Just operable. Andrew was grateful he was one of the few students at Hall High with any wheels.

After he pulled into the gravel lot, Andrew reclined the seat and plugged a joint in his mouth. Lit it, took a puff, and slowed it on the exhale. No one could take this from him.

Andrew liked this quiet time right after school. His mom worked late into the evening, and she still believed he was working part time at the Callahan's bookstore. It'd break her heart to know he dealt dope on the side.

When someone knocked on his car door, Andrew jumped four inches out of his seat. Xelan peered at him through the driver's side window. With a groan, Andrew rolled it down. "Dude, what's with the jump scare?"

Xelan grinned. "I was only checking your reflexes."

Andrew stubbed out his joint and popped the door open. Frustration wound his body tight until his neck strained from it.

After a deep breath, he cranked his head to the left. Then to the right. The pops and cracks relieved some pressure.

Andrew absorbed the sight of the trees and the expanse of mown grass around him. With the cloud coverage, dusk came early tonight. He lamented his extra hour alone.

Xelan wasn't his usual enthusiastic self. He lingered off at the edge of the parking lot, staring at the pool of light under the streetlamp.

"What's up, man?" Andrew felt closer to Xelan than the other Progeny, seeing behind the scenes of how much politics was holding their guardian back. It made Andrew more sympathetic toward Xelan's efforts.

With a heavy sigh, Xelan said, "Lucas came to see me, today."

Aw shit. "Bad news?"

The Icarus nodded. "Unfortunately."

What would it take for them to catch a break around here? It wasn't Xelan's fault, but damn. The other Icari so far had proved less than helpful. Andrew asked, "What reason could they possibly give for leaving us like sitting ducks?"

"That's the thing about The Brethren, they don't need to give a reason. Without their support, I can't risk contacting Enki for nacres or weapons or . . ." Xelan went on for a bit, pacing and muttering about their meager limitations.

But more pressing concerns plagued Andrew. "What about Rayne? Will they do anything to protect her?"

Xelan shook his head. "I couldn't risk mentioning her without exposing the truth about the Progeny training. If they wouldn't provide you nacres or reinforcements, I doubt they'd offer her any sanctuary."

There was that mounting frustration again. Andrew asked, "So that's it?! Rayne lives with a target on her back while we learn mixed martial arts and try to match your otherworldly speed? Xelan, please tell me she knows?"

Xelan looked away and bit his thumbnail. "Rayne's not ready to know. Have you noticed how badly she's been handling things lately?"

Andrew ran a frustrated hand through his hair, saying, "I know she's not sleeping because she's passed out on my couch a few times. She's dreaming of you."

"What makes you think she was dreaming about me?" Xelan's tone evened, and his posture stiffened. Either he was about to explode or he'd thought of something that didn't sit right with him.

With a puzzled frown, Andrew said, "Because she cried out your name."

Xelan closed his eyes.

Andrew wasn't sure if the alien was counting to ten or getting an image out of his head. Andrew pressed, "Over and over. It took everything I had to wake her. Every single time. Then Rayne wouldn't talk to me for like twenty minutes. The more it happened, the more she pulled away."

"Rayne wasn't calling out my name."

The quiet words reached Andrew on the breeze. The sadness in them was unmistakable. Andrew spun. At the sight of Xelan's silhouette with his head hung in shame, the younger man folded his arms, saying, "I'm listening."

Xelan cleared his throat, a rare sound. His words came rough and heavy. "She was asking for my help."

Andrew's frown deepened. "Why?"

Xelan wandered from the edge of the parking lot onto the springy grass. Off in the distance, crickets sang. The lush backdrop offset the mood.

Curious, Andrew pushed, "Why was she calling to you for help? A lot."

Xelan winced. "Two years ago, Rayne began having bad dreams. I won't betray her confidence and go into any detail. All I can say is they're recurring and they're about the invasion."

Andrew respected Xelan for not sharing more, but it added to his frustration. Their leader was secretly struggling with a turbulent case of insomnia. They deserved to know not only as her unit, but as friends who loved Rayne... "I won't tell anyone. Is there anything we can do to help her?"

Xelan plopped on the grass, staring up at the emerging stars. "We can't. I mean, not directly. She has to fight this on her own."

Andrew insisted, "Look, I know you want to protect Rayne, but I think you should tell her about the target on her bloodstream."

"I will. As soon as I think she's ready."

A few hours later, Andrew kissed his mom good night and headed for bed. The bad news from The Brethren side of things made the day seem even longer. As he laid staring at the ceiling, one arm thrown over his head, Andrew resolved not to give up. He'd try again.

Tomorrow.

Sleep took Andrew to a room filled with lilies and roses, perfuming the space with their heady scent. Humidity thickened the air, and steam wafted from the source: a hot tub was sunken in the room's center. Petals danced on the churning surface, an invitation to the waltz.

Where were Andrew's boxers? He always slept in boxers, and now he was totally naked.

"I wanted you to appreciate the oils on your skin."

Shielding himself with both hands, Andrew spun to face a woman with entirely too much ambition in her sky-blue eyes to find her trustworthy.

As if she'd heard his thoughts, the woman pouted. It was a pretty pout, with a fuller bottom lip, emphasizing her cherubic cheeks. Her voice purred as she said, "Come now, Andrius. I'd hoped we could be friends." She glided out of the steam, giving flesh to her silhouette.

Bare flesh.

Comfortable in her silken nudity, she smiled as she walked past Andrew to descend in the water. Her breasts lifted more as she wrapped her blond curls on top of her head and pinned them with an old-fashioned comb. After which, she submerged, concealing her perfect body under the bubbles.

"Join me?"

This was not a dream.

The woman's smile became more knowing. "It is, and it isn't. You are still safe at home in bed, and nothing here will affect you. So is there really any harm in joining me?" Her reasoning was sound.

Andrew, still covering himself, stepped down into the water and luxuriated in its soothing heat. He let out an involuntary sigh, feeling his muscles relax.

"There. It's not so bad." The woman braced her arms on the far side and let her head fall back.

Andrew did the same before he asked, "What do I call you, woman of my dreams?"

This seemed to please her as she said, "Colita."

Was she an Icarus? A member of The Brethren come to test Andrew in his sleep?

Silky laughter bubbled out of Colita. "Oh. No. I want to be candid with you, young Andrius. I am Nox's third-in-command."

What the fuck?!

Andrew hopped out of the hot tub, his feet pattering as he stumbled back on the tiles. He gawked at Colita, no longer concerned for his nudity but for his life.

Colita's smile took on a condescending tilt. "If I wanted to kill you, do you think I would waste my time preparing this hot tub for your dreams? I'm here to proposition you."

"What makes you think I'll listen to anything you have to say?! You're planning to invade us and hurt people I care about." Andrew felt brave for getting the words out, but he trembled all the same.

The pretty smile went away, and Colita stared at Andrew as if she could see through him. After a long moment of pure anxiety and dread, she said, "I want Nox dead, and I want to rule Cinder."

Andrew frowned. "Lady, what makes you think I can help you with that?"

Colita stood, water sluicing off her graceful shoulders and perfect, if not, small breasts. She looked less pretty without a smile as she said, "I can provide the Progeny with intelligence to thwart the invasion from the onset. Once you kill Nox and his second-in-command, I'll take the Icari back to Cinder and rule as its first Queen."

Bullshit.

The steam thickened into an unnatural cloud until Andrew couldn't see anything, including Colita. Her voice came as a harsh whisper in his ear, "Think on it, boy. Save your family and friends. Or don't."

Andrew startled awake in his bed, immediately reaching for his phone.

Xelan answered on the first ring. "What's wrong?"

"Some woman named Colita invaded my dreams, Xelan. What do I do?"

After a pause, the Icarus said, "Tell me everything."

Andrew did, and Xelan sounded certain. "I think she means it, but proceed with caution."

"Proceed with *what*, dude? I just want to sleep."

Xelan sighed. "I'm sorry, Andrew. But when Colita comes to you in your dreams, try to get information out of her."

The call ended.

School during the day. Training on Thursday nights. Training on Saturday nights. And now, espionage in his sleep. When would Andrew catch a break?

"Fuck."

Kyle knew the woman on her knees on this gigantic bed giving him the best blow job of his young life was pure evil. But that didn't stop his eyes from rolling back in his head. Or stop him from gripping her hair as he finished.

Colita came to Kyle in his dreams offering an exchange of information, and now he knew all about Nox's designs on Rayne. Designs Xelan was keeping from them.

In return, Kyle told Colita of their training schedules—Something any stalker could find out with a little persistence. It wasn't like it was vital information or anything.

Colita's blond curls fell around her angelic face as she rose on her knees, a satisfied smirk on her exquisite mouth. When the Icarean female licked her lips, Kyle was ready to go again. "That was incredible."

Kyle held his arms out to Colita, who curled up against him with a purr. She said,"We can spend every night like this. If you like."

He would like, only... "Aren't you Nox's woman or something?"

Colita's bitter laughter tinkered like broken glass before she said, "In name only. It pleases me to find gratification with his enemies." Languidly, she traced circular designs with her long fingernails on Kyle's bare chest, eliciting a shiver of desire. "Especially, one so eager."

Yup.

Kyle's soldier stood at attention to prove her point. Colita went to grip him, but he stopped her. It was so antithesis to the testosterone pumping through his system that Kyle wanted to kick his own ass. Still, he manned up and swallowed the pressing need in order to say, "I appreciate what you're willing to teach me, but this won't become anything else."

Colita smiled as if she approved of his candor. "I believe the sentiment is mutual. Now . . ." She took his hand and placed it in between her thighs, exciting him further. "If you want to impress girls—and I presume there is one in particular—then this is your next lesson."

Kyle took to it eagerly.

The next morning came too soon, pun not intended.

Kyle hated leaving his sisters alone for a Saturday afternoon with their mother, but they both assured him they'd be fine for one baseball game. J. A. Fair's parking lot was packed, more so than any other sporting event Kyle could recall. The baseball team's reputation over the last two years had pulled in the community crowds and scouts.

What little shit Kyle gave about sports made him agree to come support Matt, if only to hang out with Rayne outside of a training scenario or a boring class.

Kyle found her in the stands with Tameka, but he could tell from the end of the bleachers that something was wrong. After moving through a crowded line to claim his seat, he waved. "Hey. What's up?"

Rayne didn't answer.

Tameka only nodded toward the front row.

Oh.

Sagan was sitting down there with Justin and the other Overachievers. Not a damned one of them looked happy. But why did that upset Rayne—

Oh.

Oh, fuck no.

When Sagan turned to wave at Matt Anderson, Kyle saw the black eye. "I'll fucking kill him—"

Rayne grabbed Kyle's arm, stopping him from marching down there and beating the bastard to death. Kyle snapped around to meet Rayne's eyes and almost choked on his own recklessness.

A storm brewed in Rayne, lightning igniting her blood. She was breathing hard with the effort to restrain herself, teeth and fists clenched.

"After Rayne spent a week in detention, Xelan told us no more fights," Tameka explained, because Rayne couldn't speak for the turmoil spinning inside her. The most mature Progeny sighed with hefty regret. "And to some extent, Sagan needs to get herself out of this. She could break every one of Justin's bones, but for some reason she's letting him be a bastard."

Kyle growled, "How long are we supposed to put up with this?"

Rayne sounded hollowed out as she said, "It's already been seventy-nine hours and at least twenty-two minutes."

Despite their usual strife, Tameka and Kyle shared a concerned glance. A few days ago, Rayne had started counting everything. Tiles on the floor, people between her and the exits, and steps on the training course. It seemed like a tick or something she couldn't shake.

Tameka put an arm around Rayne.

"Hey, guys! Are you excited to see the Wareagles beat the Tigers?" Unaware of the tension in their friend group, Nikki sparkled with sweetness as she took the seat on the other side of Tameka.

"I'm only here for the hot dogs," John announced as he sat beside Nikki.

Kyle wanted to pull his hair out, but as the bleachers filled with innocent bystanders, it became increasingly more difficult to discuss the Sagan situation in any kind of privacy. Grumpy, he plopped down beside Rayne and sulked.

Tameka was better with compartmentalizing. "Hey, you two. I'm mostly here to cheer on Matt."

From behind, another friendly voice chimed in. "I know, right? He's gotten so good that he's practically carrying the team."

Tameka turned and shot Pablo a friendly smile. Kyle managed to offer him a halfhearted wave.

But the young medical science student went totally red and stared straight ahead with his mouth hanging open.

What in the world was making him—

Oh.

Lynn looked especially sexy in her drill team uniform, dancing to get the crowd hyped. Her braids swayed as an extension of herself through the elaborate twirling and flipping. When she finished a back walkover with the splits, Pablo swallowed hard enough for Kyle to hear it from one row down.

It was enough to lighten Kyle's mood some. He nudged Rayne and whispered, "Hey."

Rayne took her heavily lined eyes off the back of Justin's head and met Kyle's.

He said, "We'll talk to Xelan and convince him to make an exception in this case. I'll make it clear this isn't reckless violence, but a way to help Sagan."

A weak smile tugged at Rayne's lips. "Thanks. I hope it works."

"Shit!" John stood, revealing a streak of mustard down his shirt. The hot dog landed beneath the bleachers. "Damn, I was enjoying that."

"Do I hear swearing, young man?!" Mrs. Mendax manifested from out of the ether. "Do you want a week of detention like Ms. Callahan, here?"

Bad timing.

Kyle heard Rayne clench her jaw to keep from popping off. On the other side of her, Tameka took Rayne's hand in a show of support.

John looked abashed as he said, "Sorry, Mrs. Mendax. It won't happen again."

The principal nodded her approval. "Better not."

The second the short authority figure was out of earshot, Justin sneered from the first row, "You'd better go buy yourself a wiener, John. How else would you qualify as a man?"

Obviously, the Overachievers laughed, but many others in the crowd joined in the ridicule.

Sagan kept her gaze on the field, her stiffening was the only reaction to her boyfriend's cruel taunts.

As John's face fell and the color drained from his Osage complexion, Kyle knew just the thing.

"Yo, John."

The other boy flinched, steeling himself for more ugliness, but Kyle was tired of bullshit. He slipped out of his shirt and went to John's side. "Here."

Kyle tried not to look smug as the crowd hushed. All these years of kicking ass and training had left him ripped. That put an end to the jeering taunts.

John took the offered shirt, as the two guys walked back to the concession stands. John muttered, "Thanks."

Pleased for the excuse to show off all the hard work, Kyle grinned. "No worries, man."

John hid under the bleachers and changed into the fresh tee, scrawny and fatigued from the effort of dressing.

Now there was an idea.

Hot dog firmly in hand, John returned with Kyle to the bleachers. Kyle took up his seat beside Rayne and whispered, "Hey, I think Xelan should train John, too. Look at him..."

Rayne did. Then the most beautiful smile blossomed on her face. "You're right. We can talk to Xelan tonight about John and Sagan."

"Cool."

Matt *did* carry the team. He was humble about it even as the team surged onto the field and lifted him up after the winning home run.

Sagan remained miserable the entire game, and Rayne didn't look much better. Even though all of their friend group was watching the disaster unfold, they could only exchange concerned glances. Kyle made it home to find his mother passed out drunk on the couch and his sisters gone for the night at a friend's place. He easily 'borrowed' the Lincoln for Saturday night training, from which Sagan was absent.

By the time Kyle had arrived at the training grounds, the 'rescue Sagan' conversation was well underway. Tameka, Rayne, and Andrew all looked expectantly at Xelan for guidance.

The Icarus gave a heavy sigh. "This situation sounds awful. Kyle, have you also noticed—"

"Sagan's shiner? Yeah. I'm sure that's why she's not here tonight so she can hide it from you." Kyle didn't bother keeping his exasperation out of his voice.

Rayne looked wrung out and left to dry. "Please, Xelan. Just this once?"

Tameka even agreed. "The jerk needs his ass kicked."

Xelan staved them with both hands. "I understand what you're saying. Talk with her again, if you can. Give it a little time, and if the situation doesn't improve. Well... Try not to kill him."

With a grateful cry, Rayne jumped up and threw her arms around Xelan.

Kyle folded his arms, skeptical. "Why not sooner?"

Tameka scowled at Kyle. "We can't go around assaulting people."

Kyle glared.

Andrew got between them. "She's right, Roberts."

Kyle huffed. "Benedict Holt."

"That's enough."

They all faced Rayne. "We love Sagan, and I hope she'll deal with it herself. But if not, *I'll* step in. Until then, we train as usual and try not to push her further way."

Xelan gave Rayne a look of pure affection. "Well said."

Kyle let it go only so he could bring up, "Do you have more time in your schedule to train another of Justin's victims to defend themselves?"

A little taken aback, Xelan asked, "Seriously? What is up with this little snit?"

Tameka laughed.

Andrew shrugged. "Not everyone is trained in self-defense or has the confidence to stand up to dickheads."

Xelan bit his thumbnail, murmuring, "Fair." After some time, he said, "Yeah. I can fit another trainee. Nikki's doing great, so I don't mind."

Rayne hugged him again. "Thank you."

Sure, Xelan got all the credit, but all of this was Kyle's idea.

That night, Colita agreed. "You deserve more recognition, but it's hard being in the shadow of someone who shines as brightly as the traitor."

Rested on his chest between rounds of sex, Kyle ran his fingers through her hair. "You know him?"

"Oh, yes. We were once friends."

With some playful force, Kyle flipped Colita over on her back and settled between her legs. "Can you tell me more?"

She laughed, and it was a pretty sound, before saying, "That depends on how well you perform."

Kyle performed very, very well.

SIX

DECEIVE YOURSELF BUT YOUR HEART AND SOUL KNOW THE TRUTH

{JANUARY 2006}

FOR OVER FOUR YEARS, RAYNE WENT TO SCHOOL, HELPED HER MOM OUT AT THE BOOKSTORE, TRAINED WITH XELAN UNTIL MIDNIGHT, AND THEN DIED AT NOX'S HANDS IN HER SLEEP. She was eighteen going on two hundred, but Rayne barely felt it. She felt like a fighter, like a killer.

Crazy.

That's how Rayne felt. If she ever told her family, they'd surely lock her up. Sagan was the only person she could turn to, but Sagan was battling her own demons. While Rayne loved Tameka, her most pragmatic friend would tell Rayne to ignore Nox. Simply don't engage the King of Cinder until he left her alone—improved fighting skills be damned. Or Tameka would tell Rayne all the strange feelings mixed up in the dreams were hormones, and that Rayne should get over her immature notions about virginity. In that same vein, there was no way Rayne was talking to Kyle or Andrew about it.

No.

Rayne was alone in this storm.

She entered the dream dressed in black tactical pants and a black sports bra, this one with extra straps. Black ribbon coiled around her biceps and swirled down her arms to lace around her fingers. Rayne touched her hair and found it pulled back in a fishtail braid from her face. Practical, but cute.

The loose red soil sifted beneath Rayne's toes. Was it too much to ask for combat boots? Why did Nox never grant her sensible footwear?

"All those nerve endings let you feel the dirt and predict my attacks a mite faster. You need every advantage I'm willing to afford you."

Finally, an answer.

Like always, Nox addressed Rayne through the black pyre between them. Even with the obstruction, she knew how he'd dressed. The same as every night: black leather pants, no shirt, and no shoes.

A filter still distorted Nox's face. He'd tied his hair back as if finally acknowledging Rayne as a challenge. It emphasized the impression of a sharp jaw, angular nose, thick brows, and sculpted cheekbones.

Why must Rayne's tormentor be attractive?

Nox's carriage was one of self-regard, but not so much to suggest conceit. It was a natural esteem probably born of his station.

But that's not why Rayne's thoughts had drifted to Nox lately in a non-fighting sense. Here, in these dreams, she could act however she wanted without fear of his judgment, scolding, or concern. Nox accepted Rayne in the simplest terms. Understood her even. Which was a terrible tactical advantage in a relationship solely based on enmity.

Uncertain when the fight might begin, Rayne walked alongside the blaze, keeping him within her sights. "Did I graduate to actual exercise for you?"

Laughter rumbled from Nox's chest. The King of Cinder mocked her and paid her a compliment all in the same sound. He sidled along the fire with her in a dance, respecting her as a warrior by maintaining constant eye contact. Silken in that baritone, he said, "You gain skill with every session. Soon, you'll make a formidable adversary thanks to *my* private instruction."

"You mean thanks to Xelan's nightly training, and my willingness to work my ass off in order to stop your invasion schemes?" Rayne stopped and glared at him, her feet spread shoulder-width apart in her favorite fighting stance.

Through the black fire, Nox shrugged, and it was graceful despite the breadth of his shoulders and the bulk of his chest. The gesture said Nox knew Rayne was lying to herself. Their sessions *did* make her into a better fighter. He said, "Whatever you need to tell yourself."

Nox stopped circling and faced Rayne across the pyre. "You're so eager tonight. Good. We'll test the limits of your abilities. I will hold back far less than any night before. Are you prepared, Celindria?"

Rayne held up her fists and clenched her jaw. Always with the Celindria. "Oh, I'm ready."

"Heh." Nox shook his head, impressed. "All I want is to see that fire in you."

Fast, so impossibly fast, Nox ran at Rayne from around the pyre. She kept her feet planted, bent her knees, and blocked his first blow aimed for her jaw.

Gritting from the strain, Rayne tried to quip but growled, "I thought you were coming here to snuff me out." With a cry, she sent a good hook to his ribs.

Her blow landed with little effect as Nox blocked her next jab and said, "No. I want you accelerated. I want you blazing. A bright white beacon."

Nox's words startled Rayne, and she failed to block the roundhouse kick to her temple. Her teeth chattered together, and black blossomed in her vision. There wasn't time to dwell on the nauseating pain. She recovered well enough to roll away from the next tornado kick.

Rayne used the vantage point to sweep Nox's feet.

He jumped and saved his first leg, but not the second. The giant King of Cinder fell on his ass resulting in a shockwave of red dust.

Rayne spun her legs onto her feet and stomped her foot in his chest—

Expecting this, Nox clutched her foot, twisted Rayne's leg into a painful lock that weakened her knee, and set her other foot off balance.

Nothing—not a damned thing—was more terrifying than falling on the ground at Nox's mercy.

He was on Rayne in a heartbeat, his hands wrapped around her neck. Nox said, "You're about to die and wake once more in your bed, like all the other nights. But I know you. You'll return tomorrow, ready to try again. This is the fire I stoke."

No.

Rayne refused to let Nox win. For once, she'd sleep as a victor. The knowledge of it burned in her.

Calm down.

Don't let the panic take over.

As darkness edged Rayne's vision, she squeezed her fists in the dirt and figured it out. With a strangled war cry in Nox's face, Rayne threw the loose soil in his eyes.

Nox snarled and released her.

Rayne was up on her feet and running to one of the many columns stationed around the room. Higher ground—

No!

These vibrations under her feet could only mean—

"Ugh!"

With a sickening thud, Nox slammed Rayne's back into a pillar, pinning her wrists over her head using only one hand. By the growl in his voice, Rayne knew she'd disappointed him. "Such underhanded tactics. How like you, Celindria."

For all that Nox *knew* Rayne, she often wondered if he knew she was actually a different person from her ancestor. But that was a problem for another time.

Pinned at such a height, Rayne's toes barely brushed the ground. It was a decent position to land a kick, except Nox had pressed Rayne's legs against the column with his heavy thighs. There was no maneuverability.

Shit.

Was Rayne really—

"Your opponent bested you." Nox squeezed his hand over Rayne's wrists hard enough to make her gasp. Still, his voice was rich as he asked, "Pinned and helpless, with no dirt to save you, what will you do this time?"

A test.

Through the filter, Rayne discerned the basic features of Nox's face well enough to see a smirk on his lips. Soft and full. A mouth she'd often considered kissing when drifting off in class—

That's what Rayne did.

Straining against Nox's anchor on her wrist, Rayne pressed forward and captured his hidden mouth with her own. His lips were as soft as she'd imagined, but short-lived.

Nox pulled away sharply and searched her eyes.

Rayne licked her swelling lips, tasting spearmint and warm spices. Nox watched her do it. She felt his eyes on her mouth, roaming over her shoulders, biceps, breasts, her bare stomach, and hips as if Nox had noticed for the first time that Rayne had grown into a proper female. And this female wanted to know what it would feel like for Nox to kiss back.

A heartbeat passed. Then another.

There was something warring in Nox. It constricted his muscles and wound his entire body with tension.

Was this not happening? Could Rayne survive rejection from the only person in the entire world she'd felt understood even the worst of her?

Rayne's chest heaved from their fight, flushed all over from exertion and her desire for him. The brief sampling she'd stolen was strong and left her hungry.

More.

Rayne let Nox see it in her eyes, and the King of Cinder's name left her lips on a breath.

A soft growl rumbled in Nox's chest. Rayne felt it against her breasts. It was the sound of letting something painful go, and when he finished, he gripped her by the nape and sealed his mouth to hers.

Nox's kiss seared Rayne.

Soft, starved, and burning—She answered with her own fire and opened her mouth to him on a moan. Nox's body melted to Rayne's, and she was suddenly aware of their position. Very aware. The sensation left Rayne curious, and she deepened their kiss.

Another sound echoed in the chamber of Nox's chest. It was the warmest sound Rayne had ever heard. He loosened his legs from her. Unaware of her own instinctive reactions, Rayne lifted her legs and wrapped them around his hips.

They both moaned.

Everything about this felt so good—*tasted* so good—Rayne wanted more of Nox. Wanted to touch his hair and face, but he still gripped her wrists—

Nox went stiff, and not as in... Well, he was already stiff in that way.

No, his entire body froze, hard against her.

Rayne was afraid to move, afraid to breathe. What went wrong? Was it her? Did she advance too quickly?

On a growl, Nox wrenched Rayne by her wrists in a painful twist and flung her across the room—

Rayne slammed into her bed as if she'd been floating above it. She swore the landing rocked the bed frame and everything. Her heart pounded, and her chest hurt.

"That was intense," she said into the dark room.

Right.

As if that was the only reason her heart was hurting.

Rayne winced and reached for her notebook. It was best to get this out of her system and pray no one else ever read it. Then it was off to the training grounds because how could she sleep after Nox's kiss had rocked her foundations?

Especially, after Rayne had initiated it all...

It would be hard facing her friends tomorrow. What would Xelan think?

Oh, no.

What about the inevitable post-kiss interaction with Nox tomorrow night? Would he punish Rayne? Was there no chance for their kiss to mean more? What if it could lead to peace between their planets?

Too many thoughts left Rayne's handwriting a scribbled mess. Thoughts racing faster than her hand could record them.

Enough.

Tomorrow, Rayne would face her most difficult trial: looking her friends in their faces and lying to them. They could never know that she'd nearly slept with the enemy.

It was time to run.

Nox was losing his mind. All those millennia of carefully calculating every detail of his revenge, and for one heartbeat, he'd abandoned everything.

Rayne's kiss scorched him. Sweet and smoldering, she'd invited him inside.

Not even when Nox had arranged the wager with Korac did he imagine any real chance...

Her warmth lingered on his lips, and he touched them. Hotter than his fingertips, Rayne had left his mouth feeling swollen. Nox wanted his hands on her, and hers on him.

This was too far. A risk the invasion couldn't afford—

A knock sounded on his door. Curt and professional, it could only be Nox's second-in-command.

"Enter, Korac."

With the door ajar, Nox overheard the nocturnal activities throughout the compound. The Cult of Night's monthly ritual which repelled him so. Necessary, but truly primitive.

Korac's human dress suited him in black slacks and a silk button-down paler than his skin. More regal than military in his posture, Nox's General faced his King with firelight between them. Not the roaring pyre of his chambers on Cinder, but an adequate flame to represent Nox's internal combustion confined to his quarters under the roof of this sanctimonious institution.

Korac knew better than to interrupt Nox while he sparred with Rayne in her dreams. Truly, the General should be attending his own nocturnal pursuits.

Behind his General's infuriating mask, Nox ascertained that something was concerning him. He asked, "What is it?"

"Your majesty, our soldiers guarding the Callahans' house reported unusual activity. No. Nothing like that—"

How could Korac read Nox so well? The best soldier correctly discerned Nox's minute flinch was an impulse to stop a home intruder or some such threat to his millennia-long endeavor.

"Rayne left at 1:20AM for the traitor's training grounds. She's been there ever since. It's nearly 4:30 in the morning." On the last, Korac tucked his hands in his pockets and waited.

Nox frowned as he asked, "What is she doing there?"

Korac blew the air from his cheeks before answering. "Well, running, sire. The entire obstacle course repeatedly. Without a nacre… It's impressive."

"Quite." And dangerous. Rayne was risking herself out there alone with the kind of humanity eager to steal young women from the shadows of those woods. "Keep the guards with her." Protecting their investment took priority.

For the rest, Nox needed to contemplate the situation. He turned his back on his General and stared at his pillow where he'd rested only hours before to invade Rayne's dreams. To make her a better fighter while weakening her resolve.

The kiss had introduced an element Nox had put from his mind upon first meeting her. She was too young then to make good on his wager with Korac, cruel as it was. Ultimately, Nox found fighting with Rayne far more satisfying than any interaction with the females of his past. Rayne was fierce, and he enjoyed the banter.

Nox enjoyed her kiss more, and this recent development with the training grounds spoke of its effect on her. For the first time, Nox *saw* Rayne. Not the key to his salvation, or the completion to his vendetta.

No.

Rayne's blue eyes had shone bright like sapphires and glittered with desire. Her clothes, meant to match those of the female Icarean warriors, displayed curvaceous assets Nox had ignored until that moment. Flushed, as they both were, her blood ran hot inside her. For Nox. And her lips. So full and inviting...

"Do you find her beautiful, General?"

Nox knew without facing Korac that his General wouldn't appreciate the question. Too many wrong answers. If he answered in the negative, it could imply Nox found her attractive in poor taste. If Korac answered in the affirmative, it could mean he wanted her as well. And that wouldn't suit.

When Nox turned, he'd hoped to find his General's composure at least somewhat affected. But no. Irritatingly so, Korac's cool mask stayed in place as he delivered the perfect answer, per usual.

The best soldier.

"Rayne's heart beats in time to the life around her. Her eyes, so like her ancestor's, have gained clarity as she's developed into a fighter. It's an admirable awareness of her surroundings that only predators attain. I personally prefer a woman who smiles more freely, but when Rayne finds a worthy occasion, it lights the room with warmth and hope. Not at all like Celindria."

The last piqued Nox's curiosity. "How would you describe Celindria's smile?"

"Wrong."

Throughout his answer, Korac withdrew his hands from his pockets and folded his arms, feigning disinterest or displeasure at the chore. But Nox knew better. Korac wanted to know why his King would ask him such a question.

Nox fell back in a sturdy chair behind him and gestured at Korac, saying, "Speak your mind, General."

"Your majesty, why do you ask such a question? Why is Rayne punishing herself?" The edge to his otherwise elegant voice implied unease. Nox recognized it from millennia of companionship. It's why Korac was the best soldier and his second-in-command.

Why *was* Nox ruminating over his assignment? Why did the warmth of Rayne's legs around his hips haunt him so? The sweetness of her...

"She kissed me."

Korac, knowing all of Nox's secrets, shot his brows up and let his arms fall to the side. Quick to the point, his brows came crashing back down in an angry frown Nox was surprised to see outside of his carefully constructed countenance. Korac asked, "How can you know it was sincere?"

Ah, this question. Precisely the sort of calculation Nox expected from Korac. That point also plagued the King of Cinder. How much was Rayne like Celindria? How much of this nice, righteous girl was an act?

"I'm uncertain," Nox confessed.

Korac's assignment was far more forthright. In Sagan, Nox saw a confident woman who knew she wanted her soldier, and with Sagan's ancestor being so terribly afflicted, there was no doubting her sincerity.

Rayne was a contradiction. Sweet, but forward. Strong, but vulnerable. Innocent, but designed to kill.

Nox wanted her.

Therein lied the trouble.

Korac stared into the flames, the red glow bouncing across his contemplative features. Softly, he said, "Too many coincidences, your majesty."

True.

Nox was familiar with being a target of this form of manipulation. He despised the familiar taste of betrayal in his mouth, always sweet in the beginning. "I intend to win that wager, General."

Without taking his pale eyes off the flames, Korac assented, "Of course, sire. If Rayne is anything like Celindria, you'll claim both thrones shortly after we strike."

Korac must fear Nox's threat if he won, but the General hid it beneath an impenetrable shield to the King's irritation. "Bring me another girl. You're dismissed."

By the way Korac left the room, Nox knew his General resented all of this, including the formal treatment which was so different from their early years. But revenge required a cold menace that the King of Cinder had embraced long ago. Rayne tested that. So, Nox would return the favor.

A test of her allegiances and mental fortitude. This was a dangerous dance. Caresses and kisses between strikes, forward words to shake her stance, and when she was ready, Nox would give Rayne what she needed.

Xelan grabbed Rayne by both wrists and held her aloft. Despite her struggle, he remained firm. "We're done tonight." The words came out in a puff of frozen breath.

When Xelan let Rayne go, she cried, "Why?!"

Concern almost made his hands shake as Xelan shoved the ankle weights they'd used earlier into his duffel. The zipper closed on a scream. Flatly, he said, "Because you're unhinged."

Rayne insisted, "I'm fine. You're the one—"

"You broke two of my ribs, and the six consecutive blows to my head put me off the mood to train. You want an *actual* fight, and I'm not giving you one."

Sore and emotionally exhausted, Xelan headed for the edge of the training grounds where he'd parked the Jag.

"Xelan! Xelan, come back!"

The slight whine at the last made him pause, but he kept his back to Rayne. The soreness had already abated as Xelan's hard tissue repair system knitted his ribs and skull fractures back together. But it didn't change his unease about Rayne's behavior.

She gave in with the apologies. "I'm really sorry. You're right. Something is bothering me. I want to talk about it, but I don't know how."

Xelan turned on his heel, but he didn't come any closer, saying, "Go on." He was always prepared to listen.

So much passed over Rayne's face. Pride at wounding him. Shame for her pride. And a little fear. Rayne cried in frustration, fell to her knees, and pounded the frozen earth with her fists. Loyalty, shame, and confusion consumed her in a hurricane of conflict.

Xelan took a few slow steps toward Rayne, combat boots crunching on the hardened grass. He wanted to kneel and hug her. To tell her everything would be all right. But the ball was in her court.

A gentle push couldn't hurt. "Rayne?"

"I'm losing!" Rayne winced at her outburst.

Xelan crouched down to her level. "The dreams?" He let out a deep exhale of frozen breath. "Are you ready to tell me?"

Anguish strained Rayne's voice. "Hell no!" And yet…

She lowered her head to the grass, looking desperate for reassurance, comfort—anything. It thickened Rayne's voice as she confessed, "I don't know how much more I can take."

Curse Nox.

Xelan reached out and brushed Rayne's shoulder—

She reared back and fixed him with a red-rimmed stare. "You don't know what I've done."

Rayne's shame and confusion fractured Xelan's heart into pieces. He sat back on the grass and kept his hands to his side. The moon shifted from behind the clouds. The pale light streaked through the trees, making Rayne into an incandescent, despondent sprite.

What had Nox done to Rayne that she would fear telling Xelan? Any answer worse than killing her wrenched Xelan's insides until he squeezed his eyes tight.

When a tear rolled down Xelan's cheek, Rayne said on a breath, "I'm sorry."

His eyes snapped open, and Xelan knew by her awestruck reaction they'd went into Atramentous. The midnight ring around his iris had swallowed his corneas, leaving a white slit down the center for a pupil.

Even Rayne's fascination couldn't overtake the grief carved in the planes of her face.

Xelan's words came out in three simultaneous octaves of his voice. "Don't."

Rayne flinched.

He raised a hand to assure her as he said, "Don't apologize for what Nox has done to you. Ever." Another tear spilled from his lashes, hot on his jaw.

Rayne shook her head. "No. You don't understand. I... I kissed him. I *wanted* to do more..."

Not this.

Xelan looked away, staring into the woods. How could he help Rayne with this? She was at a curious age, and Nox would certainly take advantage of it. How could Xelan convince her she did nothing wrong? No doubt she thought worse of herself since Xelan had looked away.

"Stop." He could feel Rayne's remorse, and he wanted to put an end to it. "Stop blaming yourself." Xelan's voice was thick to the point of choking. He cleared it and rubbed his face. "You've recently turned eighteen. Nox is older than your entire species. He's a predator, and he's preying on your valid, hormone-induced confusion. Also known as a sex drive."

Rayne blushed and glanced away.

Xelan fell back on the frosted grass, asking, "Do you want me to pretend you're not a human with growing needs? Believe me, I can do that. I'd prefer to do that. I hate watching the Progeny grow up, but witnessing you internalize this has been killing me. It's the most helpless I've felt since the Vacating left me on Earth."

Rayne shed her hoodie and unstrapped the ten-pound weight vest from her chest. She shivered and shrugged back into the jacket.

Xelan watched Rayne step around him, trying to keep up with her mercurial moods. She laid down on the grass behind him and placed her head next to his. They stared at each other up close. Xelan knew his eyes had returned to normal, and Rayne's were less bloodshot. She touched the streaks of tears on his face, and he let her.

Rayne said, "I never want to see your tears again. What can I do to make that happen?"

Xelan took her hand and held it. "You can talk to me about it. Or Sagan. Or whoever you feel comfortable with. You can't internalize this anymore. It's toxic, and it's eating away at you. Also at my ribs." At Rayne's wince, he grinned. "I was proud of you for landing those shots with so much force."

"I'm sorry—"

"Stop. Talk to me or promise me you'll talk to somebody."

Rayne turned to the sky, and Xelan mirrored her. The clouds passed slowly over the silver disk of the moon. Their breath left in puffs, adding to the atmosphere. The cold absorbed into his skin.

Xelan listened as Rayne told him about the kiss, and some details left him uncomfortable. He knew she'd even left a few out, but the worst came next.

"I think there's more to Nox than conquest and vengeance." Rayne sounded painfully convinced.

Xelan would need to approach this delicately or risk pushing her away, possibly right into Nox's arms. In an even tone, Xelan said, "Tell me why you feel that way."

Rayne turned her head on the grass to meet Xelan's eyes. "What happened with Nox's brother?"

Xelan nearly choked. After the initial shock passed, he forced himself to ask, "He told you about that?"

Rayne shook her head. "No. Not exactly. Nox said, 'your guardian took him from me.'"

Never in a million years would Xelan imagine this conversation. What could he say, and how could he say it without lying to her?

Fortunately, Rayne spared him from the explanation. "It seems like it's difficult for either of you to talk about it."

Yes.

Xelan took a brief detour from the subject. "At the next group training, I'll brief the team on all the key players in the invasion. I'm disappointed in myself for not doing it sooner."

Rayne gave Xelan a reassuring pat. "You take care of us, and you do it with the weight of not just one world, but two, on your shoulders. We're turning out okay, kiss with the devil notwithstanding. Don't be so hard on yourself."

This lightheartedness was much preferable over Rayne's earlier grief and shame. Xelan grinned. "I'm proud of you. All of you."

"Facing down a sleepless night, I appreciate your encouragement even more." Rayne returned the grin.

Xelan kissed her forehead, saying, "I got you to smile. For my next miracle, I'll sort Sagan out."

This time Rayne full-on beamed. "I can't wait."

Sagan cut slits up her thighs in the short silk nightgown she'd bought with three months of her allowance. A pale silver, it reminded her of the flecks in Korac's eyes. In case he missed the hint, the slits allowed her to fight in her lingerie. Sagan knew Korac would appreciate that.

Since he'd kissed her last year, they'd done just about every other physical act together aside from actual sex. But tonight was the night. Sagan could feel it.

She brushed her short blond bob, spritzed on some perfume, and shaved her legs extra smooth. The ankle brace ruined some of the effect. As Sagan's latest accessory, courtesy of Justin, the brace's presence always seemed to affect Korac's composure. He'd let Sagan see a killer beneath the mask, and it made her want Korac even more.

Was it weird to put on eyeliner before snuggling under the covers? Or was it weirder this was the first time Sagan had bothered to wear makeup since Justin trapped her in a nightmare?

A violet confusion stared back at Sagan in the mirror.

She missed Rayne. Like a valve had closed in her heart, Sagan ached to make Rayne smile. A storm hovered over her best friend, gusting away any potential for happiness.

And it was Sagan's fault.

Yet, here she was, preparing to sleep with the Icarean secret in her dreams.

"Compartmentalize and focus on what you *can* control, Sagan." She told herself in the mirror. "We can't control Justin, but by god, we can take what little joy where we can find it."

With fresh resolve, Sagan went to bed and opened her eyes in Korac's quarters. The fire kept out the January cold, and Sagan appreciated the ambiance. But where was Korac?

"You look beautiful."

Sagan turned and found him perched on the back of a chair like a magnificent bird of prey. It sent a thrill through her and stole her breath away. And that was before she could see he was shirtless.

Korac walked off his perch with a graceful step in his silk white pajama bottoms. They hung off his hips in a way which emphasized his prominent hip bones.

Sagan knew Korac was in peak physical condition, but seeing all of it exposed brought a blush to her cheeks.

Korac let out a sound between a sigh and a growl before saying, "I love the way you look at me." In response, he raked his pale eyes down the low cut of Sagan's lingerie and where it clung to her hips and thighs. "I appreciate the slits."

Sagan's blush burned deeper.

Korac smirked, taking a step closer. He reached up and gripped the canopy rail on the massive bed. The stretched pose let the firelight touch his abs, ribs, and chest.

It was almost too much for Sagan. She felt faint.

"What are your terms?" Korac didn't need to say what he meant.

By the fire reflected in his eyes, Sagan knew. "I want you to have all of me."

As Korac leaned into the pose, all that silky white hair fell forward and concealed his reaction. Desire thickened his elegant cadence as he asked, "Are you certain you know what you're offering?"

The heat in his voice gave Sagan goosebumps. She breathed, "Yes."

Contrary to his composure, Korac ran a hand through his hair and exposed the intensity in his gaze. He let go of the canopy and held out his hand. "Come here."

Without hesitation, Sagan took it and let Korac pull her close. Her eyelids fluttered shut, and she raised her chin for a kiss.

A metallic chink startled Sagan into opening her eyes, and something cold encased her wrist. Korac took both her hands and held them high to the canopy's railing.

It was a shackle.

Korac looped it through the canopy and clasped it to her free wrist. Sagan's heart pounded until she had difficulty catching her breath. He glanced at her, and there was something innocent in his expression despite the bondage.

The man of Sagan's dreams wanted to ensure she was into it. Or at least not afraid. Warmth pooled in her chest and other places. She let it show in her eyes, but in case Korac didn't get the message, she said, "I trust you."

The fire flickered, lighting the fascination in Korac's eyes. "We'll test the extent of it, tonight." Even when he held up a blindfold, Sagan kept her eyes on him. Satisfied, he shook his head as if impressed before instructing, "No sight. No touch. Don't make a sound unless I say. Safety word?"

Sagan beamed. "Butterfly."

Hours later, Korac kissed Sagan's sore wrists, assuring, "Once you have a nacre, you won't sustain injuries like this anymore."

"I've asked Xelan about nacres multiple times throughout the years, and he's always evaded me." Sagan liked the way Korac nestled her against him. The way he cared for her after...

After...

Wow. They did damned near everything, and Sagan was deliciously sore from it. For the first time since these dreams began, she wished the sensations would last into waking life.

Korac kissed her hair and scratched a light circle with one nail along Sagan's back. Being naked with him felt right, unlike—

No.

Justin wasn't welcome here.

After the spike of anxiety dissipated, Sagan noticed a tension missing from Korac. Despite the usual easiness between them, there had been a rigidity to him. Until they'd melted it away together.

Three times.

Sagan shored up the nerve to ask, "Was something bothering you before...?"

Korac scratched a little deeper, sending a shiver of desire through Sagan. With undisguised satisfaction, he said, "Management and I are competing on a project. Last night, they progressed ahead of me—further than I'd thought possible. But after you and I..."

Sagan blushed.

"Well, let's just say our time together improved my standing by leagues."

Korac's explanation went a little over Sagan's head, but it pleased her to help. "If you ever need more improvement, I'm here for you."

His chuckle vibrated in his chest beneath Sagan, almost like a purr. She loved the sound and relished her effect on Korac.

It was time.

"Korac, I love—"

He kissed Sagan, swallowing her confession. A deep, exploring kiss which quickly became more.

Tomorrow.

Before they did anything else, Sagan would tell Korac she loved him. Tomorrow.

After thirty-six hours of no sleep and running the training course all night, Rayne thought she'd imagined Sagan smiling at her across the cafeteria during lunch.

But no.

As Rayne did a double-take, she beamed. Not only was Sagan smiling boldly in view of Justin and the other Overachievers, but she was wearing something other than athletic sweats. Her bright blue sweater matched Rayne's eyes. Was she wearing a leather skirt?

Holy shit.

Sagan looked hot with her hair tousled and her violet eyes lined heavily with kohl. She *so* didn't give a damn that Justin was glaring upside her head.

A kiss.

Sagan Sterling blew Rayne Callahan a kiss.

Rayne melted.

"Excuse me. I have to go to the bathroom."

As Kyle left to do... whatever... Nikki snickered.

Tameka grinned like Xelan's trademark expression was catching. "I don't know what's up with Sagan, but I'm loving this."

Rayne beamed back. "Me, too."

Although nothing else came of it throughout the rest of the day, Rayne rode the high all the way home from the bookstore after school. She even sniffed her dinner, rather than pushing it aside with *complete* disinterest.

Xelan noticed Rayne's good mood. "I like seeing you in higher spirits."

"Me, too."

They'd kicked ass for a few hours, and after he left, Rayne ran the training course for another hour.

Unfortunately, forty-eight hours and twenty-seven minutes was a long time to go without sleep. Rayne was losing the battle. She'd avoided the post-kiss conversation with Nox for two whole days.

But this was it.

Sick with exhaustion, Rayne passed out while counting the lines on her college-ruled notebook.

Twenty-nine.

Thirty.

Thirty-one...

A waterfall spilled into a nearby basin, crashing black water under a bloated sun. Red and orange light glared at Rayne through an amber dome, shielding her from certain destruction. All around, black trees stood sentinel in a charred forest. She could taste ash on her tongue.

Cinder.

The awesome sight broke Rayne's heart.

"You cost me an important wager last night."

The King of Cinder's silken baritone from behind couldn't startle Rayne away from the majesty of an alien planet. Through the vibrations of the red soil, she knew Nox came closer. Poised to fight, Rayne let him walk up beside her. Together, they gazed at his scorched kingdom.

Although Rayne couldn't comprehend what he'd meant by 'costing him a wager,' she knew what to say next. "I understand now why you want to invade Earth. Nox, how have you stayed sane looking at this for thousands of years?"

His black eyes stayed on the view while his smirk held a secret. One, maybe Rayne should know. It sent an icy chill through her, and a shiver alerted her to the clothes. Or lack thereof.

Small black shorts and a scant black top clung to Rayne's skin, leaving more muscle exposed than ever. Black ribbons coiled around her arms, legs, and midriff. And she was barefoot. Again.

Rayne shot Nox a flat, incredulous look.

The King of Cinder laughed, and it sang to Rayne. He was beautiful and devastating in ways she shouldn't even consider. Yet, here she was.

The continuous storm raged in Rayne, while crashing waves of desire eroded her vulnerable resolve.

She bought into what Tameka referred to as the 'virginity myth.' Rayne wanted her first time to be with someone special. Tameka had tried to convince Rayne it was asking too much of a biological act, especially of the first time with no practice. But Rayne was still saving herself for…

Nox confessed, "I've missed our talks these past two days."

Rayne had to admit, "So did I."

As he faced her, the scenery spun around them in a dizzying transformation. Gone was the poisoned landscape. They'd returned to Nox's Castle.

"We wouldn't want you to lose your sanity." The smirk on his lips warmed.

Handsome bastard.

Rayne planted her feet in the soil and raised her fists.

Nox raked his glittering black eyes over her, lingering on her shoulders and biceps, abs and quads. There was pride in his voice as he said, "You've come so far."

"Dying to you night after night motivated me to become your worst nightmare." Rayne refused to relax in her stance, despite how much it taxed her exhausted reserves.

Nox settled into his favorite posture, relying on his tree trunk arms as defense. He chuckled. "Yes. A passionate fighter with an even more passionate kiss."

Rayne wouldn't give him the satisfaction of seeing her blush. She planted her hand forward and went for an overhead kick, flipping backward when Nox evaded. This let her get some distance between them, conscious of his superior reach.

The filter blurred the full effect of his reaction, but Rayne could see Nox's eyes widen in surprise. "Nice footwork."

It confused her when he paid her compliments. Rayne always fought the flush of pride at the sincerity in Nox's voice.

"But you and I both know you're avoiding this issue. Why, Rayne?"

Not Celindria.

God help her, the way Nox said her name affected her. There was so much gravity as if he was aware of it, too. Rayne said, "Because I'm scared," before feinting with a right hook while landing a left jab to his ribs.

Nox took the blow and grabbed Rayne by the throat, only he didn't squeeze. "Nothing has to change between us."

Rayne stared into his black gaze, whispering, "What if I want it to change?"

As if her skin burned, Nox released her and stepped away. "Speak your mind, warrior, but take caution. What you say, you can never recant."

"Nox, I want to save Cinder *with* you. By being together, we can heal the wounds between our people." Rayne swallowed to get the next confession out. "I want you to be my first."

Nox tried to sweep her legs out from under her, but Rayne rolled forward and sprung back to her feet. He was there, and they traded blows. Both blocked and dodged, more dancing than fighting.

Amid the combat, Nox said, "I'm honored, but I don't believe you know what you're asking. What it will mean for you. I will still invade your planet without mercy—"

"But it doesn't have to be that way. We can work together to resolve this peacefully. We can *be* together, Nox." Rayne knew this was the right course. She felt it.

Nox caught her next punch and twisted her into him, her back to his front. "Is this what you want?"

The warmth of him seeped into Rayne's nearly bare back. Against her ear, Nox's breath smelled of spearmint. There was so much of him, solid and intimidating. Yet Rayne breathed, "More than anything."

Nox lifted Rayne's mouth to his with a finger under her chin and kissed her roughly. With her free hand, Rayne reached back and did something which had only occurred to her in the fantasies she'd written in her notebook. Rayne ran her fingers through Nox's hair, appreciating the softness.

As the kiss deepened, Nox released Rayne's twisted arm and held her to him by the waist. His hand was hot but his ring was cool on her skin. She wanted this. Wanted Nox. More brazen than she thought herself capable, Rayne took his hand and placed it on her breast.

They both moaned.

When Nox's fingers trailed down her ribs from her chin, over her belly button, and lower still, Rayne knew she was in over her head. Yet still exactly where she wanted to be.

Rayne awakened from a long night of rest, finding her hands busy and wondered if Nox did too. Between that thought and recalling the way he'd said, "Is this enough for you," after the fourth orgasm—She finished a fifth time.

It was Saturday, so no alarm, but Rayne felt alive and needed a shower. Was Nox showering right then? Like her, was he thinking of how they should meet and discuss their alliance?

When should she tell Xelan?

Rayne felt different.

With the way her mother glanced at her over breakfast that morning, Rayne wondered if she looked different, too. She didn't actually have sex, but for all the intimate details which were seared in her mind, Rayne might as well have.

Nox's skin under her hands and the bunching of the muscles in his back as he moved. Their hips together. Apart. Together again. The way he sucked on Rayne's—

"Honey, are you okay? I'd ground you if I thought it would get you to eat. I'm *that* worried about you."

Like this would go over well. *Mom, last night in my dreams, I had sex with the alien king hell bent on conquering our planet.*

And I enjoyed it.

Immensely.

Rayne's face burned.

Across the table, Jack asked, "Are you getting sick? I can't afford to get sick. I got a date tonight."

Ray and Michelle turned away from Rayne and stared at their son. She welcomed the distraction.

Jack shrugged. "What?"

The parents began a deluge of questions.

"Who is it?"

"Why are we just now hearing about this?"

"Where are you going on this little date?"

Meanwhile, Rayne wondered if Nox always brushed his teeth before their dreams. She liked the idea of him freshening up for her. It made her smile the rest of the morning.

Rayne could do this. She could save the worlds with love.

{CULT OF NIGHT COMPOUND | SACRAMENTO, CA}

Korac settled into his room for a night of pleasuring Sagan. Of watching full lashes flutter closed over those magnificent violet eyes of hers. The way she gripped the sheets when the height of ecstasy consumed her.

Tonight, they'd try spanking—

Someone with a death wish knocked on Korac's door.

Short of the King, he couldn't imagine anyone else entitled enough to disturb him at this pre-dawn hour. Korac slipped back into his red silk button-down, leaving the buttons undone and cursed as he answered the door.

"What the fuck... Colita?!"

The viper's mascara ran down her face as she held herself, trembling. Deep bruises healed before Korac's eyes as her nacre's soft tissue repair system worked overtime courtesy of her superior nanites. Colita beseeched him, "Korac, something's wrong with Nox."

He didn't hesitate. "Where is he?"

But Colita spiraled into a terrified tangent. "He's always made drinking rough, but he's never... He *hurt* me."

More gentle than Korac thought himself capable of with Colita, he held her by the arms until those sky-blue eyes focused on him. "Colita, tell me where he is."

She swallowed audibly, preparing to answer, when screams erupted from down the hall and answered for her. Destructive sounds followed—wood busting, glass shattering.

Korac set Colita in his quarters and warned, "Stay here. Don't come out for any reason."

She hiccuped a sob before asking with her heart broken in her eyes, "Korac, what's wrong with him?"

For the first time in their long history together, Korac realized Colita's feelings for Nox were sincere. And she was right to worry. Korac said, "I may know, but there's nothing you can do. You did nothing wrong. Stay out of the way until I fetch you. Can you do that?"

Colita nodded after another hiccup before settling in an armchair. Almost too soft for Korac to hear, she said, "Help him, please."

A thunderous crash which shook the walls prevented Korac from providing further reassurances. It was time to face the beast. Korac emerged from the hall into the courtyard—All CoN compounds included a courtyard the size of a football field for their festivities.

Sacramento's was on fire.

Flames consumed mountains of debris where there'd been picnic tables and supplies earlier. Buildings fell apart. The water tower collapsed, and the basin spilled onto a pile of bodies.

A woman ran by Korac, and he shouted, "Stop! Go back!"

Too late.

A familiar silhouette manifested against the flames and clutched the woman by the throat. Nox wrenched her head to the side, hard enough to break some vertebrae, and tore a chunk out of her neck. The King of Cinder drank deep in his madness.

This was total collapse, and Korac feared it.

Seconds later, the woman's drained body careened across the field, landing in the pile of corpses beneath the spilling water.

Atramentous.

Korac wanted to look away from Nox's eyes, but he stood his ground, awaiting his King's orders.

The chilling depth beyond Nox's usual baritone prickled warnings along Korac's skin. The King said, "I must feed."

"Yes, sire."

Nox ordered, "Do what you must."

The Icarean King meant as far as damage control. Korac assured, "No survivors, your majesty."

Two young CoN members made a break from their hiding place, and Nox was on them within a heartbeat. Bone broke and organs squelched as he unleashed on their fragile, nacre-less bodies.

This was Rayne's fault. Celindria's descendant had failed to keep her virtue intact, and now Nox must reap a month's worth of carnage. Korac despised the girl for her weakness all the way to the barracks.

"Squadron Twelve."

The Icarean troops hopped out of their cots and stood at attention.

Korac ordered, "Defend the perimeter. No one leaves this compound alive."

They grunted in the affirmative and set about their task.

Fuck, Korac could be dominating Sagan right now, but here he was salvaging relations between the Icari and their human sponsors. Lest they risk anyone escaping and spreading news of Nox's proclivities.

Sacramento was no small sector. The invasion force would lose four hundred human resources this night, leaving Korac to redistribute the five hundred Icarean soldiers across other compounds. Not to mention manufacturing a reason these members had deserved punishment of this magnitude.

What a PR disaster.

A howling shriek pierced the night, and blood sprayed in an arc across the barracks.

Nox would never tire, and, judging by the mounting body count, it wouldn't take him long to finish the humans.

Why had Rayne given in?

Now the King and his second-in-command were on equal footing regarding Phase I of the wager. From here, they faced Phase II. And Korac already tired of lying to Sagan. He'd stopped her from confessing her feelings for him, so seducing her in the waking world would take very little.

But that's not what Korac wanted anymore. He wanted her out of the way of the speeding train coming off the tracks that was the King of Cinder.

Another wail sounded in the night to punctuate Korac's point.

The invasion came closer with each day, and they couldn't afford breaks in Nox's sanity like this.

This mess was Rayne's fault, and nothing would make Korac believe otherwise.

He sighed and went to aid his King, as always. As was right. Korac only wished he could see Sagan's smile at least once this night.

But wishes rarely came true.

SEVEN

IT'S WORSE THAN YOU CAN IMAGINE

FOR THE FIRST TIME IN YEARS, SAGAN WAS LOOKING FORWARD TO THE PROGENY GROUP MEETING TONIGHT. Too bad it was January and too cold for a sports bra. Rayne would like that. Instead, Sagan settled for extra clingy workout gear, emphasizing her curves.

She pumped her hair up with her fingers and applied heavy gray eyeshadow. The shade always made her think of Korac. Sagan had missed him last night, probably more than she should.

They'd make up for it tonight. The thought brought a smile to Sagan's glossed lips, a sexy one she took time to appreciate in the mirror.

Tonight.

Until then, Sagan kissed her mom on the way out. "I'm heading to Rayne's for movie night. I'll be back before ten. Love you."

"Have fun, dear. Drive safe."

Everything was coming together.

The chilly day had left the windshield frosted, so Sagan sat in the car warming her hands as she waited for it to defrost. She checked the rear-view mirror and tried to ignore that the gloss didn't quite hide the split in her lower lip.

Over the last year, Justin had become careful and only bruised Sagan in places hidden by her clothes. But after Sagan blew Rayne a kiss yesterday morning, he'd lost control. She'd known it was coming by the satisfied look on Stacia and Cecily's faces. The look of smug siblings who knew the other kid was about to get punished. At least Lucy wasn't smug. More curious. As if she'd wondered why Sagan kept pushing Justin's buttons.

Sagan knew the reason 'why' all too well. It satisfied the masochist in her, but she didn't enjoy facing such an ugly truth. So she stopped looking in the mirror and headed out.

The training grounds looked magical under the light of the full moon, making all the frost glow in ethereal light. Of course, Rayne was already there, sparring with Xelan.

He stopped defending against Rayne when he saw Sagan. "Hey!"

Audacious as always, Rayne said, "You look amazing."

Sagan almost laughed. She was hiding her hair under a hood and shivering beneath a puffy coat, but she appreciated the compliment, nonetheless. "Thanks. So do you, but aren't you cold?"

Rayne had on layered tanks with no extra layers for pants. "Nah. I feel great." An out-of-place blush graced Rayne's cheeks. In fact, she looked a little different. More relaxed and confident, yet somehow shy.

Rayne was hiding something.

"Well, you're making me cold looking at you," Kyle said, as he emerged from the tree line with Andrew.

The other boy waved with bags under his eyes.

Sagan asked, "Aren't you getting any sleep, Andrew?"

He glanced at Xelan, who looked away, before saying, "Oh, you know? I'm missing winter vacation already, but at least this is our last year."

"Hell yes!" Tameka appeared next. "Seniors, baby. It's almost over."

The entire group beamed at each other.

Xelan looked especially proud before clapping his hands together, killing the moment. "Okay. Tonight is more of a briefing. We need to discuss the players in Nox's camp. I know. I know. This is a matter of strategy. Something The Brethren mostly managed for the invasion." He grinned. "But now you're ready."

Sagan and the others went to the picnic table, ready for a lesson. She sat beside Rayne, and, feeling bold, brushed the other girl's fingers. With an attempt at discretion, Rayne stiffened only momentarily before lacing her fingers with Sagan's gloved ones, warming each other through.

Xelan, oblivious to the reunion, lectured in a black tee and cargo pants, impervious to the cold. "From the intelligence I've gathered through The Brethren, Cinder's royal council functions on rotation. It's impossible to know who currently holds a seat. However, there are two allegiances sworn to the King which have survived for longer than you can imagine."

At Xelan's dramatic pause, Kyle rolled his eyes and groaned. "Yeah? Are you planning on telling us?"

Andrew nudged him with a friendly chuckle.

Tameka clicked her tongue and cut the air with her hand. "Don't mind him. We know you'll get to it."

Rayne squeezed Sagan's hand before glancing her way with a beaming grin on her face.

What a silly family they'd built over the years.

"As I was saying..." Xelan winked at Tameka before continuing. "Nox keeps two people closest to him." Xelan held up a sketch of a beautiful woman with angelic features right down to her cherubic curls. "Colita mitigates trade relations and commerce, but her primary function is to serve Nox as a source of sustenance. He feeds only from her."

Beside Sagan, Rayne stiffened, and her smile disappeared as if it had never been.

Kyle asked, "So, she's valuable to Nox; therefore, should be targeted in regards to the invasion?"

Xelan glanced over at Andrew, who confessed, "In some ways, she's already invaded. She's contacted me in my dreams a few times over the last two years."

Sagan frowned. She wasn't the only one getting nocturnal visitors?

"Me, too," Kyle piped up.

Xelan tilted his head to the side in an avian gesture, asking, "Why haven't you ever mentioned this before?"

Kyle tangled his fingers in his hair and blew the air out of his cheeks. "Well, I didn't think she was real, and the nature of the dreams were kind of private."

Private.

Sagan looked between Andrew and Tameka to glimpse Kyle's reddening cheeks.

Xelan's bewildered expression while he stared at the ground wasn't very reassuring. He asked, "Did Colita tell you anything we can use?"

"She told me what Nox *wants.*" Kyle sounded a little smug or angry, even.

Without looking up from the grass, Xelan's eyes doubled in size.

Andrew shifted uncomfortably next to Tameka, who asked, "What is *that* supposed to mean?!"

Rayne remained eerily silent, still rigid beside Sagan. Her hand even went clammy.

Kyle opened his mouth to say more, but Xelan cut him off. "Let me. Please."

The younger man conceded with a nod.

Xelan ran a hand through his hair and sighed. After which, he leveled his gaze on Rayne in a way that sent a chill down Sagan's spine. There was too much fear in his eyes.

Xelan said, "The reason I know the invasion will start in Little Rock—the reason Nox will find the Progeny first—is you, Rayne. Nox wants you."

Sagan could only see Rayne's profile, and there was almost no reaction. Aside from a single tear. Sagan squeezed Rayne's hand, trying to warm her suddenly freezing fingers.

Tameka, Andrew, and Kyle likewise checked for her reaction, and Tameka wasn't having it. She put an arm around Rayne and chafed her bicep, pegging Xelan with a fierce expression as she asked, "Can you tell us why?"

Xelan crossed the clearing and took Rayne's free hand, kindly oblivious to Sagan's grip on her. He said to Rayne, "He wants your blood which is the only way to open the conduit."

Sagan frowned. "Wait. If it's the only way to open the conduit, then how could he get here in the first place?"

Andrew answered with entirely too much confidence for someone who should be as much in the dark as the rest of them. "It's not the only conduit."

Kyle said, "And they only need a drop. They could find other ways to get your blood—As far as I've gathered from Colita. A little blood; a little door. All of Rayne's blood; all of the door."

Tameka put her face in Rayne's field of vision, brushed her brunette hair from her eyes, and said, "He has to come through us, first. Right, Rayne?"

The look on her best friend's face made Sagan want to cry. Something had broken inside Rayne. Sagan leaned in and whispered, "I won't let him take you from me."

Rayne turned and searched Sagan's eyes. No other tears fell, but 'devastated' was the only way to describe the lost look in those shattered sapphires. "I wanted to save the worlds . . ." The words trailed off as if Rayne feared finishing the sentence. After the broken confession, she shook herself, her strength gathering in her eyes. "I'll kill him."

Xelan brought Rayne to him so he could kiss the top of her head. Against her hair, he said, "That's my badass warrior." It was so sweet.

Kyle disguised a disgusted sound with a cough.

Andrew nudged him hard enough to knock him off the table.

Tameka muttered, "Serves you right."

Sagan felt better when Rayne squeezed her hand and shot her a reassuring look. It wasn't anything close to a smile, but it was better than despondent grief.

Relieved, Sagan changed the subject. "So, who else should we send packing back to Cinder?"

"Ah." Xelan held up a finger as he backed up and rifled through his bag for another sketch. "Nox's second-in-command. The Silver General."

Silver.

General.

Sagan blinked.

Then Xelan held up the next sketch, and bile rose in Sagan's throat. Pale hair, eyes, and skin. Soft angles and prominent cheekbones. Xelan even nailed the smirk, as if familiar with the expression. When he said Korac's name, she cupped a hand over her mouth to keep from vomiting.

Rayne glanced at Sagan, before double-taking and staring at her best friend. But Sagan could hardly notice. The rest of Xelan's lecture floated on the chilled air, fuzzy and confusing.

Korac.

Four years.

"Xelan didn't send me. I'm here against orders not to interfere with your training, but you're so vital, I couldn't stay away."

Four years and sex.

"Xelan could face major consequences for contacting you. As would I. So please. Don't endanger him further by mentioning me, and we'll keep our sessions a secret."

In love...

With Nox's second-in-command.

Xelan continued his lecture. "Korac's a brutal fighter—quick to kill. He's more agile than Nox and—"

"Is Korac under Nox's influence like the other Icari?" Sagan blurted. All eyes fell on her. She regretted the attention, but she *needed* to know the answer. "Does he have no other choice but to serve Nox?"

Xelan's faint wince went unnoticed by everyone by Sagan as the others continued to stare at her. Clear and grim, Xelan declared, "Korac *chose* Nox."

No.

"Like Nox's ring, you can tell them apart by signatures with this symbol on it." Xelan held up a sketch of the same heart-shaped emblem as Korac's axes. "You've heard me talk about the Pretiosum Cruor. This is it. It held Celindria's blood, and now they need Rayne's for the same purpose."

Sagan's heart sank. Her body felt like an anchor, weighing her down. This happened sometimes when Justin hurt her, but this time it hurt more. Sagan's focus splintered into useless pulp as her thoughts scattered into the night.

No thinking.

No feeling.

As Xelan continued his lecture, Sagan drifted away.

"Babe, the meeting's over. Can we talk?"

Rayne.

The concern in her voice brought Sagan back to her body. How long was she gone? Did anyone else notice?

Tameka chatted Xelan up while Andrew and Kyle came over to the girls. "See you two later."

Rayne shot Sagan a pitying look, as if she knew this was hard for her. The brunette hugged Andrew and Kyle. "Good night. Drive safe."

"This ain't *The Fast and the Furious*. It's a Volkswagen for fuck's sake." Andrew chuckled and squeezed Sagan warmly.

Kyle said, "Besides, I can't get this grandma to drive over fifty miles an hour." His hugs followed, lingering a little with Rayne, but everyone lingered with her. Sagan especially.

"Goodnight, boys."

Xelan saluted them on the way out, but kept beaming down at Tameka. Her freckles even sparkled while gazing into his undivided attention. They were so cute and didn't even know it.

They were also a wonderful distraction for Sagan's broken heart.

Rayne whispered into Sagan's ear, "Stay with me, tonight."

Yes.

Sagan wasted no time calling her mom and asking for permission, easily granted after six years of friendship. Mrs. Callahan would likewise agree, assuming she was even home from the bookstore yet.

The girls clasped hands and walked over to Xelan and Tameka, who grinned at their linked fingers in delight. He asked, "You two heading out?"

Sagan couldn't smile. Not yet. Instead, she stole a hug, soaking in Xelan's kindness. She said, "I'm staying over with Rayne."

The Icarus always squeezed just right. "Good."

As Rayne hugged Xelan next, Sagan hugged Tameka. "See you, Monday, girl."

The redhead whispered to the blond, "I'm happy for you two."

It all felt good. It felt right.

Much better than how Sagan felt on the inside. A blender had taken hold of her stomach, and she feared falling asleep. In fact, without Rayne, there would be no sleep tonight.

So, yay.

The girls left the couple in the woods to their chain dart discussion and walked the few meters to Rayne's house. Ray always worked weekend nights at the hospital, but the modest two-story seemed suspiciously empty for nine thirty at night.

Sagan asked, "Where's Jack?"

"Oh, he had a date." Rayne's eyes sparkled with humor.

Sagan wanted to make a crack about him growing up too fast, but her heart wasn't in it. "Can we go to bed now?"

All the humor died in Rayne's eyes, replaced with pure understanding. "Of course. You can shower first."

No.

Sagan leaned into Rayne's ear and made a different suggestion. The girls showered together, and Rayne held Sagan in bed. While the blond wanted to cry, the brunette asked, "How long has Korac come to you in your dreams?"

Startled, Sagan sat up in the bed and faced her best friend. "How did you know?"

A tear marked a trail down Rayne's cheek like earlier in the night. "Nox comes to mine."

"Oh, god. Rayne..."

Rayne held up a hand, staving Sagan. "Tell me about Korac. Does he hurt you?"

Sagan shook her head, and her voice broke on a sob. "No. He's perfectly wonderful."

Without hesitation, Rayne pulled Sagan in for a hug, squeezing the truth out of her. Both girls shared their stories down to every last detail, including the most recent developments.

Sagan said, "I love Korac. It's different from how I feel about you, but it's almost as intense. Do you have feelings for Nox?"

Rayne looked away. Another tear rolled down her cheek as she took a shaking breath to say, "I want to get through to him that there's another way—a better way—to save our planets. Nox doesn't have to invade. He can come to humanity as a diplomat in a relationship with a hybrid of the two species. With me . . ."

"You sound like a martyr, Rayne. That's not what I asked you. How do *you* feel about Nox?"

Crumbling, Rayne said, "I thought there was something between us, but after tonight, I know he was manipulating me. He's spent all this time making me pliable. I'm so *tired*, Sagan."

Sagan kissed Rayne, and the split lip told her it should hurt. Instead...

The girls found solace in each other for several hours until sleep took them.

"We'll tell them off tonight." They promised each other as their eyelids fluttered close. "We have each other. We don't need them."

Sagan appeared in Korac's quarters, wearing a borrowed band tee and panties. This time, she studied her surroundings. Over the last month or so, this dream space had changed in arrangement, color, and texture. There was always a fireplace, armchairs, a bed, and a massive dresser—but in different places, varied wood finishes, and other upholstery—

"I missed you last night."

Sagan shut her eyes, and already the tears wanted to form. Korac's elegant cadence elicited responses from her body and heart which did not fade after the revelation.

But there was no avoiding this.

Sagan turned and faced Korac. She gave a curtsy, which he smirked at until she said, "Hello, Silver General."

In an impossible feat, the Icarus lost what little color there was to his complexion. The mask dissolved, and genuine panic widened Korac's eyes. "Sagan, please listen to me—"

"I don't care."

Korac held out his hands, placating her. "I understand. I know you're upset—"

Sagan shook her head. "No. I'm not."

In the same avian gesture as Xelan, Korac tilted his head. He stopped trying to explain and let her have the space to speak.

When Sagan crossed the room to stand centimeters apart from her enemy, she craned her neck up to maintain eye contact. Here, the gray flecks reminded her of falling ash in snow. Korac smelled crisp as the winter outside and looked like a wet dream in his black pajama bottoms. The silk shimmered in the firelight.

It was too much, and Sagan realized she was too far gone. "I love you, Korac."

His eyes widened, taken aback, but there was no other hesitation. Korac cupped Sagan's face and kissed her. Even in the dream, it stung her tender lip, and she moaned against him.

The kiss deepened when Korac caressed the soreness with his tongue.

Despite how enraptured Sagan was with him, she separated them to say, "I need you to promise me you'll never lie to me again." Korac opened his mouth, but she shook her head. "No. I mean about anything. We won't talk about work. This space is only for us, and here you don't lie to me. I will bear the shame of loving a man who means to invade my planet, but I won't tolerate your lies."

"On Elden, I will never lie to you again, lest Li steal my last breath."

For one sorrowful second, Sagan turned to steel. "Soldier, if you lie to me again, Li won't take your last breath. *I* will."

Korac shivered, and it was *not* in a bad way.

This was wrong.

Sagan was wrong.

But at least here, and in Rayne's arms, she was happy.

Nox would take Rayne in so violent a storm as to rival the one inside her. A hurricane of passion and pain to slake all his needs with enough friction to counter a lightning strike. He'd take his satisfaction in her destruction and consummated swells until Rayne drowned in turbulent ecstasy.

If only she would arrive in the dream.

Nox sat and waited on his throne for three hours thus far, staring at the emblem on his ring. His body rested in his quarters within the Bakersfield, California CoN compound. Sacramento's facilities no longer existed. An unfortunate necessity and nothing more.

Korac, ever the professional, had attended to the cleanup. The General even placated Colita back into her role—All business Nox appreciated his second-in-command for managing on his behalf. The King of Cinder would take all of it into consideration when Korac lost the wager in the coming months. While victorious, Nox would remain generous in his triumph and grant his General leniency of his choice.

But that was a matter to contend with later.

Where was Rayne?

Surely after all her precious proclamations of love and unity the night before, Rayne would arrive eager to discuss her imaginative arrangements further.

In the last twenty-four hours, the hope which had shone in Rayne's bright blue eyes visited Nox near every thirty seconds or thereabouts. Such potential, so easily stoked with words and cemented with longing kisses. The sweet perfume of Rayne's arousal, the silkiness of her skin, and the way Nox's name fell from her lips on a gasp.

Every.

Time.

Rayne was exquisite.

If not for their distance on this tour, Nox feared the loss of his control, such was the urge to touch Rayne in person. He would risk everything to claim her, to feel her hair bunched in his fist and to watch her eyes widen in surprise during her first release. The first of many, contributing to a list of Nox's conquests over Rayne.

"You lied to me."

Nox glanced up and saw Rayne's appealing shape through the pyre. As the flames licked and danced, he caught glimpses of her eyes, staring into him like cobalt glass—hard and fractured. Rayne's accusation held a deadly promise Nox could kiss out of her, she was so under his influence now.

Still, this conversation should prove entertaining. Nox said, "Perhaps. Can you be more specific?" He let the smirk into his voice, lest she not see it for the perception filter.

Rayne danced around the pyre, saying, "You never wanted to heal this rift between our people. You let me go on believing you'd actually consider diplomacy over invasion without ever hearing a word I said. Because you know what you want. Don't you, Nox?"

When Rayne stood before the throne, Nox *did* know what he wanted. The same complication which drove him to destroy the compound last night. The same complication standing before him now.

But this—her words—were all lies.

"Celindria—"

Rayne shook her head in disdain and disappointment.

"—You know so little of the history which drives the Icari. You can't understand how immature your notions of love saving our two worlds sounds to me. Don't insult the suffering of my people by simplifying this matter with a single emotion. We are *dying*!" Her innocence angered Nox until he pounded his fist on the throne and stood, towering over the young woman before him.

Intimidation was lost on Rayne, such was the case from the beginning. She squared off against him, her voice thickened with grief. "I want to help."

There it was again.

A tug, a nudge—a confusion which had occurred to Nox throughout the years of their sparring. Rayne's beguiling determination threatened his resolve to see her as Celindria's descendant. This girl was the reincarnation of evil, and Nox had spent eight thousand years planning to send her to the Wrong Side of Eternity.

But there were other ways...

Quieter, Nox said, "You *can* help."

Rayne looked away, trembling and devastated before asking, "Nox, why do you want me?"

The way she asked it assumed she already knew the answer. Still, Nox indulged her with the truth. "Your tenacity and righteousness—So potent you could form a religion with it. It's in your stance when you fight, your eyes when you're sure you're winning, and in your smile when you try to convince me there's a future for us. You're intoxicating, Rayne."

Tears spilled from her lashes, ones she forcefully wiped away. Rayne's heartache nearly convinced Nox of her sincerity. It seemed to take all her might to meet his eyes. Then she pointed at his hand—at his ring. Her voice shook, half in sobs, as she said, "You don't want me."

The certainty in Rayne's broken voice—the wound she nursed, cut by the idea Nox was lying about his desire for her—Well, it required correction.

Nox took a single step and crossed the space between them. He stared down at Rayne, letting his hunger into his eyes, his voice. "Oh, I *do* want you. I intend to spend every night until the invasion proving how much. Then after which, you'll beg me to take you."

Rayne shivered, but held firm. "I know you want my blood, not me."

"Every. Night. Rayne. And soon, I *will* have both."

Relief and self-loathing stormed in Rayne. The contrast cast clouds of doubt in her eyes, electrified by her own longing.

All according to plan.

With a pained cry, Rayne punched him.

Nox evaded, weaving left then right to avoid her next swing. He backed away from her, letting the young woman's attempts to find catharsis dissipate into thin air.

Frustration mounted in Rayne, and she threw in some impressive leg work. An effective roundhouse kick, Nox blocked. A cartwheel kick. A leg sweep.

All of which Nox expertly evaded. Even as Rayne backed him against a wall, he moved away from her fists until they smacked into the stone and left bloody impressions.

Rayne cried, the salt of her tears tasting of desperate denial. She wanted him and hated herself for it.

Nox kept close to the wall, getting some distance between them.

When Rayne shored herself for a major offensive, Nox knew it was time. She ran up to him, kicked off the wall for some height, and aimed to wrap her legs around his neck.

The takedown.

Nox killed Rayne's momentum by catching her mid-air around the waist and slamming her back against the wall.

He kissed her, rough enough to smack her head into the stone. She kissed back, the taste of her tears on her lips mingling with her natural sweetness. She didn't stop him from deepening the kiss with his tongue or lowering his hands to her hips.

Instead, Rayne ground against Nox, granting him permission to do the same.

But as delicious as this was, it would never be enough.

Nox balled a fist in Rayne's hair and pulled back enough to hurt. She gasped against their kiss, and he raised her up by the thighs with a squeeze hard enough to bite his nails into her bare flesh.

Pain.

Passion

Destruction

Consummation.

Nox took Rayne, fueling the flames of her self-hatred and tormenting her with ecstatic agony.

This was the only future for them.

"And that's how you field dress a wound sustained in combat."

The handsome nurse giving a presentation to the Medical Science class was former military, and ticked off a lot of boxes for Tameka. Apparently for Lynn, too, who stared dreamily at the grown man with warm tawny eyes and rich brown skin. He was tall, though not as tall as Xelan, and equally weary of the world.

Since Tameka wasn't getting anywhere with the object of her obsession, it was permissible to diversify her fantasies. 'I save babies for a living' Chris worked at Arkansas Children's Hospital and would make a fine addition to Tameka's older guy kink collection.

Pablo ruined the moment by asking, "What about infection?"

Chris' eyes sparkled as if delighted at least one of the thirty students in the lab had listened enough to ask a question. "Use whatever antiseptics you have and pray for a miracle."

Tameka made a quick note—yes, she actually paid attention enough to take notes—and glanced over at Rayne who did the same. But more intensely and with an ever-present frown.

There was something wrong with that girl lately. All black and white, no color. Grave eyes flitting about the room, assessing. Rayne probably knew the number and location of the exits in every building they entered, the number of people between her and them, and the number of steps it would take to get the hell out of any situation.

Cagey.

That's how Rayne was acting.

It saddened Tameka to see it, especially given Saturday night's cuteness with Sagan. Everyone pretended not to notice the blond and the brunette holding hands and sitting closer than necessary. Their 'secret' longing glances were so obvious to Tameka, who cheered them on at every turn.

Fuck Justin.

"Chris, thank you for the presentation." Their advanced Medical Science teacher, Dr. Jones, was a small, unassuming woman with a shy smile, but she wasn't fooling Tameka, either.

Tameka, Rayne, Sagan, and Kyle took this class because that one hundred and twenty pound PhD in neuroscience was a special forces operative in retirement. Xelan even encouraged the Progeny to learn basic first aid for the upcoming invasion. Unfortunately, because of some mix up with Mrs. Mendax in registration, the four Progeny couldn't take the class together. So, Rayne and Tameka got to hang out with Pablo and Lynn first thing in the morning while Kyle and Sagan took Anatomy down the hall. Further up the north artery of the school, John and Nikki were working on the last of their foreign language requirement in senior year Spanish.

It meant they could all walk to lunch together, at least.

Chris, presumably a fellow special ops, hugged Dr. Jones and waved goodbye to the class as he left. "Stay good and be nice to your teacher. Or else." His smile was too kind for the stern warning at the end, and Tameka almost laughed trying to imagine a big teddy bear like him killing enemy soldiers.

But could Tameka kill someone? Take a life in the name of the greater good?

The dark notion sent her down a spiral only interrupted by the bell for first lunch. On A-days, the crew ate early, right after first period.

The class funneled into the hall, Pablo asking, "What did you guys think about the part where the skin might be too shredded to suture?"

"Mmm." Lynn exaggerated the sound with a thick helping of sarcasm. "Can't wait for whatever meat byproduct they're feeding us for lunch today."

Tameka laughed, grateful for Xelan's lunch box diet requirements. Beside her, Rayne didn't laugh or react at all. She looked hollowed out by a melon baller. Until…

Sagan emerged from Anatomy class with a cute bubblegum-blond kind of wave. Extra on the sugar. "Hey!" She immediately fixed herself to Rayne's side, perking the brunette girl right out of her pitiful reverie.

"Hey."

The two smiled at each other like lovesick goofballs, forcing Tameka to nudge them both forward. "C'mon. This grilled chicken with veggie medley won't eat itself."

"Fuck that. I'm having pizza." Kyle had also arrived.

Tameka worked to ignore him, especially his furtive glances in Rayne's direction until the brunette girl acknowledged him with a side hug, saying, "You know you'll need to burn the extra calories."

In Rayne's embrace, the boy's entire body relaxed. "Yeah. Yeah. Extra cardio."

Tameka rolled her eyes.

John, as a tall Native American, stood out in the crowd. Nikki, the shortest blond Tameka had ever met, didn't. So she looked extra grateful for the tall boy to escort her to the center of the thickening herd, where the rest filed to lunch. They greeted the group, "Hey." "What's up?"

Tameka glanced John up and down. Since training with Xelan no one had called him scrawny. If they could see Nikki's shoulders, biceps, and back, they'd find her equally intimidating. It was reassuring to be surrounded by so many capable people.

With that thought…

"Be back in a second." While everyone else chatted, Tameka took a quick detour to her locker. There, she stole a quiet moment to reassess and consider the rest of her day. Shoving aside her weapon's cache, she traded her backpack for her purse. Hidden from view, she checked her phone for text messages. The little Nokia almost fit in her hand, making it easy to scroll discretely.

One new message. It was from Xelan. After restraining a squeal of excitement, Tameka took a steadying breath and checked it.

TOMORROW NIGHT, YOU UPGRADE TO CHAIN DART. WEAR PADDED GEAR.

Tameka beamed.

Finally.

"Ms. Phillips, that had better not be a cellphone in your locker."

Tameka dropped the Nokia and whirled to find Mrs. Mendax at her back, looking none too pleased. One day, the strict 'no tolerance' policy on cellphones in school would seem stupid and archaic. But today was not that day.

"No, ma'am. I'm just getting a tampon."

Mrs. Mendax loosened up at the mention of female problems and nodded before turning away.

That was a close one. For someone who couldn't walk in heels, their principal was awfully stealthy in them.

Tameka found the others in the cafeteria at their usual spot, but today was special. Sagan sat beside Rayne. Out in the open.

This was shaping up to be a great day.

This was Sagan's favorite place to be. Right here with her friends and her sketchbook. Even if Tameka was on her case.

"Are you disassociating again or just ignoring me?" Tameka asked.

Rayne played with the food on her lunch tray, her voice pleading. "Leave her alone. Justin's out on his only away game. This is the first time she's sat with us in a year, and you're on her ass."

Tameka pointed a fork full of veggies at them. "Hey, it's not my fault she lets that asshole order her around like a harem girl."

Sagan wanted to stay in her sketchbook rather than join in the conversation. It seemed much more pleasant to work the shading on this wing or the negative space on that antenna. She looked forward to going home and adding some watercolor.

Sagan hated tolerating Justin's brutish control. After all that shit he'd said about her being a track and field star being the source of his attraction to her, he'd decimated her ankle.

Justin told Sagan to stop wearing makeup; she did. Stop dressing like a Goth chick; she did. Stop attending concerts; she did. And finally, to stop eating with her friends at lunch and only eat with him; she did.

Basically, anything Sagan found fun or relaxing seemed to upset Justin. So she gave it all up. And what did she get? Three bad minutes of physical "intimacy" almost daily that still failed to push away the tall, devastatingly handsome invader of her dreams.

After the other night, when Sagan confronted Korac, she'd confessed the truth to Rayne, who confessed her truth about Nox. Both girls were a lost cause.

Rayne had pulled Sagan in for a hug, saying, "You're beating yourself up about it."

Sagan squeezed back, knowing Rayne was the only person in the world who understood. "I don't know how to undo it. I'm in love with *him*."

They found solace in each other.

So here, at lunch, Sagan risked Justin's spies snitching on her again for hanging out with her real friends. If only Justin had a clue. However she might act at school for his sake, she would never be the girl he wanted.

"You might have a point, Tameka," Sagan mumbled to her sketchbook.

She smiled and closed her latest drawing of a butterfly, before glancing over Rayne's shoulder to scan Justin's usual table.

There sat the Overachievers enjoying their lunches. Lucy's head popped up as if summoned. When she caught Sagan's glance, the blue-eyed blond girl quickly looked away. Cecily peered up next and snitched to Stacia beside her.

Justin would definitely hear about this.

Later that night, Sagan's training session with Xelan went sideways fast. Laid out on her ass, he pinned her, forcing a weapon to her midsection. If a car had pulled up to her driveway with beaming headlights, they'd shine on a vulgar-looking scene.

Sagan had lost this contest before it started. Xelan was thousands of years more experienced than her. Thanks to his sleeveless tank, she saw that his exceptionally chiseled muscles weren't even straining. And maybe for half a second Sagan considered giving in and letting him plunge the axe into her chest.

At that exact moment, Xelan rolled off Sagan and extracted the blade. He laid there beside her until he was suddenly standing on his feet. Anxiety and fear crippled Sagan.

Don't move.

Don't breathe.

And don't meet his eyes.

Xelan was upset. "Kyle and Andrew train with no drama. Why are you, Rayne, and Tameka so troublesome?! I swear you three girls will be the death of me."

Sagan stiffened, afraid to answer. She reacted the only way she knew how to that tone of voice from a man. Sensing herself moving further away from her body, Sagan curled on her side, drifting.

It was okay. It would be over soon.

"No!" Xelan knelt on his knees and shook her gently by the shoulders. Terrified, he begged her, "Come. Back."

Sagan slammed back into herself, gasping. The compassion in Xelan's kind midnight eyes forced the tightness in her chest to loosen.

"Don't go, Sagan," Xelan pleaded. "Rayne was right. What is that bastard doing to you?" He reached out then thought better of it, lowering his hand.

Sagan uncoiled herself from the fetal position and knelt on her knees in the dirt, mirroring him. She couldn't bear to tell Xelan about her nightly tormentor. So there was only one other 'bastard' in question.

Sagan's voice came out softly as it often sounded after leaving herself. This was the first time it didn't involve bruising on her throat. "How can I be a soldier if I'm broken?"

Did Sagan hear right?

No, she must be mistaken.

In all this time Sagan had known Xelan—four years—he'd never once shed a tear. Now he was weeping.

Silhouetted against the moonlight, Xelan cried for Sagan, saying, "I can't protect you in the daylight. We can make you physically strong. We can even make you defend yourself against the hordes of Cinder. But this… I can't protect you against this." He stood with a sigh and walked toward the only tree in her backyard.

Sagan stayed on her knees in the dirt.

Xelan said, "This will take a toll on your human soul that I can't bring you back from. Your face during our fight? You wanted to die." He let that hang in the air.

"Xelan—"

"All of you are struggling with this in ways I couldn't predict. This wait is causing suffering I wasn't expecting. You're warriors with nothing to fight. Where else would you take that fight but inside yourselves?" Xelan walked back to Sagan with gentle movements, and his hands loose at his sides. Non-threatening.

She loved him for it.

Xelan said, "Tell me everything. Everything that's eating away at you. It's the only way I can help you."

And Sagan did. Mostly.

Korac would remain her darkest secret, for Rayne's ears only. But after Sagan told Xelan everything about Justin, the midnight ring around his eyes swallowed the whites of them.

Xelan's voice had triplicated. "I should've let Rayne kill him in the beginning."

Sagan took his closed fists in her hands and spread his fingers against her palms while she promised, "I'm getting better. Rayne is helping me, and once school ends, this will all be over."

The lovable Icarus regained enough control to revert his eyes to normal before saying, "I don't want this to go on for another second let alone five more months."

Sagan squeezed Xelan's hands and sighed. "But what if he tells Rayne's parents? This is a small town, Xelan. Mine and Rayne's secret could ruin her."

Xelan pulled Sagan in for a full-on hug, warm and welcoming as he said, "Promise me, you'll take care of yourself from now on. You know Rayne wouldn't want you to risk yourself this way. If she knew the truth, even *I* couldn't keep her from jail."

It was a kind of reassurance Sagan understood. "I promise, Xelan. No more."

After separating their hug, Xelan gently gripped her chin and examined the split in her lip. "If you'd had a nacre, this wouldn't have lasted but a minute or two."

Sagan winced. "If only."

"So, aside from making me a wizard in the bedroom, would you say you've accomplished your mission here in my dreams?"

Kyle owed Colita for his now vast inventory of sexual positions and innovative elicitations of orgasms. He was grateful, but beyond suspicious of what exactly she'd hoped to gain from these nocturnal encounters.

Colita stretched like a satisfied cat against Kyle in her big four-post bed, each night different from the last. The invasion crew had moved around the past few months. When the mood struck him, Kyle would report descriptions of their surroundings to Xelan. Unfortunately, late night texts to the Icarus turned into two-hour long phone conversations, souring Kyle's morning at school. The only balm for his agitation was...

"Rayne. Tell me about her," Colita demanded with a sexy pout on her way to kneel between Kyle's legs.

Kyle's eyes rolled into the back of his head as he closed them and arched for her. "Good god, I love when you do that with your tongue."

Colita stopped.

Instantly frustrated, Kyle growled, "What makes you think I want you to stop?!"

Colita's sky-blue eyes stared at Kyle with her lips poised on the brink of pleasuring him. She purred, "Tell me about Rayne, and you'll have your release."

Kyle didn't like the direction of this inquiry, but he was clever. He could find a smart ass way around it. He said, "Her eyes are bluer than yours. Brighter, too."

Colita wrapped her hand around Kyle and stroked languidly. "And?"

"She works out endlessly, to the point where we're a little worried about her. I haven't seen Rayne eat in months, and even then I think she was only choking down enough to build muscle mass—Fuck, that feels amazing."

Colita had returned to her oral ministrations, and Kyle was sure she meant to suck his soul out of him.

Fine by him.

When Colita stopped mid-suck and rolled her eyes up at Kyle, he knew what she wanted.

This game was stupid.

Kyle said, "Because Rayne trains more with Xelan, she's stronger and faster than the rest of us. She also knows all the fancy kicks and flips and shit. When she does a perfect tornado crescent kick, I like the way her ass looks in those tight workout pants—Ow, fuck! You're supposed to warn me before you bite."

Venom hardened the edge of Colita's voice as she said, "Never mind about the girl's ass. I want to know what it is you see in Rayne. Do you imagine her when you're with me?" Colita sat up on her knees and folded her arms, petulant and bratty, while glaring at Kyle.

Seriously?!

This hot alien woman was thousands of years old and jealous of a girl from Little Rock, Arkansas.

Kyle sighed, refusing to lie. "Life beats in time to Rayne's smile. Making her laugh is an addiction with a sweet reward and almost no downside, aside from unrequited love. And I can't even hold that against Rayne. She loves Sagan, and they're kinda made for each other. I'm happy for both of them."

Colita quirked a brow, less than happy.

Kyle realized he'd neglected to answer her question and sat up to meet Colita head on. He cupped her nape under all those curls and kissed her until he left the Icarean female breathless.

After breaking the kiss to stare in Colita's eyes, Kyle said, "No. I don't imagine Rayne when I'm with you." How could he? They were nothing alike, but if he wanted Colita to finish the blow job, that was best kept to himself.

Kyle sat next to Rayne in calculus, watching her stare at a notebook she let no one read. Chocked full of her secrets, he could smell the pencil lead and see his reflection in the shiny graphite.

What haunted Rayne so to warrant hundreds of words in private confession? Was Kyle mentioned anywhere in those pages?

Determined to make Rayne smile, he leaned over and whispered in her ear, "Want to crash Sagan's practice tonight?"

There.

Rayne beamed for Kyle, and he felt ten feet tall. His chest swelled with pride as he grinned back at her.

The bell rang, and Kyle followed Rayne to her locker. She traded one well-worn notebook for another, but in the brief glimpse of her personal storage, he noticed a machete.

Leave it to Rayne to prepare the wildest cache. How did she even sneak that shit into the school?

Tameka appeared at her locker across North Hall with a wave for Rayne, purposely ignoring Kyle. There was an extra skip in Tameka's step which grated on his nerves.

Kyle taunted, "What about your nights with Xelan always puts you in such a good mood?" Ugh, he hated the raw bitterness in his own voice.

Tameka rose to the bait. "What is it about your nights with Colita that leave you in such a foul one?"

It was a strange enough thing to spout across a milling student body to make some people stop and peer between the bickering pair.

Matt Anderson being one of them. He spared them both a glance before nodding at Kyle like a bro.

"Hey, Matt, wait up. Rayne and I will walk you out to baseball practice."

Rayne finished up and shut her locker, hugging her notebook to her chest. "If you don't mind the company."

Matt's all-American smile didn't quite reach his ridiculously dark eyes as he said, "Sure," a little tightly.

In their four years as the class of 2006, Kyle couldn't recall Matt ever having a date or a partner or even a rival. Except maybe Justin, but nobody liked that cocksucker. It seemed Matt liked to keep to himself.

Kyle could get behind that. He joined Matt on the walk down the hall, leaving Rayne to say goodbye to Tameka. As much as Kyle loved Sagan, he hadn't really thought this afternoon through. It would be him on the bleachers playing third wheel to Rayne and Sagan's discrete flirting.

Shit.

Conspiratorially, he leaned in and muttered to Matt, "Hey, man. You got a joint?"

Straight-faced, completely non-bullshitting, the baseball star said, "Naw. I don't do drugs. It's bad for the game."

Kyle knew his eyes widened a little, but he let it go as Rayne ran up behind them. To Kyle's dismay, her eyes flitted over the heads in the hallway, counting.

To distract and comfort Rayne, Kyle wrapped an arm around her shoulder and side-squeezed her for good measure. It seemed to break her of the habit.

"Oh, hey. Coach is looking for me. I better head over. You two have fun." Matt's half-sincere smile looked practiced out of social necessity, but Kyle got the gist of it.

He gave Matt a nod. "Thanks, man. See you."

Rayne waved. "Bye, Matt."

After leaving the baseball diamond, Kyle and Rayne walked in silence up the hill to the track. Sagan was already warming up, gentle on her ankle, when Rayne whistled.

The blond lit up, and Kyle was glad he'd thought of this. The girls ran into each other's arms, as he found a seat in the bleachers. Not for the first time, he wished Andrew went to the same school if only for a joint.

Hey...

Where were the girls headed?

Nosy as fuck, Kyle followed along the stands until the girls settled against a support column beneath him. Through the risers, Kyle watched Sagan and Rayne—

Oh, yes.

This was way better than getting high.

The girls made out in a coordinated frenzy. Aware of their limited time and privacy, they stole each other's breath away. After five minutes of them making out, Kyle felt more lonely than turned on until...

"I knew it!"

Cecily.

The annoying Overachiever had brought company. Lucy followed her under the bleachers, looking more curious than disdainful. She warned, "Cecily's already told Stacia. She's gone to get Justin."

Breathless from fear or from amazing Rayne kisses, Sagan said, "But he's not back from the away game."

Cecily put her hands on her hips and sneered, "Their bus just pulled in. Wait until Justin hears about this."

Rayne put herself between Cecily and Sagan, turned to her girlfriend, and muttered reassurances.

Sagan looked freaked out.

They'd also attracted a bit of a crowd as Stacia stormed by the baseball diamond with Justin parting the sea of people on their way to the girls.

Kyle jumped off the risers to back them up, but Rayne held up a hand. The look in her eyes...

Justin was so dead.

The crowd following Justin included the entire Wareagles football team and half the baseball team. Matt's eyes stayed on the back of Justin's head like he was ready to remove it himself.

No shortage of enemies here.

Still, Justin got in Rayne's face, saying, "Move."

Sagan broke into a sob behind Rayne, but their leader never batted an eyelash. "No."

"Move or I'll make you move."

Kyle almost took a step forward, but he knew better. Rayne had this.

She smiled a most dangerous smile. "Put your hands on me and see what happens."

Justin laughed and placed both his hands on Rayne's shoulders to set her bodily aside.

Coiled tight, she sprung loose and punched him in the gut.

The air whooshed out of Justin as he doubled over. All around people gaped, but Rayne wasn't done.

With a deft blow, she kneed Justin in the face and spin-kicked him into the support beam. He slid down the brick, where Rayne jumped on his leg.

The crack whipped through the crowd, and Justin finally gathered enough air to bellow in agony.

Kyle didn't know if he should grin or frown. On the one hand, the drama with that prick was over. Finally. On the other, there was no way Rayne wasn't getting suspended.

"What is happening down here?"

On cue, Mrs. Mendax made her way through the underside of the risers and the crowd. "Ms. Callahan, what have you done now?"

Before Kyle or Sagan could offer a defense for Rayne, Matt said, "Justin fell off the bleachers. We all came to check on him."

Justin still couldn't form coherent words. All the piece of shit did was howl like a little bitch.

Lucy peered between Cecily and Matt, looking ready to speak. Before Lucy could say a word, Stacia said, "That's not what happened. Rayne—"

"Came to help me first. God, Mrs. Mendax, I need an ambulance."

Everyone whipped around to glare at Justin. He was staring daggers at Stacia, apparently playing along with Matt's pretense.

Either Justin feared Rayne enough to keep his mouth shut, or, more likely, he didn't want the entire school to hear about a girl kicking his ass.

Kyle would bet on the latter.

Mrs. Mendax broke out a cell phone, breaking the zero tolerance policy. "I'll call an ambulance. Don't move."

As she stepped away to call, Justin glared at Rayne, who smiled beatifically back at him. She mouthed, "It's. Over."

Justin mouthed back, "That's. What. You. Think."

Sagan took Rayne by the arm. "C'mon. I want to get back to practice."

Kyle followed the girls back to the track and glanced over his shoulder at Justin. The abusive football player kept his eyes on Rayne's back, but he glanced at Kyle for a brief second.

Kyle flipped him off and nodded at Matt, who waved before heading back to practice.

This school was a drama factory, but at least they'd built some solid allies over the last four years.

Here's hoping they survived the invasion.

"Xelan, I had a dream—not a memory—about Celindria last night," Rayne confessed.

Concerned, Xelan lowered the throwing knife he was about to launch at her, asking, "Is that unusual?"

Rayne sounded a little defensive as she said, "Not entirely, but this one seemed different."

Despite how much the stress had altered her mood lately, he maintained his patience with her. "Why is that?"

"I think she's trying to warn me."

Every muscle in Xelan's body stiffened as he asked, "Warn you?" Since Celindria's death, he could say his grief had manifested more than one dream about his First Progeny. It wasn't unusual. But with Nox invading Rayne's subconscious, only Elden knew what else was happening in Rayne's mind.

Surrounded by the peace of their training ground, Rayne's eyes darted from obstacle to tree to picnic table.

Anywhere, but meeting Xelan's eyes as she admitted, "Celindria said I couldn't trust anyone. That someone would betray our group. Someone already had in the past." When he kept silent, she pressed, "Do you know what she's talking about?"

Divide and conquer.

Someone was playing a game with Xelan's Progeny.

He cleared his throat before speaking. Twice. "There are many differences between you and Celindria. Like in this situation, you came to me and you told me about this dream. Celindria wouldn't. She'd always suspected there was a traitor among us, but she never told me who she'd suspected, and I never asked."

Rayne finally gave him the full force of her stare and asked, "So you don't know who it could be, either?"

He shoved the knives and other training materials into his duffel. Now *he* was the one who couldn't meet her eyes. "I don't think you should tell anyone about this. It was only a dream."

Rayne said, "But she was—"

Slightly on edge, Xelan didn't mean to move faster than she could see. The alien-ness of it always took her breath away, setting him further apart from her. That was the last thing he wanted.

Xelan gently took both her hands and tried to communicate his sincerity with his eyes. "Your unit only works strongest when it's whole. If it's pulled apart by even a single member, every one of you would be vulnerable." He knew because he'd seen it happen after Merit's passing.

Rayne started to object, and he gave a gentle tug on her hands. "A single thread, frayed with doubt, could unravel the unit. No matter what you suspect, no matter what she told you, keep the unit together for now. I will work on discovering any potential threats."

Rayne asked, "So don't tell them?"

"Absolutely not." Xelan shook his head.

"What will you do when you find the traitor?"

"End them."

Then Rayne asked Xelan's least favorite question. "When?"

She need not specify. By now, he knew what she meant. Xelan appreciated Rayne's determination and dedication, but tonight it bordered on obsession.

"When will they come?" Rayne asked for the fortieth time. She walked away from Xelan, leaving his hands empty. Although the training session went well, she'd clung to the subject of the invasion like her sanity depended on it.

Maintaining his patience, Xelan said, "I told you it could happen at any moment."

Tonight, any attempts to placate her only seemed to push Rayne further away as she said, "But you've been saying that for three years!" She unwound the boxing wrap from her knuckles in violent, rough jerks. "How much longer do we have to wait?! How long before we say the Icari called the entire thing off, and we can let everything go back to normal?"

Xelan rushed over to Rayne and took her bleeding fists in his hands again, trying to stem her angry fretting. Like before, he shook them once until she met his eyes.

The eighteen-year-old girl with all those muscles and all that aggressive training met Xelan's gaze.

He recoiled and almost dropped Rayne's hands at the callowness on her face. Xelan asked, "Why? Why do you want this so badly? Wherever you are, whatever you're doing, Nox will find you and slaughter everyone around you. Why are you asking for this?"

"Because I want it over with."

Xelan gently opened Rayne's hands and took them in his own.

She continued, "I hate this constant preparedness. I hate waking up every morning from terrible dreams only to live the day wondering if they'll come true this time or tomorrow. Or are we safe now? Did it blow over?"

Xelan squeezed her hands. "Rayne, sometimes I forget how young you are and for that I'm sorry. But as long as you have those dreams, you know it isn't over."

Into the dark of the surrounding night, Rayne spoke one breathy word that carried on the wind.

"When?"

Xelan drove to his installation upset on Rayne's behalf, lost in his own determination to find her peace. He gripped the Jag's steering wheel tightly, bothered by the direction of his thoughts.

This was a risk. A huge risk. It would jeopardize Xelan's entire operation, but Rayne was worth it.

No time to stop. No time to plan. Because if he gave this even one iota of consideration beyond, "Just get it over with," then Xelan would lose his nerve.

Three in the morning meant the IONA-01 skeleton crew was sitting down to lunch.

Perfect.

Xelan whipped the car into the hangar and rushed into his office unimpeded. There, he dialed Lucas' number.

No greeting. No preamble.

When Lucas answered, all Xelan had to say was, "It's time," to get the ball rolling on an irreversible decision.

Rayne's peace.

That's all Xelan wanted.

So when Lucas escorted Caedes and Frullop into IONA-01 at 4:00AM, Xelan clenched his jaw and faced the music.

For Rayne.

"I have intelligence I want to exchange for a favor."

Frullop eyed Xelan suspiciously, but Caedes' eyes sparkled with intelligence as he asked, "What favor do you seek from The Brethren?"

From behind his powerful cohorts, Lucas gave Xelan a reassuring nod.

He cleared his throat before saying, "I request an investigation into the conduit. I believe there's been a breach."

Frullop and Caedes exchanged a glance before the sturdy bald Icarus folded his arms and asked with more gravel in his voice, "What makes you suspect a breach?"

Lucas winced, knowing what Xelan would say next. "I've been in contact with the Progeny, and Nox torments young Rayne Callahan in her dreams. He's invading her mind." Concern clutched at Xelan's heart as he worried about what else of hers Nox had invaded.

Xelan expected more surprise at his confession, but the only reaction was Frullop's sneer turned into more of a snarl as the rabid Icarus said, "You've violated the terms of your exile. We should report you to Enki's Tribunal."

'Should.'

Interesting.

With his hands up in a placating gesture toward the other members, Lucas stepped between them and Xelan. "I think we understand why Xelan aided the Progeny—They're helpless without our protection."

Caedes wasn't having it. "We walk a fine line with Enki, and your disregard for their authority endangers us all."

"So, we'll take over from here," Frullop announced with entirely too much delight.

Xelan looked between them with an entreating glance at his ally.

Lucas put a hand on Xelan's shoulder and shook his head.

There was nothing to do about it.

Fine. But...

"What about my request?" Xelan would not give up, for Rayne's sake.

Frullop gave a cavalier shrug.

Caedes huffed. "You think we don't know about the breach?"

Xelan felt his eyes triple in size.

Lucas squeezed Xelan's shoulder with an apologetic look. "I didn't want to burden you with this, but yes. Nox invaded around the time you first approached the Progeny in 2002. They've been squatting in the Cult of Night compounds, but believe me, old friend. I never suspected they were tormenting the Progeny. Spying on them? Yes. But not hurting Rayne."

Xelan swallowed the sinking feeling in his stomach to say, "Well, Nox is. This explains how, but can you do nothing about it? And what are your plans to stop the invasion? Is there an army to combat their forces? How many are there—"

"Those questions are none of your concern now." Frullop never said anything productive or assuring. "We're confining you to this installation and depriving you of further contact with the Progeny." The bastard turned his back and headed for the exit.

Xelan made to stop him, to confront him—

Lucas held Xelan off, golden eyes filled with grave concern. He shook his head, trying to stop Xelan.

But there was no stopping this. Rayne was in danger.

"What about Rayne?!"

Caedes was on his cellphone, calling in the order to surround IONA-01 with their soldiers. He finished and faced Xelan with regard in his gruff expression. "From what we've gathered, the Night King plans to invade within the next few months. Perhaps preparing for the primary assault will occupy him enough to leave the girl alone."

Still restraining Xelan, Lucas whispered into his ear, "I'll see to it."

Helicopters arrived, and trucks barreled down the drive.

The Brethren ceased operations in IONA-01 and brought an end to Xelan's preparations. And he'd told no one.

Rayne.

Tameka.

Xelan prayed to Elden they didn't believe he had abandoned them, because there was nothing he could do about it now.

EIGHT

THE END IS COMING SOONER THAN YOU THINK

{LITTLE ROCK, AR | APRIL 2006}

NIGHT AFTER NIGHT, KORAC STALKED RAYNE AT NOX'S BEHEST. They'd ceased their nocturnal pursuits of their targets four months prior. No dreams. No sweet laughter or the scent of watermelon arousal for four months. Absent from exhilaration for so long, Korac was downright unpleasant to be around.

Pissy didn't cover it.

Nox's mood had fared even worse.

Why had the King ordered his General to abandon the dream facet of their mission? Was it because Korac was winning the wager? And then to demand the General follow Rayne around seemed like a taunt. 'Enjoy watching my girl kiss your girl from afar.'

Fuck off.

At least, the new objective had proved entertaining.

Rayne fancied herself a superhero. Since The Brethren reigned in the traitor, the young Progeny woman acted out by dressing all in black and pitting herself against the terrors of the night.

Robbery.
Assault.
Rape.
Rayne thwarted it all.

And when she wasn't up to those hijinks, Rayne sang at a dive bar to a seedy crowd of men with appetites darker than she could imagine. Her rich alto begged for a man to put his hands on her. A man with a cold ring and about a foot of height difference between them.

Rayne beckoned Nox to take her.

Korac waited at the back alley for the rebellious girl to exit after her set. She did so, flipping her curled hair out of her heavily lined eyes. If Korac hadn't seen Rayne climb out of her second-story window, he'd wonder how she'd left the house in a fishnet top and a bra. From following her, he knew she'd bought those skin-tight leather pants with her bookstore earnings.

'Trouble' was Rayne's new middle name, and she never bit off more than she could chew. At least, as far as she knew. Korac would intervene if necessary.

"Don't worry, Sagan," Rayne said into her cellphone on her walk to the main street. "If Justin comes near you again, I'll break his other leg." She gave a flirty, fake-modest laugh. "Well, how was I supposed to know steroids would weaken his bones? Dosing must've shriveled his brains along with his balls—Hang on, Sagan. Let me call you back."

From the rooftops, Korac watched a human male step in Rayne's way. She stopped walking as she hung up and squared off with the stranger. Behind her, another potential threat emerged, boxing her in.

Korac was remiss to admit, he appreciated Rayne's smirk as she asked, "Can I help you, boys?"

The greasier of the two said, "We were hoping to make your wish come true."

"Yeah, pretty girl. Think you could 'skin me with your tongue'?" Thing Two chuckled, amused at his reference to Rayne's lyrics.

Perched on the roof, Korac inhaled the humid April air. In the time it took him to exhale, Rayne had laid the greasy guy low and stomped him with her high-heeled combat boot.

The second assailant snarled, "Bitch," and flipped open a blade. "Hold still, or I'll cut that grin off your sweet face."

Rayne *was* grinning broad enough to make her guardian proud. She flicked her hand, encouraging Thing Two to come at her with the knife.

Foolishly, the brute charged at her.

Rayne kicked off one wall of the alley, spun and kicked off the other to match her opponent's height. Up there, she boxed his ears.

He growled and backed off with his head between his hands.

Rayne stood over her quarry and said, "Next time, pick on someone your own size. Or how about not picking on anyone at all? Creep." She kicked him the ribs and even from this vantage point, Korac could hear them break.

He followed along the rooftops as Rayne headed back to her parents' car. She'd borrowed it without permission, like every other night. The Callahan's worked hard and slept heavy.

Korac tailed Rayne home in a discrete SUV, but the girl didn't stay inside the modest two-story for long. After thirty minutes, she reemerged in workout gear.

Ah…

To the training course Rayne went, like clockwork. There, she ran and vaulted obstacles, counting her heart rate in a merciless tick Korac couldn't help but commiserate with.

There was no further need of him this night. Korac left Rayne in the care of his soldiers, who guarded the periphery to prevent anyone from encroaching on Nox's investment.

What exactly had the King of Cinder invested in Rayne Callahan? Korac wished he knew.

Why ask the General to watch her? All it accomplished was Korac's begrudging approval. Rayne had grown into a competent fighter with a twisted side. The girl simultaneously baited Nox to take her or Xelan to rescue her after both had disappeared from her life in the last four months. There was a temptation to respect Rayne or worse, like her, but Korac would never forget the destruction Celindria had wrought. Her descendant had to pay for the ancestor's sins.

Right?

Korac pondered this the entire way back to the compound. Above all of the static of Rayne and Nox, Korac's libido begged for a hot bath with Sagan. She was never far from his thoughts, evident by the violet pocket square the same shade as Sagan's eyes. He'd commissioned a matching belt, hoping to use it on her. Soon.

In some ways, Korac both anticipated and dreaded the invasion. Finally, they would reap what Celindria had sowed. But would Sagan still want him after? Could she compartmentalize everything to come? As he pulled into the compound, he could only pray to Elden Sagan saw the coming future as Korac did.

The Little Rock Justice greeted him, wobbling after a long day walking incorrectly in those kitten heels. "Silver General, greetings. May I have a word with you?"

No.

"What is it?" Korac wasn't even two steps out of the car before this haughty human bore down on him with her pretentious demands. So, he hurried through the halls to the royal quarters, forcing her aching feet to keep up.

Huffing with the exertion, she said, "Well, everyone is wondering when can we expect to serve the invasion? The other Justices are eager to deliver the message of faith to mankind."

Eager for nacres. Eager for a slightly elevated station at the end of the world.

Korac resisted the urge to roll his eyes with a groan. Instead, he grasped for some eloquent rhetoric to shut her up. "Your fealty is every Icarus' greatest treasure. We will reward you beyond your imagination. No dream could match the prosperity you'll soon know. We only ask for a little more of your patience." He stopped outside the hallway to the royal quarters where Icarean guards prevented humans from entering aside from feedings.

The Justice bowed deep enough to impress Korac. "Thank you, Silver General. We patiently await your orders."

"Soon, Justice, you will have everything you deserve." Korac turned and left her on the threshold before knocking on the door to Nox's quarters.

"Enter, Korac."

How did he always know?

Korac entered to find Nox staring at the fire once again, as if it were the black flames of his pyre back home. Could he see Rayne's shape in the orange flicker?

Nox said, "If you're here, she must be on the training course for the night. Am I correct?"

Korac bowed with his head. "Yes, sire."

The King of Cinder smiled. "Good. Let her tire. Let her ache. Does she eat?"

"No, your majesty. Rayne survives on meager snitches of calories forced on her by a concerned mother."

With his eyes reflecting fire, Nox humphed in satisfaction. "Quite."

After a long second in silence, Korac stared into the flames, saying, "When we invade, she *will* fall to you."

Nox met Korac's eyes then, and the General *knew.*

This was it.

A thrill shot through Korac, and he said, "I'll mobilize the troops immediately, sire."

"See to it, General."

Before Korac could leave Nox's quarters, the King called, "Good luck with the wager, soldier."

It set the General's teeth on edge for his King's mood to sour so. "You as well, your majesty." He left Nox to his obsession before knocking on Colita's door.

After Sacramento, she answered with the first knock. "Yes, Korac?"

"It's time."

Her sky-blue eyes widened before her face transformed into a wicked smile. "Finally."

Korac needled her. "Did you ever manage to seduce any useful information from Andrew?"

Colita actually stuck her tongue out at him. "No. Did you ever get anything but amateur sex out of that girl you've been fucking every night?"

Korac chuckled and dug in his spurs. "I'll wager our King prefers Rayne's company to yours because the younger woman is less bratty."

Acid replaced the petulance as Colita spat, "Maybe you can give her lessons on her future as a slave—"

Faster than Colita could see, Korac cupped her cheek. As he put his face in hers, the viper's lips parted, releasing her heavy anticipatory breaths. Cinnamon perfumed the air, and she leaned closer for a kiss.

"Say what you want, Colita, you'd bed this former slave in a human heartbeat. If only I'd ever be desperate enough to resort to bestiality, blood whore."

Colita's eyes flashed Atramentous as she shouted, "Fuck you," and slammed the door in Korac's face.

He smirked.

It wasn't as gratifying as sex with Sagan, but it was almost as much fun.

Sweat dripped in Rayne's eyes. Her skin burned. Not even the early morning air could calm the storm in her. It had swelled over the last year, and this morning it raged.

Rayne had abandoned Xelan's old buddy system. Restless and even a little reckless, she worked out alone. Why bother? Danger pressed into these woods, and Rayne welcomed it. She invited anyone or anything to take her on.

Where did Xelan go? And her dreams… Why did they stop around the same time he disappeared?

In the last one, Rayne was sure she'd gotten through to Nox, but when he didn't return the next night or the night after...

Hope couldn't save her now.

So Rayne ran. She ran until every fiber in her quads and calves begged her to stop. Ran until her lungs shriveled and popped. Ran as if an imminence chased her. And she dared not slow down, never look back, because one day it just might catch up—

Rayne turned and screamed behind her, "Why?!"

Why did he go away? And which 'he' was she more upset about? Xelan or—

A gust in the darkness carried an ominous chill. A light whisper disguised in the breeze. It was a message. The words faint. A deep voice asked in hushed tones, "Is this enough for you?"

Great.

Now Rayne was hallucinating.

Alone and armed only with her anger, Rayne bolted down the familiar route once more. Eight hundred meters until home. The wind howled through the woods, and the underbrush swirled at her legs. She called on the last reserves of her strength and sprinted the final five hundred meters as fast as her fatigued legs would take her. Her heart rate skyrocketed well over 200BPM. She spared a glance behind her. Nothing, but...

Rayne couldn't remember the last time she'd felt completely alone.

With a grunt, absolutely not a whimper, Rayne vaulted the seven-foot privacy fence into her backyard. She lost maybe three seconds of her advantage.

Rushing to her front door, Rayne checked the knob. It was locked. When did she lock it? In her scramble for the key, she fumbled it out of her hands. "Shit!" Leaves rustled behind her. She turned slowly, facing whatever waited.

The front door opened, and Rayne recalled some trials frightened her more than others.

"Rayne. Echo. Callahan. What are you doing out at this time of night?"

If Rayne's heart pounded any harder in her chest, it might burst through her sternum.

"What's the matter with you, girl?" Michelle Callahan demanded a response.

Rayne lied, "Nothing, momma."

"How long have you been out of this house?"

Uncertain of the truth, Rayne lied, "About thirty minutes. I couldn't sleep."

"You don't sleep, and you don't eat. You don't even do your homework anymore. Then you run up on the front porch, scrambling for your keys like you're terrified of the dark. You make no sense." As her mom listed off her keen observations, it occurred to Rayne that she sucked at appearing normal. "Why are you half naked? It's freezing out there."

Rayne stifled a groan. She dragged her dying legs into the house and across the living room. Every step felt heavy. She glanced at her feet to check for cinder blocks. Nope. She said, "Mom, I went for a run—"

"In Southwest Little Rock?! In the dark? I know I raised you to be smarter than that. Just last week, that Night cult abducted two girls from Wal-Mart. All their bodies turned up on Granite Mountain." Her mom shook her head and pointed up the stairs. "Go to your room. I need to think about what I'll have to do with you."

Eighteen years old—almost nineteen—and her mom still treated Rayne like a child.

"And before you go thinking you're grown, you better remember this is *my* house. As long as you live under my roof you will go to school, make good grades, get into college, and live to be eighty years old. And you're gonna stop that running around Southwest Little Rock after dark or before dawn or however you want to word it." At last, Michelle tossed her hands in the air. "I've half a mind to make you close the store every night for two weeks. With no breaks."

Rayne trudged up the steps, tempted to crawl with her fatigued legs. Upstairs, she collected her clothes for her shower. Black and white. Her walls white. Her furniture black. The carpet black.

Although the hot shower had rinsed away the workout, Rayne still shivered. She needed to contact Xelan, but how? She needed his help to tell if she was hallucinating in her deteriorating mental state or if something had actually happened outside.

As Rayne prepared for the day, she passed her backpack on her desk. A short stack of homework mounted. Evidence of her apathy. Rayne brushed a history essay prompt with her fingertip. She loved history and writing. With a certain future ahead of her, what was the point? She closed her eyes, and the storm roared.

Rayne asked the empty room, "When?"

No answer.

Frustrated, she swept the stack off her desk. She considered throwing the lamp and busting the bookcase, but contained herself. Her mom might lock her in a padded room.

Downstairs, Michelle waited with breakfast. Rayne almost asked where Jack was, but then remembered he'd stayed the night with a less than reputable friend.

Her mom pulled out Rayne's chair. "Eat."

Homemade pancakes with real maple syrup, scrambled eggs, and sausage. Rayne waited for her mouth to water. Instead, her stomach turned while she fought not to groan.

Why didn't Rayne want to eat?

Four years ago, she'd shovel this feast in her face faster than her mom could pile on seconds. Thirds. Where did her appetite go?

"You're stressed, baby," Michelle said, her tone softened.

The storm abated. Why couldn't Rayne go back to being a kid? She pleaded in a tiny voice, "Momma?"

"C'mere."

Rayne rushed from the table to her mother's embrace. She ignored her initial urge to stop Michelle from smoothing her hair.

"Shh... It's okay. Listen." Her mom withdrew enough to meet Rayne's gaze. Her soft brown eyes shone with tears. "This is normal. You're in a tough place. Adult, but not enough to go out and live on your own. Your senior year. Going to college next year. It's a very stressful time." Michelle's face grew contemplative before saying, "Although, not as bad as when you were thirteen."

Rayne giggled. The thought of college made her frown again. Not for her.

"I'm worried about you. Will you promise me something?"

"Anything," Rayne answered, meaning it.

"Let's you and I have a chat tonight. Tell me everything. All of what's bothering you. Even the stuff you think I won't understand. We can get some milkshakes." Michelle held up a hand before Rayne could grimace. "Or whatever it is you have an appetite for these days. I'll even go on a run with you if it gets you talking to me. Deal?"

How would Michelle handle the truth? Would Xelan be mad at Rayne if she told? Well, he wasn't exactly around to answer the question, now was he? She said, "Yeah. I'd like that."

Michelle patted her daughter's arm. "Good. Now sit down and eat half your breakfast, and then I'll let you finish getting ready."

Rayne looked down at the heaping plate of carbs and proteins, and this time, she groaned.

"Nox is making his move, today."

Andrew stopped fishing his backpack out of his mom's Volkswagen. This was the last thing he needed on this nice spring day. He'd like to say Xelan's appearance had startled him, but the Icarus had been doing this a lot lately.

Andrew said, "Good morning to you, too," as he retrieved his bag. Only five minutes until the late bell. He wouldn't make it.

Xelan pulled the backpack from Andrew's grip with a sharp tug, panic written all over his Icarean features. "This isn't a drill."

"Look, dude, you're making me regret parking in the shade. All I have to do is walk one meter that way, and you'll have to harass someone else. While I'm glad Lucas is letting you out of your cage, I'm tired of The Brethren's false alarms. Every day last week, you told me Nox was coming with all of Cinder to tear our planet apart, and nothing came of it except a lot of marks on my truancy record."

The Icarean fighter hauled Andrew up off his feet and slammed him onto his mom's car, leaving a huge dent on the roof. Xelan stood over him. "I can't be there to warn Rayne, and The Brethren picked you to do it." He emphasized 'you' by jabbing his finger into Andrew's chest.

Xelan leaned over Andrew, on the verge of a breakdown. His voice shook with it as he said, "If anything happens to her because you weren't there to help the others, we all lose. If you don't go, Nox might take Rayne." As quickly as he'd thrown Andrew onto the car, Xelan leapt to the ground and straightened his coat.

As Andrew lay in the crater of the VW's exterior, he felt torn. On the one hand, he really wanted to blow Xelan off and go about his day. On the other, he'd never seen the Icarus' eyes filled with such unadulterated terror before. Clearly, this was it, and Andrew wasn't about to fail Rayne.

With a groan, he rolled himself off the top of the sedan and asked, "Do you know which plan they're going with?"

After Xelan explained, Andrew felt light-headed. He raced to a tree and lost his breakfast all over the roots. The Icarus, for all his earlier animosity, spared Andrew the shit-talking for once.

In a soft voice, Xelan said, "I'd offer to hold your hair, but I can't get to you."

It was a small comfort, but still appreciated. After a hard swallow and a gasp for air, Andrew choked out, "Will anyone survive?"

Kyle sensed Rayne's irritation long before her eye twitched with the ring of the first bell. Moody was a nice way to describe her behavior ever since Xelan abandoned them, but today seemed even worse.

From behind Rayne, Sagan mouthed to Kyle, "What's. Wrong?"

He shook his head and grabbed his bag. How the hell should he know? And there Rayne went about counting all the exits and how many people stood between her and the nearest one. They could tell by the way her eyes flicked and her lips moved with the numbers.

Something was up.

Acutely aware of the tension, Kyle led the girls to North Hall's riot gate. There, the security guards worked to roll the gates high above their heads, allowing the students access to their lockers with a scant five minutes before class started.

Assholes.

Sagan asked, "Why do they always put it off until the last minute?"

Rayne said, "For the power trip."

Kyle humphed his agreement as they made their way through the halls.

As Sagan rummaged through her messenger bag, it was hard not to stare at her cleavage in that red corset top, but Kyle managed. She said, "Great. I think I left my cheat sheet for the Anatomy exam in my locker."

In exaggerated alarm, Kyle's eyes widened, and he gasped. "Oh, no! You might get an 'A' minus!"

Rayne smiled at his joke at least.

Sagan stuck her tongue out. "Some of us want to get into good universities."

There it was. The big bomb. He blew out his breath on a whistle.

When Rayne whirled on Sagan, it nearly gave Kyle whiplash. Incredulous, Rayne asked, "Are you serious?!"

Sagan flinched.

Even Kyle winced at Rayne's tone.

At their responses, she softened a touch, opening her mouth to say something—

Rayne spun around, her eyes darting everywhere, counting and scanning the crowd.

This was not a drill. Kyle asked, "What's wrong?"

Sharp and alarmed, Rayne said, "I saw someone... White hair."

Sagan stiffened and joined the search. "Do you think...? Was it...? But it couldn't be."

Kyle had seen nothing, but he trusted Rayne's instincts.

"Are you three okay?" Tameka broke the tension.

With a sigh, Kyle stared at her. Rayne and Sagan did the same, blinking as if she were an apparition.

Tameka recoiled slightly. "What?"

In a show of vulnerability Kyle wanted to cure, Rayne hugged herself, stretching her white blouse across her defined arms and shoulders. "Nothing. I thought I saw something."

Sagan put an arm around her, and Rayne let her come in for a side hug.

It was more affection than Kyle had seen Rayne spare anyone in the last four months.

Tameka blew the air out of her cheeks before asking, "Is there anything I can do to help?"

"You can move expeditiously through the hall, young lady." Mrs. Mendax's voice rang off the wooden lockers to make up for her tiny stature.

Two students mocked in shrill, unified voices, "Expeditiously, everyone! Expeditiously!"

Kyle burst out in laughter. Sagan's grin made Rayne smile while Tameka shook her head.

The small woman threatened, "Gentlemen, straighten up before I write you up."

It made Kyle laugh even more. As if Mrs. Mendax would give herself the paperwork.

More students mocked her further down the hall, and for the first time in Kyle's tenure at J. A. Fair, Mrs. Mendax stomped her kitten-heeled foot and stormed off toward the office.

Sagan watched her go. "Did something finally get to her?"

Rayne nudged Kyle. "Come on. Let's get to class before the late bell rings."

Sagan broke off to her locker, making her tiny skirt spin. "Stay out of trouble. See you guys at lunch!" Her knee-high stilettos tapped as she walked away.

Tameka went to her locker next, grumbling about their quiz in Medical Science.

As Rayne went to her locker, Kyle leaned against it, trying for casual. Xelan taught them all the same covert methods of relaxed posture and unassuming stance. They couldn't let the world know they were trained to be murderers.

Was it even murder if it was an alien?

After a quick glance in Rayne's locker, Kyle noticed her weapons cache had doubled in size since their guardian had disappeared. He kept his voice low as he said, "Rayne, if you want to talk about anything, I'm right here."

She switched out worn notebooks, sparing Kyle an appreciative glance. Then she lied to his face. "Everything's fine."

"Rayne, I think—"

"Don't you have somewhere to be?" The sass, the salt, the scorn. Tameka knew which buttons to push, and she loved to push them. Often.

Kyle scowled at her.

Tameka's eyes narrowed like emerald shards. "Why are you always following Rayne like a puppy?"

Classmates passed through the hall. Some paused and took notice of the scene.

Instead of rising to take Tameka's bait, Kyle smirked and said, "Everyone's gotta have a hobby." To Rayne, he added, "I'll see you at lunch." He considered ruffling her hair, but then thought better of it.

A whistle caught his attention, and Kyle looked over to see Nikki waving from the door to Spanish III. He crossed through the milling bodies to get to her. "What's up?"

Tiny and sweet, Nikki's shy smile always made Kyle feel like a giant. She asked, "Is Rayne doing better today?"

"Unfortunately not," Kyle answered with a frown. When he glimpsed John further in the class, Kyle nodded at him while saying, "I don't think she'll be okay until Xelan comes back or something else gives."

Nikki's sad frown was adorable and disheartening all at once.

Kyle lifted her chin with a finger until she met his eyes again. "Try not to worry, okay?"

Some light returned to Nikki's pale blue eyes, and she smiled in a way that made Kyle appreciate her pale freckles more. "Atta girl. See you at lunch."

Anatomy was further down the hall, and Sagan was waiting for Kyle by the door with a wave. On their way to their seats, Sagan asked, "Was that about Rayne?"

Kyle nodded, not at all prepared for this morning's exam. He knew all about stabbing holes in an Icarean body, but not all that much about human anatomy. "Hey, let me copy your cheat sheet real quick."

Sagan's violet eyes widened cutely. "Are you serious?"

"Yeah. Just for a second. I'll give them right back—"

The lights in the hall went off, raising the hair on the back of Kyle's neck. They were motion-censored, and students were still rushing to their classes. Combine that eerie fact with Rayne's earlier freak out, and a chill shot down Kyle's spine.

"Sagan."

"I see it." She sounded as unnerved as Kyle felt.

That's when the first scream tore through the school, followed by a chorus of terror and mayhem.

The two trained fighters breathed the same word at once.

"Rayne."

When Rebecca Mendax heard her office door connect with the jamb, she wrenched the kitten heels off her aching feet. Checking the clock, she groaned. Eight-thirty in the morning. "Seven more hours to go."

But Rebecca had signed up for this. Fifteen years ago, she'd agreed to promote out of teaching into principal duties. She'd understood long hours came with the territory. She'd just underestimated how hard the work would be.

J. A. Fair had always scored beneath public school standards, but never as bad as the last five years. These days, the guidance counselors replaced college brochures with Burger King applications.

All that mattered was the reason Rebecca got into education and accepted the principal position at this school. She'd never forget that.

Clicking her tongue, Mrs. Mendax walked over to her desk. Why so much footwork? Five days a week, she'd patrolled the halls on a near hourly basis to catch kids skipping or up to no good. Then there was her least favorite time of day: class change. At four foot nine, Rebecca hardly impressed her students as she shouted for them to move faster through the halls.

And her feet always hurt.

With that in mind, Rebecca swept a hand over the cushion of her seat and lowered herself onto it. Before the back of her skirt even touched the leather surface, a knock sounded from her door.

Rebecca groaned. "Yes?"

A muffled voice wavered from beyond the door. "Mrs. Mendax, we need you at the front office. Urgently." The vice principal, sounded upset or bothered.

Something was wrong.

"I'll be right there." Lamenting the interruption of her down time, Mrs. Mendax re-shoed her feet and hurried to the door. With narrowed eyes, she examined the VP. "How may I help you?"

The woman's eyes brimmed with tears as she said, "Please. The front office. Please." Her voice shook and carried an edge of panic.

Alert and irritated, Mrs. Mendax pushed past her simpering subordinate and stomped to the front office. After an increase in the trend, mass shootings had become a constant concern of school staff. Except for Rebecca. That wasn't her destiny. But why else would one of her VPs knock on Rebecca's door on the verge of pissing herself? Prepared to talk some sense into a crazed teenager, she barged into the front office.

How could Mrs. Mendax prepare for this?

A man with white hair an inch longer than his ass examined their intercom system and muttered, "Yes, this will do nicely." He flipped a switch with leather fingerless gloves. When he stood, his leather coat creaked, and it swayed around him. He smiled brilliantly at the sight of Mrs. Mendax, saying, "Hello. I'll bet this works great as a sound system." He indicated the intercom speaker.

Two men entered both front doors to the office and shielded the exits.

Rebecca resisted the urge to recoil. Instead, she asked, "I beg your pardon?"

"Oh, that's not all you'll beg for," the white-haired man assured

Mrs. Mendax gave in and recoiled this time. Did he have any idea who she was?

As if in answer, a remote, disturbing smile crept onto his lips. "Rebecca. May I call you Rebecca?" He paced away from the intercom system and draped an arm across a secretary's cube.

The secretary tried to shrivel further into her work space.

Mrs. Mendax straightened herself and shuddered as she shook off the nagging sensation of impending doom. "You may." She used the same firm tone as she would use on some of her toughest delinquent students.

"Thanks." The smile dialed down into something that could be mistaken for charming. "I'm having girl troubles."

Rebecca blinked. Was he serious? She stopped herself from laughing. The situation grew more ridiculous with each moment.

He ignored her discomfort and carried on. "There's this girl I like, see? Brilliant. Beautiful. Blond. And I'm trying to impress her with the perfect entrance."

Mrs. Mendax nodded to show she followed along.

He shone her another winning smile, saying, "I'm glad you understand. This school . . ." He circled his index finger around. "Is the perfect place, but it's missing something."

Rebecca rose to the bait, "What's that?"

"A soundtrack. Boys!"

Two men by the door lunged for the staff behind the counter. The secretaries and counselors burst from their desks and tried to bolt for the doors. The white-haired man grabbed the woman nearest him, and, in an act of mercy, snapped her neck. He ran, jumped onto a desk, and leapt onto a retreating counselor.

Mrs. Mendax heard the woman scream, then a snarl, and finally nothing. The two men at the front lay sprawled dead across the counter. From behind Rebecca, where two people had escaped, she heard muffled cries. More men waited back there. In a few minutes, the invaders had disposed of the entire office staff.

Rebecca swiped blood off her lapels. "So this is it, then? His majesty didn't inform me it was happening so soon. I thought you would notify me to make preparations."

The Silver General stood and wiped the blood from his mouth before saying, "He's been most impressed with you, Justice Mendax, and the other followers."

Justice Mendax nodded. "I make good on my promises." Four fucking years of housing Icari across the world. Feeding them scraps from the lower-end of the socio-economical table. The Cult of Night had even earned themselves a reputation after the FBI had investigated them for cultist ideology. Humans understood so little.

Rebecca straightened her jacket as she took in the blood all around the room and on the office doors. After clearing her throat, she asked, "What does the Master wish for me to do next? I can help find the girls or all of the Progeny, if you like."

The Silver General smiled down at her, saying, "There'll be no need for that. The Night King said it was time for you to receive payment."

Rebecca flushed with excitement. Finally, her time had come. Laying on the humility never hurt. "Payment? I am but a humble servant to the Pretiosum Cruor. I only wish to assist the Night King."

The second-in-command chuckled, and his genuine smile curled into a cruel smirk.

Strong arms grabbed Justice Mendax from behind. She cried out, "What's the meaning of this! I did everything I was told, and I brought the Progeny together! I serve the Master! We all serve the Night King!"

"To put it simply, he'd suspected you'd want a meet and greet. Picture. Autograph. You know? And this being the culmination of thousands of years of work, he doesn't want to waste any time on fans. You understand. Now, hold still. This will hurt a lot."

The Silver General stepped toward her, and Justice Mendax screamed. Her screams were the last sound she'd ever hear. The blood-smeared face of her Master's second-in-command was the last sight she'd ever see. And her aching feet were the last sensation she'd ever feel.

NINE

'ALWAYS BE PREPARED' ISN'T JUST A MOTTO FOR THE SCOUTS

CELINDRIA'S DESCENDANT WOULD KNOW NOX WAS HERE. He wanted Rayne to feel him nearby. Wanted her quaking and terrified. She would soon surrender her entire race to him, and had no way of knowing, yet. Although she must know...

This was always meant to be.

The cloth across Nox's back itched and pressed into him. He resented the heavy cloak, and his need to cover himself on this planet. He'd ruled Cinder as its King for thousands of years with no need to hide from their sun. But no matter. The cloak served for dramatic effect. This moment, eight thousand years in the making, called for some theatrics.

Colita's warriors flanked Nox, where they stood at the mouth of North Hall in menacing dress. Frightened students ran into the nearest classroom. Some were too petrified to move or scream.

Until the first shriek sounded. It came not from a young student, but from an adult. A teacher. She walked out to investigate the commotion, took one look at Nox, and broke into a shrill fit before hurrying into her classroom.

The scream resonated to the opposite end of the school, where Colita was cutting the sprinkler lines and preparing the explosives. At present, Korac took care of a most inconvenient errand for Nox. Each of them had prepared for their own moment. Each of them were electric with anticipation.

Nox flexed his ringed fist around a nacre in his palm, and Colita's soldiers deployed to cover the exits. Poised on the brink, the tension intensified as the aroma of amped-up human adrenaline enticed Nox's predatory senses. Weak humans pressed their faces to the glass of a nearby classroom. He glared through the window, and the people stayed inside.

Oh, how Nox wanted the buildup before the climax to last. For the shrieks to announce his presence. He knew Rayne's heart pounded as if he'd held it in his hand. Tears would breach her lashes. Overcome, overwrought, and oh, just a tad bit...

Excited.

Nox flexed his fist again until the nails bit into his palm. The amber glass pearl refused to break in his grip, no matter how often he tried. Soon, he would convince Rayne to swallow it—Force her, if he must. Then afterward, passion would consume them. There was time enough for that in a few hours. An eternity waited for them after today.

Nox approached the first bank of lockers, and Colita's men grunted on cue. He continued his stroll down North Hall, passing classrooms filled with intoxicating donors. He stopped at the end where cursed light beamed through the glass exit, drawing a line the Icari couldn't cross.

For now.

Rayne was so close. Around the corner. Utterly frightened. Dread would drain her lovely fair skin, almost as pale as the most beautiful women on Cinder. Her wide, bright-blue eyes shedding tears from the delicious adrenaline spike. Her delicate mouth parted, allowing short, quivering breaths.

Nox desired to taste Rayne's lips, splashed with salty tears, for the first time outside of one of her dreams. He wanted her to look exactly as she did now, underneath him on their pallet beside his fire. He imagined his fingers tangled in that beautiful midnight hair.

There would be time enough for that. Here and now , the security guard approached, and Nox flexed his fist one last time.

The invasion began.

Screams from North Hall alerted Tameka to the darkness outside the Med Lab door. Before she could even ask what was wrong, Dr. Jones pushed two lab tables against the jam, barricading them in.

"Get behind the incinerator!"

Med Lab was the size of three regular classrooms. Rows of desks made up the front third of the space, and chunky black lab tables comprised the middle of the room. The last third contained stainless steel gurneys. Upper and lower cabinets consumed the wall space and hugged the incinerator, which divided the medical space with a large glass door, resembling a massive microwave oven.

Tameka stood and found the rest of the class frozen in terror. She shouted, "Go!"

Pablo jumped up first and nudged the student next to him, saying, "C'mon. Let's move!"

Lynn spared Tameka a concerned glance before rushing back with the rest. The only person who didn't move was Rayne. She stared at the inky darkness outside the door with her eyes so wide a tear fell out of them.

Dr. Jones crouched until her eyes were level with Rayne's. "I know it's terrifying, but you need to get back with the rest. I'll hold them off for as long as I can."

Tameka whispered in Rayne's ear, "We have to move. Talk to me, Callahan."

"Nox."

The word hit Tameka as if Rayne had slapped her. Tameka cried, "Are you fucking kidding me?!"

Another tear spilled from Rayne's lashes as she said, "He's here. I can feel him."

Dr. Jones looked between them, concerned and confused, before asking, "Do you know the terrorists?"

This was it.

Tameka shivered before kicking it into high gear. As she rushed to look out the door, she said, "They're aliens, and they're invading Earth."

Some gasps followed, but the teacher frowned. "Please. This isn't a game. Get behind the incinerator with the others—"

Glass shattered from the window along the ceiling—the only source of natural light in the sunken room. Closer to it, behind the incinerator, the students shrieked as massive claws swiped for them through the window. More screams echoed their panic from deeper in the school as other classes opened and spilled out into the hallway.

"Back this way—No! Don't run out!" Tameka cursed. This was so out of hand. She turned to Dr. Jones and said, "I don't have time to explain everything to you, but that is an alien monster attacking the window. And bet your ass, it's intentional. They *want* us to flee the classrooms."

Pablo, Lynn, and the others huddled together in the center of the room, far from the window and the door. But nowhere was truly safe. Tameka scanned outside the door, barely able to see anything for the pitch darkness. Bodies stampeded by to the chorus of shrill cries—

A face appeared in the small window, with angles chiseled from gray stone and eyes the bright yellow of a citrine. He assessed Tameka in equal measure before hissing in her face, revealing elongated canines.

She recoiled an entire step back, and he dismissed his interest in her by marching for the emergency exit.

"Get back from the door," Rayne ordered, her bright blue eyes clear once more. "You're right. They want us afraid." She faced the class of frightened students and one confounded teacher, who looked more convinced with every passing minute.

When Rayne took a steadying breath, Tameka knew she'd donned the leadership hat. Rayne addressed the class, "You will survive this. Tameka and I will see to it, but you have to listen to everything we say."

Dr. Jones glanced back at the broken windows, muttering, "The entire school knows you're involved in something, Rayne. No one fights the way you do at such a young age without excellent cause. Is this it?" She turned and met Rayne's eyes. "Is this what you've been preparing for?"

Rayne and Tameka shared a glance before nodding simultaneously.

Dr. Jones shored herself and joined the students in the center of the room. "Then we'll listen."

The nod from Rayne gave Tameka the floor. She took out her cell phone, saying, "Try calling anyone for help—Yes, I know we aren't allowed to have our phones, but maybe they'll save our lives today. So everyone, call." She tried her parents first—

No dial tone.

No signal.

Tameka tried to move around the classroom, searching for a signal, and almost ran into Lynn, who was doing the same. Her dark brown eyes were grim as she shook her head.

"I got nothing."

"Same."

"Me, too. No signal."

All the students with cell phones agreed, there was nothing.

Another scream tore through the hall, closer, followed by gurgling wet sounds—

"Rayne, what're you doing?" Dr. Jones stayed with the students, calling after the martyr.

She was scouting the broken window with half her head in the sunlight.

Tameka ran over, chiding, "What the hell do you think you're doing? Those things might eat you—"

"They're gone." Rayne hopped out of the window. "I think they meant for those monsters to scare everyone into the hallways." She explained to the huddle of classmates, "The aliens can't go into the sunlight. They're like vampires. You'll be safe outside, but just in case those things are guarding the perimeter, wait for us at the football field."

Dr. Jones glanced at her charges before asking, "What about you two?"

Tameka looked toward the door where the Icarus had glared at her. "We have work to do."

Lynn held up a hand, saying, "One minute." She opened the nearest cabinet and grabbed some gauze, wound packing, and antiseptic. "Like Chris showed us. You two might need this out there."

Rayne clasped Lynn's shoulder. "Great thinking. Actually, we could use some volunteers to stay in the Med Lab in case we send anyone needing medical help. You can tell the survivors to hide at the football field."

"I'm your girl." Lynn stomped on a table leg at the joint, breaking it off. She inspected the sharp shiv before flipping it in her hand. "Nineteen years of survival training might finally come in handy."

Of all the times for Rayne to smile, of course it was amid the apocalypse.

Tameka raised her brows, impressed. So the Progeny weren't the only ones with a doomsday plan. Setting that story aside for later, she said, "You'll need someone to stay with you."

Pablo licked his lips nervously, fight or flight warring in his warm brown eyes. He looked ready to haul his ass through that window to the football field, but also like he needed a nudge to volunteer and help Lynn.

Tameka gave him that nudge. "Pablo, do you think you can handle this?"

He glanced from Tameka to Lynn, and wet his lips before nodding anxiously. "I want to help."

Rayne beamed. "Good. Make do with what you can."

Lynn gave him a considering look, but shrugged with her arms full of supplies. "C'mon. We need wound packing."

Pablo's rich brown complexion paled, but he did as she'd asked.

Tameka kept her eyes on the window in the door as she muttered to Rayne, "We need to get to our caches."

"You're right, but what about the Icarus outside?"

With a crack of her knuckles and a stretch to loosen the tension in her neck, Tameka said, "Leave it to me."

A chorus of screams from the hall prompted Dr. Jones to say, "This is impossible. You can't expect me to let my *students* defend this class from an alien invasion."

As Rayne cleared the tables from the door, Tameka snatched two giant bottles of peroxide out of Pablo's arms and loaded them into her messenger bag. "Watch me." She tested the swing of the heavy parcel. Ready or not.

At Tameka's nod, Rayne opened the door and stepped out, calling, "Hey, lemon eyes. Looking for me?"

It was a risk using Rayne as bait, but Tameka trusted Xelan's training. Sure enough, Rayne darted inside, and Tameka wound up the bag as the soldier's heavy boots ran closer. She timed it just right and swung the improvised weapon into the Icarean warrior's face.

He stumbled back into the hallway with a snarl as Dr. Jones and the class drew in a collective gasp.

Rayne went to work with a solid roundhouse kick to the Icarus' diaphragm.

While he was unsteady, Tameka didn't waste time and swung to take out his knees.

"Lynn!" Rayne called.

Their friend tossed her the makeshift stake, and Rayne stabbed up through his ribcage into his chest until he fell still.

Pablo breathed, "Just like a vampire."

Tameka stared at the cerulean blood welling around the puncture site. "Well, not exactly. Their brains and hearts are switched from ours, but most everything else checks out."

"Come on, class. Let's get to the football field." Dr. Jones led her charges to the window, peered out, and gave a boost to the first student.

Tameka glanced at Rayne, who nodded her approval. This was a nightmare, but at least they'd saved a few students today. Tameka knelt and helped Rayne search the Icarus' cloak and pants for anything useful.

Pablo and Lynn helped Dr. Jones out of the classroom. She spared one last glance at Rayne and Tameka. "Are you sure you're prepared for this?"

Honestly, Tameka didn't know. All this time, Xelan told them the Icari couldn't withstand the radiation from their sun during the day. While she'd stashed weapons in her locker, Tameka had never truly expected the invasion to happen at school.

But there was something about Rayne—a shift in her behavior since the invasion started.

Purpose.

There was almost an eagerness to her which left Tameka unnerved.

With that fervor gleaming in her eyes, Rayne said, "We're ready."

Tameka supposed they'd need to be, or this was the end of everything. "Rayne, are you—"

A deafening roar thundered through the building and rocked Tameka unsteady. Horrific shrills followed the disruption. Structural debris—glass, beams, ceiling panels, duct work, cinder blocks—spattered and echoed from deeper within the school. An acrid smell filled the air.

Tameka and Rayne steadied each other. Pablo hit the floor, tangled in a pile of gauze. Lynn ducked under a lab table, as one should during an explosion.

An explosion.

It went off in South Hall. Goosebumps rose along Tameka's skin, her heart pounded in her chest, and the adrenaline unfocused her eyesight for a few seconds. The invasion was really happening, people they knew were dying, and Xelan wasn't around to help them.

For one heartbeat, Tameka allowed herself to feel the fear. To experience trauma in the making. She muttered, "What do we do?"

Rayne unsheathed a sword from the Icarus' gear and gazed at the Pretiosum Cruor emblem on the pommel. With enough confidence for the both of them, she said, "We send them back to Cinder."

Get to the weapons caches.

Find Sagan and Kyle.

Stop the invasion.

Tameka's faith was restored. "We got this."

"Oh my god." So much smoke.

"Oh my god." Everyone was screaming.

"Oh my god." The ground was shaking.

Lucy tried to right herself as the school rocked. Squeezing her hands over her ringing ears, she stood still in the dust, smoke, and debris. The fire alarms never went off. Shouldn't they go off?

Never mind. The screaming was noise enough.

Left alone in the programming classroom, Lucy staggered her numb limbs toward the door. Out in the hall, students squealed and funneled out of classrooms to escape the fire blazing in the technology hallway. So many bodies stood between her and the exit at South Hall. Lucy joined the crowd at the back and pushed her way through. She wanted to see the sunlight from the doors just at the end there.

A rumble elicited more cries from the terrified teenagers. Lucy gazed up at the ceiling in time to watch an enormous beam collapse and crush in a classmate's face. With fresh panic and screams, any semblance of order flew out the window. Chaos reigned. A wave surged through the crowd. Rushing forward became the only priority.

Lucy squeezed between her neighbors. Hands pushed on her back, elbows punched her ribs, and someone's ankle entangled hers. Lucy thought for sure she might fall down, but the other girl lost her footing and fell under the heaving heap of stampeding students.

The girl screamed as one foot mushed into her, another bashed her head, and another stomped her until the screams gurgled into nothing. Lucy knew if she ever slept again, she would hear that sound in her nightmares for the rest of her life.

The herd of people thinned as one hall spilled into another. But why was everyone turning right? The exit was on the left. Lucy emerged from the technology hall and stopped so abruptly the crowd sent her sprawling onto the floor. She slid shy of a man's combat boots.

The boots belonged to a behemoth guarding the exit. He snarled down at her with huge teeth and a sword. Startled, Lucy scurried onto her feet to rejoin the herd. After sparing a glance behind her, she noticed the man didn't give chase.

Lucy ran outside the flood now, and it refused to let her back in. Where the elbows had annoyed her before, they pained her now. The aggressive jabs forced her out of the way. In one last ditch effort to keep her place, she dove into the mess of them.

Someone smashed the side of Lucy's face against the lockers. The girl flattened Lucy there and ran off. Bodies brushed against her, feet rushed across her, her head smacked against a combination lock, and, without a doubt, Lucy would fall under the churning battery of shoes. Her screams would die after a time, like the trampled girl.

While the screaming never ceased, it took on a desensitizing rhythm. As the herd approached the cafeteria, that rhythm changed into an orchestra of sounds. Cries, grunts, groans, guttural sounds, wet sounds, crunching sounds. All of it awful. Some blood-drenched students ran screaming back into South Hall. They didn't get very far before arms reached out from the cafeteria and pulled them back inside.

Swept into a break in the lockers, Lucy opened the door next to her and popped inside. She recognized the recently built band room by the smell of new industrial carpet and paint. Cast in darkness, focusing on the new-room smell helped Lucy ignore the smell of smoke and a faint odor she didn't recognize. The stench made her pull her wrist to her mouth to stifle the urge to gag. Fumbling around the location of her fourth period class, Lucy stumbled over a desk. Beyond that was the podium, beyond that was the stage, and beyond that was the door. The way out.

Soundproof. Lucy no longer heard the violent deaths of her classmates.

What the hell was going on? How could this happen? Well, it certainly wouldn't happen to her. She planned to get the hell out of there.

When Lucy hopped around the podium to claim the stage, something grabbed her arm. She yelped and jumped back, knocking over a sheet music stand with a terrible clang. It rang in the eerie silence until a wailing moan came from the dark.

"Who's there?"

Someone coughed in response.

Nothing attacked Lucy. Was someone in the dark? Maybe hurt? She found the courage to walk back to the podium. No grabby hands this time. She blindly reached forward. There, denim. Wet denim.

A moan answered Lucy.

"Who are you? Are you hurt?"

Lucy cursed the darkness as she recalled her cellphone. One thing at a time. Check on this person. Then call the cops. As soon as she hit a button, Lucy's Nokia screen illuminated a patch of denim. She raised it slowly from the pants leg up to the hip then along the waist.

Lucy stopped.

The light bounced as her hands shook. So much blood. The person's shirt was soaked black with it.

Another moan made Lucy jerk her hand up higher. Mr. Kent's face was swollen black and blue.

Lucy dropped her phone and recoiled. She screamed as stands fell like dominoes around her. She tripped and landed with the lot of them and tried desperately to unhinge her foot from the base of one.

All the while, Mr. Kent echoed Lucy's screams to the best of his abilities. Frightened and in pain, he needed help, but how could she possibly help him?

Pulling herself out of the frenzy, Lucy lifted her phone from the ground by Mr. Kent's feet, slow and careful. This time the phone rattled in her hand. The light bounced around the room. She took a deep, calming breath and tried her best to be a decent human being. She refused to be like those students who'd crushed her against the lockers.

"Mr. Kent?"

He groaned and gargled.

"Mr. Kent, can you move?"

He thumped the podium.

Lucy swallowed as much apprehension as she could, resulting in a huge gulp that echoed in the room's nice acoustics. She examined him again, careful not to shine the light on his face. If Lucy possessed an empathetic bone in her body, it told her that discretion mattered here. Mr. Kent might not know he looked like a monster, and screeching in his face was not the kindest way to tell him.

"...Me."

Did he just say a word? "What was that, Mr. Kent?"

He moaned, "Mmm... me..."

Lucy moved closer, saying, "I'm sorry. I can't hear you. Can you try again?" This close, she found the source of the smell. It came from him.

"Ki-kill... me..." The words were faint. Would they be Mr. Kent's last? They should strike Lucy to the core, but it was odd how a battered face had numbed her. Somewhere in her subconscious, she'd already reached the same conclusion.

"Mr. Kent, I don't think I can do that," Lucy lied. Physically, it might prove harder than she'd expected, but she'd worked at her parents' vet office on the weekends. She helped euthanize animals. Lucy understood ending another's suffering, and right now Mr. Kent had suffered enough to warrant euthanasia. But letting other people know she took a cold, clinical approach to mercy killing could brand Lucy as a sociopath. So she lied.

Mr. Kent gripped a shard of wood in his hands. To Lucy's surprise, he'd filed a shank out of it against the podium.

She winced and asked, "Mr. Kent, can you move?"

He muttered again, "Kill. Me." He tried to hand Lucy the shiv.

"No, Mr. Kent. That won't work, anyway." She promptly shut up and used her phone to scan him one more time. Except for his face. No need to see that again. Those blue eyes beseeching Lucy against all that puffy flesh would haunt her nightmares forever, right alongside the trampled girl's screams.

Lucy shuddered.

There.

Mr. Kent's bleeding abdomen presented a more complicated case. A gut wound. Lucy turned her head away and tried to breathe shallow breaths. She refused to vomit. But damn it! She'd resigned herself to killing him.

Lucy said, "Okay."

Mr. Kent tried to hand her the shiv, and she pushed it away once more.

"No, it won't work." As Lucy contemplated her options, she scanned the room in the Nokia's dim light. Then she realized. "Of course."

Walking over to the music stands, Lucy picked up the bigger, sturdier of the bunch. The teacher's.

How messed up was this day that she was about to kill the band teacher with his own stand? At his request?!

Lucy divided it in half and poked the top to see if it was sharp enough. She wanted to put him down as painlessly as possible. Oh, who was she kidding?! This was gonna hurt like hell.

"Mr. Kent, are you sure?" Lucy said, trying to clear her conscience as she walked back over to him.

The band instructor gave one slow nod.

"You were one of my favorite teachers," She offered as some cold comfort here at the end.

Mr. Kent coughed and groaned louder than he had so far. A sob caught on the end.

With his head resting on the podium, Mr. Kent was already in the optimum position for what Lucy had planned to do. Before she allowed herself to think about it, she lifted the stand over her hand with both hands and thrust it into the back of his neck.

Mr. Kent's entire body convulsed against the podium. It wasn't terribly violent. More like a prolonged shiver. Desperately, Lucy looked anywhere else. After a second, she considered retrieving the stand and trying again. But then all went still. No more sounds.

Lucy stepped as close to Mr. Kent as she ought to and held her breath. She listened beyond her pounding heart for any signs he was still breathing. Still in pain. Nothing. Mr. Kent was dead, and Lucy had killed him. It wasn't anything like the animals.

Something burned Lucy's face. She pressed a hand to her cheek, felt the tears through her shock, and said, "Thank you, Mr Kent."

Sagan and Kyle tried to stop their Anatomy teacher from running out the door, but when beastly claws shattered the window at the back of the room, he bailed. The class followed his lead, and shortly after, their screams rose in a haggard chorus through North Hall.

And those claws...

Sagan recognized them from Korac's sketchbook. She ran to find Rayne and Tameka, but Kyle grabbed her arm, saying, "Wait. There's a reason for the pandemonium."

"But Rayne..." Sagan didn't need to finish her sentence looking into the concern in Kyle's eyes. He got it. She said, "Okay. What should we do?"

Kyle flipped open a ten-centimeter blade. "We work our way to them, one-by-one."

Sagan nodded, deciding to save the whole sketchbook conversation for later. "Got it." She turned a desk over and wrenched off a metal leg, asking, "Where were you hiding that thing, anyway?"

"Don't ask."

It was enough to make Sagan smile, and she caught Kyle checking for her reaction. They shared a moment of solidarity, certain they would live through this day. The chair leg gave, and Sagan twirled it. "Let's do this—"

Something erupted deeper in the school, and a cacophony of screams followed.

Kyle's eyes widened. "Holy shit. Explosives."

This day kept getting better and better. Sagan went to the door. "Come on. We need to get Rayne out of here before Nox finds her."

Kyle's frown deepened. "What makes you think he's even here?"

"Earlier, Rayne said she saw 'white hair.' I think she meant Korac's—I mean—the Silver General's hair. And sure, maybe Nox would trust Rayne with his second-in-command, but something tells me he'll want to confront her personally. He'll enjoy her fear." Sagan glanced around the door frame into the dark hallway and hurried back into the room. "There's one guarding the foreign language hall." She didn't mention the lumps of shadow surrounding the guard to herself, not willing to acknowledge the body count just yet.

Even as Sagan thought it, the vibrating buzz of the flood lights accompanied their red glow. They illuminated the blanket of dead students in a harsh crimson glare like a nightmare.

Kyle pressed against the wall alongside Sagan, saying, "All right. We get to Nikki and John, find Tameka and Rayne, and go from there. If we get outside, there's a chance we could survive until nightfall, except..."

Sagan clued into his train of thought. "Except how did they get in the building in the first place?! Shit. Well, one thing at a time. I'll provide a diversion; you get to Nikki and John. Got it?"

"Yes, ma'am. Being in charge suits you, by the way." Kyle gave her a nod of approval.

Instead of hiding her blush, Sagan ran into the hallway.

The Icarus stopped gnawing on the throat of a student and dropped her lifeless body to the ground. His expression wasn't murderous or hateful. It was devoid of emotion or understanding. So when he spoke in such a reasonable tone, it took Sagan aback. "The Afflicted One, your presence is demanded in the cafeteria." He took a step toward her.

Sagan could guess who'd demanded her presence. Was that spike of adrenaline from fear or excitement? She'd analyze that later. Right now, she used the adrenaline to fuel her mad dash to the science hall.

When the Icarean warrior pursued Sagan at a Michael Myers pace, he'd confirmed a theory for her: they wanted the Progeny alive. His slow pursuit afforded her a thirty-second advantage.

The chem lab welcomed Sagan with the smell of old textbooks and dry erase marker, the formula for decomposition half-written on the board. She ran to the back of the room, nudged the lab tables along the way, and hid behind one, hoping the Icarus would stalk past.

When he didn't, it confirmed another theory for Sagan.

"We can smell your fear."

Yikes.

After searching through the backpacks beside her for what she needed, Sagan stood and faced him, nudging the table closest to her. All the while she prayed he didn't notice why.

He came closer with his hands loose in a non-threatening posture, but the glyphs written on his handsome face added to the intimidation of his broad figure. He held out a hand like a vampire in every horror movie Sagan had ever seen and said, "Come with me."

She couldn't help it. Sagan cupped a hand over her mouth and snickered. At his frown, she said, "Oh, sorry. I know you can't help it, but that was so cheesy. Almost as bad as me saying, 'You're fired,' or 'Let me help you go out in a blaze of glory.'"

The frown deepened, marring his attractive face. It flickered with uncertainty as Sagan held up a lighter.

Yes, this was mayhem.

No, nothing would ever be the same after today.

Still, Sagan smirked as she lit the flame and tossed it into the center of the room into the cloud of gas leaked from the Bunsen burners after she'd disconnected their lines.

A hair-raising whoosh followed Sagan to the ground, and heat kissed her back as she curled into a ball, prepared for the worst.

Would Rayne forgive her prom date for burning off her hair and eyebrows in the apocalypse? Probably.

The Icarus shrieked in agony, and the odor of burnt flesh replaced the smell of knowledge in the classroom. Sagan crawled for the door, daring to glimpse for only a second at the figure ablaze in the room.

Some part of her heart ached. Why didn't he stop, drop, and roll? Was he too encumbered by his repressed intelligence to know any better? Should she help him?

But, no.

No, this was war, and Sagan needed to remember he was eating a human being when she found him. She locked the door on her way out of the room.

Surely, Kyle had found Nikki and John by now—

Sagan rounded the corner to North Hall and almost walked smack into two more Icarean warriors.

They were all dressed in the same gear—loose black pants and cloaks. And these two had yellow eyes as well. One was dark-complected, with the branches of an alien tree painted on his face. The other was pale, though not as pale as Korac, with the bone structure of a Roman bust.

Unsure if she could take two on at once, Sagan offered, "Has anyone ever told you two you should consider a career in modeling?"

Without regard for her banter, the Roman said, "The General waits."

Korac.

Sagan's confused heart fluttered, but before she could say anything, the Icarus with the tree on his face shrieked as a metal rod pierced through his chest from the back.

The Roman snarled and choked on a blood-smattering growl with more rage than anguish. A piece of metal also impaled him, but below his diaphragm.

Kyle's voice rang through North Hall. "John, you missed the brain!"

The tree warrior fell to the ground, revealing Nikki's tiny frame, coated in cobalt arterial spray. Never underestimate a short blond with freckles.

"Look out!"

John collided with Sagan hard enough to rattle her teeth together, biting her tongue. "Fuck!"

Tangled in his limbs, Sagan struggled to pry them apart, asking, "Are you okay?"

"Yeah, I'm just trying to remember how to breathe," John croaked. Where he rubbed his neck, mottled palm prints would later form bruises.

"Nikki!" Kyle shouted.

Sagan got to her feet as the Icarus lifted the teeny young woman by the throat and threatened to break her neck. Sagan ran into the fray, clawing at his hands as she cried, "The rod! Shove it in his brain!"

Kyle's tornado crescent kick landed and shifted the rod higher and deeper.

Further wrenching Sagan's heart, the Icarus' death throes screeched like an avian creature. Sagan would hear them in her dreams, reverberating off the wooden lockers in the dark.

The Icarean warrior succumbed to his wounds, fell to his knees, and curled further forward on his face. Dead.

John, panting from exertion, said, "We... did it."

Kyle cradled Nikki in his arms on the floor, asking her, "Are you all right?"

She shook her head, unable to speak for the terrible constriction visible around her neck.

"Wow. You guys are awesome."

The group looked toward the newcomers to find Rayne and Tameka were alive and safe, haloed by the red pool of floodlights.

Sagan closed her eyes on the verge of crying tears of gratitude.

The sassy redhead asked, "Are you ready to raid our stashes and stop this invasion?"

Kyle and Sagan answered, "Hell yes."

On their way to the other Progeny, Rayne and Tameka had evacuated most of the students—the remaining ones, anyway—to the football field, assuming the clawed beasts were guarding the perimeter. All the while, shrieks had ricocheted from North Hall.

The school's major artery pumped blood into the mouths of the invaders. The intruders craved this pandemonium. They lusted for the aphrodisiac of fear, the temptation of helplessness, and the enticement of adrenaline.

Now, the flow of human blood trickled, clotted by the Progeny. The unit made their way through the red-lit darkness, where Rayne counted twenty-two bodies. A girl was slumped against the next bank of lockers. She scrambled to check her pulse, but found her wrists were punctured. She was drained.

Beside Rayne, Sagan looked away. Tameka shook her head. Kyle carried Nikki on his back, stone-faced.

They kept moving.

John said, "I don't think I ever thanked you for sending Xelan to my house that day. But, yeah. Thanks, Callahan."

Rayne understood. If not for Xelan, Nox would have her already. No matter how many times Xelan warned her, this wasn't what she imagined the invasion would be like. Rather than meeting with Nox and resolving peace between them, there was only carnage.

Nox was insane.

She glanced at Sagan. Was she having similar thoughts about Korac? And how—

"Shit!" Rayne drifted on debris beneath her combat boots. The sharp remnants of a door caught her fall until she slid against her locker.

"Are you okay?" Tameka and Kyle cried at once, much to their irritation.

Rayne groaned as Sagan lifted her by the arm. She assured, "I'll be fine." There was no point in telling them about her hands. The broken glass bit into Rayne's skin like sharp gravel. "You get to your stash. I'll grab mine." She belted the sword she'd claimed from the first Icarus they'd killed in the Med Lab. Sadly, the last three were unarmed.

Tameka hesitated like she wanted to force the issue. Instead, she hopped over to her locker while mumbling, "Got it."

Kyle nodded at John. "I'll take these two to our lockers. We'll see you there." They headed further into the school with Nikki.

Rayne's hands reminded her of hamburger meat. The tiny chips coalesced into the tissue of her palms. There was no use in trying to pick those out. Rayne ripped the sleeves from her white blouse and gritted her teeth as she wrapped the wounds, glass and all. She hoped Tameka and Sagan weren't watching her.

Sagan gasped, pointing at Rayne's locker.

Rayne spun and examined the wooden cabinet under the dim light. Closer, she could see her machete was used to pin a folded sheet of paper to the door.

No.

No, no, no.

Tameka asked, "What is it, Rayne?"

With more effort than she'd expected, Rayne yanked the knife out. She said, "It's from my stash." With her back to Tameka and Sagan, Rayne opened the note.

Nox wrote it in blood. She almost rolled her eyes at how predictable it was, but, as she read on, a leaden weight sank in her gut.

IT STILL WON'T BE ENOUGH.

Icy dread calmed the storm in Rayne, suppressing any desire for Nox.

Behind her, Tameka sucked air through her teeth, and Sagan swallowed with an audible gulp. There was no sense in telling her best friends now that they'd read it for themselves.

Rayne broke the combination lock and rummaged through the disarray of her ransacked locker. She promised, "We'll get through this."

Inside, she located a leather bag stowed in the back. A small, tactical backpack concealed—originally—four knives, a Zippo lighter, two flares, and a bundle of twine. They didn't bother stealing their weapons, but all of Rayne's personal notebooks were missing.

She returned the machete to its sheath on a strap and wrapped it around her thigh. Between that and the sword, she imagined she made for quite the fearsome sight.

'It won't be enough,' her ass. With a quick glance in the mirror, she tied back her hair before turning to find Tameka and Sagan doing the same. Both of them armed to the teeth.

Tameka asked, "Do you think we'll be able to find hair-care products after the world ends?"

Bemused, Sagan smiled.

Rayne embraced her friends. "We'll make these aliens think twice about invading Earth."

Sagan's smile broadened into a grin. "We'll make Xelan proud."

Tameka leaned back into Rayne. "We'll save everyone, right?"

Rayne refused to lie to her. Instead, she said, "We'll save as many as we can."

The three girls found Kyle, John, and Nikki armed and ready at their lockers.

Kyle asked, "Should we check classrooms for survivors?"

They all looked to Rayne for the answer, and she wasn't sure.

What would Xelan do?

As if she'd read Rayne's thoughts, Tameka said, "I think we can best help any survivors by stopping the invasion before the fire spreads."

Smoke already formed a blanket overhead, deepening the darkness.

Nikki croaked, "But where?"

Sagan said, "The cafeteria. Two of the Icarean soldiers threatened to take me there."

Korac was seeking Sagan. Rayne searched her best friend's face for signs of internal struggle—

There.

Sagan's eyes darted away for a millisecond. She was hiding shame or curiosity.

Rayne wrapped her arm around Sagan's waist and squeezed before agreeing, "Then let's head to the cafeteria—"

"I'm sorry," John interrupted. "I know the Icari are here to invade Earth, but you've left out some details. Like who would want you in the cafeteria and why?"

Kyle opened his mouth to answer, but someone from behind cut him off.

"The King of Cinder, and he wants the five of us."

"Andrew!" Tameka cried out. She ran over to hug him, while everyone else gaped in shock.

Except John. He grumbled about people withholding information.

Andrew returned Tameka's embrace. He'd tied his long brown hair back from his face, baring the concern in his teal eyes as he examined their crew. Standing at five foot eight, he appeared solemn and suspiciously uninjured.

Rayne scanned him. Did Andrew walk into the middle of an apocalyptic invasion unscathed? How was he even here? He went to Hall High School, which was on the other side of town from Fair. Had the assault spread so far already? There was that icy dread in her veins again.

First things first. Rayne asked, "Is Hall under attack, too?"

Andrew shook his head. "I don't know. I was skipping class."

He just lied to Rayne's face. She narrowed her eyes at him and opened her mouth to call him out—

"Never mind that. We don't have much time because your school is seriously on fire. Are we going in after them?"

Everyone turned. They stared at her, expectantly.

Rayne smiled at Andrew. She might find the circumstances of his arrival suspicious, but having their fifth teammate here made a world of difference to their morale. Rayne said, "Exactly. And if we come across any victims, we can send them to the Med Lab."

Andrew dropped his duffle bag and spread it open to reveal medical supplies. The others dove in. Rayne watched everyone fill their bags and pockets. Their expressions were stoic and focused. She noted scrapes, wounds, cuts, and bruises on every single one of them.

A wave of guilt and shame washed over Rayne. Earlier this morning she'd wanted anything to come of Xelan's warnings, and now that it was here...

Rayne squeezed Andrew's shoulder. "Good work, Holt. I'm running to the restroom. You explain to John and Nikki about Nox and the Progeny. They deserve to know what they're dying for."

Andrew stared a little too long into Rayne's eyes before saying, "I don't think any of them are planning on dying, today."

She looked away then, mumbling, "Just tell them," and headed for the restroom two doors down.

As Rayne went to leave, she glimpsed Kyle spying her exit. He opened his mouth to say something to her, and Andrew swatted his arm. Kyle promptly made to cuss him out. At the shake of Andrew's head, Kyle listened for once.

She was grateful for the respite from her friends and ashamed of the relief.

As Andrew filled in the gaps, Rayne closed her eyes to it, turned her back on it, and walked away from it.

Confusion and ferocity. How could Rayne harbor feelings for a being capable of so much merciless destruction? And Nox wouldn't stop here. If Rayne couldn't fend him off back to Cinder, he'd conquer the Earth. Would that even be enough?

Is this enough for you?

"You can't think I'd let you walk away like that."

Sagan.

She'd followed Rayne into the restroom.

Rayne glimpsed her through the mirror in the red-lit room. As she watched, Sagan draped her arms around Rayne and rested her chin on her shoulder. She said, "Talk to me."

"I'm scared of myself," Rayne confessed, meeting Sagan's eyes.

The other girl stared back, and Rayne wondered if she could see the storm raging inside.

Sagan said, "Me, too." The next part she whispered, "And all those dreams of you and Nox or me and Korac? They'll never happen. Rayne, I want you to listen because this is important. If some part of you wants something to happen, forgive yourself. Don't hate yourself over something you can't control. We're young, impressionable girls, dammit, and they fucked with us in our dreams for four years. Don't you dare blame yourself for that or any of this. We're being invaded by aliens. Hot aliens who want to murder us. Whatever conflicting shit you're traumatizing over, it's okay. Take all of it and stab them in the face with it. Do you understand?!"

Rayne questioned Sagan's bravado. The girl's body trembled around her. Sagan was as terrified as Rayne. Maybe more.

But Rayne couldn't let that speech go to waste. "Yes." Her voice was tight with unshed tears. Not tears of anguish, but appreciation. She opened her eyes and pulled back from her friend. "You're right. No time for trauma. No time for tears."

Sagan shook her head. "No, you're wrong. There'll always be time for those things, but we have to be ready to fight with them, and everything else we've got."

"How are the others on supplies? Has Andrew finished briefing them yet?"

"They were just finishing up when I left. We could honestly use more medical supplies. Or a bazooka."

TEN

WARRIOR BEWARE, HERE BE MONSTERS

WHEN IT ALL STARTED, THE SCREAMS BLENDED INTO A MASSIVE CHORUS OF PAIN AND DEATH. From the moment the windows broke, Matt Anderson knew this wasn't a school shooting. The claws breaking the glass had tipped him off. As everyone in his biology class stampeded out the door, he'd slipped unnoticed into the drop-ceiling panel over his desk. The teacher didn't even spare a backward glance as she rushed after her students.

Matt tried to use his cell phone to call for help, but no signal. He'd kept his cool until the explosion rattled the school from South Hall. He'd never imagined himself as a soldier, but this felt like a war zone. Why would anyone reign an assault on J. A. Fair of all schools? And this was Little Rock, Arkansas for god's sake, not Washington D.C. or L.A. or New York. Something didn't add up.

Despite his concerns over the logic behind the attack, nothing changed the facts. It happened, and he needed to get out of the ceiling. Smoke permeated the tiny space, and he suspected the intruders had disabled the fire alarm and sprinklers.

In the last five minutes, the screams had died down from a chorus to an occasional solo. Matt was tough. He could handle a few one-on-one altercations.

Also, no gunfire. Not yet, anyway. Someone had emptied the entire school, blew up a portion of it, and never fired a shot? He definitely needed to find someone who knew what was going on.

Matt lifted the nearest tile back from the wall and surveyed the immediate area. Notta. He stuck his head out and observed the upside down classroom. Nothing. Now was as good a time as any. He hung one leg down until it found footing on the desk underneath, and the other leg followed right after.

All clear, Matt dropped out of the ceiling and laid flat on the ground. He crawled over to the door, trying to keep low. Careful not to scrape on the broken glass. He stood and planted his back against the door. He checked the window. Left. Right. Nothing.

Well, nothing but bodies. So many students' bodies littered the science hall. Should Matt have convinced a few classmates to climb in the ceiling with him? There was no way to guarantee he might live through this, so he couldn't vouch for the safety of others. But what would his friends think if they knew he'd let everyone run out while he'd suspected the broken glass was a diversion?

Matt shook the doubts from his head and assessed his current situation. Alone, he needed weapons, and he knew nothing about the 'enemy' except they used weapons other than guns. After ten minutes of breaking up furniture into makeshift shanks, he collected his bag of dangerous goodies.

Tentatively, Matt opened the door to the hallway. He approached the closest body, a brunette he'd never met. He nudged the girl's leg with his foot. No response. He searched her body over for any wounds. Leaning down, he pushed her hair aside and glanced over the marks on her neck. Some kind of bite. It caused alarms to ring in his head. She wasn't covered in blood. There was no pool of blood. There was no blood anywhere other than right at the wound. Exsanguination. Her murderers had removed the blood from her body.

Matt checked the black-haired guy next to her, same thing. He examined one more body. They all appeared to be exsanguinated. Bite marks. Blood loss. Vampires? That didn't seem right, aside from the fact that they didn't exist. But he knew all too well monsters were real.

He picked up his gear and headed for the exit. A very low and deep grumble carried from North Hall. Goosebumps pricked his skin. Matt's hair stood on end, and his spine went ramrod straight.

Was it one of them? Had he lingered too long?

Next came a sigh. Not really sounds he'd expect from an elite fighting force attacking the school and draining the students of blood. Especially not from vampires.

Matt spun on the spot and listened again, peering into North Hall. His instincts were at odds with himself. A chuff whispered from the hall.

That was it.

He needed to satisfy his curiosity. Marching down the hall, Matt stopped at the edge with his back pressed to the corner. Carefully, he took one searching glance and immediately withdrew. Two of the biggest dudes he'd ever seen were laid out in a heap in the hallway. The one with paint on his face laid still aside from the occasional whimper. A metal pole stuck out from his back.

Ignoring the morbidity of it, Matt reached down and unlaced a dead classmate's shoe. His breath came hard, and his pulse pounded as he contemplated all the years of his life leading up to this moment. He lifted the sneaker, steeled himself, and tossed it at the impaled guy.

"Umph," the stranger groaned. His head lolled over, and yellow eyes rolled around in his sockets.

Matt recoiled at the sight of them, but the stranger continued to lie on his back. Matt hugged the wall and crouched like he was a practiced member of the armed forces. He crept along the hallway until he reached the pile of weird looking dudes in cloaks.

The chiseled one looked dead with a chair leg stuck out of his chest. He wasn't going anywhere. But the guy sporting the tree on his face was alive, if unresponsive.

Matt pulled out one of his shanks and dared to poke the guy. Just a groan. With a piece of metal sticking out of the soldier's chest, Matt wondered how the hell he was breathing?

He knew what he wanted to do next, and he didn't want anyone to see him do it. He looked down the foreign language hall. Nothing. He looked back the way he came. Nothing. All clear. Rather than retract the metal already inside the guy's body, Matt plunged his shank in right next to it.

The stranger's tongue rolled out. A gasp escaped, but no more sound. Dead. Matt lifted the stranger's hand, and it fell limply to the linoleum with a splat. He knelt beside him and got to work.

Blue blood. Probably vampires. Maybe even alien vampires.

Chest punctured. He removed those implements of death.

With the metal chair legs gone, Matt explored the wound and cavity a little better. Between the unacceptable red emergency lighting, and the blood seeping into the wound, it proved difficult, but he found what he thought might be the heart. At least, if it were human, it would be.

From inside the chest, Matt lifted a human-like brain and brain stem, but they came from where the heart belonged in a human.

Bizarre.

Blood and very thick fluids slid down his hands, wrists, and elbows. He'd set the brain aside when something else caught his eye. There was an extra connection at the base of the brain stem to something inside the chest cavity.

Matt laid the brain down, gently, and dipped his hand back inside. There was a small chamber there, not dissimilar to the sac around a heart. He felt something hard in it. A nerve cluster, maybe? Feeling on the verge of something important, he pressed into the mucus lining and grasped the hard object inside. He retrieved a tiny, shining sphere.

An amber pearl.

Embracing the inner-scientist Matt usually ignored, he left his things in the hall and rushed back to his biology classroom. Microscopes, Bunsen burners, and vials lined the counter, but most importantly, a sink. After washing the pearl, he placed it under a microscope to examine it. Beautiful, but indiscernible. He couldn't glean a single bit of information from it. Still, he shoved it in his pocket until he understood the situation better.

After retrieving his bag, Matt froze when voices rose from North Hall. As they carried on, his body relaxed. He recognized them. Without checking, he turned the corner. Sagan and Rayne left the restroom halfway down the hallway. He whispered, "Hey."

They both startled as if he'd interrupted something. Matt thought better of apologizing, considering there were vampires attacking the school. They seemed to come to the same conclusion because Sagan said, "You have to get out of here."

Rayne joined in. "Go to the football field."

Matt held up a hand. "First, what's going on?"

Nikki only half-listened to Andrew's explanation of Nox, Korac, Colita, and their grudge against Rayne's ancestor. Instead, Nikki kept peering around Kyle to see if Rayne was on her way back from the restroom, yet.

"Don't worry. Sagan's with her," Kyle assured, clued into the direction of Nikki's distracted thoughts. As he discretely laced his fingers through hers, she soaked in the comfort.

At least there was someone else who shared Nikki's secret misery—A support group to pine in silence after the blue-eyed, midnight-haired beauty. Like with all unrequited love, Rayne was oblivious to their suffering. So, it was nice to see Kyle's eyes flick toward the hallway for the same reason Nikki couldn't keep from doing it.

When Rayne emerged through the terrible lighting, Nikki fought not to cry in delight. There was an additional sobering at the sight of Rayne and Sagan holding hands.

Rayne said, "Matt survived."

Sagan pointed behind them. "We just sent him out to the football field."

Well, there was some good news. Still, the reminder of peril filled Nikki with shame. This was an apocalypse, not an excuse to moon over Rayne, who looked perfectly content with Sagan.

Kyle squeezed Nikki's hand before releasing it. He said, "We're all caught up and ready to move on."

Tameka punched her fist into her palm. "Let's kick some ass."

Even though some tension had surrounded Andrew's arrival, the other four Progeny—Tameka, Sagan, Rayne, and Kyle—all gained some confidence by Andrew's presence. Nikki found it infectious. Even John stood a little straighter and gripped his knife tighter as they made their way down the hall.

Rayne took point and as they approached the library, Nikki heard her mutter, "Please, don't let there be anything around the corner."

Rayne, Andrew, and Kyle popped their heads around. Kyle cursed, and Andrew shook his head.

Nikki asked, "What is it?"

Rayne's eyes were on Sagan as she said, "Have a look."

Tameka and John went with Nikki to catch a peek.

An Icarus, almost as tall as the door, lingered inside the 'Media Center.' By the glare of the emergency lights, Nikki saw the attractive man was wearing black leather. Coat, pants, gloves with the fingers cut out, and heavy boots.

His straight, white hair flowed down to his waist, looking like a stereotypical Anime villain.

Nikki whispered, "Think we can slip past him to the cafeteria?"

Kyle shrugged. "Yeah, but we can't be sure if there's more waiting on us."

Rayne never took her eyes off Sagan, who looked as though she were afraid to peer into the library. Rayne said, "We take that chance."

John asked, "Is that Nox?"

Nikki said, "No. Remember? Korac has long white hair."

"Right. Hard to keep track of all these players."

Rayne beamed so brightly at Nikki's correct assumption that the wattage melted her heart. Rayne said, "Good eye, Nikki."

Sagan, on the other hand, hid something close to panic.

Tameka continued the briefing. "He's armed. Two weapons, but I can't tell what they are. We can't fight him with these." She shook her tiny knife for emphasis. "He's between us and the cafeteria, but we can make it."

John ticked off on his fingers, saying, "Okay, so we'll sneak by the library and hope like hell Krack or Borak or whatever his name is doesn't catch us?"

Sagan smiled. "To put it simply, smart ass, yes."

He shrugged. "Just making sure we're on the same page. Oh, and sorry, Kyle. I didn't mean to come for your title."

Sagan snickered. Nikki rolled her eyes. Kyle, resident smart ass, added, "Don't get cute."

Andrew muttered to the ceiling, "We're all gonna die."

Rayne took a deep breath before saying, "Okay. When I count to three, Tameka and I will run by the library. Andrew will go last with Kyle to be sure everyone gets there safely." She inched a little forward. "One. Two—"

"Wait, wait," Nikki said. "Do we go on three or after three?"

Tameka laughed.

"Three." Rayne and Tameka ran alongside the wall, past the Media Center entrance, and slipped around the corner.

Tameka signaled for John, Nikki, and Sagan to follow next.

As Nikki ran past, she glanced inside. Korac took a drag on his cigarette as he examined a 'Stamp-Out-Smoking' poster. He blew a smoke ring at it. Adrenaline kept Nikki from staring and blinking at his magnificence.

Andrew and Kyle brought up the rear.

As Andrew slipped into the hall, he muttered, "Man, I could really use one of those."

Sweat from stress cleared a streak through the soot on John's face. "Oh, yeah? Why don't you go ask him for one?"

The two glared at one another.

Nikki snickered—Again, inappropriate response, but she'd heard once that a morbid sense of humor in the face of adversity was healthy.

Someone put their hand on Nikki's back, and she peered up to find Rayne beaming down at her. The person Nikki wanted most said, "You're doing great."

As they made their way into the bowels of the burning school, Nikki knew there was nowhere else she'd rather be.

Andrew hated J. A. Fair. Why the fuck did someone build an underground school? There were no windows in the inner hallway. And what was with all these crazy gates?

One blocked their way out of North Hall, leading to the offices and the cafeteria.

Kyle, Rayne, and Tameka rattled it some, trying to raise it, but Andrew discovered a padlock keeping it in place. He said, "I guess we have to go around."

This was Andrew's first time meeting John, since they didn't attend the same school, and so far Andrew had kept from forming an opinion until the Osage teen said, "We'll march right into the deathtrap they've obviously made of the gym."

John's observation was likely spot on, but was this really the time for negativity?

Also, Andrew hated the side glances Rayne was shooting Andrew's way. She clearly found his arrival suspicious—And for good reason. Andrew's appearance at their school on the very day Nox invaded was suspicious as hell, but he couldn't live with himself if her wariness toward him distracted Rayne from the fight.

Nikki, a saint as far as Andrew was concerned, nudged John playfully as she said, "We won't let anything happen to you."

Kyle humphed.

With a reassuring smile, Sagan said, "There's only one way to find out."

Tameka cried, "What the fuck, Rayne?!"

The brunette's hair trailed behind her as she went headlong into the gym without checking inside.

They followed Rayne into the lion's den. Andrew breathed, "Oh, shit."

Six cloaked soldiers spanned the breadth of the gym, acting as personal guard to the woman who led them. Long legs, softly rounded hips, a tiny waist, and a modest chest made up her tall, athletic frame. The mass of blond curls around her face and shoulders emphasized the sky blue of her eyes.

Colita smiled. Large, curved canines protruded.

Andrew blinked, but no matter how hard he tried, the nightmare didn't go away.

Colita bowed her head, saying, "Celindria, Merit, and The Afflicted One." She greeted the three girls in front as she scanned their unit.

Kyle swallowed audibly, and Andrew knew instantly Kyle had let the Icarean female seduce him.

Tameka glanced at him.

Kyle's face filled with blood, and his eyes found the linoleum very interesting.

Rayne blinked at him. "Really?"

"What?! It was a dream!" he cried.

Andrew noticed John also looked elsewhere.

Sagan gaped, asking, "And you, too?"

Heat reddened John's complexion.

Rayne's jaw slacked open.

Tameka whistled. "Colita's been busy."

John shrugged.

Andrew understood.

Colita gasped in mock surprise. "Andrius. My, my. Our spy said you wouldn't be here. I suppose we were misled." She glanced over her shoulder.

The other soldiers took a step away from one warrior with mahogany-colored hair and skin the color of rust.

He stuttered over his apology, "Mistress, there was no way I could know—"

Colita cut him off with a sharp, "Silence!" Her voice echoed off the walls in one harsh hiss.

Tameka took point on this one. "Colita."

Colita grinned. As if remembering something unpleasant, she stamped her foot and sighed. "I was told to deliver you a message. Korac awaits you in the cafeteria." She rolled her eyes. "Not that you'll make it there. You bleeding hearts aren't a threat to me."

"You *should* worry," Tameka countered. "You know not all our hearts bleed so easily."

The cold iron in his unrelated sister's voice impressed Andrew.

Colita went still, the silence in the wake of it was painful before she said, "I will *make* them bleed." She smiled that twisted grin again. The malice in it turned her otherwise angelic face ugly.

Tameka glared at her as she said, "You don't have a heart or a brain."

Colita's sky-blue eyes narrowed into vertical slits. Her hands tightened into fists, and her voice came in layers. "I don't care what his majesty wants. I'll kill you myself, Merit."

"Then stop talking, bitch, and let's see you try."

Holy.

Shit.

Without taking a single step, Colita appeared in front of Tameka, lashing out with a backhand.

The redhead was ready for her and took one step back.

The Icarean female stumbled forward.

Tameka impressed Andrew by gripping Colita's hair and kneeing her in the stomach.

Colita choked and shrieked with rage, wasting precious time and energy.

Tameka slammed the other woman's head into a cement wall. With a dull crack, Colita dropped to the floor.

Sagan called out, "Tameka?"

"I'm fine."

Andrew breathed, "That was amazing."

Colita straightened and faced them. Her nose oozed a bright-blue waterfall. Both eyes were already black and blue.

Kyle raised his hand.

Andrew rolled his eyes with a sigh. "Yes?"

"Did we win already?"

John groaned.

Nikki blinked in awe.

Rayne grinned.

Far too soon, Colita's breathing improved. A force emanated from her which thickened the air. Then came an odd sound, subtle at first until louder it came. The sound of someone chewing popcorn, crunching and cracking. It came from Colita's nose.

The bleeding ceased. The color of her nose faded into lighter shades of green. Then yellow. The cartilage filled back into place, and blood receded from the wound, as the swelling faded. The blow would have killed a human. More's the pity.

Tameka whistled, impressed, before saying, "Instant plastic surgery… Nice. Where'd you learn that?"

Andrew clenched his jaw and said through his teeth, "The regenerative upgrades Xelan warned us about."

Kyle scoffed, "How the fuck are we supposed to fight that?"

Rayne admonished him. "Let's start by not admitting out loud that you don't know how."

Colita smiled with icy rage in her narrowed eyes. In a silken voice, she said, "I'll bury you in a mass grave under the rubble of this school, but first, you'll repay the lost blood of my soldiers." She made a gesture, and the six Icari marched forward.

They discarded the black cloaks, revealing similar monochrome uniforms, with shiny armor over black tunics and laced slacks. Each male was modeled after a different time and place. One exotic warrior after the next. From ancient Chinese to Nordic Norwegian, each Icarus distinguished themselves with Earth heritage.

Tameka shook her head. "Someone has a fetish."

Rayne counted everything in the room before saying, "Nikki, John, and Kyle?" At their nods, she continued, "You take the three on the right. Sagan, Andrew, and I? The three on the left."

Tameka bounced, asking, "What about me?"

Andrew almost smiled. It was obvious Tameka wanted to fight Colita.

Rayne *did* smile, and it was bitter while making Tameka's day. "You get Ms. Facelift."

Colita responded with a snap of her sizable teeth.

"Yes, ma'am!" Tameka grinned with anticipation.

The good guys took one collective step forward. The invading horde took one step back. Colita took two, so that she stood behind a barrier of muscle. Everyone gripped their knives tight and relaxed into a stance.

Rayne held her sword firm at her side.

Tameka stared at it and broke the silence. "Do you mind if we trade for this fight?" She waved her ten-centimeter knife. Child's play compared to the sword.

Rayne smiled and handed her the shining weapon, saying, "Only if you promise to kick her ass."

Colita cried from behind her meat wall, "Fuck you!"

A crackle sounded through the gym, and all fighters present turned to the intercom speakers. Except for Andrew. He was the only one with his eye on the prize as a smooth tenor came over the line.

"Now, Progeny, don't waste too much time on the opening act. A few more surprises are still in store, and the main event awaits you."

Colita glared at the speaker, asking, "Whose side is Korac on?!"

Music started playing and signaled the start of the fight. John, Nikki, and Kyle rushed their assigned set of alien soldiers. Andrew barreled into a Russian Icarus, shoved his substantial blade up through its ribcage, and let the soldier drop dead with a grunt.

So began the first battle of Invasion Day.

"Vampires are real, my ass. Those are just dickheads on PCP or some shit. Or fucking terrorists," Sagan's ex-boyfriend shouted abuse in Lucy's face against the backdrop of the football field.

Justin's stark white skin flared red with anger. Unfortunately, that was an all too familiar sight, and every day until six months ago he'd directed that fury at Sagan.

Even the teachers cowed and looked away, dipping off to smoke with the students at the other end of the field.

Cecily tried a calm and even voice, "People are dead. We have to stay here. Rayne was the only—"

"Since when in the fuck do you listen to Rayne, huh?! Or any of those freaks she hangs out with? They're probably in on this. Don't you know the freaks are the ones that shoot up schools for being bullied and shit?"

Another football player, Michael, shouted, "Yeah, man, what are we doing sitting around here?!" He joined Justin on the edge of campus, just beyond the football field.

"Those assholes will slaughter y'all and y'all are just gonna let them do it. Starting with Rayne."

"Rayne has never been one to stand for bullying. That's something you should know pretty well, Justin."

Matt noticed everyone looking at him as he walked onto the bleachers.

He pulled the battery out of his Nokia and replaced it while he spoke. "You'll get in Cecily's face and Lucy's face, but you won't get in Rayne's. Not after what she did to you at the end of football season. If she says she knows what's happening in the school and that I need to sit my ass in this football field and wait for her, then fine. That's what I'll do. But I won't sit here and listen to you bitch and call her shit you wouldn't say to her face while I wait." He never even spared a glance at Justin, but he knew what would come next.

Justin lunged forward like he meant to haul up the bleachers and beat Matt's ass. Michael made a show of holding Justin back. More importantly, Justin let him while he squealed, "You don't know a fucking thing, Anderson. You wanna talk about saying shit to people's faces, you get down here and say all that to mine." And he said many more lines to that effect.

Meanwhile, Matt powered on his cellphone and tried to find a signal.

Michael calmed Justin down while Lucy and Cecily approached Matt. The latter asked, "Did you get anything?"

"Naw, I don't think there's any signal to get. Did you notice the smoke plumes around us?" He nodded in various directions.

They followed his line of sight, and dread filled their eyes.

"I think this is bigger than our school."

Stacia screamed, "Hey, where are you going?!"

Justin and Michael had bolted to the student parking lot. Matt jumped up and raced the girls to the edge of the football field. Other students gathered to watch the spectacle.

While Matt trusted Rayne implicitly with their safety after she explained some things, he had wondered what would happen if someone tried to leave the school. "Justin! Michael! Get your asses back here!" Ah, fuck it. Why should he care what happened to a girlfriend abuser and his crony?

The guys climbed into Justin's truck—lifted, of course, thanks to his daddy's money. The ignition started fine, but for a brief second the fellas froze. They looked like they were thinking long and hard about this decision. They seemed too scared to move. Then Justin said something and hit the gas in reverse. They pulled out of the parking spot and drove along the pavement to the only exit on campus.

Matt, Lucy, Cecily, and the others watched them stop the truck at the bottom of the hill leading out of the parking lot. He debated if he wanted to see them turn back or press on while the truck eased up the hill toward the open gate.

That's when Matt heard a sound he would never forget if he lived through this.

A keening howl echoed through the trees and buildings comprising the campus. It raised the hair on his arms and gave him goosebumps. If that noise wasn't disturbing enough, he heard something too loud to describe as a rustle but definitely sounded like vegetation moving around by heavy force.

A tree fell over close to the truck and a giant monster, for lack of a better word, thundered out of the tree line heading straight for Justin's vehicle. A massive thing and all wrong—Its skin looked charred red and black, like a lit coal. It had horns on its head, and a snout like a big lizard. So many teeth—more than he wanted to count. Each one was longer than Matt's arm. The creature's wing span spread wider than Justin's extended cab with claws at the tip of each wing.

It bounded up to the truck on all six of its taloned feet. Every muscle honed on its twelve-foot mass strained as it rammed into the vehicle. The truck flipped once on its side, then stopped upside-down.

The girls next to Matt screamed as if they'd just found the air to do so.

His lungs refused to draw air. He stood frozen to the spot and filled with a mixture of fright and anticipation.

The beast stomped on the truck's undercarriage with its front four claws. The truck flattened with ease.

Lucy sank to her knees beside Matt as they watched the spectacle in horror.

Surely Justin and Michael were already dead. Unfortunately, as soon as he thought it, a pale hand stretched out of the driver's side window.

"No," Matt muttered. While he had no love for the two trapped inside, he didn't wish this demise on his worst enemy.

Cecily shrieked, "Save them!"

The gargoyle snatched onto the hand with its immensely large teeth and pulled. They heard Justin scream all the way across campus when the beast ripped his arm from its socket. A few people behind them retched, and at least one or two followed from the sounds and smells.

Matt searched internally for a response. He was numb. Desensitized. Nothing.

A howl pierced the air, followed by another and another. A chorus of beasts sang to each other inside the tree line bordering the entire school.

Cecily sobbed hysterically, "We're all gonna die!!"

Lucy went catatonic beside Matt.

More tears and desperate cries filled the air. Children. All of them were frightened children who were worried about their families and friends.

Although only eighteen himself, Matt shared little in common with the surrounding people, emotionally. People he liked and cared about were inside and nearby, but he didn't want them to know how much fun he was having.

"I won't tell you we'll be all right, but I will say that they warned us not to leave the perimeter. Now we know why. We need to stick together, wait this out, and help anyone who makes it out of that building alive," Matt said as he pointed to their high school. "As crazy as it is, we've always known Rayne, Sagan, Kyle, and them were different. They're inside there, now, trying to save us. We have to believe they're gonna make it."

He looked down the hill at the student parking lot to his Chevrolet Malibu and then turned back to his captive audience of terrified teenagers. Matt said, "I'll go down there to get my car."

This was met with many cries of "No" and "You can't."

Matt talked through it. "I'm just driving it back up here and seeing if I can get any kind of news on the radio. Does that sound like a plan?"

Students and teachers glanced at each other with nervous eyes, and he understood their reservations. But Matt had watched Justin and Michael closely. The monster didn't make a move on them until they attempted to drive through the gate. He had no intention of doing that.

"I'll go with you," Cecily announced.

A thrill of panic crawled up Matt's spine. "No!"

At the hurt look on her face, he raked a hand through his auburn hair.

In a calm voice, he reasoned, "No. In case something goes wrong, I don't want to be responsible for anyone else getting hurt."

That seemed to smooth things over.

Matt walked toward his car, offering over his shoulder, "I'll be right back." As he approached the student lot, he felt nothing. He hypothesized that the beasts were meant to keep the students within school grounds. He wasn't technically violating that rule.

The white interior of his little sedan was immaculate. The machete he kept under the passenger seat was the only thing dirty inside. He pulled it out for good measure. The Malibu crept back up the hill to the football field.

As Matt made his way up, he wondered if his kit in the trunk contained anything useful for this situation. He shook his head at the notion. Although he could explain the machete away as protection, there was no way he could explain the rest.

At the top of the hill, the students gathered around Matt's car. He winced, uncomfortable with their proximity to his dirty secrets, but there were bigger issues to deal with here.

"Turn it on." Stacia always came across as too bossy for his liking.

Matt turned on the radio, anyway. The sound of static filled the air. He said, "I'll try another station," as he turned the knob. More static.

"Try AM," someone in the crowd offered.

He obeyed with a deep frown on his face. They listened to the static for a moment, and then a beeping came through the airwaves.

The crowd murmured in response.

Matt leaned in closer to the speaker. "Shh, quiet."

The static cleared and the beeping droned into a message. The most terrifying message they would ever hear.

"Earthlings, humans, homo sapiens, we have weapons capable of destruction you cannot imagine. As you can see. We demand surrender from your leaders. The sooner they deliver it, the sooner we can begin administering mercy. Not a moment before. If you resist, we have no choice but to provide another demonstration and another. If you surrender, the populace will suffer almost no casualties. We want the human race to live. Surrender."

Pablo closed a cabinet door as soft as possible to avoid detection.

Lynn slammed one.

They definitely had two separate minds at this.

Rayne and the rest had left maybe thirty minutes ago. He and Lynn had been at it ever since. They opened every cabinet, scoured every drawer, and even busted the lock on the good stuff. Between them, they found suture kits, wound packs, and cast plaster.

"I know we promised Rayne that we'd help, but I'm kinda hoping we don't have to use this stuff," Pablo confessed.

Lynn rolled her eyes before she said, "First you won't fight, and now you're telling me you won't help the wounded?"

Pablo held up his hands, warding her off. "No! No. It's not that. I just hope no one shows up in bad enough shape to use it."

"They're probably all dead, anyway."

He blew the air out of his cheeks before saying, "You know? I used to like you."

Lynn gave him the finger without looking away from her work. "Oh, fuck off."

"No, I mean it. Lynn, you're funny in class, but not like a bitch to the teacher or anything. You pretend to struggle with the material, and I'm not the only one who figured that out. You even lent me your pencil once, and that really meant something to me." He pointed at her with a pack of gauze.

Lynn busied herself with organizing the supplies on the exam tables in the back of the class as she said, "I've lent that pencil out to plenty of people."

"Yeah, but that day you didn't have another one." Pablo's smile spread, assuming his flirting was making some headway. He licked his lips and made his way over to her, saying, "You're kind, and I don't know why you hide it."

Lynn mused, "Boy, everyone knows you flirt with anything in a skirt."

Pablo approached her at the table. "But few know how observant I am." His smile softened as he leaned against her. "When you think no one's looking, you do the kindest things. You compliment and build up other girls. You help the teachers grade papers. And you'd do anything you can for anyone in choir. You're a modest saint."

Pablo brushed a braid away from Lynn's face. The softness in her brown eyes told him that he was finally getting through to her. While it's true, he didn't want to die a virgin, he also really liked Lynn and wished he'd made his move before the world ended.

"Pablo," Lynn spoke his name in a husky whisper.

"Yes?"

She said, "Lick your lips one more time."

Pablo, aware of how much the girls liked his full lips, gave Lynn what she wanted very, *very* slowly. She smashed his face down to hers and pressed their lips together. Going with it, he wrapped his arms around her waist and pulled her tighter.

Unexpectedly, Lynn jumped up and wrapped her legs around Pablo's hips. Because of his undue lack of preparedness, they both tipped over and fell to the ground. She landed on top of him and didn't miss a beat.

Lynn's nails raked along his skin as her warm hands snaked under his shirt and made their way up his abs. Thank god for his workout routine. The softness of her lips, and the sweet merciful give of them as he tested his tongue for permission to enter, forced his hips to undulate under hers.

Slow. Easy. Don't push.

Lynn moaned, and all systems were go. His tongue explored the inside of her mouth; she unbuckled his pants. It all seemed to move a lot faster than Pablo had expected for his first time. It was as if both of them clawed desperately at each other for this fleeting moment of normalcy.

Voices from the hall made them bolt upright. Lynn rolled over to let Pablo fix his shirt while she adjusted her hair. His heart pounded for so many reasons. She made to stand, but he stopped her.

Pablo whispered, "I'll go check."

He stood and tried hard not to take offense at the amused twinkle in Lynn's eyes. With caution, he approached the door. All the while, the voices grew louder. An entire crowd of people gathered outside the Med Lab door: five of them students and two teachers. The teachers braced one limping student between them.

Pablo rolled up the sleeves on his overshirt, saying, "Lynn, there's some people hurt out here." He opened the door and stepped outside. "Hey, hey, we're human." He put his hands up to show he was unarmed.

Lynn followed his lead and raised her hands. He smiled sadly when he saw her braids were still tousled from their make-out session. If he ever got the chance to muss them up again, he wanted to do it right and alone with her spread out beneath—

"Hi, we have supplies in here," Lynn assured. "Mr. Palmer, are you all right?"

"Yes, but not all of us." The history teacher nodded at the girl between him and the other teacher.

"Bring them in here. We can help," Pablo said as he waved them inside.

Pablo and Mr. Palmer lifted the girl with the limp as gently as they could and placed her on the exam table Lynn had set up. She and two other students helped another onto the second table.

Mr. Palmer searched around the classroom and at all the supplies they'd gathered. "Where's Dr. Jones?"

Pablo said, "She's out on the football field, where you'll be headed as soon as we finish here." He grabbed a pair of scissors.

The girl flinched and hissed. The panic stressed her injury and caused her to groan.

"I won't hurt you. I only need to cut your jeans to see better."

She bit her lip and looked over at Mr. Palmer for reassurance. He patted her hand. "He's going to do what he can to help."

Well, except maybe setting a bone without an X-Ray, which is exactly what this girl needed.

After Pablo pulled away the blood-soaked material of her jeans, he shook his head as if that might remove the image from his brain. Her tibia, the lower leg bone, had broken the skin of her shin. He tried hard to see it for all the blood and tissue, but he thought maybe her fibula was broken beneath it. Monsters like these didn't settle for flesh wounds. They went for the bone.

Pablo didn't know what was happening outside of the school, but if Rayne and Sagan thought it was on a global scale, they were screwed. He worried that if any hospitals were still standing, they'd be full and run out of supplies and doctors quickly.

Lynn inhaled sharply across the room. Even with her back to him, Pablo saw the fine tremor of her shoulders. Everyone around her patient stared at the girl as if they were wondering how she'd made it this far without dying.

Determined, Pablo prepared the splints, readied the wraps, and smiled reassuringly at his patient. He said, "I'll tell you the story about a girl named Rayne and how she and her friends will save the world."

Pablo set to work.

Four out of six of Colita's guards fell to the floor with gulfing wounds in their chests, eyes, and necks. The remaining two would soon join them.

Sweat beaded against Tameka's topaz skin as she stood over a prone Colita. The Progeny girl held the swordpoint to the Icarean woman's chest. The realization this was the end dawned in the alien's sky-blue eyes. Those same eyes sought mercy in Tameka's expression who gave her nothing but icy justice in return.

Colita licked her lips before pleading for her life. "Nox is here for Celindria; not you. Do you really want to go any further? Do you have any idea what he'll do to you?! He wants her blood and her soul. He'll spare you for her!"

Tameka knelt, straddling Colita's waist. She enjoyed the exaggerated show of pointing the sword against the blond murderer's sternum.

This was for Merit.

As if Colita saw it in Tameka's eyes, more begging followed. "I wouldn't wish that fate on even my worst enemy. Not even on you!" The last she screamed with a glance at Rayne. "You should try to escape this place! Do you really believe that you could defeat him? That you could kill him?!"

Rayne finished defeating an Icarean soldier before she knelt, put her lips to Colita's ear, and said, "Yes."

With a deep sense of satisfaction, Tameka's fiery curls bounced as she pushed the sword until the point punched linoleum. Colita's eyes were wide open with shock. Tameka stood withdrawing the sword, drenched in fresh blood. She passed it back to Rayne.

Her best friend accepted it with a smile and a pat on Tameka's shoulder. She said, "Thanks."

Kyle nudged Colita with his foot, staring as she shifted without response. He asked, "Do you think she's dead?"

Nikki's eyes widened. "Can they come back?"

Sagan shuddered.

Rayne glared at Kyle, who gave a casual shrug. He seemed unconcerned by the death of his dream lover.

Andrew spoke up, "It's time to go."

Rayne turned to the others, saying, "They'll patrol the area outside the cafeteria. I want everyone to spread out, but not so far that you're out of hearing range. Make sure you can see at least one of us at all times."

Even Tameka nodded along in agreement with no questions and a sense of anticipation. She said, "Let's go."

As Rayne took point, Tameka glanced at her best friend's hand where it held the sword. Tiny red droplets fell from the soaked bandages. Their leader turned and stepped over Colita's body.

As they walked away, Tameka spared a furtive, longing glance at Colita's head.

"What the hell?" Rayne halted outside the south entrance to the gym.

"What is it?" Tameka strained to see around Sagan, who also stopped short and stared at something on the ground. She squeezed through them.

Someone had laid out a black sign on the blood-soaked tiles.

STAMP OUT SMOKING.

Tameka frowned.

Sagan hissed, "He knows we defeated her."

John asked, "Did that Sephiroth-looking dude really just leave this here for us to find?!"

Andrew snarled, "He's messing with us. Focus on the priorities. Remember?"

Rayne squeezed Sagan's shoulder. "Are you good?"

Tameka felt a little left out. Why was Rayne so worried about Sagan every time Korac came up? She wanted to press, but it wasn't really the time.

Sagan gave a weak smile before saying, "I'm fine. We can do this."

Rayne patted her hand and went ahead. Tameka and the rest followed.

"Are we going straight in there?" John whispered.

"I am," Rayne announced loudly to anything that might overhear.

Tameka wondered why Rayne was acting so reckless. She and Sagan were keeping secrets, and it was affecting their A-game.

As they finally reached the end of North Hall, the group spilled into the school center and froze. In the open space separating the school offices and the cafeteria's main entrance, someone with an artistic inclination had gotten very busy. In blood, they drew a heart impaled by a dagger surrounded by a spiraling vine. The emblem of the Pretiosum Cruor.

A human head marked the center, unlit beyond the reach of the emergency lights.

Kyle circled the emblem, saying, "You'd think in the middle of a war zone they'd have better things to do than leave us all these love notes."

Tameka hated agreeing with him.

Andrew said, "They don't think they're in a war zone. This is a playground to them."

Sagan walked by Tameka and Rayne and stepped over the lines of blood.

"Do you really have to know?" John asked.

Nikki scoffed, "If your loved ones wanted a list of this battle's casualties or survivors, you'd want your name marked so they could mourn you."

Sagan knelt by the head and gasped. "It's Justin!"

Tameka wasn't surprised when John murmured, "Good riddance."

Even Kyle rubbed his neck and looked off elsewhere. No one wanted to comment on how little Justin's death affected them. But it affected Sagan.

She picked up an object beside Justin's head and shoved it into her skirt pocket. Tameka almost didn't catch the movement, and she supposed Sagan wanted it that way. Tameka would ask her about it later in private. They needed to press forward.

Behind her, Kyle said, "I don't know about you guys, but severed heads are more disturbing than they make them out to be in the movies."

Andrew grunted his agreement.

Tameka just shook her head.

ELEVEN

THERE'S ONLY ONE WAY TO CHECK FOR RABIES

KORAC LOVED MAKING AN ENTRANCE, AND THIS TIME WAS DIFFERENT. IT WAS SPECIAL. He needed to impress Sagan to distract her from the devastation. Not to mention, this was their first time meeting outside of her dreams.

Dreams where they shared beautiful and intimate secrets, though Sagan would never admit it. In breathy tones, in piercing cries, and in little giggles, she told Korac she loved him. He considered each confession a triumph and drew from them her soul.

Korac was so close to possessing it. It might take a few scratches and bruises to convince her to leave with him, but having been in her life for four years now, he knew where to leave his marks. What a puzzle she was.

Korac gleefully popped his new CD into the disc player and connected the converter for the headphone jack. This moment he planned to relish on the long drag back to Cinder with both Sagan and Rayne in tow. He expected neither one of them to say 'yes.'

Their training with Xelan all these years had granted them a false sense of confidence. He had to give them credit. They'd worked their asses off. Every night, they devoted at least two hours learning how to kill his kind, and the Icarean Traitor showed them every method known as of ten thousand years ago. Even with Xelan gone, others came forward to improve their technology beyond the predictable deaths. It was unlikely Xelan possessed this information.

As Korac considered the song selection, he recalled how he kept his secrets from Sagan the first three years since they'd started seeing each other in their dreams.

And then Justin came along.

It was interesting to follow Sagan's development as a young woman living a double life. She needed the punishment during the day for the forbidden lovers she enjoyed so much at night. The guilt and danger gnawed at her.

Korac respected pain, punishment, and torture. In all honesty, all of those were his favorite things. But it lacked art... a finesse. The adolescent puke didn't understand the subtlety of keeping a woman on the brink of orgasm, and then refusing to let her finish for four months. *That* was pain. That was art. Brutishly bruising her or ruining her ankle, that was just juvenile.

Korac rolled his eyes and hopped off the counter. The link between him and Sagan tugged as he walked closer to the cafeteria. He watched through the blood-washed windows as she stepped into the middle of the lobby and collected the gift he'd left her.

Yes.

That was the expression Korac had longed to see. Ecstatic torture at its best. Take the lock from his hair of which she'd told him so many times she loved. Feel him nearby. Know that Korac was coming for her.

The eight long tables served as a gathering place for students to eat crappy food and let off steam, but in the dark they stretched like rows in a graveyard, forever staining Nikki's memories with nightmare fuel.

Several of their unit closed their eyes to the bodies, but Nikki knew they could see it behind their lids. She certainly could.

The entire time they absorbed the horrific sight, they held a collective breath. Their lungs forced them to breathe, reluctantly. Nikki wasn't sure which smell hit her first. The sickly sweet scent of blood or the burnt discount food from this morning. Everyone pulled either their arm, hand, or shirt over their nose and mouth. They groaned and gasped.

John took too deep a breath, fell to his knees, and retched.

The sounds of another person vomiting cost Nikki her self-control. Though, unlike John, she found the nearest waste container, and lost her breakfast there.

Everything was too much. How could the invaders kill so many people? And how was Nikki spared but for the grace of Rayne?

"Jesus Christ," Kyle murmured against his arm.

Rayne closed her eyes tight and held the back of her hand under her nose. At Nikki's side, she coached, "Take small gulps of air."

Too much.

It was all too much.

When Nikki looked up, Rayne recoiled but recovered quickly. "Nikki, you can't afford a panic attack right now. Come back!"

{October 2004}

Nikki's mental retreat paled compared to its usual splendor. The man of her dreams sat across from her puffy chair on his rock throne with a frown.

This bothered Nikki because he knew full well how the stern treatment from her parents unsettled her. She told him when he first appeared two years ago. Around the same time, she took an interest in a freshman girl with black hair and shocking blue eyes.

Nikki loved Rayne's hair.

To the man in her dreams, she whined, "What is it?"

Nox sounded sullen as he said, "Your mind is elsewhere. It's not here with me."

True. Thoughts of Rayne were distracting Nikki.

Nox growled.

She stammered as she asked, "Wh-What's wrong?"

Nox stood and rolled Nikki out of her chair, and the dreamscape rolled with her. She lay on a rough, earthen floor with a massive black fire beside her.

"Where are we?! You've never taken me here before!" Nikki's voice trembled, and she tried to steady herself on her knees.

"Silence!"

Nikki went stone still.

Nox stood before her, unveiled. An icy chill shot down her spine. Nikki closed her eyes. Her blond lashes laced tight.

Wake up. Just wake up. It's a dream.

There was so much finality in Nox's rich baritone as he said, "It is more than a dream, and you've always known that."

Nikki's eyes snapped open and locked onto the face she'd never seen until now. His long hair brushed against his forearms and ribs.

Terrified of pain, her voice carried an edge of desperation. "Will you hurt me?"

Nox knelt down in a motion so sudden it made her flinch, but he only brushed against her hair and cupped her face, saying, "Not I. Look into the fire. Look and see what you fear to know."

Nikki trusted him. She did. He gave her advice on everything from what part-time job to get to what colleges she should apply to. She got into every one of them, and the job she worked qualified as valuable experience on those applications. Nikki *needed* to trust Nox.

Slowly, as if afraid to take her eyes off him, Nikki turned and looked into the blaze. The images she saw there took her breath away.

Rayne sat at the lunchroom table beside Nikki. They both looked content. But when Nikki looked away, Rayne peered at a table on the far side of the white-washed space. Sagan sat there searching the room. When she caught Rayne's eyes they both exchanged a smile Nikki had never seen from either of them until now.

It glowed radiantly, and their eyes shone in equal brilliance. In love. They were in love. Before Nikki or Justin turned back and caught them, both girls glanced away. The moment ended as quickly as it started. Heart broken, Nikki wanted to squeeze her eyes shut and turn away.

But the images went on.

The next scene took place in this very cavern. Nikki recognized the rough dirt floor and the fire blazing away. Bare limbs peeked through the dancing of the black flames.

Nikki made out Nox's bare backside. His long hair was swept aside. There was some motion, like he was moving. And then the sounds finally reached her.

Oh, it was those kinds of movements. Why would Nox share his sex life with Nikki? Such a terribly intimate scene. She opened her mouth to ask him, when the face of the woman appeared over his shoulder.

Dampness matted her black hair to her face. Pale skin beaded with sweat from the heat and exertion. Nikki need not see her eyes to guess their color.

The girl kissed Nox long and deep. Her satisfied moans echoed from across the vast chamber. Their kiss ended. Rayne's eyes opened and looked right at Nikki, startling her.

Nikki shut her eyes tight. She couldn't take much more.

When she opened them again, the latest scene choked a scream in her throat. Nikki laid face up, her mouth open in a never-ending scream, and her pale-blue eyes glazed over in death.

The initial horror subsided, and Nikki leaned closer to discern the cause of her future death. She was the same age as now. So, no comfort there. Bruises streaked her body. She glimpsed a terrible sight under her loose blouse and forced her eyes closed.

Nikki would die in agony. She gagged, and the fire took the image away. A small mercy.

"I don't understand. Why did you show me those awful things?" Her voice was devoid of hope.

Nox said, "To protect you."

Nikki glared at him. "Protect me?!"

He assured in a gentle, reasonable tone, "Every single image is avoidable. Do you want to know how?"

"Yes! Yes, of course!"

"Let Rayne go."

"What?!" No. Nikki wasn't about to do that. She loved Rayne. Although…

In that same reasonable tone, Nox said, "Let her go. She isn't and won't be faithful to you."

"But I love her," Nikki argued, her voice weak.

Nox shrugged. "She didn't appear to reciprocate those feelings."

Nikki said, "You don't know. You know nothing about how relationships work!"

He offered, "I believe relationships are in actions like that smile shared between Rayne and Sagan. Or passionate like her efficacious liaison with me."

Nikki wasn't the most secure teenage girl to begin with. Add a realistic image of an interaction between two exes and a dash of crazy sex scene with a handsome alien King, and some doubt might worm its way in. "I don't understand the third scene," she whispered, defeated.

Nox said, "Simple. You avoid that end entirely if you avoid Rayne. You will never know that kind of pain."

Ashamed of her weakness, Nikki hung her head.

Nox leaned forward and placed a gentle kiss on her pale hair.

"I love her," Nikki sniffled.

"We all do."

{INVASION DAY | APRIL 2006}

"Come on, Nikki!" Rayne continued to shout. John and Kyle gathered closer in case they could help.

Kyle asked, "A panic attack?"

Rayne nodded, unwilling to look away from Nikki.

"It's been two years since she's had one, right?" John pointed out.

Nikki came around. Her pupils shrank from the dilation during the attack.

"Are you with us?" Rayne checked her vitals.

"I want to be with you," Nikki finally answered, her voice quiet.

Kyle and John stepped back out of Rayne's line of sight. She appreciated the privacy. She spared a sad smile and pulled Nikki into a hug, saying, "I can't let you break down on me right now. We have to get through this together."

Nikki clung to Rayne tighter than expected.

Sagan shouted from the kitchen area, "There's two people alive back here!"

Andrew shouted back, "I don't want to know your definition of 'alive!'"

Rayne gave Nikki a reassuring smile.

Nikki let her go, and Rayne knew she was lying when she said, "I'll be all right. Go to her."

She, Kyle, and John hurried to Sagan while Tameka and Andrew stayed behind to search for their sanity. Nikki recovered on the floor.

Two students sat upright on the linoleum near one of the warming stations. As far as Rayne could see, they showed no signs of external damage. She asked, "Are they injured?"

Sagan shook her head. "They don't appear to be."

Kyle knelt and snapped his fingers in their face. One of them stopped trembling long enough to focus on his eyes. Kyle asked them, "What happened?"

Rayne groaned. "What kind of question is that to ask on today of all days?"

Sagan reprimanded them, "Be quiet both of you." She turned back to the students. "Are you able to walk?"

The trembling freshman nodded.

Sagan said, "You know the Med Lab? Try to help your friend up and head that way. Two people there can help you. Okay?"

There was no response this time. The boy just put his arm around the girl and staggered away.

Sagan and Kyle walked back to the open area. Sagan chided him, "What kind of question is 'what happened' in the middle of an invasion?"

"C'mon, I was asking for specifics, sheesh," Kyle answered. The two carried on around the corner.

Rayne glanced around the kitchens, her frown deepened with confusion. Why was there no blood back here?

The chatter stopped.

The panic in John's voice broke her concentration. "Hey, Rayne?"

Music played over the school's intercom system. Not just any music. After the quiet electric guitar intro, the lyrics to *Sweet Dreams* played. Marilyn Manson performed the soundtrack to her worst nightmare.

Only one Icarus would make this kind of entrance.

Rayne stepped around the corner, sword in hand. She looked up and contemplated how much she wanted to lose her shit on this dude right now.

Apparently, Sagan and Kyle made it only this far from the kitchen before they, too, realized they had company. They both stood only one meter away from Rayne in the lunch line doorway.

The bad guys turned the lights on in the cafeteria. The contrast of the bright blood across all the white walls, white floors, and white table tops overwhelmed Rayne at first. She caught herself counting the bodies before she forced herself to quit.

"Celindria," an elegant voice said.

At the mention of her ancestral designation, Rayne went empty. No movement. No response.

The elegant voice belonged to none other than General Korac. His long white hair was pulled tight from his face and held by an Asian hair pin, letting the ponytail cascade down his back in silver waves. His stark pale eyes, even lighter than Colita's, held absolutely nothing as he faced Rayne down. No rage, no searing hatred. Just business.

But when he looked at Sagan, several emotions crossed his face. Passion, obsession, hunger. It shone in his eyes and pulled his lips into a secretive smirk. Whatever turmoil churned under the surface of Rayne's self-control, his eyes on Sagan, crested the waves.

Korac brought his friends with him. More Icarean soldiers, without their cloaks, holding tools from the janitor's closet in their hands—broomsticks and hammers—one or two of them wielded swords like their fallen brethren. Twenty-two warriors total. Did they bring a small army to attack the school? How the hell did they get this many Icari in here during the day? Three stood sentinel at each entrance to the cafeteria, and three flanked their General.

Kyle muttered a soft, "Shit."

Rayne checked, and Sagan's eyes darted anywhere, trying to avoid Korac's gaze. The more uncomfortable she seemed, the more loose and relaxed he became. He was a very insistent stalker.

Andrew spoke gently, "Rayne, are you with us? Come on, we have to finish it."

There was no need to reply once Rayne finally looked into the Icarus' face. He switched his focus from Sagan to her.

"What say you, Celindria? You and Sagan come with us, and we'll leave. No more of this..." he spread his hands, indicating the entire room, "...carnage. You and I both know this is pointless. All this fighting—Nox will take you, anyway. But if you go now, no more innocent people will have to die."

"Why did you say Sagan goes, too?" Nikki spoke up. She stepped forward with a cobalt coated knife.

Korac observed Rayne's reaction as he replied, "His majesty promised her to me, and I have waited a very long time."

Rayne must not have reacted the way he wanted. He frowned in disappointment at her unchanged expression.

Sagan turned and inspected Rayne behind her.

The lyrics droned on about submission and abuse. Rayne gripped the sword tight in one hand. So tight her knuckles mottled white. She clenched her free hand so hard she wrung drops of blood from the glass in her wounds. Rayne didn't feel a damned thing. She just wanted the fucking music to stop.

The lights flickered above.

"What the fuck?" John asked.

Andrew called softly, "Rayne?"

Everyone in the room glanced up except Korac. No, Rayne held his undivided attention. Likewise, she never moved her gaze from his, but that anger in her swelled with every line of that song. His lips stretched into a gruesome smile. He knew.

The intercom speakers crackled, the music distorted, and eventually everything stopped. Korac's smirk never wavered. "Do you have any idea how hard it is to find decent music on Cinder?"

Footsteps approached the door. Shadows appeared through the glass window. The door knob turned slowly.

Come on, just try it. Lynn stood flush against the wall. She swung a metal pole before she recognized the two intruders as frightened students.

"Shit! Sorry!"

Lynn dropped the scrap and urged them inside, asking, "Are you all right? You're not hurt, are you?"

Pablo sat the girl down in a chair.

Lynn didn't recognize her or the boy. She looked over at Pablo and said, "Maybe they made it to the cafeteria." Maybe this would all end soon.

Ever since the fight team left, people escaped hiding places in droves and made their way here. The injuries were all fearsome and almost every single one required hospital treatment. Historically, field medicine didn't provide a suitable answer for broken limbs on the battlefield, and that's exactly what this was. A battlefield.

The boy nodded. His eyes were full of shock.

The girl kept to herself, too frightened to speak.

Pablo wrapped a blanket around her shoulders. He looked up at Lynn, saying, "I think she's in shock."

Lynn turned her back on them, rummaging through the bag of supplies.

The boy stepped closer, talking loud and clear. "It was horrible. Blood everywhere." He continued speaking, but Lynn concentrated on her search for the materials. With her back to him, she didn't see the pole hit her at the base of the neck.

Damn. Darkness swirled in her vision.

The girl sprung for Pablo, screaming. Now they knew why she was so quiet. She didn't have a tongue. Choking him, she forced him back against the lab table.

Pablo gripped her hands and croaked, "Hey, wait a minute!" He pushed her hard enough that she stumbled back.

She screamed and lunged for him once more. When she fell on him, he used her momentum to throw her over his head. She landed on one of the upturned plastic chairs with the metal leg impaling her.

The alien girl shrieked her last.

Pablo grabbed the bastard attacking Lynn by the back of the neck, pulled him off her, and slammed him into the incinerator. He pounded the red button and watched as the monster's head exploded inside the purifier.

From the floor, Lynn sighed in relief. "Thanks, Pablo!"

He checked the scratch on her neck. "It's minor." He grinned. "Next two are yours."

Lynn laughed. Their eyes locked. She stared into his gaze, longing to finish what they'd started, but this sneak assassin thing meant that the time for distractions was over. They couldn't afford even ten minutes together.

Lynn stood, and sadness softened her voice as she said, "I don't know if there's anyone else to save."

Pablo frowned. "I think there should be more people to help. We've only seen maybe three dozen."

"I know."

He frowned harder in confusion, asking, "So what do you mean?"

Lynn's tone was gentle. "Either they're at the football field or they're all gone."

Pablo lowered his head and sniffled.

TWELVE

STAY OUT OF THE WAY OF A MAN WITH AN AXE TO GRIND

RAYNE TURNED HER WRIST, SPINNING THE SWORD IN HER HAND. Icarean blood spilled onto the floor, and mingled with the human blood. So much gore and soot covered her body. Of the twenty-two Icarean soldiers, only thirteen plus their leader remained.

Andrew tried to help John relocate his knee, Kyle bled from a sword gash on his bicep, and Nikki killed the Icarus which had blackened her eye.

Twelve left.

While surveying Rayne's troops' progress, an Icarus hauled her from behind and slammed her onto the nearest table. She kicked at the monster's face. "Fuck you!"

He dodged and pinned Rayne to the wet, bloody surface with a meaty hand. He took the time to lean down and snarl all his many sharp teeth in her face.

Rayne ground out, "Your breath wreaks, wingless." She knew at least she and Sagan couldn't be harmed as long as the Icari delivered them whole to their Icarean masters. So no matter how much this guy snarled at her, he wasn't about to hurt her much. There were other ways to torment her, unfortunately.

From where he gripped Rayne's no-longer-white blouse, he pulled her along with him as he ran down the length of the entire table. With every slippery meter, blood soaked into the back of her shirt and her disheveled hair. He lifted her from the table by the shoulders and slammed her against the wall with her feet dangling off the ground. Her back squelched against the blood-drenched cinder blocks.

"What's the matter? Afraid to take me out without daddy's permission?!" Rayne stuck her tongue out at him. Her breath came hard against the press of him on her chest.

That did it. He pressed harder.

But if he killed her, what would he tell the boss? It was an accident?

Fortunately, Sagan ran up behind the Icarus and shoved a knife through his chest. Brain impaled. Girl power!

He screamed and released Rayne. She slid down the wall, resting on her feet. She needed a second to recover from the sternum pressure.

Eleven.

"Are you all right?" Sagan asked.

Rayne answered, "I'll be—Down!"

Sagan dropped without hesitation and missed the blow from a sledgehammer. She swept her assailant's leg out from under him, and Rayne stabbed him through the chest.

Ten.

A little breathless, Rayne said, "Nice leg sweep."

"Badass bitch impaling."

Oh, what the hell? Rayne threw up a hand, and Sagan gave her a high five. Both grinned despite the apocalypse.

When the girls turned around, they stopped dead in the center of the cafeteria.

Korac awaited there in leather-clad splendor. Who was his stylist? They needed a bonus. He switched eye contact between Sagan and Rayne. Emphasis on Sagan.

The General's face was locked in that permanent, condescending grin. He spread his arms wide, and the two soldiers flanking him removed his leather duster. Like, seriously. Swept it off him and away.

Rayne straight-up rolled her eyes, but he paid her no mind. He maintained eye contact with Sagan for the spectacle's sake.

To Rayne's surprise, the blond girl peered at him with wide eyes. Her chest heaved from her shallow breath, and her lips parted. Not good.

Underneath his coat, Korac wore a sleeveless black shirt which bared his corded arms and the hilts of some kind of weapon at both hips.

One of the blood suckers ruined the moment by barreling into Sagan, knocking her over. Before Rayne could help, the assailant landed on Sagan's knife when he fell on top of her. Impaled himself. She rolled the dead body off her, but retrieving the weapon from the corpse wasn't happening. So she collected his sword instead.

Back on her feet, Sagan smiled at Rayne. "Sweet."

Korac seemed a smidge disappointed by the interruption and frowned. He looked back to the soldier holding his coat. In a nonchalant tone that suited his irritatingly pleasant voice, he ordered, "Kill the rest."

One went for Andrew and John, one went for Tameka, and the other stalked toward Nikki and Kyle. Apparently satisfied, Korac turned back to Rayne and Sagan. His infuriating smirk returned as he asked, "Shall we continue, then?"

With a flourishing cross draw, Korac unsheathed both weapons in a fluid, simultaneous motion. He'd practiced. Probably in a mirror. He'd probably practiced naked in said mirror.

Silver battle axes. Both polished to a gleam and worked with intricate designs at the grip and pommel. It boasted the symbol of the Pretiosum Cruor in the center of each blade. Predictable. And they glinted in the light, sharpened to perfection.

Beside Rayne, Sagan's eyes widened, and she thought her best friend even gulped.

Rayne's hair stood on end, and her muscles constricted with pre-fight tension. Her breathing shallowed, and her heart rate quickened. In her peripheral vision, two Icarean bodies fell. Eight more to go.

But looking at Korac... Damn, this would be harder than Rayne had originally thought. The smell of smoke gnawed at her subconscious and distracted her. Not afraid. Totally not afraid. Were her hands shaking?

Korac advanced first. With one foot he took a step forward, and Sagan took a step back. Rayne glanced at her bestie and tried to read her. Sagan was fighting a losing battle inside. Hell no. This was not happening on Rayne's watch.

In his single-minded determination to obtain Sagan, Korac ignored Rayne altogether. He stepped right in front of her with no sign of defense.

Here goes.

Rayne plunged the borrowed blade right into Korac's center.

Before she sunk anything home, Rayne jolted when Korac's eyes locked right onto hers mid-attack. His smirk was no longer condescending. It molded into something determined, focused. He was here on a mission and he'd be damned if Rayne got in the way. He reacted to her move by disappearing.

"What the fuck?!" Rayne's startled cry was both shrill and embarrassing.

Korac disappeared without a trace.

"Behind you!" Sagan sounded terrified.

Rayne's entire body froze to the spot. Stiffer than she wanted to be about it, she turned around. Korac, in fact, lingered behind her, looking entirely too pleased with himself.

Over the course of their training, Xelan taught them to track, and even imitate his speed moves, which to untrained eyes looked like disappearing tricks. Not only couldn't Rayne track Korac's movements, but she couldn't even sense a spatial disturbance. That wasn't speed. How was she supposed to fight an enemy who could disappear and reappear? Xelan never told them Icari were capable of those abilities. This wasn't going well.

When Korac spoke, Rayne startled to her own irritation. "In no uncertain terms am I allowed to injure you. The Night King reserves that pleasure all unto himself, as is his right."

Rayne smiled, slowly. "Is that so?"

Korac nodded, still pleased with himself.

"Then you don't mind if I—" Rayne feinted a punch and thrust her sword at his ribs. The sword pierced air.

Korac had disappeared, again.

Sagan cried out.

Rayne whirled around to find Korac holding her best friend in his arms, his front pressed to her back. He crossed the axes over Sagan's chest with the points of the blades too close to her throat.

Rayne glared at him through a whirlwind of rage and promised, "I will kill you for this."

To her disgust, Korac pressed his face closer to Sagan's hair and took a deep breath. Sagan's eyes went even wider with what Rayne hoped was terror. This was such a fucked up way to abuse their dreams. Only, they had an advantage.

"Sagan," Rayne said in a calm voice, belying the storm within.

Sagan's eyes focused a little. "Rayne?"

"You're my girl, and I know you won't stand for a man hurting you again."

With her confidence returning, Sagan gripped the sword tighter and gave a single nod.

Rayne charged at Korac. As before, his relaxed expression came across as unconcerned. The shine of his eyes told her they amused him and little else.

When Rayne tackled him, he let go of Sagan and disappeared. Rayne crashed to the floor, grabbing at air.

So, Korac didn't take Sagan with him. More than likely *couldn't* in this case. No passengers aboard Icarean Airlines. Where she knelt on the floor, Rayne heard a low grunt. She stood up, pulling her sticky hair from her eyes.

Korac staggered a few feet away from Sagan. His neck bled from a fresh wound, and the blond girl held her sword ready for the next strike.

A hint of concern marked the tightness around Korac's eyes as he said, "I see Xelan trained you *very* well."

Rayne approached her best friend. What was happening?

Korac took a step toward them to start the fun over again, but Sagan stopped Rayne with her hand. Sagan turned, risking her back to Korac, saying, "The smoke is growing thicker. It won't be much longer before we can't breathe. We still have to fight Nox, and this is such a mess. Tell us what to do, Rayne. What will make this stop before we all die from suffocation?"

"Fall down at my feet and beg me to take you with us?" Korac suggested, his pale eyes shining with silent laughter.

Rayne glanced around to take in the fight itself. Tameka fought two. Andrew helped John regain his footing, and together they took on three. Kyle and Nikki battled three of their own. Kyle knocked off the head of one as Rayne watched.

Fifteen alien soldiers down.

The one Nikki was fighting stopped, looked around at the fifteen Icarean bodies, and retreated to South Hall. The smaller girl pursued him on her own.

Only six left, now.

Rayne ordered, "You kill Korac, Sagan. I'll follow Nikki to see if that Icarus reported to Nox."

Korac chuckled. She wanted to kill him for the silkiness of it. What a crime.

Sagan shook her head, saying, "No way. I won't let you go alone."

Rayne pulled her into a one-armed hug. "If you come with me, he'll use you to hurt me. I go alone. I'll find you when I'm finished." She pulled away and gazed into Sagan's violet eyes.

Her best friend's reassuring smile satisfied Rayne. Sagan nodded. "Be careful."

Rayne wondered if Korac would let them have enough time for a kiss? The creak of leather caught her attention. She peered at him over Sagan's shoulder. He shook his head as if answering her unspoken request. The stormy darkness cast over his eyes suggested he was tired of their parting gestures.

Fuck Korac.

Rayne gripped Sagan's neck and kissed her like it was the last time. Then Rayne turned and went for the opening where John and Andrew struggled with their three warriors. She walked up to one from behind, thrust the sword into its brain, and withdrew it. She smiled at Andrew.

"Rayne? Where are you going?!" Andrew called before another Icarus tackled him about the waist.

"Take care!" John shouted.

Rayne nodded, running to Nox with fresh, blue blood on her sword. Her friends would be safe. They could take care of each other.

Only five left.

She took one last glance at the opening event.

Sagan turned to face Korac. A vague sense of apprehension occupied the scene. He stood there, smirking with all his amusement and arrogance. He spun both axes in his hands. Sagan charged for him, and he met her halfway. Her sword fell between the two crossed axes, and there they faced one another like they'd met that way before.

One of Colita's harem fled right into Nox's path. He flexed his fist, and the Icarus disintegrated into dust. Running from human children. How pathetic.

Nikki barged around the corner in pursuit of her quarry. She stopped short, recognizing him.

Nox grinned with satisfaction. He had a promise to fulfill.

"You really are here," Nikki whispered, her voice hoarse with exertion and smoke inhalation.

"Yes." Nox chuckled. She was such a tiny thing. Measuring below his chest, she hardly weighed over eight stones. He considered her frame delicate. Her facial bone structure was like that of a pixie. And her beautiful fair skin and hair would elicit instincts of possession and protection.

To a human, anyway.

To a being like Nox, he interpreted her weak, fragile body as a challenge. How many ways could he break her? How much could he gain?

His predatory instincts must've shown on his face because those lovely gray eyes of hers widened. So enticing. She surprised him by brandishing her sword. Nox resisted the urge to taunt her.

Let her own this moment. Die with some dignity.

"It's a dangerous game you play," Nox said instead.

With grave eyes, Nikki vowed, "It's not a game. I won't let you take Rayne."

Nox nodded in approval. Her death wouldn't be quick, but he would honor her as a warrior. Well, as much as he could without bothering to draw his sword. "Then be swift in your actions, woman. I won't play pity to your stature."

Nikki lunged at him.

He feigned a narrow evasion of her weak demonstration. He trusted the Icarean Traitor did a better job training Rayne. Otherwise, they'd wasted four years.

Nikki lunged again.

Nox exaggerated the effort to jump aside. He took cruel enjoyment watching the confidence build in her moves and the determination to slay the dragon grow on her face. Maybe this wouldn't be such a bad appetizer to the main course.

It was time to get a few of his own offensive maneuvers in. While dodging another attack, Nox asked, "What do you think will happen after you defeat me?"

Sweat beaded across Nikki's brow. This close to the fire, humans would have trouble withstanding the increased temperatures without a nacre. She withheld an answer but grunted cutely as she attempted to slash him.

Nox intentionally inflated the twirl of his cloak as he spun away. All the while Nikki made her advances, he drew her further into the smoky corridor of South Hall.

Nox asked again, "Do you think you'll be the prince rescuing the princess?"

Nikki's slashing intensified, and a fierceness cast a deadly look on her face. Meanwhile, Nox maintained a cavalier air even with his flourishes to boost her confidence.

Nikki breathed heavier in the denser smoke as she stepped back in a defensive pose.

"I save the day," she finally answered him.

But Nox wasn't satisfied. "And then what?"

No response. Nikki need not say anything. He already knew what this girl's childish mind imagined for the outcome of this battle. Nox tsked before he said, "You get the girl, and you both live happily ever after?"

Nikki faltered. For a second, the confidence drained out of her. Between heavy breaths, she said in a small voice, "If that's what Rayne wants." The sliver of desperate hope in those words almost broke what remained of his heart.

It was time to end this. "Well..." Nox took the gloves off his fingers and cracked his knuckles. He rolled his shoulders back and rotated his neck.

All the while, Nikki watched and her eyes grew less fierce and more aware of her surroundings.

Nox said, "I'm afraid that's just not how your story will end."

In the empty hallway, through the building's silence, in the smallest voice he'd ever heard, Nikki said, "No. No, it was never going to."

Ah, so she understood. It was meant to end this way. Well, Nox gave her credit for her bravery and her devotion. Her loyalty was not unlike Korac's to himself. Nox respected that. He said, "It won't be quick, and it won't be painless."

The small woman squared her shoulders and gripped the sword tightly. Lacking the strength for anymore words, Nikki nodded.

Nox swung one fist into her face. He used the other to grab the sword she attempted to impale him with. He ripped it out of her hand and sent it flying toward the technology hallway with the worst of the fire. With not even a sliver of effort, he grabbed her upper arms and hauled her off her feet.

Nikki never screamed. Just grunted, and even that was involuntary. She tried to kick Nox, and he admired that. He threw her into the nearest wall.

Nikki's eyes were already swelling shut. Her ears and lips bled. She tried to pull herself back up. There. Hot tears streamed from her good eye. It was enough to send him over the edge and make him drain her dry.

But Nox refused to drink from her. Since the Vacating, Nikki's affiliation with the Progeny was a contamination to his kind. Only Celindria reserved the honor until now. He would pass it on to Rayne.

Nox slammed his fist into the other side of Nikki's face. He might as well make the bruising even. That time, she screamed and spat out something solid. Humans were such weak things. She tried to punch him in the crotch. He grabbed her fist and wrenched her arm back.

"Now, I think you've had enough fun." Nox lifted Nikki by her throat and threw her into one of many heaps of flaming rubble.

She screamed until her voice went ragged. She rolled and turned until she doused the flames.

Nox smiled with satisfaction. Ever since he saw the construction of this school, he really, really wanted to try this. He lifted one hand into the air and pulled the riot gate down.

The gate slammed into Nikki's midsection. The writhing of her partially cooked body treated him to an aphrodisiac. Again. He had to do it again. He raised the gate high and paused.

Nox wanted to see the futility in her eyes.

Nikki disappointed him, barely looking at him at all. Her head lolled in a pitiful sight to one side. Blood oozed out of her mouth and ears. Her swollen eyes left her unrecognizable from the delectable creature he'd started this little tiff with.

Nox demanded, "Come on! Put some fight into it!"

Nikki shook her head.

This was pointless, but before he finished her, he leaned in close and whispered, "You remember your visions I showed you?"

Nikki struggled to glance at him, but he saw the recognition in her eyes. Good.

"If you think about it, the one about you dying in pain came true." Nox paused, waiting for her to acknowledge it.

After a long time, Nikki nodded.

He smirked, saying, "And you know without a doubt the one about Rayne and Sagan was true."

Again, a weak nod of the head.

Nox said, "Then, I promise I'll do everything in my power to make the third one happen. And when I finally do, I will think of you while I'm enjoying my time with our girl."

The human heart. Despite the painful swelling, fresh tears forced their way out of the corners of Nikki's eyes. And there, on the edge of his hearing, came a sob.

"Mmm," he purred as he stood back to his full height. "Good night, little prince."

Nox slammed the gate for the last time.

The thick curtain of smoke hung in the air, darkening the red-lit hallways. The smell of charred wood and rot combined thick enough to cake Rayne's tongue and make it hard to swallow. With every inhale, her lungs screamed.

Something bothered her. Nikki came this way a while ago. Where was she?

Gripping her sword tight, she stopped at the South Hall opening. Fear knotted her stomach so tight, she almost walked back to the cafeteria. No one would blame her.

Rayne took a deep breath and that last step. Her eyes swept across the destruction. Dizzy with distress, she clutched the first riot gate for support.

Flames climbed the walls of wooden lockers and licked the drop-ceiling tiles. Charred and melted clumps of rubble were all ruined in flames. South Hall's riot gates were half-raised, searing in the fire.

These were props and a backdrop for her living nightmare. Her friends' weapons clanging in time with grunts and cries from the cafeteria were the soundtrack.

Rayne took a step back from the gate and shoved both hands in her hair. She took this moment to get a grip. Once she crossed that threshold, this ended only one way. After a not-so-deep breath, she slipped under the gate.

Rayne strained to see through the caustic smoke. Beyond a fallen bank of crumbled lockers, she made out a dark figure. Her heart slammed into her chest. The man towered almost to the ceiling. Beneath the cloak, heavy muscle forged his body. She knew from their dreams. Even so, the garment failed to contain the unearthly strength radiating from his alien being.

As if on cue, the Icarus swept back the hood and stripped his broad upper body altogether.

How? How was Rayne supposed to do this? Look at him and not think about—

She refused to see his face. But how else could she fight him? Her heart pounded to escape her chest as she surveyed his hands. He wore the same heavy silver ring with the Pretiosum Cruor insignia from her dreams. He had much to answer for.

After agonizing over it, Rayne lifted her chin and examined the rest of him. Heavy boots, black leathers trousers, and bare skin from the waist up. He'd plaited his long black hair down his scalp. A few loose strands framed his ruefully handsome face with heavy, angled eyebrows, high cheekbones, and soft, full lips.

Rayne admitted to herself that if he'd ever shown his face in her dreams, she might have slept forever. After reminding herself of his atrocities, she met his gaze.

There was nothing more calculating or sinister as the black depths of his ravenous eyes. And those eyes smoldered with a thirst, a hunger for primal power. Almost as if he lusted for nothing else and could not be sated of it.

Dizzy. So dizzy. Rayne reached her hand out to steady herself against another riot gate. Four years, haunted and enthralled by him, her body knew no difference. She was drawn to him all the same.

Rayne shook her head and straightened. Her grip on the sword tightened. Rage burned in her. She was more determined than him. She had more to lose, and she wouldn't let that happen. Rayne was ready.

"Nox."

Sagan's pulse threatened to strangle her as if her heart was lodged in her throat. It beat so hard that her wrists ached with it, making her grip on the sword uncertain. She refused to give even a centimeter. The blade of her sword fell solidly between Korac's axes in a demonstration of strength. No, she wasn't winning. And the smirk on his alluring lips suggested he knew it. She had to think of something.

"What's the matter, little butterfly? Are you struggling more than Xelan said that you would?" Korac teased and exerted more pressure against her sword. He said, "All those up close and personal sessions with our wayward brother amounted to a lot of show and little strength."

Korac gained against her offensive, and with every detail of her life he divulged, Sagan lost the strength to keep Korac down.

"And how steamy some of those sessions were. Did you ever ask *him* to scorch a blade and sear you with it? You did it enough when you were alone, I suspect you considered it."

A strained cry escaped Sagan as Korac reached his full height, towering over her. And he continued on with his banter, "But my favorite—oh, yes—my favorite moments were when you thought no one was watching you and Rayne—"

Sagan screamed in Korac's face. Anger lit her skin on fire. Sick of his mouth and his intrusion on her life, she decided. No way. No way would she make this an easy win for him.

She kicked his ankle, unsteadying him. That wiped the smirk off his face. He stumbled back, lowering the axes.

Sagan seized the fault in his guard and swung for his midsection.

Korac regained his balance sooner than she'd expected and evaded her strike. He used one axe to block her sword and sliced at her with the other.

Sagan spun outward, away from him. She avoided the worst of the blow, but caught the blade in the meat of her shoulder. The wound bled immediately, and she hissed through gritted teeth.

It was Sagan's turn to step back and regroup. She examined the wound. Small, but deep. Unlike the weaker Icari before Korac, her dream lover would hurt her. When she met his gaze, her eyes burned with rage.

Korac blew Sagan a kiss, and she lunged for him, sword first.

He disappeared before her blow landed. She jumped to the side, fast and agile, and swung a punch into the air in front of her.

Korac materialized, and Sagan's fist connected with his face. She immediately mourned not stabbing with her sword instead. Hopefully, she'd live to regret it.

He lashed out with an axe, and she fell back onto her ass to avoid it. Rather than take advantage of her current vulnerability, Korac concerned himself with the mark on his jaw. He rubbed it back and forth, checking his reflection in his blade.

Sagan stood slowly and stepped away. Korac's total disregard unnerved her.

Come on. React.

The hair on her arms stood on end, and her skin bubbled in gooseflesh. A force emanated from Korac which thickened the air like with Colita. The mark Sagan had given him faded away to her dismay. When his striking, pale gaze returned to her, she watched him assess everything from her height to her muscle mass.

"You don't have a nacre," Korac contemplated aloud.

"What the fuck are you talking about?" Sagan's skin burned under his scrutiny.

Korac disappeared in response. She whirled around, and his face appeared right in front of her. His expression was filled with bewilderment.

He vanished again.

Sagan scanned the corner of the room near John and Kyle. Korac appeared on the table beside them, perched on a stool.

She shouted, "Look out!"

Busy with their own issues, the guys kept their fight on the perimeter.

Korac paid her team even less regard. He crouched on the stool like a magnificent bird. The confusion on his face vanished, replaced with calculation.

When he disappeared again, Sagan spun almost out of reflex now, and he reappeared before her. Displeased but curious, Korac asked, "How're you doing that?"

Sagan said, "It would be stupid of me to divulge a tactical advantage." In all honesty, she thought about where he might go and that's where he'd be, but she wasn't about to share the simplicity of it with him. Flushed with pride, she grinned. Her shoulders straightened. She held her sword and her stance with more confidence.

The displeasure melted from Korac's face. His eyes shone with something that frightened Sagan.

Excitement.

His smirk held a secret, as if only the two of them were in on it. Korac said, "I'm afraid I brought this on myself. No matter." He dematerialized.

Sagan gawked up at the ceiling. She wasn't sure what to do when he appeared directly above her, but getting out of the way seemed like a good idea. She darted over, but too late.

Korac cleaved her back open.

Sagan shrieked and sprawled onto the floor.

Korac landed in a three-point stance, saying, "That's twice now you've passed on the opportunity to kill me."

Like last time, Sagan tried to crawl away without drawing his attention. But unlike last time, Korac was utterly fixated on her.

Feeling braver than she ought to, she quipped, "You're making me regret those little mercies."

Korac struck with one axe.

Sagan blocked and held back with her sword.

The angle felt all wrong, and judging by the gleam in his eyes, he was toying with her.

Korac struck the linoleum next to her head with his free axe and said, "Don't forget. I have two."

Sagan yelped, sure he meant to strike her in the face with it.

He twisted the axe locked with her sword until it bent her arm so painfully she dropped it beside her head. Flushed with triumph, Korac knelt and straddled Sagan's waist. She feared him, but not because he planned to kill her.

He wanted to take her with him.

She feared herself more because a part of her wanted to go.

Korac leaned closer until Sagan stared into the darker gray flecks in his otherwise colorless eyes. She breathed the peppermint of his breath. He said, "I will convince you to come with me."

Korac's voice. The deep timbre, the elegant cadence, and the silken tone of it drove her crazy in her dreams.

In reality?

Sagan's breath hitched, and her heart pounded against the linoleum beneath her back. She half-lied, "Not willingly. Never."

"By the time I am done with you here, you will cry my name for every sexual encounter you allowed that prepubescent thug to force on you when you could've easily defended yourself." He brushed his fingers through her hair. "Those moments were meant to be mine."

Hot tears streamed from Sagan's eyes, down her temples, and into her blood-soaked hairline. She whispered, "I know."

Korac lifted his hand, a tear delicately balanced there. He brought it to his lips and tasted it. His eyes closed, and the muscles in his neck strained.

The moment Korac let his guard down, Sagan grabbed the sword, and slammed the pommel against the top of his spine with a cry.

He grunted and rolled away from her. She backed farther away from him on the floor. Where she crawled, she trailed a considerable pool of fresh blood.

Korac retrieved the buried axe. Sagan's eyes grew wide when it lifted a chunk of foundation with the linoleum tiles. He smirked at the shock on her face.

"My name. Three hundred and two times."

Everyone had drifted away from Matt's car by now. Listening to the message repeat on the radio didn't comfort anyone. They needed to focus on the here and now. They should prepare for what came next. These students, who belonged in hallways lined with lockers, waited around a parking lot surrounded by acrid smoke. What was next?

Lucy sat in the grass behind the school, knees hugged to her chest. Someone called, and she lifted her head.

"Lucy?" Cecily called again, approaching her friend.

"I'm here." Timidly, she touched the bandaged injury on her forehead.

Cecily sat beside her best friend on the grass, saying, "I never asked. What happened?" Her voice was full of concern.

Lucy said, "I saw one of *them* in the hall. I was running when someone ran into me, and someone else slammed me against the wall. They nearly crushed me." She felt her eyes hollow with the memory of it. "Do you remember when Sagan came to school with that bandage on her forehead?"

Cecily sat in silence, her face stricken.

Nearby, Lucy noticed Stacia eavesdropping with very little subtlety. Well, good. She needed to hear this, too. Lucy said, "I remember wondering what happened. I thought, 'Oh. I guess Justin happened again.' Now, all I can think is, 'That must have hurt like hell, and Justin was a piece of shit for doing it. I'm glad he's dead.'"

Cecily rolled her eyes, saying, "You don't mean that. She has responsibility in it, too. She stayed with him. We don't know—"

Lucy had more to say. "No, it gets worse, because we were pieces of shit, too. We told him everything she did when he wasn't around, and we were almost eager to tell him when it was something he wouldn't like. We just wanted him to quit bullying us for a minute, so we let that girl be the whipping boy."

Cecily's eyes widened as she frowned with enough hurt to contort her expression.

Stacia stepped into the spotlight as always, saying, "You can't talk to her like that. We weren't there. We don't know what Sagan did to Justin."

Lucy looked straight into her face, filled with all that indignation. "And we deserve to die, too."

Stacia spat in Lucy's face and stomped away.

Cecily gaped with her brown eyes fuming.

Lucy let the full force of her own self-loathing show on her face.

With a sudden hop, Cecily popped off the grass and ran after Stacia.

So much for the Overachievers Club. R.I.P.

"You did the right thing."

Lucy glanced up into the brilliant, sunlit sky, and squinted under the shade of her hand to make out Matt's face. She said, "Thanks, I guess. I don't think I deserve it."

The grass crunched under him as he sat beside her. "Well, I wasn't exactly giving you a compliment. Sometimes doing the right thing, especially if you're a little late for it, isn't something to congratulate yourself about."

Matt's words stung, but they were the truth. Which, if Lucy was honest with herself, was something she hadn't heard from another person in a long time.

She wanted to go deeper and share more of the truth. "When his truck flipped over and what happened, happened... My first feeling was relief. I knew that was awful, so I went with my second feeling, which was mostly horror. But I was more horrified with myself. We let him push us around for four years, and I assisted in a terrible cycle of abuse. And you know, maybe sometime down the road I could make amends for that. Before today. That message on the radio... I'll never get the chance."

Matt replied in that reasonable tone of his, "There is no making up for it. Own it and move on. Don't feel guilty for feeling relieved. Justin didn't have the best impact on the world. But you still could."

Lucy said, "Thanks, Matt."

They both sat in silence for a bit. The day seemed to stretch on in its horrific torture, as if they were separated from the world beyond that barrier of smoke plumes. As if the sun had blacked out.

Lucy squinted harder into the sky, and then realization struck her. She cried out, alarming Matt.

"What is it?" Matt asked, peering around.

Someone close stood and pointed toward the sky. "Look! It's the sun!"

That's when Matt noticed what Lucy saw. A fraction of the sun was turning dark, and this strange blackness consumed the fiery ball in a gradual filter. The surrounding daylight weakened, diminishing, growing darker through the smoke. All around, people cried in collective terror. The monsters could come outside, now.

THIRTEEN

PET THE TIGER THROUGH THE CAGE BUT NEVER RELEASE HIM

THE ATMOSPHERE CLOSED IN AROUND RAYNE, INDUCING CLAUSTROPHOBIA. Soot and ash clung to her skin. She sipped air in quick breaths. This made her throat raw and her chest burn. Her eyes watered as she focused through the acrid fog.

Nox fared better with a nacre in conditions so similar to his homeworld. The predator's eyes glinted in the darkness. What did Rayne look like to him? Did he notice the blood dripping from her fingertips? Did he see how hard it was for her to breathe? After her fight in the cafeteria, mixed blood covered her white shirt and gleamed on her throat. Her sword dripped cobalt blood. The blood of his fallen soldiers.

"Is this enough for you?" Nox's voice resonated like a roll of thunder through the blanket of smoke and flame.

Rayne closed her eyes against him. He knew. He knew how she felt. How he affected her. She opened her eyes and asked with a tremor in her words, "Why did you keep me waiting so long?"

Nox noticed her reaction. She knew it as sure as he enjoyed his influence over her. He said, "You needed time, Rayne."

He always spoke her name with so much finality, as if he'd waited his entire life to say it.

"I allowed you to gain strength and learn defense. I want to fight a warrior, not a helpless young woman. Now you've proven you can handle yourself. Do you think you're prepared to fight in this war, Rayne? Are you ready to protect your world and your friends?"

Rayne spun the sword, saying, "I dedicated years of my life to fighting you. No eating. No sleeping. No future. Barely seeing my friends. I will not lose to you, Nox. I'm saving the world today, even if it means ending you."

Nox roared with laughter, and Rayne flinched. Every hair on her body stood on end. A chill shivered down her spine, and a shaky breath passed her lips.

Eyes on him. Don't lose him in the smoke.

The soot collected on Rayne's lashes. So dry. So heavy. In one blink, Nox vanished.

"Shit!"

Nox reappeared in front of her. Rayne peered into his eyes, shining like black pools. This close, she recalled those many nights when she'd wanted nothing more than to see him in person. To stand this close to him.

His ringed fist collided with her face, scoring her cheekbone.

Stars burst in Rayne's eyes, and blood filled her mouth.

Nox wrenched her up high by the collar of her ruined shirt.

Rayne stared down into the face of the Icarus who she loved and hated. Who beat her to death in a hundred dreams. And who unmade her in a hundred others. All along, he manipulated her to his advantage.

Rayne held the real advantage. Xelan told her they needed her alive. She seethed through gritted teeth. "I won't go with you, Nox."

He growled in her face, "I will drench these walls with your blood, and take what's left of you back with me."

"Only if I'm dead." She spat blood in his face and kneed him in the crotch.

Rayne thought Nox would drop her. Instead, he took her biceps in a firm grip. She groaned in frustration before asking, "Do you even have anything down there, your highness? Or is it all made of iron?"

Nox's fingers bruised, and his long nails bit into her skin. Something swam in his eyes. Determination. No matter the cost to Rayne, he would see this through.

He slammed her into the nearest wall of lockers. The combination locks pressed into her back, reverberating through her lungs and kidneys. Rayne's breath left her in a pained gasp. Least favorite thing. Ever.

Again, Nox gripped her hard, drug her feet, and slammed her into the opposite wall. She cried out. Black blossomed in her vision again, and she lost all her strength. The sword fell to the floor. She sank beside it, painting the lockers with her blood.

Nox loomed over her. "Rayne, where's that storm you promised me? How will you end me from the floor?" Not a single bead of sweat marred his gray skin, and she hated him for it.

Meanwhile, sweat pooled everywhere imaginable on Rayne's body as flames licked the surrounding walls. She almost sobbed as Nox unsheathed a gnarly serrated sword. A slow, agonizing reveal. A show for her.

"Don't worry, your majesty. I'm just warming up," Rayne said as she reached for her sword.

Nox kicked it away from her and grabbed her outstretched arm.

Rayne let out a strangled breath.

He wrenched her hand closer to him, balling it into a fist around the wrapped wounds.

"No. No. What the hell do you think you're doing?!" Rayne fought with everything in her. His grip was like a vice.

In that rich baritone, Nox said, "Lover, struggle like in our dreams. Feed that need in me as I feed the one in you." He kissed one finger, then the next. With morbid fascination,

Rayne watched as he cleaved into the bony flesh of her knuckle. The exquisite pain surprised her.

"No!" Rayne wrenched and screamed for her hand back.

Nox asked, "If I offered you a nacre to heal these wounds within seconds, would you take it?"

Even if it could heal the cuts within seconds, the nacre would come with too many strings attached. Rayne swallowed the pain and ground out, "No."

Fascination gleamed in those obsidian mirrors. Nox asked, "Doesn't this remind you of our third night together?"

It did, and Rayne hated it. In a breathy voice, she promised, "I'll make you pay for this."

"You're welcome to try." Nox sliced another clenched knuckle. He repeated this process on the following fingers, slicing down the white joints. She writhed, tugged, and screamed. This was profane. Every. Single. Time.

Tears streamed down Rayne's cheeks, leaving pale ruts in the soot. Fed up with it, she steadied herself, risked a chance, and kicked his knee.

It bent the wrong way and brought Nox down. He let go of her arm.

On her knees, Rayne grabbed her sword and turned in time to block.

Nox recovered and gave her a devastatingly attractive smirk when his sword struck down on hers. She held him off.

He purred, "Not so wise, my sweet killer."

At a twinge in her wrapped palm, Rayne cried out, "Fuck!" The sharp edge of her blade bit into her injured hand.

"You're not thinking quick enough, Celindria," Nox said with a smile as he pushed his substantial weight against her. He liked to hurt her.

"Wipe that smirk off your face." Rayne gritted her teeth and pushed back, forcing the blade in faster. With a primal cry, she pushed him back enough to stand. Still straining, she feigned a weakness on one side.

Nox took the bait and fell into it.

Seizing the opportunity, Rayne kneed him in the stomach. He doubled over, choking for air.

She raised her sword to decapitate him, but Nox recovered too quickly.

He clutched her wrists, and Rayne knew by now what she was in for. He enjoyed throwing her into things. With every slam, her lungs and kidneys vibrated, and her breath left her.

"What's your deal with the lockers? Don't you have anything new to show me? I'm getting bored."

Nox's deep voice went husky with anticipation as he said, "In this, I obey."

He slammed Rayne one last time and took both her wrists in one hand. He stretched her arms high above her head. Her abused, sore muscles strained. Nox leaned his face into hers. So close that their lips brushed with spearmint on his breath.

Emotional. Turbulence.

Rayne regretted the little thrill of excitement it gave her. She searched his eyes for anything at all resembling the tamer creature from her later dreams.

Nox gazed into hers, and in the black she saw nothing.

Distraction. Rayne needed a distraction. Further down South Hall, she peered through the broken doors.

The sunlight. Where did the light go?! Were they too late? There was darkness inside and out.

Flames kissed the walls and ceiling. Smoke escaped in black plumes.

Nox brought Rayne back to him with a caress. His fingers felt like velvet. He plunged them into her hair and gripped a fistful until her neck arched at a painful angle.

Did she scream? No. Did she whimper? No. After two years of wet dreams and nightmares with the king of an alien race. While remaining practically abstinent in real life. What sound did she make at the first intimate contact with him?

Rayne moaned.

She could never tell her friends about this part of the fight.

Nox's breath left his lips on a satisfied sigh against her hair. "I'm so pleased you're coming… around, lover."

Rayne's eyes fluttered closed. She tried to squirm, pressed firmly between the lockers and his muscular build. A wall of wood and a hard place? Very hard.

She let out a pathetic cry when Nox's soft lips brushed her neck. He said, "I've not taken Progeny vein in eight thousand years." The bass timbre of his voice vibrated against her throat.

Almost recovered. Just a little longer. How did she distract him without distracting herself? She strained against the hold on her hair. When her lips brushed his ear, she whispered, "My King."

Nox snapped to her. Suspicion ladened his voice, "Rayne?"

Why couldn't he be dumber?

"I'm prepared to negotiate terms." She leaned back against his hand, letting him cradle her nape.

Nox laughed, a full, throaty sound. A genuine one. It suited him. He said, "You're not exactly in a position for negotiation." Something passed over his humorous expression. He leaned in close again, his lips over hers. "However, I will grant a few amenities to you and one other you choose in return for a willing surrender."

Rayne both wanted and really didn't want him to kiss her. Every fiber of her being yearned for both.

Nox trailed his free hand lightly along her neck to her collarbone. Staring into Rayne's eyes, he admitted, "I am a generous King."

Ready to go.

His holding her entire weight at her wrists afforded her an advantage. Rayne tucked her knees to her chest and kicked Nox in the diaphragm. He growled, "Snake!" and tossed her closer to the flames.

Rayne tumbled in the hot debris. After two rolls, she leveraged enough momentum to spring into a cartwheel and right herself. Before her heart took a beat, she started a flat sprint.

Nox straightened and waited for her.

She jumped and kicked one foot off the locker to gain some height. Rayne wrapped her legs around his neck and swung them both to the ground. The takedown. Straddling Nox's neck, she boxed his ears for good measure, and hoped they rang like hell.

Rayne wrenched back for a good right hook to his jaw. Her knuckles were sore from their wounds.

Too late.

Nox caught her fist and ground his thumb into the pulpy injury of her palm.

She shrieked, "Damn it!"

His expression betrayed no pain or fear. In fact, his eyes sparkled in the depths of those abyssal pools. Was he toying with her? Nox bucked Rayne to the side.

"My turn?"

Lynn was forming the stirrings of a plan. Pushing the mass of braids behind her shoulder, she continued searching through drawers. "Great," she muttered to herself after finding at least one thing she wanted. Unscrewing the bottom of the flashlight took a short eternity. When it opened at last, she groaned in disgust. "It's empty."

"Yeah well if they left the batteries in it they would die. Check the same drawer," Pablo offered unhelpfully. She knew he meant well.

"Check the same drawer for the batteries," Lynn repeated in a mocking tone. She rifled through the drawer, louder than ever to cover her complaining.

How could she let herself fall for Pablo's front? How could she pounce on him like a thirsty woman? Lynn cringed every time she relived the 'lick your lips' line. Worse yet, she couldn't get a single second of their contact out of her head.

Visions of Pablo's velvety, brown eyes behind low lids as he sneaked peeks at Lynn during their kisses harassed her non-stop. When she wasn't treating a dire and devastating wound, her brain tormented her with their entire scene on perpetual replay. In slow-mo. And with an embarrassing soundtrack.

Lynn roused a happy, "Aha!" when she found the batteries in an altogether separate drawer. She wanted Pablo to witness the moment in which he was wrong, but when she looked up, he was staring out the back window.

She shrugged and continued her task while her inner monologue berated her. Sure, the kissing was amazing. Lynn would give him that, but it was only because Pablo had so much practice. He flirted with every girl in his grade. Despite all that, she always had a thing for him.

Pablo was nice and funny. It was hard to determine how smart someone was in this school. Most people hid it, aside from the Overachievers, of course. But Pablo was quick on the uptake and applied new skills with confidence.

He was handsome, and he hadn't even grown into his face, yet. It's a wonder the boy was single. Come to think of it, Lynn couldn't remember him ever having a public relationship—

"What the fuck?" Pablo barked from the window. It was a small mercy as it broke the dangerous spiral of her thoughts.

Lynn diverted her attention away from the flashlight to spare him a glance. "What is—"

Before she finished asking, she saw what made him swear. She stood and walked over to him.

They both watched in horror with mouths wide open as the daylight receded. The light was diminishing until only a deep shade of darkness remained. It was unnatural. Noon cast in a blanket of reddened darkness, for the sun's rays still graced the smoky clouds. Yet it was dark. If the Icari could really leave the shelter of the building, then all was lost.

"Lynn?" Pablo asked. She turned to him, and he continued. "How many do you think are left?"

"Aliens or students in the building?"

He stepped forward and glanced through the doorway. "Icari."

Lynn took a hair tie from her bag and began gathering her braids away from her face. She responded with the tie clenched in her teeth. "Well, if Nox is anything for Rayne to worry about, then we should definitely assume he came prepared for this..."

She slipped the weight of her hair through the tie and walked back into the Med Lab. Lynn tried hard not to think of him as a sensual piece of meat while they dealt with an apocalyptic crisis.

Pablo followed, asking, "Where do you think they came from?"

Lynn proceeded to the large cabinets in the left corner of the room. "What do you mean?"

"These anemic posers came from somewhere, right? But they can't be out in daylight, so..."

"So how did they get into the school to begin with?" Lynn finished for him. Curious. Wait, did she just finish his sentence?

Lynn shook her head and rummaged through storage. She retrieved an industrial-sized bottle of denatured alcohol and fifteen empty glass specimen jars. She relished the mixture of confusion and surprise written on his expression.

While Lynn talked, she applied labels to the bottle and filled them with alcohol. "They had to come from somewhere underground, but where is an underground entrance to this school? Hand me your over-shirt, Pablo."

Lynn wrote on the labels: DO NOT FUCK WITH.

He complied. "What are you doing?"

Rather than answer Pablo, Lynn tugged his shirt with her teeth and ripped it into strips. She ignored how much it smelled of him.

"Hey!"

"I'm making a surprise. It'll be useful for where we're going." Lynn soaked the strips of cloth in the alcohol and shoved them into the tops of the containers.

"That's not what I meant. Here." Pablo handed her a pair of scissors openly displayed on Dr. Jones' desk. She tried to keep her eye roll to herself. He asked, "Where are we going?"

This was exactly the distraction she needed. Lynn shoved eight bottles and four shivs into a bag. She marched to the door with her mini armory, saying, "To find where the Icari are coming from."

"What?!" Pablo exclaimed as he ran to catch up with her. "Hey! Wait a minute!"

Water sluiced from Kyle's face. His hair dripped in a waterfall, and his biceps and forceps strained where he gripped the toilet. Twenty seconds of precious air remained before it filled up again.

How could Kyle get this boot-licker off of him? Where the hell was Nikki, anyway? She was supposed to back him up. Was she okay? Guilt twinged his already overloaded conscience. He couldn't afford this distraction.

The unreal strength of the Icarean soldier pressed down on the back of Kyle's head. He gulped a lungful of smoky air and reached for the toilet handle again. The sight of the water filling up the bowl sent him into a panic. How many times had he done this now? Two? Three? Was he developing a phobia?

The water washed over Kyle's face, rushing around and pressing at his eyelids and nostrils. It wanted inside. For the first time in two years, Kyle wished he'd cut his hair. In the water, it loomed around his face, inducing claustrophobia. It made his heart race and incited the urge to thrash.

Kyle and Xelan never practiced drowning torture techniques. But in all those years of training, Kyle recalled one important thing. *"To remain calm is to remain in control."* So he remained calm, and it paid off.

He pushed himself enough off the floor to kick the Icarean soldier's hip, and the bastard stopped drowning him.

Kyle stood in a rush and rolled his eyes in growing frustration. "Man, I was hoping that was your nuts." He sniffed blood back against his sleeve. "If you even have any..."

The monster's eyes flared, and rage seeped into them. He screamed wordlessly and lunged.

Kyle's shoe squelched as he sidestepped the soldier and clotheslined him. The Icarus doubled over, choking. Kyle shoved into the soldier's chest with one hand and slammed an elbow into the middle of his back with the other.

Before the monster recovered, Kyle pounded his knee into the alien's face. Blue blood sprayed the white-washed walls. After which, Kyle asked, "Do you understand English?"

The bastard stumbled back. Cerulean liquid rushed from his nose and mouth. No answer.

"Do. You. Understand. English?"

The soldier snarled.

Kyle said, "Good. Because I want the next thing I say to be clear between us. I'm about to fuck you up."

Oh, yeah. He got it.

The alien launched at Kyle. Kyle turned, centered his balance with ease, and side-kicked the vamp-wannabe square in the chest. It went flying into the bathroom stall. The cherry on top? His head fell into the toilet.

Kyle jumped on the stall door. The soldier righted himself as the Progeny swung the door back at him. If they'd built the school from sturdier materials, the blow would have decapitated him. Alas, it only crushed his opponent's throat perfectly. Kyle grabbed the knife and finished him before the alien recovered. Right in the chest.

The young man swung his soppy hair back and laughed, nudging the corpse with his foot. Luckily, these cloaked guys didn't teleport like Korac with Rayne and Sagan. Maybe not every single blood sucker on Cinder was super gifted.

"Ooo... What's this?" Kyle knelt beside the body, shoved aside the folds of his cloak, and snatched something from his belt. The familiar gold dagger fit in his hand. From the pommel to the blade, a golden-leafed vine swirled in delicate metallurgy. This could only be...

{Near 6,000 BCE}

"You forged this?" Celindria stared down into the magnificent vessel.

Pride warmed Devis' chest. His smile broadened at the awe in her eyes. Grateful for the rare gift of her praise, he said, "I named it 'Pretiosum Cruor,' which means—"

"Cherished Blood," they said in unison.

She smiled at him over the surveyed artifacts. "How does it function?"

Devis understood Celindria only focused on business. She desired nothing more than to save humanity from the Icarean horde. He respected her for it, but he also wondered if she ever got lonely. Many in their group had paired off. Even Xelan and Merit stopped dancing around it and started spending time together. But Celindria went off on her own, planning every detail of their revolution. Devis would never stop loving her.

"Devis? Is something wrong?" Celindria pressed.

"Oh, apologies. The work has taxed me greatly." He laughed away her concern. "Here," he said as he laid the dagger and vessel on a silk display. Both were forged with smelted gold. A metal which harbored adverse effects on their oppressors.

Devis touched the empty heart-shaped receptacle. A golden sword pierced it, and a delicate golden vine surrounded both. "This is for the blood as we talked about. I designed this to chamber it. Releasing the blood will unlock the conduit and set the last step of our plans in motion. Once we gather The Brethren and discuss our strategy, we can vet volunteers for the process. One person. One bond. Forever."

Celindria asked, "How do we get the blood into it?"

Devis said, "This dagger." He touched a ten-centimeter golden blade surrounded by the same swirling vine. "The technology Xelan provided us will prevent oxygen from reaching the blood. Straight from the vein to the glass with no exposure."

Suddenly, Celindria faltered and let the podium hold her weight.

"Are you all right?" Devis asked, holding her elbow.

In a breathy voice, Celindria said, "Yes. I apologize. It must be the heat from the forge."

"I can fetch water." The young man rushed to the center of the camp and collected the ladle from the trough.

After filling the flask, Devis rushed back to his forge. Upon entering, he knew without words something was wrong. He dropped the flask and gaped. "No." His voice went quiet and thin.

Celindria offered a sad smile as if afraid she'd disappointed him. "This is the way," she offered.

Devis said, "You can never understand what you have done."

"The nanotechnology will recognize my blood for the Vacating. It will accept no other."

"Forever, Celindria. It will not accept the blood of another so long as the technology exists," Devis elaborated.

Celindria touched him on the shoulder gently and relaxed a little. "It could be no other way. Never would I ask another to take on such a charge. All generations that follow would suffer. Please tell no one of the consequences."

"How could you ask me to accept such a thing?" Devis countered. "And what of the generations to follow *your* bloodline?"

Celindria said, "We must all bear our burdens. I, too, wish I did not have to ask you to bear mine."

Devis nodded. When she left, he stared at the podium. A tear fell from his eyes, and then another. Inside the glass vessel pooled the most cherished blood, and he blamed himself.

{Invasion Day | April 2006}

Kyle stuck the fine instrument in one of his deeper pockets and chuffed at the fallen soldier. "This belongs to me. How did you get it?"

A scream alerted him back to the battle in the cafeteria. There were only four left after this one. Not counting Korac, of course.

John's knee hurt. It's all he could think about as he ducked again. For the fourth time that day he felt the air displacement of something swinging over his head, narrowly and fortunately missing. Four attempts on his life in a matter of six hours. That had to be a world record, and of course it's the first and only accomplishment in his life. Now, he wouldn't have a world to share it with.

This entire day was seriously fucked. The worst part was how much the people John was with kept eating it up. They're all, "Oh Rayne says let's do this, so this is what we're gonna do." And, "We don't want anything happening to Rayne." Pfft. Out of all of them, she looked like she could handle herself the most, but Tameka made better leadership decisions.

Throughout today's events, John allowed a sparse momentary thought for himself. He reflected on that day two years ago when Rayne's mystery trainer first approached him.

{March 2004}

"So you followed me all the way home because Rayne Callahan asked you to teach me how to defend myself in an oncoming apocalypse?" Why the hell was she even mentioning John to strangers? They weren't close like that. This girl tortured him daily in their late afternoon classes for the last two years. Listing off delicious food while he complained about his empty stomach. Diabolical.

"If you must put it in terms so simply, then yes. That's what I'm here for." The annoyingly good-looking and tall man—and John was tall so anyone taller than him was really tall—agreed almost as if it was a chore to him or an errand Rayne had him run.

John stopped at the end of his driveway and said, "Look. I don't want you here, and you don't seem to want to be here. So let's just tell her whatever we can to make this go away." He turned to walk away, and the X-men guy appeared in front of him several meters away.

Did John blink? Or have a seizure? His mouth gaped. He couldn't help it. Gravel crunched as his bag dropped from his hands. It was like his brain had shut off or something.

After dinner, he followed Xelan two houses down to Sagan's place. Apparently, this was their regularly scheduled night, and superhero guy wanted to *"ease John into it with a preview of the training."*

John felt more than a little self-sufficient in defense. He said, "I know Aikido."

Xelan offered a simple nod without turning back or stopping. He said, "That should prove useful. I studied under Takeda Sokaku and Morihei Usehiba in the early 20th century. Turning your opponent's momentum against them is a very valuable aspect of the style I teach."

John allowed his mouth to fall open again as he gaped at the back of Xelan's head. "Osensei?"

Xelan threw a glance over his shoulder, saying, "The very same."

The teenager didn't know what bothered him more. That Xelan claimed to train with a guy who'd died several decades before John was born. Or that he wasn't even bragging about it. He stated it as a simple fact.

Sagan called to Xelan, "Hey, I was worried. You were later than usual—"

John waved from behind Xelan.

After a flash of confusion, Sagan smiled. "Hey, John! This is my new boyfriend, Xelan. He goes to college. Did he miss my driveway and park at your house?"

John said, "Well, actually—"

Xelan groaned in frustration.

John shot the ancient dude a glare for interrupting him.

The tall Aikido master pinched the bridge of his nose before saying, "Elden, that was pitiful. I never thought I'd have to teach a teenage girl how to tell a decent lie. But it looks like I'll have to add an hour of 'covert operations.'"

John didn't want to get involved with this, but after a few moments of watching them spar, he agreed. "I can't believe you can move so fast." He stared at Sagan with a new light of appreciation.

She swiped a grass stain from her pants and groused, "Yet somehow I always end up on my ass."

Xelan indicated in front of John. "Your turn."

Reluctant and a little nervous, John assumed a confident, balanced stance. He said, "Before we get too far into it, I want to know how likely all this is to even happen. Like, how much of a chance are we talking here? An invasion sounds ludicrous."

Sagan chimed in, "We've been waiting for two years. But I can tell you that in those two years, weird shit has happened, and we accept in good faith that Xelan's training is best for us."

John scoffed, "How many of you are there?!"

"You don't need to worry about that. Just get ready to block this punch," Xelan commanded.

John posed his hands for the best defense and waited with easy breath.

Xelan kicked him in the face.

"Oh, ow! Fuck!" John shielded his nose and mouth and whined when he tasted blood. Filtered through his cupped hands, he shouted, "What the fuck, man?!"

"Shh!" Sagan passed him an ice pack. "Don't wake my parents."

"Jesus Christ!"

"You were watching my hands and not my moves," Xelan explained.

John defended himself. "Yeah cause you said you would punch me."

"Do you think someone intending to kill you will tell you the truth and fight fair?"

{Invasion Day | April 2006}

Well, John knew for sure now: Icari did not fight fair. Despite the time he'd spent training with Xelan, he didn't find himself all that good at fighting them, either. But the others?

Man, sometimes they actually smiled during these fights. The harder it got, the more likely it was to catch one of them grinning. It bothered John on a spiritual level.

He only wanted an ice pack for his knee.

John felt more than saw Andrew tackle the blood sucker behind him to the disgusting table top with a squelch. John gazed longingly at the space under the table beside him. He gave serious thought to crawling under it and waiting until the fight was over, but he knew that wouldn't fly.

He jumped up, ran over to the soldier under Andrew, and forced the thing's arms down. He hoped Andrew got a clear shot for the kill.

There! As if Andrew considered the battle already won, he grinned.

John shivered in revulsion. What was wrong with these people? The Icarus below Andrew surprised them both by wrenching his hands from John's grip and grabbing Andrew by the throat.

Andrew squeezed out, "Oh. Fuck."

Fang-face threw him to the floor.

The alien whirled on John.

"Shit." He turned to run away. A loud and disrespectful 'pop' erupted from John's knee, making him scream. As he crumpled to the floor, he cursed himself for not hiding under the table earlier. The end was upon him. He squeezed his eyes tight and wished he stood even a slim chance of receiving Last Rites.

The bastard breathed on John's neck.

Oh, hell no, this was not the way he wanted to go! Understandably, he whimpered. The moment wet teeth touched his neck, the fucker dared to screech in his ear.

"What the hell?!" John needed to look. His eyes popped open, and he spun all the way behind him to see the wannabe vamp flailing around with his arms at his back. He clawed at something there. Beyond him, Andrew faced the Icarus with that perverse smile slapped back on his face.

The fighter taunted, "Come and get me, alien scum."

As John watched the "alien scum" pursue Andrew around the room, he realized how much he really didn't like being Rayne's friend.

"I hate what you did to me," Sagan confessed as she punched her assailant.

Korac evaded. "Aww, baby. That's mean. You were never this mean before. Has Tameka rubbed off on you?" He disappeared.

"Why? Don't you like my best friend?" Sagan anticipated his next materialization and shoved the heel of her palm into his nose.

The Icarean General took the hit and stumbled back. With one hand over his nose, he said, "Let's just say I don't want her to give a speech at our wedding."

Sagan lunged with the sword.

Korac turned to the side, evading the attack, and hammered an axe pommel on her wrist. Hard.

Sagan staggered, dropping her weapon with a curse.

Korac's arms encircled her from behind and pulled her tight. One axe dug into her hip, the other on her shoulder, pressing the blade against her face. His presence surrounded her, overwhelmed her, trapped her. No, not like this. Anything but this. She broke out into a sweat, gritted her teeth, and swallowed her pulse.

The Icarean General purred against her ear, "Seems like you can't stay out of my arms, My Afflicted One."

Sagan closed her eyes tight and tried to steel herself against what she knew would follow. This close to him, she smelled the crisp winter of his skin and the fresh peppermint of his breath.

It was hard to admit, but Sagan wanted him. Even after all this destruction. She'd kept the braided lock of Korac's hair, and even now she felt it in her skirt pocket. Yet, this wasn't right and the way he held onto her said he knew it too.

So Sagan would play the game. Through clenched teeth, she said, "Fuck you."

Korac chuckled maliciously as he drew the axe down Sagan's cheek. She cried out when the skin submitted under the sharp silver, and blood flowed liberally from the wound. The entire time, the General kept his lips on her ear as he tested her limits with pain and pleasure.

"Love, why are you doing this?!" The desperation in her own voice made Sagan wince.

Korac breathed against her, quiet, meant only for her to hear, "If you come back with me, we can fix it. Just like that. No scarring." The silky tone took on a hard edge. "But if you don't, you'll always have this to remind you of me. And when you tire of seeing it in your reflection, you can come for me anytime."

Nope. Sagan was done.

She stomped on his foot and shoved her elbow into Korac's ribs.

With a grunt, he backed away to catch his breath.

Sagan grabbed the axe he held above her and landed a high kick square into his chest.

The blow forced him to release the axe to her. Korac growled in frustration.

Nervous about his retaliation, Sagan put a few meters between them and tested the feel of the axe in her palm.

Korac recovered too quickly. He straightened, towering almost a foot above Sagan. His sense of humor was unphased as he purred, "The reality is more enjoyable than the fantasy."

Sagan confessed, "With you, this wasn't what I fantasized about."

Her honesty struck him, giving her time to assess him. Why wasn't anything affecting him? No heavy breathing. No sweat. Not even pain.

In a voice wrought with yearning, Korac shared, "We thought about this day for so very long."

Wait, there!

There was a tiny trickle of blue blood at the corner of his sinful smirk, and something in his silver eyes seemed transformed. They smoldered like melting pools. Korac tasted his own blood on his lips before saying, "The way you look at me..." He chuckled in that silky tenor. "You're the warrior I wanted you to be. How would you tally this fight so far, Lieutenant General?"

Smoke polluted Sagan's lungs. Even her eyes watered. This couldn't go on any longer, but she just couldn't resist a jab. She swallowed a dry lump in her throat, spun the axe once, and said, "You can't seem to stay off the floor."

Korac mirrored her axe spin. "Isn't this familiar? How good do you think you are with that?" He inclined his head at her.

Sagan shrugged. "Feels right at home." And it did thanks to his training.

His cold and bitter laugh startled her before he swung his arm high and threw the axe.

Sagan dove to the floor and somersaulted toward Korac. She straightened upright on her knees and plunged the axe with a strong two-handed grip. Her final desperate attempt to rid herself of his power over her.

Korac froze. His eyes went wide, the mercury in them shining. He lowered his gaze to his nightly lover.

Sagan's chest heaved with her teeth clenched and bared. She refused to let go of the axe embedded deep inside his chest. When she heard him grunt, she raised her violet eyes to meet his.

This wound should be fatal. It should kill him. Xelan taught her so. The bone resisted until his chest gave under the honed blade. The apex of the axe penetrated his brain just enough to affect its functions.

Unsteady, Korac sank to his knees. His breathing grew more labored than her own. He grunted with every inhale. Sagan stared into his eyes. What was this feeling? Why...? With his blood spattered across her face and clothes, she searched for relief. She released the axe, gasped for air, and tried to feel something else through her exhaustion.

Korac reached for her with a pale hand.

Sagan recoiled and crawled back away from him. At last, his body fell lifeless to the side, his eyes unblinking.

She touched her face to wipe away his blood. What was that?

Tears.

They tugged from her heart. Another monster had died. That was all. Even so, Sagan cried for him. When the magnitude of it hit her, she fought not to weep. Loss. She grieved for Korac, or maybe just a chapter in her life closed before she was ready.

Kyle shouted, breaking Sagan's reverie, "John, down!"

With shaking hands, Sagan forced herself off the floor, and took stock of the surrounding battle. Why the hell were these last four still fighting? Their leader was dead. Yet, they continued to attack her friends. They were fighting to the last man. Were they stalling for something?

A shriek resounded throughout the building and rang through Sagan's ears.

Rayne.

FOURTEEN

LOVE AND WAR ARE TWO OF THE MOST UNFAIR GAMES WE PLAY, SO WHY NOT PLAY THEM AT THE SAME TIME

"WHAT'RE YOU DOING?"

Rayne couldn't keep the fear out of her voice.

Nox had pinned her to the floor and stretched his hand over burning debris off to the side. The heavy, ornate ring shimmered with firelight. His deep voice rumbled as he assured Rayne, "Patience." Flames reflected in his obsidian eyes when he added a vicious smile.

Rayne's heart raced. She needed longer to recover. Two more minutes. Come on.

Nox hurled his adorned fist at her face. Rayne closed her eyes and braced herself for the strike.

Nothing came.

Holding her breath, Rayne cautiously opened her eyes. When they met his gaze, Nox cupped her cheek.

Rayne screamed. Her skin blistered under white heat as the perversion of the Pretiosum Cruor branded onto her face.

Despite her thrashing, Nox gently pressed his forehead to hers. "That's it, girl. You're mine. Until you accept my offer of a nacre, you'll look in the mirror and think of me." He pulled away to watch her suffer.

Trapped under his legs, Rayne writhed in pain. Her eyes blazed with hatred. She knew he could see it. He licked his lips, enticed by it. The only one who knew her darkest needs and her gravest fears. Nox personified her worst nightmares.

He gripped a fistful of her hair and brought her face to his. This close, Rayne burned in the flames reflecting in his eyes. "Destiny is patient. So unkind that it would make us mortal enemies."

Rayne recovered. She grabbed the nearest heavy thing, a cinder block, and smashed him in the face with it.

Nox stood and backed away from her, snarling.

She spun her legs to hop on her feet.

He swung at her.

Rayne caught his fist, hooked her leg onto the bend of his elbow, and used that fulcrum to climb onto his shoulders. From there, she broke the cinder block on top of Nox's head.

He growled and slammed her to the floor with enough height and force she knew this was the end. At the last second, Nox twisted Rayne into his arms, a breath away from the tiles.

He said, "You're too fragile. Killing you takes nothing."

Rayne's heart pounded against her heaving chest. Breathless from the near-death experience, she asked, "Nox, why do you want me?"

The King of Cinder brushed her tears across the fresh brand on her face as he said, "Salvation."

Rayne ground out, "Then why are you hurting me?!"

Nox frowned at her words. "To touch you. I've waited eight thousand years to break you and bring you back with me. And now that we've begun to dance, I'll take my time with you."

"Give me enough time and I'll kill you," Rayne said before she wrapped one leg around his neck and squeezed.

Nox tossed her casually to the other end of the hall.

Rayne slid across hot debris and missed a fallen beam by a breath. She groaned.

Sit up. Regroup. Start again—

Rayne stared at something beside her, frozen. Nikki's body was spread out amid the rubble.

"No!" Why? Why would Nox do this? The young woman had died an awful death. A weapon hadn't caused her injuries. Then what—

Rayne looked up at the riot gate through the dense smoke. Nox appeared beside her. Before he hauled the gate down, she rolled out of the way.

Almost out of the way.

"Shit!"

The heavy metal of the riot gate crashed into Rayne's left arm. A sickening, guttural pop erupted from the smashed appendage. Her entire body spasmed in pain, and she screamed through clenched teeth.

"Powerless." Nox raised the gate.

"No!" She swallowed three heaving breaths, pinned to the spot, and he slammed it down again. Her body jumped and writhed.

"Hopeless." Solemnly, Nox raised the gate again.

No, no, no, no...

"Accepting." Staring into Rayne's eyes, he rolled the gate down one more time.

Rayne hated the tears. Hated the way her limbs flailed outside her control. But most of all, she hated that the pain dissipated in its entirety. Numb was bad. Her arm stopped responding. Her mind begged her not to look.

Rayne crawled onto her side and opened her eyes. "Oh... no..." Was this it? Would it never move again?

Judging by the limpness of the socket, Nox must have dislocated the shoulder. Blood pooled and poured from the middle of her bicep. Something peeked out from the blood. Stark. White. Bone.

Rayne groaned.

Nox stood over her pulverized arm and admired her, staring at the exposed bone.

She scrambled to get away. Right. Now. But she couldn't move.

He chuckled. "The fighter in you never stops. Good. You'll need that for your inevitable future. So much worse awaits you."

Get up.

Rayne pushed. Nothing.

Get up!

Nox was about to fuck her up, and her body refused to move. She'd tapped out her reserves.

Nox fell upon her with a thirst Rayne recognized from her nightmares. "May I have this dance?" Mock gentility dripped from his words. He lifted her numb hand gingerly and placed a soft kiss on the back of it.

Rayne locked eyes with the devil, and for a moment contemplated falling into them. When his lips curled into a gruesome smile, she held her breath, knowing what would come next. Nox gripped her hand and pulled her by her broken arm.

Rayne didn't scream. She didn't give him what he wanted. Time. She needed time.

Survive. Recover. Kill.

That was her plan. She just hoped to survive Nox long enough.

"Where do you think it is?" As they reached the junction to North Hall, Pablo contemplated if all this hero shit was nonsense. But he knew deep down, if he lived through this, he wanted history to count him among the heroes. Because of *her.*

Lynn peered around the corner, checking right, then left. Nothing. She asked, "When this first started, did you hear someone shouting orders?"

He nodded, admiring her face with her braids tied back. They framed her beautiful brown eyes—

Pablo dug his fingernails deep into his palms. He had to quit thinking like that. Treating their injured classmates had kept him distracted in the Med Lab. But out here they were on their own and facing certain death. His more primitive instincts wanted to focus only on her.

Lynn inhaled deep and cleared her throat. The smoke got thick, fast. She headed left down North Hall. "I think they came from down here. Maybe the gym or the library?"

"Oh." Pablo wished he had more to contribute, but he was running on fumes here.

Lynn walked around the next corner, and he followed closely. When their hands brushed, he snatched his back to prevent himself from holding hers.

She was all business, searching the library through glass doors. Dark with no sign of movement. She waved for him. "C'mon..."

Why does the sign say MEDIA CENTER? It never made much sense. It wasn't like students could check out videos or anything.

"I wonder why the sign has always said 'Media Center?'" Lynn asked.

That was it. If they survived this and she would have him, Pablo would ask Lynn to marry him.

He made a guess, "The computers, maybe?"

She scoffed, "What media can they run? Eight-bit porn?"

Pablo barked out a laugh, and Lynn snickered.

Pablo and Lynn deserved this inappropriate laugh in the wide open. The sun was eclipsed, and their friends were fighting aliens to save humanity.

Cautiously, they pulled the library doors open and walked through the theft detectors. Shelves lined the walls stuffed with musty books. A long table of student computers occupied the middle. The librarian offices were off to the right. If anyone wanted to speak to them, they could tap the large, glass windows.

Pablo and Lynn searched carefully, trying hard to stay quiet. Both of them gripped their weapons firm in hand.

They'd made it past the checkout counter when something caused Lynn to whimper.

"What?" Pablo rushed over to her, but stopped short when he glimpsed the cause. "Oh, god..."

They found Ms. McGreen, the librarian. Dead and on display like a warning.

The entire room spun. Pablo crouched to the floor and spilled the scant contents of his stomach. He suppressed a sob when Lynn started rubbing his back in soothing circles.

She said, "It's okay."

Pablo was definitely marrying her. When he finished, she offered him a bottle of water. He took it with a nod of gratitude.

Lynn asked, "Are you all right?"

Pablo swallowed hard and choked on the air. "You know? I'm really starting to hate that question."

"Are you okay?" Kyle asked Sagan as he offered her his hand.

She nodded and let him lift her off the floor. After all the wet, slippery shit Sagan had touched today, she still wiped her hands on her skirt and grimaced. "Why are you all wet?!"

Kyle shrugged and said, "I got my first swirly, and I don't recommend it."

Okay. Sagan was not asking for those details. Instead, she assessed the situation in the cafeteria. Only four Icari were left to fight, and Rayne had yet to return from Nox.

Sagan hated this. It took every ounce of her self-control not to run and help Rayne, but staying away was the right thing. After listening to Rayne's dreams about Nox, Sagan knew he'd simply torture or even kill anyone who came to help Rayne. He'd get off on her misery all because his hatred for Celindria made him blind to anything else.

Besides, the fight wasn't over yet.

John favored his right leg as he faced down a Russian soldier. Andrew stood over his latest kill after putting a large blade through its back. Nikki running off and not returning weighed heavily on Sagan's mind. Tameka fought off two Icarean soldiers. Alone.

With no time to mourn the lover she'd slain, Sagan burst into action. Tameka's curling mass of red hair bounced from the table where one soldier held her arms down. Another straddled her with a knife raised high. Tameka snarled in his face.

Sagan retrieved the axe Korac had thrown at her and rushed over. She kicked off a wall and vaulted at the soldier holding Tameka down. She swung the axe mid-fall. The monster's head landed on the ground before she did.

Two more to go.

Andrew took out the Icarus with a knife on Tameka. Both crashed to the floor, and he stabbed the soldier with his own knife. It wailed as cobalt arterial spray drenched Andrew's already messy face.

Andrew shouted, "Aww, nasty!"

Sagan's head snapped up, and Andrew bolted upright as John cried out across the cafeteria.

An Icarus was dragging John away by his bad leg.

Kyle leapt from the nearest table onto the soldier's back hard enough that he rode it down to the floor. "Where the fuck do you think you're going?! John, are you okay? John?"

John made achingly slow progress to stand on his good leg. The agitated Icarus threw Kyle and retrieved him from his landing site, only to throw him again.

John called out, "Hey, you blood-sucking son of a bitch!"

The Icarus snapped his teeth at John and rushed him. "Yeah, you know? You shouldn't turn your back on an enemy."

Kyle hit the Icarus over the head with a toilet seat he'd pulled from god knows where. He threw the soldier up against the wall, and John staked it.

Sagan surveyed the room. By some miracle, they'd killed all the invaders, and the unit had stayed alive. A twinge struck her as she wondered about Nikki.

Kyle searched the space. "Is that all of them?"

"Yeah, it is..." Sagan answered with a smile spreading across her face.

They did it.

Andrew stared at Sagan as she tore the bottom of her tank top and wrapped her wounds with her midriff exposed. If she caught him looking, she might think he was perving on her. But he meant well. Just checking her for injuries after her fight with Nox's General. She carried herself as if affected by more than the cuts and bruises.

John examined his knee while Kyle checked his potentially broken nose in the reflection of a knife.

"Where's Nikki?" Tameka rubbed her bruised throat.

John groaned. "She never came back."

Kyle walked over. "What about Rayne?!"

Sagan and Andrew exchanged a look, and both said, "She'll be fine."

Tameka shook her head. "But what if—"

Sagan spun an axe, saying, "No, leave her to it."

"Well, at least *they're* gone." John nudged a fallen soldier's corpse with his foot. "What do we do with their bodies? We can't leave alien bodies lying around."

Andrew waved the smoke around, saying, "The fire will take care of it." The way it was spreading, it might take care of them first. He opened his mouth to move this evacuation along—

"It was one hell of a fight, huh?" Kyle smiled when they gave him confused faces.

Why the hell did Kyle have to be so weird? Andrew said, "Dude."

After an awkward silence, the group broke into a fit of laughter. Andrew needed that, no matter how much it hurt. What a day. Both he and John sagged to the floor, holding their ribs.

Tameka knelt to check on Andrew.

He said, "Thank you," appreciating her small smile in return.

Kyle gave his nose a more thorough inspection. When the laughter faded into sighing and a deep, mutual relief, Andrew glanced up to see Sagan standing over him.

"How did you know to come here, today?" Straight to the point.

Andrew blinked. "What do you mean?" He did *not* want to do this right now.

That lit Sagan's fuse. "You couldn't have known to come today unless someone informed you about the attack!"

It was true. Andrew stood and faced her. "All right. He told me not to say anything but..."

"Who?" Kyle joined the interrogation.

Andrew hesitated. How could he phrase this without breaking his oath? "Xelan."

One word—one name—said all too much. Shit.

Tameka gasped. "Xelan?!"

The news surprised everyone, save for Sagan. She grew further impatient. He couldn't blame her.

Sagan asked, "When? When did you speak to him? No one else has heard from him in four months. How long have you known?" She backed him against a wall, advancing toward him, gripping the axes with renewed vigor.

Andrew raised his hands in surrender. Time to lie. "This morning, I swear. I had a nightmare of Fair in flames and there he was, all dark and full of warnings." He lowered his arms and relaxed as Sagan loosened a little.

"What did he say?" Tameka flanked Sagan like she might have to hold the shorter girl back.

Andrew couldn't tell them the truth. No matter what. It's not like they'd appreciate him for meeting with Xelan secretly these last four months. Besides, he was deep in the weeds, and he had more questions than answers, himself. This morning was a prime example.

Xelan's initial estimates had turned out fairly accurate so far, and now the Icarus wasn't around for the team interrogation. The truth, but not all of it.

Andrew explained, "Xelan said Rayne would die today if I didn't come here. And if that happened, we would all die. Something about the aftermath." He swallowed before saying, "I actually didn't believe him at first, but I was late to school anyway and could afford to drop by. The Icari are dead now, so it's over." Okay. He managed it.

As he finished his explanation, the foundation shuddered beneath their feet. His eyes searched the quaking room.

Sagan bolted for the cafeteria's entrance. Everyone formed a line beside her, and a sense of dread filled the air.

"No... It's not over."

Pablo and Lynn advanced at a creep down the library's short corridor into the break room.

As they passed the dead librarians, his complexion must've paled because Lynn asked, "You good?"

He lied, "Yeah. Thanks. Let's keep going." Pablo gestured her forward. He wasn't really ready to press on, but how was he supposed to salvage her opinion of him if he kept retching? Besides, something gnawed at his morbid curiosity further down the hallway. Despite his fight or flight begging him to give it up, he needed to see it.

The darkness smothered Pablo like a velvety, tangible blockade. He wished for some light. As if summoned, a beam pierced the veil of darkness all the way down the hall.

Lynn glanced back at him, flashlight in hand. "I'm glad these batteries work."

"You can say that again. The smoke just makes everything so much more..." Pablo fought for the right word.

She offered a few, "Terrifying? Claustrophobic? Horror movie atmosphere?" Searching, she swung the beam out of one door and into another.

Lynn was so fearless. God, he was falling in love with her. As he watched her be brave enough for the both of them, Pablo said, "Claustrophobic was my favorite. I like when you use four-syllable words. Smart chicks are hot."

Lynn snapped around to him.

Pablo almost clapped his hand over his flirtatious mouth. He did not mean to say that out loud. Instead, he gave into a nervous habit and licked his lips.

And she watched him do it.

Seconds ago, Pablo came close to puking his guts up. Now, he wanted to sweep Lynn in his arms and plant a kiss on her lips. He wanted her to know how much she affected him.

Before Pablo could put his plan into action, a dry rasp penetrated the darkness. The mood died as both of them stiffened, alert.

"Did you do that?"

Pablo shook his head. Any words he wanted to answer with choked in his throat.

To his absolute horror, Lynn inched forward.

He communicated his disapproval in rigid, frantic gestures. The whisper of his hands moving caught her attention.

Lynn mouthed, "We. Have. To. Know."

Pablo cocked one eyebrow sky high. "Do. We. Really?!" And hoped all his incredulity seeped into his lip talking.

Lynn just turned around and kept going. Pablo threw his hands in the air with frustration. How could he reason with her? Exasperated, he clutched his knife, huffed, and followed.

The corridor ended in a large storeroom. It was some kind of archive. Files and crates of books piled up the walls on all sides. Lynn made it to the back, peeking at the corner. Her head vanished into the wall.

The atmosphere was playing tricks on Pablo. He crossed the room after her. At the seams of the wall where they met in the corner, Lynn found a narrow hallway. A well-hidden optical illusion. She glanced at him. He nodded, and they both took the corner.

They gawked at what they found inside. An open access hatch—enormous in size—was in the floor beneath a large patch of removed carpet. Glancing at one another again, Pablo held one palm flat up, and a fist on top of it. Understanding, Lynn rolled her eyes and mimicked the gesture.

Rock. Paper. Scissors. He got rock. She got scissors. Sighing, she passed the flashlight over to him.

Pablo was of two minds about winning. On the one hand, he wanted to keep Lynn out of harm's way. On the other hand, he didn't want to put himself in danger. But this was a chance at redemption, and he couldn't pass it up.

Slowly—painfully slowly—Pablo edged over to the open hole in the secret room of their scary library. He examined the hatch and predictably found a ladder. Next step, look in the hole. He really didn't want to look, but he shoved his face to the frayed carpet and peered in with the flashlight. It led down a passageway to a basement he never knew existed. Even in the dark, he spotted a connecting tunnel.

As soon as he found it, the ground shuddered as if it wanted to rupture and swallow them whole. Something was coming. Pablo panicked and dropped the flashlight.

"What is it, Pablo?!" The tremor in Lynn's voice upset him because he wanted to keep her safe.

But that was too damned bad.

He jumped up. "Go!"

Lynn didn't argue. Pablo reached her, and they both ran. The thunderous roar of stampeding boots followed them. Whatever came out of that hole was chasing them.

As they turned the hidden corner, he cried, "Pass me a Molotov and a light!"

"Here!" She tossed him the supplies.

They rushed down the smelly corridor. Pablo dared to glance back. Not far behind, a pasty, tall S.O.B. pursued them around the hidden corner. He was more advanced and suped up than the others. Bigger. Faster. More aggressive.

Pablo lit the rag and tossed it as they broke into the stacks of seizing books.

"Nice shot!" Lynn shouted.

It connected and burst into flames. At least one caught fire and stopped chasing them. Not bad. Not bad.

They passed the checkout counter. Once more through the theft detectors, they fled the library. The thunder chased them.

When Lynn and Pablo made it to the North Hall junction, they found Sagan and the others standing bloodied in front of the cafeteria. He spared a passing thought that he hoped it wasn't all their blood before he kicked it into high gear.

"Run!" Pablo and Lynn shouted in unison.

The others didn't react fast enough.

Kyle glanced them over and asked, "I thought all the Icari were dead?"

Sagan's complexion lost all color. "Those were Colita's soldiers."

"Yeah?"

"These are Korac's warriors."

As Sagan finished explaining, sixteen men in chrome armor and silk robes stampeded around the corner behind Lynn and Pablo. One sported some nasty burn wounds. His skin was damned near melted off his face.

Time slowed down. Everyone turned to retreat as Pablo and Lynn ran by them. Lynn turned, lit one bottle, and threw it on an advancing Icarus. He whooshed up in flames as the alcohol poured over him.

Yup, Pablo was definitely marrying Lynn. He planned to ask her the moment this battle was won. And they were winning. Because he knew Lynn wouldn't let them lose.

The ground shook with the weight of blood suckers as if a stampede of elephants were quaking the earth.

Sagan and Kyle led in front. "This way!"

They ran past the gym and made for the exit down a narrow corridor. The lights of the back-up generator flashed red across their faces.

"Come on! Just a little further!" The corridor twisted and turned as they ran in a single file line to the exit. Riot gates blocked the entrances into the auxiliary gym. Why would those be closed? The only thing in there was—

They came to the exit. It was chained shut with a massive lock.

Kyle shouted, "Fuck!"

The only other exits were through the aux gym, blocked by the gates. Smoke billowed into Sagan's lungs, and huge aliens were on their way to butcher them in the school's rectum.

"Sagan, how do we get out of here?" Tameka asked when she turned the last corner and saw the door. Her words came a little too sharp and fast. Tameka couldn't panic. If she felt like panicking, then they really were screwed.

John stared at the doors as the rumbling came closer. He whispered, "We're gonna die here."

Sagan turned to him. "No, we're not—"

A loud crash brought her attention back to the door. Kyle rammed into it with his shoulder. Andrew and John joined him.

"Shit!" Kyle sank to the floor. The wound on his arm gushed from his efforts. "It's no good. We can't get through here, and the gym is closed off."

Andrew and John didn't give up.

Sagan glanced back to the corridor. Shadows moved in a stealth formation amid the red lights. "Oh, fuck! Move! Clear the door!"

They backed off. She swung her axe on the chain. Sparks flew. The strike point of the blade went red and smoldered. The chains smoked.

Silently, Sagan thanked Korac for the weapon. Only then did she realize she'd lost the other one in the cafeteria. She almost pouted.

"Damn," Pablo said with feeling.

"Come on. We gotta get out of here!" Tameka kicked the doors open.

That's when they realized they weren't safe from the Icari outside at all. Where was the sun? Sagan cursed, "Fucking underground school."

Several of her friends grunted their agreement.

Andrew said, "Yeah no offense guys, but your school is so jacked."

Plumes of smoke billowed from the technology hall across the way. It was beyond jacked now.

Students were scattered across the parking lot, looking like a cat had jumped into a jigsaw puzzle. When they noticed everyone escaping from the building, they cheered in celebration and relief.

"No! Run!" Sagan and Tameka screamed. No one moved. They didn't understand. They were still overjoyed to see them alive. "No!" The girls ran into the gathering crowd.

Sagan pointed the axe at the school. "They're coming. We have to leave."

Kyle shook his head. "There are fifteen of them and like a few hundred of us. We can take 'em."

Andrew protested, "We can't just hand weapons to civilians and expect them to survive."

John threw down his bag of weapons and opened it. Sagan rummaged through it. She reserved any Icarean swords for her immediate team. Tameka muttered only loud enough for their group to hear, "I'm not even expecting the students to survive, but I am expecting them to take one or two Icari with them."

Andrew stared at her, open-mouthed.

Sagan addressed the surviving students, "The bastards who attacked our school brought reinforcements. Look at us." She swept her hands at her crew. "We're bloody, bruised, and tired. We've killed at least thirty of these things already and one of their leaders. Look at you."

Students glanced at one another.

"There are at least three hundred of you. We fight more than any school in Little Rock because we never back down. We will not back down today. Are you with me?!"

The crowd cheered. Each student straightened, stood taller. Every one of them proud of their misguided reputation. Not so misguided right now.

"Fifteen. We only have to kill fifteen. Run away, back to the football field if you have to. I won't ask you to fight if you're afraid, but if you think you can do anything to help, grab a stake, a knife, or a sword, and hold the line."

Only three students walked back to the football field. Surprisingly, one of them was Matt. Sagan was sure he'd be up for the fight. It was a misjudgment on her part. The crew passed out make-shift stakes and unclaimed swords to the crowd.

Kyle walked over to Lucy and asked, "Are you all right?"

She glanced at him with little recognition in her eyes.

"Take this." He put a sword in her hand and touched her shoulder.

Some people grabbed materials for weapons out of the dumpsters. When everyone was armed, they formed a line. An organized mass of people. A small army.

The fifteen super warriors emerged from the building at a casual pace, serrated swords unsheathed. A few laughed, mocking the school's pitiful resistance, but several took a fighting stance with serious, cautious expressions.

What were they thinking? What's the best method for julienne Fair student?

Sagan stood at the front line. No fear. She'd fought stronger and killed worse not even thirty minutes ago. Kyle was unafraid next to her. Andrew stood amongst the mass of students like a great, unwavering statue. He did *not* look happy. Tameka nodded at Sagan from the throng.

Their strength helped the others gain confidence, and a wave of defiance surged through the crowd. They would win. Or so they thought.

Thirty or more of Colita's warriors emerged from behind the fifteen super soldiers. Each of them were armed with a shining sword.

The army of students took a collective, hesitant step back. Sagan and the rest stayed put.

Tameka growled, "That bitch! How many models did Colita collect?"

Two Icari pressed forward, and the tension surged in Sagan's gut. Before she called for the attack, a loud horn blared through the battleground.

"What the fuck?" Kyle called out.

A white Chevy Malibu barreled down the hill from the football field. The mass of students rushed out of the way, but the Icari stood there. Had they never seen a car before?

John muttered, "No way."

Sagan peered into the driver's seat and grinned.

Matt smashed his car right into the crowd of bewildered Icarean soldiers. The impact wasn't pretty. Two warriors went under the car, four rolled over the top, and two went flying back into the school. While one of them made a fine hood ornament, the others had survived.

Not messing around, Matt threw his car in reverse and backed over a few of them. Sagan startled when he jumped out of the car and decapitated six on the ground with a machete.

Now was as good a time as any.

Sagan screamed, "You fucked with the wrong school!" And charged into the line of Icari.

The mass of students surged around her like water parting around a stone, and the Icarean forces charged forward. The two masses collided with Machete Matt in the center.

FIFTEEN

A PARTNER MIGHT MAKE YOU FEEL GOOD FOR A NIGHT, BUT YOUR WRATH WILL KEEP YOU WARM FOR A LIFETIME

NOX DRAGGED RAYNE ALONG WITH HIM BY HER BROKEN ARM. Debris and glass buried inside her back. Grasping, she scraped her nails across the floor until her fingertips bled. He raised her up by the ruined arm, forcing her to climb to her feet. He smiled all the while.

She screamed, "I look forward to ripping your nacre from your chest."

Nox laughed with genuine mirth again. "There's that storm. All these years of training. No eating. No sleeping. Barely spending time with your friends. And spending *all* your nights with me... With a nacre of your own, you'd make a formidable opponent." He put his face in hers. "Now, all you require is some incentive to take one." Nox wrenched her arm until it popped again.

Rayne spat in his face. "Incentivize that." Her blood spattered across his mouth.

Much to her dismay, Nox licked it from his lips. "That's a rude way to address your dance partner." He spun her away from him by her broken arm. She crashed against the riot gate, hitting it so hard her vision blacked out.

Appearing behind her, Nox twisted her bad arm against her back. The elbow bent inward.

Gasping, Rayne murmured, "I never agreed to dance with you."

Nox pressed his ear to her lips, asking her to repeat it.

She ground out, "I never. Agreed. To Dance. With you."

He had that signature villain laugh down to an art. A lot of evil with a dash of sexy.

Rayne hated it.

Nox suggested, "Let's make a deal between warriors then. I convince you to dance with me, and you wear something outstanding."

"Never. Going. To happen."

He bent the elbow again and wrenched her arm the other way until she screamed.

The fire spread. Ceiling panels warped and melted, landing all around them. Looking up, the beams above shifted as if they wanted to give. She missed the numb feeling in her arm. The pain came close to making her faint.

Nox leaned his full weight on her mangled limb. Against her ear, he whispered, "Show me you're ready. Are you prepared to defend your world or not?"

Rayne clenched her teeth. "Fuck. You."

"We could do that or…" Nox whirled Rayne around to face him. His smile disappeared. This unfamiliar expression frightened her even more with its emptiness. He brushed his knuckles against the brand. "We could do this."

Rayne hissed at him.

Nox clutched strong fingers around her throat, squeezing firm enough to choke her. She sipped raw breaths into her dried husks for lungs. He bent her backwards. The debris in her back buried deeper, but that pain was minuscule compared to what came next.

Fire. There was fire. Rayne craned in Nox's firm grasp to see the flaming heap of rubble he held her over. The shredded cloth of her shirt gave way to the flames licking across her back, kissing the bloody scrapes. Unable to scream, she wept.

Rayne drove her nails into the skin of his wrist. Nox clenched his jaw and squeezed his fingers. How could he burn her with no remorse?

"Let. Go."

He raised Rayne high above him by her throat. She choked in convulsions, trying to find air. Raking her nails down his wrists made little rivers of blue blood that he ignored.

Nox asked, "Wouldn't you say your lessons were woefully incomplete? Tell me, did you ever ask yourself if an Icarus would really teach you how to take another of his kind down?"

If Rayne could speak, she would say that Xelan wanted him overthrown for his abuse of power. But was that the only reason? Or was that reason enough?

Her vision blurred. Spotty. She couldn't breathe.

Nox threw Rayne into another section of lockers near where the fight started. The fire was less here. She drew ragged gulps of air. Blood dripped into her eye. She touched her fingertips to it and winced. Letting her hand fall to her side, she touched something cool. Grasping it, she suppressed a smile.

Was she supposed to answer his question? Rayne said, "No. The thought never occurred to me, being only fourteen and all."

Rayne lifted her eyes. Nox stood over her, sword in hand, with that empty expression which unnerved her so. He wanted a challenge.

Ready to give him one, she stood carefully until she was stabilized. The storm in her surged on. This ass kicking stopped now. She leveled her eyes with his dark stare, and rage filled her.

Nox didn't miss the renewed confidence in her stance. Smirking, he swung the sword at her face. Her sword met his above her head, clanking loudly. He reached for her, seized the meat of her left shoulder, and pushed.

A sickening sound emitted from her arm, and Rayne screamed, "Son of a bitch!" Staggering back, she realized some mobility had returned to her left arm. It was painful with the bone pulverized.

Nox lunged for Rayne, and she crouched to the floor. She swept his legs out from under him, and he fell on his back. Rayne made to strike for him, but he kicked her in the leg like a little bitch. She crumpled to her knees.

In a sheer defiance of physics, Nox pulled himself upright, feet planted to the floor. He kneed Rayne in the face, and she grunted as she went down again. After a perfect kip up, she waited in front of him, sword in hand.

That twisted smile returned to Nox's lips. "Now, you look ready."

Rayne wasn't sure which expression she hated more.

The battle outside raged on. Bodies littered the rear parking lot of the school. Twenty-four of Colita's brood yet lived.

The pavement was no longer pooled in blood. It bathed in it. A great splashing lake of deep sanguine colors. Once the blue mixed with the red, it all just looked black. Like oil. The abyss swallowed their feet as opponents clashed together. The battle was even more intense than Sagan had imagined.

Out in the open air, the Icari found almost no limit to their abilities. They were capable of carnage unimaginable unless witnessed. After four years of training and preparation, their unit had gotten so much wrong.

Colita's men were the enemies they'd expected and were easy enough to kill. Their sheer numbers posed a problem when the good guy army consisted of untrained students.

Korac's men were a distinct challenge. Not long after the fight began, the good guys learned that piercing the brain wasn't enough. Decapitation was the only way to go.

"Sagan!"

She whirled around the massacre. "Matt?"

About ten fighting pairs away, Matt shouted at her while forcing his way through the throng. Above the screams and grunts, she barely made out his words, "—In the woods."

"What?"

He shoved an Icarus away. This was really important to him. She maneuvered through the crowd and met him halfway. "What is it?"

Matt stopped to catch his breath. He opened his mouth to say, "There are—"

A high keening sound interrupted him. A sound unlike anything Sagan had ever heard. It raised goosebumps all over her arms. A primal instinct screamed at her to get far away.

"Gargoyles."

"In the fucking woods?!"

Matt nodded, saying, "They've kept us trapped on campus." An Icarus bumped into him, and he shoved him off like a mosh pit veteran.

Sagan glanced at the tree line to ask, "What's stopping them now?"

Matt said, "I think they're only meant to keep us in. We've experimented. We can go anywhere on this campus, and they don't bother us. Like really well-trained guard dogs. The biggest ones you'll ever see."

The creatures from Korac's sketchbook...

One problem at a time. Sagan said, "Thanks for the info. Are you okay?" She scanned him over for wounds.

Matt smiled. A genuine, good-looking smile. "Lieutenant General, I think you have bigger problems right now." And he disappeared into the throng.

Sagan really did, too. The extreme underestimation of the Icarean super soldiers bothered Sagan. It was all she could do to evade their blows. She'd only killed one, and several students had died during that time, and if *they* were so hard to kill, then why—

Sagan recognized Andrew's scream. She spotted him through the crowd as one of the excessively serrated blades impaled him.

"Andrew!" She pushed her way to him.

He waved her off and knocked the Icarus in the jaw, staggering him. The effort was too much and Andrew fell to the pavement. He laid there unmoving.

John, even with his worn knee, severed the head of a super warrior. He took over fighting Andrew's Icarus.

Deeper in the crowd, Tameka traded blows with another one. Sagan shouted, "Look out, Tameka!"

The redhead evaded a devastating lunge, blocked the attacking blood sucker with her sword, and landed a well-aimed kick to his face. She thrust the sword into his throat. The blade lodged in his vertebrae.

Tameka shouted in surprise. It was still alive. A blow like that would kill a lesser Icarus. The redhead turned the sword in his neck and split his spine apart. The beast stayed down this time.

Tameka shouted, "Thanks for watching my back!" She tried to retrieve the sword. "Shit!" It appeared to be stuck.

Sagan pushed through the crowd to help. All the fights between the students and Icari swallowed any path to her friend. She only caught glimpses of Tameka now. Something glinted. Metal. Serrated metal behind her best friend.

Sagan screamed, "Tameka!" Another echoed her.

The rough blade erupted from her best friend's right shoulder. She screamed, and her knees gave.

The blade withdrew, the large teeth tearing as it exited. After a flash of fire, the Icarus shrieked. Lynn knelt beside Tameka.

Sagan sighed in relief as she burst into the clearing. "Are you all right?"

Tameka nodded and swallowed before asking, "Is he dead?"

Lynn scanned the few dozen people that surrounded them. She said, "No. He's just gone."

Tameka searched. "Where's Pablo?"

Lynn pointed, and both girls turned. Pablo and Kyle shared the honor of serving as one of the Icarus' punching bags. Each of them had lost their weapons. Their lips were bloodied, and their eyes were blackened.

John knelt on the asphalt beside Andrew. Three bodies laid around them and more followed suit. Swords clashed, people shouted and screamed, flames roared, and bodies fell. Only six super Icari remained, but the good guys had gained the upper hand, and proved more than enough to finish them all off.

Tameka allowed Lynn to help her stand and retrieved her sword from the dead monster's corpse. "Give me one of those bottles."

"Yes, ma'am!" Lynn tossed her a bottle and a lighter.

Tameka collected the items and pushed into the crowd.

"What will you do?" Sagan asked, worried about the girl's wounded shoulder.

Tameka announced without turning back, "I'll save Pablo! And Kyle, too, I guess."

The Icarus was content with the distracting task of beating the two to death. Tameka set fire to the Molotov cocktail and wedged it inside the soldier's armor. Flames erupted and clung to his clothes. He screamed in agony and panic as the alien fell to the pavement to battle the fire away.

Pablo said something to Tameka that Sagan didn't catch. He reached out his hand. She passed him the sword, still covered in the other Icarus' blood. Vicious rage mottled Pablo's face as he decapitated the alien.

Five super soldiers left.

Sagan enjoyed the swell of pride in her chest. Her people made good on their training. They even acted well together as—

She shrieked in agony, and the entire crowd turned to her. In the middle of the action, she faltered backwards. Her hand came away from her bare stomach covered in blood.

The Icarus behind her tried to lunge for her heart. She spun and caught the sword in the crook of her axe in a test of strength she couldn't afford to spare.

Sagan fell. Just before the blood sucking alien impaled her, his head came loose from his body, and Cecily stood where he fell.

"Cecily?"

The other girl smiled and offered her hand to Sagan.

"Thanks."

Regretful tears sprung to Cecily's eyes as she said, "I'm—"

Her face contorted in agony. A jagged sword burst through the center of Cecily's body. She clutched Sagan's arm in a death grip, trying to speak, but her voice only gargled.

Sagan held on. "No, Cecily! It'll be okay. Don't go."

Blood sprayed from the dying girl's mouth across Sagan's face, and then she fell.

Sagan glared up at the Icarus with his partially burnt face. With one powerful swing of the axe, the bastard fell on top of Cecily, a headless corpse.

Only three left.

Sagan winced at her midriff. A nice diagonal gap crossed her stomach, losing blood. She stumbled and supported herself on Korac's axe. She stayed there on one knee, head bowed, wrist perched on the pommel. One minute to rest. That's all she needed.

The dream team executed the last three super Icari quickly, but not before Korac's soldiers had reaped maximum carnage. At substantial cost, the students dispatched Colita's soldiers. At least eighty students had died.

Andrew was still unconscious. Kyle and Pablo swelled like tenderized meat. Tameka's shoulder bled severely.

This wasn't right.

Kyle shouted, "Check the bodies. Make sure no one's just unconscious." He marveled as people complied, and a secret, satisfied smile spread over his lips. He finally got to give an order.

Sagan shook her head.

Pablo and Lynn came over to check on her. Tameka and Kyle checked on John and Andrew. Bleeding wounds needed packing and tending. Everyone needed well-deserved rest. No one had really thought of a plan for broken bones, yet. There was far too much horror for one day. Surely this was the last.

The only thing left was Rayne.

The back of South Hall crumbled in on itself, and the sounds of collapsing beams warned Rayne to get the hell out. The smoke acted as a black blanket, burning the eyes and searing the lungs. Sweat glistened on Rayne's pale skin, mingling with blood from her open wounds.

Her left arm, though mobile, lay all but useless. Blood dripped from her ruined bicep, burns, and hair. Periodic waves of nausea reminded Rayne of the concussion. Gory injuries hindered her grip on the sword. She was such a mess.

And yet, Rayne stood before Nox with a perfectly balanced stance. She kept her eyes on him as she held the sword over flaming debris. It smoldered.

Nox stared down at her, sparing a glance at the sword as it caught fire. He asked, "Is that for me?"

Firelight flashed across Rayne's face. She said, "I don't see anyone else around here. Do you?"

They shared a moment in silence. There was no need for more words. Rayne's eyes seethed brighter than the fire as Nox's stare became an icy void. A loud crash signaled the end.

Nox charged for her, and Rayne blocked the attack with her sword. The sound of metal clashing against metal rang through her ears. The impasse proved only temporary.

Nox backhanded her with his ring hand. She wavered before recovering her balance and returned his assault with her fist. Nox faltered. He brushed the back of his hand across his mouth. Smiling over the blood from his lips, he gave one long stroke of his tongue. He lapped up his own blood like some kind of feral beast.

Rayne's eyes narrowed at the intimacy in his stare. "How can you get off on that?"

"When you lose this fight, I'll teach you." He sounded absolutely certain.

She lunged, and he rose to the challenge. Their swords crossed, and their faces met way too close.

Nox asked, "Did anyone try to teach you the finer points of intimacy? Aside from what we shared?"

Rayne answered with her best impression of a growl and leaned harder into her sword. "You know the answer."

"Beautiful Progeny girl. Breaking hearts to save herself for a lover in her dreams. One of them will betray you for it. Perhaps, even your guardian isn't trustworthy." He said this as if it were a secret between friends. Not as if he'd just dropped a nuclear bomb on her entire world.

Rayne let her reaction show on her face before she thought to stop it. Wide-eyed and terrified. Traitor?

Nox took advantage of her momentary hysteria and pushed her back. She didn't resist. Although Rayne moaned when he pinned her up against the lockers, her mind wasn't with them.

What he said made so much sense. A traitor in their midst. The dream with Celindria. She told Xelan about it right before he disappeared.

Misinformed. Under-prepared. No help. No one to save the day. Was Xelan a traitor all along?

Distantly, Nox's fangs pierced the skin of Rayne's neck, but she couldn't bother to pay attention.

Was this the reason Xelan disappeared after she told him about the dream? No one had heard from him in the last four months. Not even her.

Reflexively, Rayne sighed when Nox's tongue pressed to her throat at the open wound and tasted her blood there.

What would she do if Xelan betrayed them after all this time?

Nox punched her hard enough that Rayne understood the metaphor about seeing stars. "Am I so little a threat to you now that you can just disengage in the middle of battle?!"

Rayne spat blood on some cindered rubble. She confessed, "I want to call you a liar."

He stepped away from her. Walked away from her. His back was to her and everything.

Nox kept dropping bombs. "You know I tell the truth. Xelan trained your brood all along to fight an enemy that proved more powerful and more difficult to kill than you'd ever imagined. You should pick your friends more wisely, my sweet killer. Why would an Icarus betray the rest? Unless he never intended to betray us at all."

God damn him. Rayne cried, "You're wrong! Xelan trained me to kill you, and that's exactly what I'll do."

Rayne charged to strike him. Nox stepped aside and retaliated by backhanding her with his ring hand across her eye. She took the blow. Spinning away, she sliced his ribs. He tried to hit her again, only this time she expected it.

She obstructed the blow with her bad arm. Agonizing and jarring, Rayne recovered quickly. She kneed the pommel of his sword, sending it into the air. Reaching up, she caught it with her bad hand and thrust both blades straight into the center of his chest.

Nox swayed, lowering his onyx eyes to the blades crossed inside his flesh. Rayne pushed with everything in her. She swallowed with exertion and gasped for air. Rich cobalt blood seeped from his brain. As thick as tree sap or molasses.

Rayne unclenched her jaw and apprehensively released both weapons. Her hands shook. She let her battered arm fall to its side. Her good hand tentatively touched her throat, and she winced at the bruises.

Needing more air, she gazed as the monster of her nightmares fell roaring to his knees. The shout seemed to shake the earth, itself. She forced herself back and covered one ear.

Crackling and groaning alerted her once more to the blazing structures surrounding them. Her reflexes acted faster than her body. Rayne jumped away from Nox. Beams, paneling, and a set of scorched lockers crashed down around her. Her ankle refused to move. Heart pounding, breathing rapidly, she glanced down the line of her body, and sucked air through her teeth.

A flaming beam pinned Rayne's ankle to the floor. She barely lifted the heavy thing with her other foot to get free. She spared a moment to examine the newest burn wound.

The massive pile of debris had crushed Nox beneath it. The entire building fell, and the smoke rose so thick she couldn't see. She tried standing, applying as little pressure on her right leg as possible. Her bad arm went limp. Slick with sweat and dripping blood from everywhere, she sought the newly expanded band room. Her only way out.

As soon as Rayne cleared the door, the ceiling fell out behind her. The burning insulation and panel tiles melted away. She rushed through the rows of desks, ignored the body chained to the podium, nearly got entangled by the music stands, and busted onto the stage.

That exit sign was the most beautiful thing Rayne had ever seen.

Emerging from the burning school, she heaved in great lungfuls of relieving, fresh air. This led to coughing. Then to limping further into the cleaner air. The coolness of it was worth enduring the sting on her back.

Was everyone else all right? Had they defeated Korac and survived? Was Sagan alive? Rayne would feel something if she'd died, wouldn't she?

Rayne expected someone to rush to her side and help her, but the figures in her hazy vision stayed back. Her knees buckled, and her legs fell out from under her. Something in her pocket jabbed her until she pulled it out. Small and hard, she instantly recognized it. The mark she now carried on her face.

The Earth shook.

Rayne clutched the ring in her hand as she put her feet back under her. "Run! Get the hell out of here!" Why weren't they moving? Were they too shaken up? She didn't have time for this.

Rayne ran back to the building, prepared for another fight.

Time slowed down. Debris flew everywhere. Two winged beings erupted from the burning structure. Her sprained ankle gave way, and she slid across the pavement.

Nox and Korac glared down at her from the sky with matching sets of beautiful, black wings. Their wings were fashioned with feathers like angels. The King of Cinder recovered his sword and sheathed it at his hip. The two gaping wounds in his chest had healed. In their place was perfect, unmarred skin.

Rayne cried out in frustration.

Korac cradled Colita in his arms, alive and hanging on. Rayne knew Tameka regretted not taking Colita's head. The King and the General waited patiently. But for what?

Screaming students scattered for the wooded hillside behind the school. In the distance came a bizarre, keening howl. The likes of which Rayne had never heard before. Goosebumps pricked along her skin. The students' screams intensified. Other awful, garbled sounds followed. What the hell was happening in the tree line? She dared not take her eyes off the two Icari to check.

Between one beat of Rayne's heart and the next, Nox dove for her. She watched from where she lay on the ground, unable to move, and remained calm. He wouldn't kill her. He needed her.

The alien King stopped within a few inches of her face, his body aligned along the length of hers. His dark, remorseless eyes shifted into chrome. Alien. Terrifying.

Above her, the dark angel hovered with fluttering wings. With every beat, gravel blew back, and her hair mingled with his, sweeping across her face. Rayne was at the mercy of someone who had none to spare.

Nox reached for her by the throat and lifted her bodily ten feet from the asphalt. She tried to scream. No sound came. His wings beat the surrounding air. He swept an arm beneath her, relieving her throat. Maybe he would kill her? Maybe he'd found another way to his salvation?

Nox brought Rayne closer until their eyes were level. He sought something in hers, and she in his.

Invade Earth. Destroy a school. Fight all five of the Progeny. Sow the seeds of doubt. Fake their deaths. But don't love her. Don't ask her to go with him because that's what he wanted. No.

"Why, Nox?!"

Quietly—So quietly she almost didn't hear his voice layered in three pitches.

"My brother trained you well."

Nox released his grip on her. Rayne fell to the ground, the air rushing around her. She couldn't help herself. She reached out to him to save her from the fall.

Her breath rushed from her lungs when she landed on the rough pavement. Sagan knelt at her side, her face horror-stricken.

The three Icari soared away to an unknown destination.

There was no relief. No joy. Just pure, icy fear. Fresh tears streamed down Rayne's cheeks. She couldn't breathe, and not only from the fall.

Sagan checked Rayne over, asking, "What did he say to you?"

Several pairs of feet came into Rayne's line of sight.

Andrew shouted, "Xelan!"

Rayne turned to look over the roof of the auxiliary gym. Five men stood there draped in all black. She recognized only one familiar face. She hadn't seen him for months, but she would never mistake him.

Xelan's shoulder-length black hair caught the breeze perfectly over his kind features. How had Rayne never made the connection before? They looked so similar. Sure, she never saw Nox's face completely in her dreams, but—

"Rayne, what's going on?" Sagan asked, again.

Xelan stood taller than the other four, almost as tall as his brother. This was The Brethren he never allowed her to meet before today. They were undoubtedly Icarean, but not entirely evil. Or were they?

Anger incensed Rayne's entire being. After everything Nox had told her, after disappearing for four months, Xelan was here in time for his brother to end the world.

Confusion and anguish muddied her thoughts. Did they watch the entire time? Would they have even bothered helping?

Rayne wanted to shout and cry all at once. Her body screamed at her. Aching, stinging, burning, bleeding, sweating, and numbing. It took everything in her to keep breathing.

Cold traveled up from her fingertips and toes. Her legs became unyielding. Both arms went immobile. Nothing would move. The painful sensation reached her eyes and a blood-curdling, heart-wrenching scream tore from her throat before Rayne fell back on Sagan's lap.

And the world went black.

EPILOGUE

THE MESSAGE PLAYED ON REPEAT.

"We have surrendered. Can you understand us? Have you received the message? The southern United States surrenders. We await further instructions. God save us all."

Students hauled supplies and material possessions into cars. Some people braved the fire to collect keys from bags and purses. They needed the unclaimed vehicles for the evacuation. Sagan recommended it before disappearing with Rayne and her friends.

"Do you think this is enough?" Lucy carried tons of assorted snacks she'd stolen from the vending machine outside, using her shirt as a basket.

Matt placed an outward smile on his lips to display his approval. "Yeah, this is exactly what we need. Thanks."

"Can you pop the trunk for me?" Her voice was strained with the effort.

"No," he answered, tersely. "Just put it in the backseat with the rest." When he glimpsed the constraint in her eyes, he considered the abuse she'd suffered over the years from Justin.

Matt aimed for a more gentle approach. Even if it went against every one of his instincts. "We'll want them accessible to us on the drive. No unnecessary stops if we can help it."

This seemed to satisfy Lucy as she visibly relaxed and stored food rations in the backseat. Well, she tried, anyway. She had every right to ask about the trunk, seeing how the back of the car was piled up with makeshift weapons, an abundance of medical supplies, and unstained clothes they'd scavenged from North Hall lockers.

The fire engulfed the school at a terrifying pace after South Hall collapsed. All the insulation combusted and withered, spreading it faster. They had a thirty-minute window where they could access the safer classrooms before the entire school went up in flames.

Lucy mussed around the backseat. "Where are we going?"

Matt tried hard to ignore her perfect heart-shaped, jean-clad ass as she rifled through their shit between the front seats.

He wet his lips and looked straight ahead out the windshield. A few cars pulled away. After the two Icarean leaders had flown off, the beasts guarding the perimeter followed. As in, hefted their great bodies into the sky and flew away into the darkness. After that, every single individual looked defeated. Matt asked, "Uhm, do you want to check on your folks?"

Lucy paused in her task. "Wow."

He raised an eyebrow. "What is it?"

"I forgot about them."

He knew exactly how she felt. Until he'd asked her, Matt hadn't given a second thought to his parents. It was like he survived a battle, and now he had to contend with a war. He asked again, "Yeah. So, do you wanna check on them?"

"Of course."

"Where do you live?" He peered at her through the rearview mirror.

"Oh, uhm." Lucy's cheeks warmed a little, and she started concentrating on packing the food away. Her movements became awkward. "I live in Mabelvale."

Matt understood. She was ashamed of her neighborhood, but he'd learned a long time ago that all the students living in Southwest Little Rock, the primary zone for J. A. Fair, lived in lower income areas. He said, "That's the opposite of where I'm headed."

"Where do you live?"

"Oh, I live in Otter Creek, but I'm not going home. I'm headed to Kavanaugh. Did you know Rayne well or at all?"

Lucy shook her head.

Matt explained, "Her parents have a bookstore in the Heights. I plan to start there in case that's where her crew went."

She spun around to face him again. "You're going after them?!"

"You got a problem with that?" The thought amused Matt. As if Lucy could persuade him not to go.

She got closer to his face. "Take me with you."

That was the last thing he'd expected her to say. "Whoa, this ain't an adventure. People are hurt and dying."

Lucy said, "And if anyone knows what's going on, it's that group of freaks."

Matt worked hard to keep his voice very calm and very still. "Nobody is a freak." He examined the effect his voice had on her.

She pulled back from his face and returned to her chore. After a few moments of silence, she made a disgruntled sound. "I understand the food, but can't we put some of this in the—"

"Shh!" Matt interrupted, his tone sharp. He strained to listen, and he noticed her face shift as she realized it, too. Deafening static had replaced the message on the radio. For the first time since nine that morning, the message had stopped.

Lucy jumped into the front seat, and they both leaned forward. Matt's hands gripped the steering wheel until his knuckles went white. With bated breath, they waited for anything to take the message's place. When a man's deep voice invaded the radio waves, Lucy startled and slapped a hand against her mouth. Matt watched her out of his periphery. She appeared frightened, and he wondered if he should act the same.

The insidious voice delivered its address across every station, "Earthlings, humans, homo sapiens, in a presentation of surprisingly sound wisdom the leaders of your planet have surrendered all assets, resources, and possessions to me."

Lucy whimpered and shivered.

Matt's skin grew chill, and his palms went damp. The pearl in his back pocket prodded him.

"Henceforth, you shall know Nox as your King. You serve me in all things without question. This obedience extends to my people whom you will come to recognize and know very well. You are no longer the dominant species on your planet. The Icari are your Masters, now. There will be no period of adjustment. Effective immediately, we will collect you from your shelters. All of you: men, women, children, and the elderly. Any attempt to resist will result in the total destruction of the surrounding thirty acres. The only hope for your feeble race is to fetch me the woman, Progeny Alpha One. Code Name: Celindria. Bring her to me, and we will consider negotiations. Make what peace you will and enjoy the following news reports."

As soon as the voice departed, Matt jumped to turn the volume down. The station flooded with sirens and explosions. "I don't know how much longer I can go on. I've been reporting since eight this morning. This is Longview, Texas. Please send any help. Wait, something is coming in from the station. Oh, god. No. It seems… It seems Houston is entirely gone. I repeat, they wiped Houston off the map. Austin, Dallas, and San Antonio. Still no word from Western Texas."

Matt changed to the next station. The FM radio tuned into a signal, but he wished it hadn't. "The west coast is gone. It sank into the seaboard around 10:00AM. California, Oregon, and Washington state. All gone."

Lucy pressed the next preset. A female voice whispered, "Please send help. They're outside the building. I know they're coming for me. I just hope—" Silence. Then a shrill scream, the rustling of furniture, and a very unusual whoosh sound. Rubble scrambled in the background.

Lucy turned the radio off. Matt met her eyes at the same instant. They both looked away and closed the car doors.

Matt started the engine. "Put your seatbelt on."

AUTHOR'S NOTE

Was that the ending you were expecting?
Keep reading for a sneak peek at *By the Pale Moonlight,*
Book II of the Vast Collective Series.
And sign up for news of future books.

BY THE PALE MOONLIGHT

RAYNE WAKES

{INVASION DAY | 2006}

FAMILIAR COMFORTING VOICES PIERCED RAYNE'S NIGHTMARE. While they filled her with warmth, the words they spoke sent a chill down her spine.

"Will she live?" Rayne heard Tameka ask.

Whoever spoke the answer did so in a whisper. So soft she couldn't make it out. The grim silence that followed answered the question for her. Rayne opened her eyes. Well, tried to anyway. One of her eyes refused to open, and any attempt to force it hurt. When the light pierced her eye, she instantly regretted it. With a flinch and a groan, she squeezed her eyes tight and curled into herself. That was a mistake.

Rayne's body wanted none of it. Her porcelain skin was canvassed in a mosaic of deep purples and blues. Making a fist required closing her fingers, and when she tried, she winced. The angry, red slits on her knuckles needed stitches. She tried to clench her left fist, and her breath hitched in her throat. Nothing.

That was it. Rayne's pulse hammered in her throat. Sweat beaded on her brow and stung her shut eye. Her chest heaved with each gulping breath. With her eyes closed as tight as a vice, Rayne released a strangled, panicked cry. Then another.

Once she started screaming, she couldn't stop. With each scream, Rayne remembered more of the horrors she'd survived that day and more of what lay ahead of her. Every blow, every cut, every bruise, and so much to come. Her heart fluttered through the panic. Her lungs couldn't swallow enough air.

Something shuffled near her. Voices dented the wall of screams. She remained unreachable.

"Celindria," one calm voice said.

The word didn't reach her; the voice did. And it set her blood to boil. The emotional turmoil wrought from his voice opened her uninjured eye and squelched her screams.

Rayne needed her voice to tear into him. She focused on him through blurry vision. Close around her, she heard others speaking, but they would have to wait.

Xelan's black hair was swept back into a hair tie. Every pale, angular feature seemed harsher, free from his hair. His concerned, midnight-blue eyes lit her insides ablaze. With his face this close, she discerned the resemblance. How could she be so blind? For four years?!

Xelan knew. He saw it in her expression as his posture straightened, and his eyes tightened with regret.

Enraged, Rayne spat, "Liar!"

Xelan recoiled.

The others hushed, almost as if a switch had flipped.

Hoarse from hours of smoke inhalation, Rayne screamed again, "LIAR!"

After the initial shock wore off, Xelan relaxed. His eyes connected with hers without wavering. His lips tightened into a thin line, and he spared a quick glance at the others. "Can you please give us a minute?" Before she protested, he held up a hand. "Allow me to talk to you alone, and then you can kill me if you like."

Someone gasped.

Without taking her eyes off Xelan, Rayne waved to her friends off. "It's okay. I'll call if I need you." Several pairs of footsteps left the room. One person stayed.

Sagan lingered in the doorway of what Rayne recognized as the back storeroom of her family's bookstore. "Are you sure?" her best friend asked, weary eyes flicking to Xelan.

"I promise. He won't hurt me." Xelan winced at Rayne's choice of words.

The blond promised in a stern voice, "We'll be right here. With the door cracked."

Rayne didn't know how much time had passed since J. A. Fair fell and the world went to shit, but it felt like days since she'd last smiled. She smiled as she nodded to her best friend. It melted as soon as the door pulled just shy of closed. She turned back to Xelan and flinched. Unsure what to expect from him, she didn't expect to see him cradling his head in his hands.

Wisps of his hair contrasted against his pale complexion. He straightened himself upright and slowly dragged his hands down his face until he steepled his fingers against his lips. Meanwhile, his eyes scanned the room, careful to look at anything but Rayne. Xelan folded his fingers together at his chin and finally focused on her left arm.

She refused to look at it. The cold appendage was dead from her shoulder down. For the time being, she considered it a mercy. This was more important. Xelan stared until sadness dawned in the midnight of his eyes. The guilt which was carved into his face arrested Rayne.

The shame.

It was so long before he spoke that she jumped at the sound, "I think the longer I live here the harder it is for me to divulge information about myself."

Rayne narrowed her eyes at him.

Xelan continued to stare at the ruined limb. He said, "Regrettably, your life spans are but a mere heartbeat to me. One breath, you're here and gone the next. In the early years, I formed connections. I wanted to help humanity, but

I was recently separated from my species, my homeworld. I wanted to create personal friendships. Especially with the descendants of the Progeny. Maintaining a link to the few with Icarean blood on this planet was critical to my mental survival." He paused and turned away.

Despite the awesome fury which had overwhelmed Rayne at Nox's revelation, when she stared at Xelan, she saw her mentor. The man who trained her struggled with an inner turmoil she could only guess at. She found a wealth of patience for him.

Xelan cleared his throat and continued, "I formed strong, familial relationships with my remaining kind. For two thousand years, I tried. As the centuries carried on, and it became more difficult to explain my ties to them despite their shorter lifespan, I became a legendary uncle or a family friend. Eventually, the excuses ran dry. The Progeny line delineated and diluted until their lifespans were as short as humans. With the rise of civilization and the Judeo-Christian religions, I risked the descendants dying for their heretical knowledge of other worlds."

His knee bounced. Rayne had never imagined Xelan, always level-headed, always patient, feeling the need to bounce his knee. He turned and found the floor in front of him rather interesting.

"It's been six thousand years since I told anyone Nox and I are siblings."

www.ingramcontent.com/pod-product-compliance
Lightning Source LLC
Chambersburg PA
CBHW020248030826
48979CB00030B/2654/J
* 9 7 9 8 9 8 6 8 2 2 0 2 0 *